One Full American Life of a First-Generation Immigrant of Mexican Descent

The story of the eleventh of twelve children of
Felipe Pérez and Amalia Charpes-Pérez

Mexican Immigrants to America from the year 1927
and whose family had five sons and four grandsons in
the American Armed Forces during times of war.
One life lived within two centuries, in three
states, and in four continents.

ROBERTO PEREZ

(1952 at age nineteen during the Korean War)

Fulton Books, Inc.
Meadville, PA

First originally published by Fulton Books 2018

ISBN 978-1-63338-625-9 (Paperback)
ISBN 978-1-63338-626-6 (Digital)

Printed in the United States of America

Contents

Foreword

We are well into the seventeenth year of the twenty-first century. The author of this memoir is now in his eighty-fifth year since his birth. As the reader will discover, his life has been very much *nontypical* as a native-born American. You see, while he was born in America, he is also the son of Mexican-born parents. Thus, is seen by a substantial percentage of native-born Americans as a *hyphenated* American…a "Mexican-American." But enough of third-person referrals, after this sentence, all referrals to this author will be in the first person. *I* am writing this memoir. I am also the only surviving member of this fourteen-member American family named Pérez.

I turned 84 this year. For the sake of using percent-ages when I refer to portions of my life (the reader will find that I *love* to use numbers because they describe more vividly the essence of reality), I will use phrases like *50 percent of the time* or *80 percent of the time*, and often. So a word to the wise, be prepared.

This is mostly the lifelong personal story of a first-generation American of Mexican descent, who is also the eleventh of twelve children born to Felipe and Amalia Pérez. Eighty-five percent of this story occurs in the twentieth century, but because I am still alive in the twenty-first, this tale will dovetail into the current century as well. Call it a memoir. Call it an autobiography or a biography or even a biographical sketch. More than that, it is also the story of an American family of the twentieth century. Throughout this book, this author will bring up this fact. It is done somewhat cynically because in the eyes of many Americans, no one named Pérez could possibly be American. To continue the cynicism, when I reflect on the contributions this family has made to make America great (to use the words of a certain presidential candidate who emerged on the scene in 2015 but who was well-known by most Americans and *never* considered as a viable candidate for the highest office in the land, and yes, in my eyes he is still a candidate. He held rallies in South Carolina and Florida the week of February 12–18, 2017, long after he won the presidency). I am proud to say that if all American families were like mine, *America would truly be a great country.*

As you will read below, the period covers a lot of ground. I was born in the middle of the depression, one year after Franklin Delano Roosevelt won election as our president (and also just three years before FDR-installed social security, six years before Ted Williams hit .400, eight years before Joe DiMaggio hit in fifty-six straight games and eight years and four months before the Japanese bombed Pearl Harbor). This book covers the lives of fourteen people of one family living in America starting in the year 1927.

My mother's birthday is May 5. When I was born, she was 40 years old and my father was 50. On her birthday in 2017, my mother would have celebrated her 124th birthday. On his birthday in 2017, my father would have celebrated his 134th birthday. My paternal grandfather was 27 when he and my grandmother had my father. I remember both paternal and maternal grandmothers back in the 1930s before they died. One was rather frail, the other much bigger. I can find their graves in San Antonio today if I had to because I accompanied my mother when she visited their graves, as she did several times each year, and would know more or less where to look.

Oh yes. There will be a quiz at the end of the book asking what year my parents and grandparents were born. So, pay attention. On August 17 of 2016, I turned 83. (Are you writing all this down?) I often surprise my readers with five- to ten-dollar gift certificates if they can answer simple questions. This is always done on a first-come-first-served basis, of course.

For some time now I have reflected on the many things that have happened in my life and how I should find a way to record the most memorable of all the events and milestones of one's life here in America. It would be one thing if my life had been one dull and dreary experience. It was not. The questions are, should I record all this information by putting it into a book? Does it matter to anyone? After all, doesn't everyone have a story to tell? And if I decided to tell my story, how would I do it? Chronologically? Should I tell the story of each member of the family as a separate chapter? Some would be very long, others very short. Should I remember only the good things I did in my life, or also mention my errors in judgment and bad decisions? I have a quick answer for the latter question. Bad decisions and errors in judgment will be here, for sure. They are a part of everyone's life.

I suppose the best thing to do is to begin with a synopsis (a summary of the story), and perhaps pursue this general outline in chronological order, starting from the very first things I can remember. Reading the summary here at the beginning will also serve to tell the reader what lies ahead. Additionally, perhaps I should list the most significant things in some order so that I can be sure they are included in this narrative. But even before starting at this point, perhaps this century-old picture of my father with other professional associates of his, taken around the year 1913 in Mexico, will give the reader a better picture of who my father was when he decided to give up on his home country and immigrate to the north. There is little I can add to the picture because my father was not accustomed to sharing much information with members of his family. Knowing what I know now and tremendously hungry for more information, I now wish I would have been more inquisitive of just who my father was. I knew him as a good parent who wanted only the best for his sons and daughters. I knew precious little else, to my regret. By the way, my dad is the first person on the lower left.

Before starting with my family members, I must tell my readers why I am doing this (writing this book). It is a simple fact. Hmm, now I have to mention my interpretation of the word *fact*. I will endeavor to be as factual as possible. I will also endeavor to add IMHO, or *in my humble opinion*.

Back to the purpose in this work. It is true that I, perhaps mistakenly and very judgmentally, considered my parents, six brothers, and five sisters as *special people* and who should be remembered for the lives they lived in this country. This *is* how I really feel, but I developed this feeling after *walking on this earth with my eyes open*, reading the literature on the history of this country, and experiencing the sometimes blatant racism that continues to be a big part of America. My plans for putting the lives of these fourteen Americans of Mexican descent in writing started sometime during the school year 1977–78. It was the same school year that I completed my dissertation to earn my doctorate at the University of Texas at Austin. No, it is not strange at all that I first thought about this possibility during this time. You see, there is a reason there are tens of thousands of ABDs (all but dissertation) among American doctoral students. Writing one's research study in a chosen field can be next to impossible to complete when the doctoral student has to have approval to proceed from chapter to chapter of one's study from five different full professors before proceeding forward with each chapter of one's work. When I went through this process in that school year (1977–78) my thoughts frequently were "Holy Shit! I'll never finish this!" Two or three of my professors were very negligent in returning my requests for approval of each chapter. I had trouble getting their approval even with my proposal at the very beginning.

There will be more on this topic when I reach that particular portion of this "story." For now, here is a picture of my mom and dad, with my oldest sister Jovita, taken in 1913 when my dad was very much a citizen of Mexico, a land owner with status, a professional who was forced to choose sides in a continuing conflict in Mexico between civilians, "*generales*," and opportunists like Pancho Villa who attempted to take charge of a troubled country.

Yes, my family is special. Consider this: My father, Felipe Pérez, was a railroad engineer in Mexico. He wore a suit, with shirt and tie, when he went to work every day. He married an equally educated Mexican woman, Amalia Charpes. He was 27, my mother 17, when they married in 1910. Mexico was mired in political upheavals constantly during this period. A vicious and deadly revolution began in Mexico. My father chose Pancho Villa's side and lost everything but his home in Monterrey. He struggled to make a living. In 1927, he had had enough and immigrated to America with his seven children. My father and mother would have five more, four of them born in America. Of the seven boys my parents had, five wore the American military uniform and served proudly as four grandchildren would as well. All nine members of my family served proudly when we were involved in armed conflicts around the world.

I knew that if I could complete a doctorate, which I did, I could write a book about my special family. When billionaire Donald Trump surfaced in the year 2015 as a candidate for president, and he called Mexicans rapists and drug dealers, I felt an obligation to complete my task as soon as possible. Donald Trump literally drew a fire under my ass.

Before reaching the end of this book, I will mention my experiences with some ten or eleven different incidents that reveal both institutional and individual evidence of racial discrimination and/or incidents of blatant prejudice. They occurred during different times in my life, like when I obtained my Texas driver's license at the age of 15; when an obviously angry junior high school teacher who lost her composure in front of my class, a class where all the students were of Mexican descent, and let loose an angry barrage of demeaning and ugly words about our culture. There was an incident when my son was denied the first place ribbon during an athletic competition among American youths while living in the Canal Zone in the late 1960s. There was also the time when my brother Ramiro had to correct several white men at Carswell Air Force Base in Texas in the 1970s when they began talking under their breath about my brother who was there as a representative of the air force conducting a study of man hours required to work on B-52 jet engines. Ramiro was a civil engineer out of Kelly Air Force Base in San Antonio.

There were other incidents. Perhaps the most glaring is growing up these many years and seeing that only white people had positions of authority or were the teachers we faced every day. They were the doctors and nurses and pharmacists and more. They were the movie stars, the major league baseball players, and football players. They seemed to be the only people who really mattered, and no one else who had skin darker than theirs could possibly be considered as capable or held in high esteem. We grew up with this detriment in our thinking.

Psychologically, it was damaging to our mental health. I still remember one Latina student I met in graduate school at the University of Texas in the 1970s and who wanted desperately to show her emotions when she heard our national anthem or heard the singing of "America the Beautiful." She was angry that even this small pleasure was denied her.

My father was a captain in Pancho Villa's army in Mexico in the early part of the twentieth century. As an engineer, he could drive coal-fed railroad trains (and the reason Villa made him a captain). Yet, in the twenty-eight years I had my father in my life, he never put a pistol in his hand and never hunted for wild life. That I know of, there was never a gun of any kind in our home. So, why mention guns in this manner? Until we started piling up statistics about gun deaths in America, guns did not matter in this story about an American family of the twentieth century. But do they matter today in the summer of 2017? *Yes!*

I have already mentioned that five of us (brothers) and four of my nephews served in the armed forces during times of conflict. Three of my four nephews were marines. My brothers were all in the army. I was a volunteer for the air force. The wars included World War II, the Korean Conflict, the Viet Nam War, and the Gulf War. None of us served in either Afghanistan or Iraq. These last two are wars America was involved in that occurred in the twenty-first century. My three oldest brothers served in the army during World War II. The third oldest served in the Army Air Corps (before it branched out and became the United States Air Force in the late 1940s). He remained in the army air corps through the Korean conflict. I served during the Korean and the Vietnam conflicts. One nephew served as a machine gunner in the marines during the Vietnam conflict. His brother also served in the marines but did not go to this theatre. A third nephew also served in Vietnam and the fourth nephew served in the army and in the Gulf War.

My grandfather was 27 when my father was born, making him 161 years old in 2017. My parents were born in Mexico. My mother became a naturalized American citizen on September 16, 1954 (yes, "el diez y seis de septiembre") at the age of 61. My mother never talked about the irony of it all (becoming a U.S. citizen on Mexico's Independence Day, and no, Mexico's Independence Day is not "el cinco de mayo"). My father used his green card all his life while living here in America. My parents came to America in 1927 with eight children. (Actually seven, but my mother returned to Mexico to give birth to Jaime [/"Hime-eh"/] "Jimmy," the fourth son, thus "evening the score" at four boys and four girls.) The remaining four (three boys and one girl) were born in America. While my father owned his own home in Mexico, he never aspired to buying a home here in America. His plans were to return to Mexico and die and be buried there. He accomplished the former after he retired, but not the latter. He is buried with my mother in San Antonio, Texas. It was not a case of not complying with his wishes, it was a case of what our family could afford. My father is buried in a Christian (Catholic) cemetery even though he was a nonbeliever his entire life. My mother's remains are next to his.

My brother Jimmy was born on July 2, 1927, after my mother returned to Monterrey to give birth under familiar circumstances. As an aside, and to add to the political talking points of American politicians of today, none of the Republican political talking points about immigrants apply to my family (coming to America to have their babies born here in order to be declared Americans). The word *absurd* does not do justice to such a mistaken perspective. Besides, we're talking about the year 1927. This is long before anybody from Mexico even thought of coming to America. Many still carried psychological wounds from the armed conflicts, from the mid-nineteenth century to the early twentieth, when General Pershing was in hot pursuit of the so-called "rebel," Pancho Villa. Pershing wanted Villa to stop raiding places this side of the border. It is true that Pancho Villa was labeled a bandit by the Mexican government, but

Villa was more anti-government than he was a bandit. Villa was known to take only from the rich to give to the poor. He was more like Robin Hood than anything else, a sort of redistributor. Yeah, my father was on Villa's staff, but my father was an "anti-Carranzista," more than he was anything else. Venustiano Carranza was the latest corrupt Mexican president at the time. The period is early twentieth century (1910–1920).

The seven who came with my parents in 1927 were Jovita, Carolina, Felipe Jr., Armando, Graciela, Luz María, and Ramiro. Their ages at the time, oldest to youngest in the same order, were 15, 13, 10, 8, 7, 5, and 4, respectively. At 15, Jovita was very much in charge when my mother was absent, as she was when my mother returned to Mexico the same year she came to America to have her eighth child. Enrique "Henry," Elida, me, and José "Pepe" were born in Texas. The years were 1929, 1931, 1933, and 1936, respectively, in the same order as noted here. Of the first six children my parents had, four were girls. Throughout their developing years, even past their adolescent stage, the four were together whenever possible. Here is a picture taken in 1941 when all four were under thirty years of age. Pictured clockwise starting at twelve o'clock: Carolina, age 27; Jovita, age 29; Graciela, age 21; Luz Maria, age 19.

My five sisters all graduated from Catholic high schools. Only Ramiro and José (Pepe from this point on) managed to accomplish this among the men in the family, although I later acquired the equivalency and three additional college degrees. There will be much more information on our education in America in later chapters of this book. The youngest of my sisters, but almost two years older than me, was born in 1932 in San Antonio. Elida came eleven years after Luz Maria and was never close to her older sisters. Here is her high school graduation picture from 1950:

Because my father kept his home in Monterrey, it was easy for my oldest sisters—Jovita, Carolina, and Luz María ("Chacha" from this moment on)—to return to Monterrey with their high school diplomas and find much more meaningful and appropriate employment than they could obtain in America. All three were perfectly bilingual, and Luz Maria eventually became the executive secretary to the CEO of the National Carbon Eveready Company that was located in Monterrey. With their proficiency of both languages,

Jovita and Carolina were immediately employed by the telephone company in Monterrey.

Regarding the statement "more meaningful and appropriate employment...," Chacha graduated from high school at 16 in San Antonio in 1938. Carolina and Jovita had already graduated, and were now 26 and 24, respectively. While I never heard of their experiences in finding jobs here in America, my guess is that they were still seen as three Mexican American girls, diplomas or not. Okay, I will go out on a limb and say they couldn't get jobs because their names were Jovita Pérez, Carolina Pérez, and Luz María Pérez. More than that, we're talking of the years America is mired in a depression and jobs are scarce. As it is today, companies were looking for the best qualified and, for women, those with good communication skills. Eventually Chacha would completely lose her accent, while Jovita and Carolina had gone through most of their school years in Mexico and never lost theirs.

With the exception of Ramiro, all my brothers worked as laborers in San Antonio, Texas, or were self-employed. I don't remember Armando ever working for anyone. Pepe also became self-employed soon after moving to Houston while in his twenties. Details of what they did will come in later chapters. The following picture was taken in December of 1955 at Pepe's wedding. The picture was taken because it was probably the only time my parents' seven sons were together for anything. (Left to right: Armando, age 37; Felipe Jr. age 39; Jaime, age 28; Pepe, age 19; Ramiro, age 32; Enrique, age 26; and Roberto, age 22.)

Since my family was maintaining two homes, one in Monterrey, Mexico, and the other in San Antonio, we traveled frequently between both homes. Those of us in school would only travel to Mexico during the summer breaks from school. My father became a boilermaker and worked for the Missouri Pacific Railroad in their "Roundhouse." Felipe Jr. joined him there as a boilermaker assistant before going off to war and after returning from his stint in the army during WWII. We had free passes to travel by train anywhere in the continental limits of the United States. When we reached the border to Mexico, we had to buy train tickets to transfer to the Mexican railroad. Occasionally, we couldn't afford train tickets in Mexico, so we would take a bus. Monterrey is 150 miles south of the Texas-Mexico border.

Every student in my school (John B. Hood Elementary School in San Antonio, Texas) was Mexican American. My junior high school (Washington Irving Junior High), where I attended for grades seven through nine, was also 100% Mexican American. While my high school, San Antonio Vocational and Technical School was composed of both white (about 30%) and brown (close to 70%), there were no black students in any of my schools. Remember, Brown V Board of Education did not occur until 1954. The entire country was separated by the color of a person's skin. It was like living in one country with three very separate "worlds" inside of the one country.

The Korean War started in 1950. I was seventeen. We had a military draft then, and unless one (male citizen) was in college (and only those in upper class families could afford going to college since there were no student loans at the time), one could count on being called for active duty. The draft then, as I remember, was for males ages eighteen to thirty-five. Most of my friends in high school were called for military induction as soon as they turned eighteen. Many didn't wait to be called. They volunteered. I was in this latter group. In fact, I quit high school to try to qualify for the air force. When I took the aptitude tests to qualify for an Air Force Specialty Code (the famous AFSC), I was told I qualified for Air Traffic Control Tower operator. I joined in December of 1951. I was not sent to this chosen tech school. Instead I received training as a logistician. My immediate thoughts were that the school I didn't get must have been full and also that the air force needed logisticians more than they needed control tower operators. My cynicism, acquired over time, eventually led me to the conclusion that the air force didn't think I had enough command of the English language to communicate with flight personnel. There are several incidents later on in this book that will bring up this aspect of life in America for a citizen whose first language is not English.

I spent twenty years, close to a quarter of my life, in the air force. I became a military training instructor (for basic training) and spent two tours of duty at Lackland Air Force Base in Texas (1957–1961 and 1964–1968). I spent eight years as a logistician in Germany, Korea, Okinawa, and Panama.

With the exception of Jovita, all my siblings, including me, were married and had left home by 1957. I was the last one to get married. The first marriages occurred immediately after WWII ended. My first wife, Grace Campos, and I had four children, two boys and two girls, born in girl/boy/girl/boy order. My sister Chacha died in 1957. Her only son preceded her in death at the age of five in 1956. In 1964, I started my college career after turning 31. I attended college on a part-time basis for all of my degrees (bachelor's, master's, and doctorate). I lost my father in the summer of 1961 and my mother seven months later, when I was 28 and 29, respectively.

I started my second career in January of 1972 after giving the air force twenty years of my life. It was to culminate forty-one years later when I stopped teaching as an adjunct professor during the summer of 2014. I officially retired when I turned 65 in the summer of 1998, although I continued teaching as a substitute teacher at first and then settling into adjunct professorships at two different universities from the year 2000 until 2014. I spent sixty-one years working as a professional, twenty years in the United States Air Force, and forty-one years in education. As I will show in later chapters, I really began working for money when I was just 6 years old. I should add that there was a time in America when it was perfectly acceptable to look for a job at any age. More on this fact in later chapters.

This period of my life, at the age of 38, from January of 1972 on, was also a time for transition. I had spent twenty consecutive years in the air force, including tours in Germany, Korea, Okinawa, and Panama. After retiring in December of 1971, I found myself teaching as an Air Force ROTC Instructor at a Catholic High School in San Antonio the following month. I had already earned a bachelor's degree by attending classes after work and on Saturdays, while still being in the air force. I then earned two advanced degrees, my masters in 1974 and my doctorate in 1978. After obtaining my doctorate, I became an associate professor at a private university just one month after graduating. Even though I was on a tenured track, I eventually resigned from this position after three years in order to maintain my integrity and dignity because of an impossible supervisor-supervisee relationship I found myself in at St. Edward's University.

Regarding this incident, I can still hear my oldest sister, Jovita, as she looked at me somewhat disapprovingly when she found out I was no longer a "college professor." She had evidently told many of her friends that her brother was a professor. In fact, I remember her words: "What's the matter, Bobby, couldn't you cut it?" I remember, too, that I was not going to tell her I had told my immediate supervisor of the college department where I was an assistant professor to "take this job and shove it" and to find another fool to "put up with his shit." I loved my sister, and I could stand her short sightedness. I was used to it. These were stupid things to say on my part to someone who had the poison pen to write a bad evaluation on me. Still, I look at myself in the mirror every day and ask myself, who I am? Well, I know who I am. I had spent twenty years in the air force and that had to be bad enough insofar as always being told what to do and where you are going next. Also if all this education I had gotten was wasted, well then, I should do something else with my life. Yes, I was willing to do that. But I wasn't willing to lose my integrity and dignity because of someone's incompetence. I knew my profession. I lived it, slept with it, ate with it, and even dreamed about it such that I would get up in the middle of the night to write notes about my dreams, about my job. For most of my forty-one years in education, I have been on duty 24/7, and yes, I'm a little cocky about it because I have never been unemployed and have always engaged with other professionals in my field. I know what I know. Forgive me for tooting my horn. I have been excellent as a classroom teacher, as a principal, and as a college professor. I have the evaluations and comments from people to prove it.

I remember the incident at St. Edward's like it was two to three years ago. It was summer of 1981. I'd had my doctorate for only three years. I waited for the director (the one I told to take this job and shove it) to either yell back at me, try to strike me, or something. No, he simply walked out of the office, his office, and left me standing there. I went to my office and called Dr. Peder Matthews, principal at Williams Elementary School in Austin, Texas, and a former doctoral student with me at the University of Texas. I informed Peder of my situation (hoping I could get a teaching job at his school. It was also summer—the right time). I added that he should call the Dean to ask of my three-year record there at St. Edward's. I was that confident of my work. He told me to hang up and he would call me back in a few minutes. Less than fifteen minutes later, he calls me back. "Roberto, he told me you were 'prolific' in everything you do. I want you to teach sixth grade at my school. Just drop everything and get over here." I did. Going back to the classroom also meant doubling my salary. I still wonder to this day how St. Edward's, or any other Catholic university, can keep its instructional staff on board. Use your imagination: a college professor, with a doctorate, who easily qualifies for food stamps. As a caveat, remember also that the year is 1981, thirty-six years ago.

I spent the next three years teaching sixth grade under Peder Matthews, and I learned to truly fall in love with my profession. During those three years I also earned a certificate in educational administration. I never lost sight of my doctorate in educational administration and had every intention to reap benefits from it and go wherever my terminal degree would take me. I spent a full year working on my dissertation, after completing all my required courses, in a lengthy and costly study. It was all I did, 24/7, as I had resigned from my university position where I was a member of the Teacher Corps staff. All this occurred before graduating with my doctorate in 1978. I had four children, three in college and one in high school. I felt a lot of pressure to finish my studies and get back to earning a living for my family. I was hired right away by St. Edward's University in Austin, albeit at a salary that was less than that of a beginning classroom teacher. Yet, it was a tenured-track professorial position. This is why we get doctoral degrees, to seek a professorial position at a university. Grace was working, and I had borrowed $10,000 to pay bills for the one year I gave myself to complete my dissertation. I met my goal.

After three years in the classroom under Peder Matthews and having earned my certificate in educational administration from Southwest Texas State University, I was immediately selected as an assistant elementary school principal in Austin, Texas. One year later, I was appointed the principal at Bryker Woods Elementary School, also in Austin. The year was 1984.

My two oldest brothers died in the mid-1970s. One was in his sixties, the other his late fifties. Chito died of cancer four months shy of his sixty-first birthday. Armando died in Houston at the age of fifty-eight of pneumonia. Henry, only four years older than me, was murdered in a bar in San Antonio in 1976. While no one has been brought to justice for his death, what I do know about Henry is that he was dealing in drugs at the time. Ramiro, who was four years old when my father came to America in 1927, died in 1984. His death was due to a stroke caused by a clogged carotid artery. All four of my brothers will be mentioned again in the chronological narrative I will include in other parts of this book.

I also left my wife of twenty-four years in 1984. To this day I have a hard time explaining why I did this. Trying to answer the question posed by Peggy Lee in her hit song "Is This All There Is?" simply does not do justice to a milestone event that impacted a lot of people I love. Hurt most of all was Grace Campos Perez, my first wife, and my four grown children (Maria at 26, Robert at 24, Patty, at 22, and Rey at 19).

I was an elementary school principal from 1984 to 1998 in three different states. The first six were with the Austin Public Schools. Because of my divorce and, as probably happens in all divorce cases, friends and family divided into "camps," my ex-wife's and mine. Nonetheless, I wanted to be the best I could be, so I still had the desire to continue growing professionally. I began submitting applications for employment in the northeastern part of our country. I had now married again, and my second wife was originally from New York so that also had something to do with my wanting to leave Texas. I was hired as a principal in Maryland, stayed five years, and then left for Massachusetts during the summer of 1995. I soon suffered the same fate I imposed on my first wife. The difference was that my second wife and I had two children, ages 10 and 7. That brought on many issues.

I took a few too many risks as a principal that caused me to leave Maryland. I burned one bridge too many in my confrontations with an administration that, to me, was not truly invested in student learning.

Bridgewater State University, at the time producing more classroom teachers than any other university in the northeastern part of our country, selected me as a tenured associate professor. This was a tremendous feather in my cap because their search was nationwide. I felt quite privileged to be selected. To be selected as tenured and an associate professor meant I jumped many hoops that normally take fifteen years or more to accomplish. I eventually turned their offer down because my second wife begged me to take a different position elsewhere in Massachusetts. It was the stupidest decision I ever made. While I lost a lot of sleep over my divorce from Grace, this decision was one that would have me prop up in bed in the middle of the night for weeks, months, and even years. I wondered if I had dreamed that I turned that job down. The associate professorship was my goal when I spent four years in doctoral studies and in a very expensive research project. I cannot blame my second wife for this very stupid decision. It was mine to make. Yes, there were two children involved that influenced my decision. I wonder if my second wife ever gave the sacrifice I made (turning down this job offer) a second thought. I still have that long-lasting picture of her sitting in a chair in the living room crying her eyes out, like a baby, because her husband had accepted a professional position that was the culmination of a lifetime of hard work. This was a learned behavior that she used very effectively for most of her life, and this time with me. Like an idiot, I succumbed.

The job I ended up taking was as the principal of Wildwood Elementary School in Amherst, Massachusetts, a job from which I retired in 1998 when I turned 65. While I was in Amherst, my sister Nena died. My retirement soon became the start of my present situation and what has become the very best part of my entire life. I want to say that there is a reason for every decision one makes, that some "higher calling made that decision for me." Honestly, my beliefs have always been that if there is a God up there somewhere, he (she, it) helps those who help themselves. I have believed this from day one, and I have never believed anything else (even though I "thought" I was a good Catholic). I made things work for me because I worked my ass off to get the job done. I am by nature one of the hardest working people I have ever met. In fact, I have obsessions about perfection. I have had them all my life. I had them while I was in the air force, as some of the experiences I will mention later on prove to be the case. I have them today.

I want to say a few more things about my decision to turn down that associate professor position. There were a lot of factors in front of me that were tugging at me to *not* turn down this position. At least two were professional administrative members at Bridgewater State. One of them was a woman, also an associate professor, who asked to speak to me. She said she understood my attempts to satisfy my wife, and she applauded my consideration of her wishes. However, she added that in time, if I went ahead and took the position, both my wife and I would live to be thankful I accepted the position. I didn't internalize (enough) her words of wisdom. I did not think for one second of satisfying my wife and not accept the position. It was the thought of losing my two children. In fact, as I reflect more and more on this today, it was the fear of having my wife walk out on me and take these two wonderful lives out of my life that made my decision a little easier to make. Within a year, she walked out on me anyway. I have remained very much in my children's lives, in spite of her actions. Here it is, two decades later, and I can honestly say I am as close to Josef and Sofia as I have ever been.

This last period in my life has been the very best due to finally settling down to a healthy lifestyle. Much of the credit has to go to Carol Parker, who became my third wife. As I word-processed "my third wife," I had this slight feeling of embarrassment. You see, once upon a time I was a hard-core Catholic who wanted my faith, my marriage, my role as a son, father, brother, grandfather, uncle, and friend to be perfect. I wanted to go to heaven when I died and join my parents, brothers, and sisters. I no longer feel this way. My failure to comply with my marriage vows was the beginning of starting to feel inadequate in many areas. I eventually overcame my feelings of having failed, but only when I accepted life as being what one makes of it. I dropped everything in my life that made demands of me, demands that required me to be someone I was not. I had to be who I was, what I had become from living a rather full life. I had lived in Europe, Korea, Okinawa, and in Panama. I had married three times, had six children, had bought and sold five different homes in the states of Texas, Maryland, and Massachusetts. I was also seconds away from drowning in the Sea of Biscay ("mar Cantabrico") off the coast of France at the age of twenty. I earned a bachelor's degree from Florida State University and two advanced degrees from the University of Texas. I earned all three degrees going part-time between the years 1964 and 1978. Fourteen years! I never asked for any help, strength, or for prayers. I knew it was up to me to do. I gave up believing God could make a difference in my life. I was the only one who could make a difference in my life. The decisions one makes are the things for which only the individual himself can be responsible. I have to be responsible for me. If there is a God, he can only help me when I help myself.

This period also saw me truly become much more philosophical about my chosen career. I read the literature on teaching and learning from the perspective of human development and many related theories I believed in started to fall into place. Chief among these was the theory on building brain cells through aerobic exercises. It's true the jury is not exactly "in" on this, but there are many positive theories out there in the literature that say nothing but good things about exercise programs. And exercise is not only good for the brain, it is beneficial for almost every part of one's body.

About Carol. She and I are "cut from the same cloth." We are very different in ways that don't matter. I let her be who she needs to be. She lets me be who I am. She concerns herself with a healthy lifestyle. I do, too. I am attracted to her for many reasons. She cares about my six children (even though, today, they are 58, 56, 55, 52, 31, and 28). Carol is 63. She cares about all people, generally. There are examples galore of specific actions she has taken that prove where her heart is at all times. If a homeless man, dirty, and showing every indication he has other problems, such as a drinking problem, were to come up to Carol with his hand out, Carol would pull her wallet out and not give him a dollar, a five, or a ten, but would instead give him a twenty. I saw it happen as well as other incidents like this. She is a wonderful mother to her three grown children and a wonderful grandmother to her five grandchildren. She cares deeply about her two brothers and one sister. When her youngest sister Julie died recently, she substituted for her mother, who had preceded Julie in death by only a couple of years, and was there for her whenever Julie called her, and it was often.

This last period of my life also dwindled my previous fourteen-member family down to only me. My brothers Jimmy and Pepe, my sisters Jovita and Elida, died during this latter period. My sisters' deaths were more of a blessing. Jovita was only one year and a few months from reaching 100. She was mostly ambulatory, immobile, and wanted to die. However, Jovita kept her vivid awareness and was alert, conscious, and cognizant of almost everything around her. She even kept up with the news. Elida, on the other hand, had been fighting Alzheimer's for well over ten years and, as I said in my eulogy for her, her death was a blessing for her sons and daughters. Jimmy died in February of 2010 at the age of 82. Jimmy suffered with heart disease and diabetes.

An amazing fact for me personally is how beautiful life has become. It is a cliché to say one is *smelling the roses*, but I can honestly say this with a sense of honesty. I have never enjoyed a sunset more, or a colorful garden with multiple colors of flowers, or a well-manicured lawn, as well as a beautiful landscape. It can be dry, wet, hilly, or tree-studded and a deep green in color (as summers are here in Maryland). I would love it all. I love anything that looks clean and natural. I enjoy watching birds and I could easily join a birdwatchers group.

Is there a message here for the reader?

There is. Being a person of color* who was born into an American society where, for probably the greater part of its history, one's skin color has meant everything insofar as to how far one could advance economically, socially, and in acceptance in this country, I have always been conscious of this fact. It rears its ugly head even amongst people of color themselves, whether Mexican American, African American, or any other group that I consider among the people of color. I have become an octogenarian who has lived his entire life as an American, and I have more negative experiences about this fact than most people would care to know. They will come up in the chapters ahead.

I need to add that I believe this same prejudice probably exists all over the world. It just may be normal behavior for our species of animal. That is, we have this penchant to need to be better than others, or at least to *feel* better than others. Nonetheless, I don't care how the rest of the world behaves. I care only about this country, the country where my six children and I were born and live.

In America, prejudices and discrimination go farther than feeling better or superior. It is also calling people of color as not really being "American." If the reader could only see my face as I type this sentence. No, it isn't a scowl. It is a smile as I reflect on the irony of it all. When the white Europeans landed on this continent, they were, for all intents and purposes, greeted by people who look like me. In time, these European newcomers began to see the people who were already here as also not being American. There are so many clichés about American behavior, both here and abroad, that I am still thinking about, that the smile on my face hasn't left me. There's the one about the wealthy American middle-aged white woman vacationing in France and, while walking along an avenue in Paris, overhears some children speaking French as they play together. She stops to pat one on the head and says to the child, "My, my, so young, and already speaking a foreign language." This behavior is what earned us the label "the ugly Americans."

So what possible message could this book have for the reader? The message is that it is insulting to hear, read, and witness, from those Americans of European ancestry, that people who do not look like them cannot possibly be Americans. I am particularly offended for my family because four of my brothers and I gave a combined thirty-five years of our lives to be in uniform during the twentieth century, when we (America) engaged in three different armed conflicts. Add another nine years for the years four of my nephews also served in uniform and one should be able to understand how sensitive this issue can be for me. It would be one thing if my parents came to America in 1927 to have babies born here so they could receive benefits and to become wards of the state. The Perez family, my family, has only contributed positively, and has modeled the desired behavior for all of our citizens. We are judges, lawyers, teachers, and skilled artisans who, together with our children and grandchildren, have been among the most loyal and contributing members of the overall American population.

The color of one's skin has always dictated how one is perceived by the society at large. At this very moment I am remembering a time from the past when I listened to one of the ladies, a Latina, with whom I came in contact during the 1960s. The Civil Rights movement encouraged many American minority groups to speak out about the discrimination they were experiencing in this American society. At the time, I was attending college as a part-time student. People in these progressive environments have a tendency to speak from the heart and with emotion. This Latina I refer to was telling a sociology class I was taking that she resented very much being denied an honest, sincere appreciation to the words in the song "America the Beautiful." Yet while she may have been seen as a Latina, she thought of herself as an American who felt emotional whenever we celebrate special days like Memorial Day, the Fourth of July, Veteran's Day, and when her father and other relatives returned from the wars in which they were involved. I had that same feeling quite frequently, especially since I also spent twenty years in the United States Air Force.

The message I would like to convey to the reader is that, in spite of this prejudice on behalf of many Americans, we are not going anywhere. We have nowhere to go. We are home. It is an amazing *postulate* (here used as a basic principle and, of course, a noun) that I assume to be the truth. I say *amazing* for several reasons. When the pilgrims arrived here they did not find an uninhabited land. The people who were here were the first Americans. Many of us are descendants from these first Americans. Secondly, there is no written definition of who are truly Americans that even resembles such a postulate. Thirdly, this prejudiced perspective makes the rest of us feel abused, discriminated against, insecure in one's own country, and yes, as our former president is sometimes accused of being, angry as hell.

One final note on this issue. I received an email this past June from a nephew of mine who lives in New York City. He is my brother Ramiro's son, now 71 years of age and a retired lawyer. He is married to a Jewish American woman. He attached a picture of his grandson, born to his daughter who married a young white man from California. I met him and he is a delightful person who, at the time, was working for *Sports Illustrated*, a publication to which I always subscribe. My nephew's grandson, is also my great, great-grandnephew. He looks like any white European two-year-old. He, like many others of my own grandchildren, nephews, nieces, grandnephews, and grandnieces, looks less and less like his uncles, aunts, granduncles and grandaunts. My own grandson looks as European as anyone. He does not look like he has any Mexican American blood in him. But he does, as does my great-grandnephew.

In the ninety years since my parents arrived here as immigrants, we now have Pérez offspring in Texas, Missouri, Kansas, Florida, New York, Maryland, Delaware, Colorado, and California. With exception of the wars in Iraq and Afghanistan, the Perez men have been in some branch of military service in every war our country has fought in during these same ninety years. How much *more* American can we be?

I have given the reader a "capsule" summary of my life. I have included many of the major milestones of the life of an American family of Mexican descent during the twentieth century. Many more will come up in my narrative in the rest of this book. My objectives for this forward are only to put the premise of this story in its proper context.

The following picture was taken on St. Patrick's Day, 2017, of my sister-in-law Cruz visiting her son's grave. Enrique Junior was my nephew and one of my father's four grandsons who served proudly in our American armed forces. Enrique was a marine machine gunner in Vietnam.

Now for the details.

*A person of color is anyone who is not considered Anglo-Saxon or "white." Native Americans, African Americans, Latinos, Asian Americans, and every member of a third world country are, for me anyway, members of this group. While Latinos are from over twenty countries in the Americas, many people from these same countries remained European and their blood never mixed with indigenous peoples from their adopted new country. They don't qualify for the Latino label. The Spaniards who settled in Mexico and never mixed with the local natives were among the most discriminating groups in the Americas. But they were also in all the other countries. A recent "pure" European Venezuelan was overheard to say that the worst thing about Hugo Chavez was that there were more people of color eating in their fine restaurants. The speaker, a woman, was not being complimentary. These people, and the people from Spain, may be called "Hispanic." I am a Latino, but an American first.

My Earliest Years

Our community was made up of mostly Mexican American families. There were a few white families and even fewer families from the Middle East, Asia, Europe, or any other parts of the world. A homogeneous society we were not. We were segregated to a great extent. As Mexican American workers began to get better jobs and make more money, many would move out of the working-class areas and into the middle class communities north of the downtown area. As this happened, the white families began the extension of the city of San Antonio farther and farther out and away from the center of downtown. If one were to divide the city, at this time in its history, the southern and western parts of the city were where most of the Mexican American families lived. The eastern part of the city was where most of the African-American families resided. Most white families lived north of the city and have continued extending the city farther and farther north since that time. The Middle Eastern and Asian families lived for the most part near the downtown area. This, of course, is not the case today. We are in the twenty-first century and one's income determines where one lives, regardless of what we look like. I could easily add "one's income *ideally* determines…"

My initial recollection of how far west the city of San Antonio extended was from what was probably my first work experience. I remember being five years old, sometime after August of 1938, and my family not having much money. I can honestly say we didn't have much money because we didn't "buy" material goods and the talk around home was always to conserve and "to make do." There were no monetary allowances for anyone. Still, the word *poor* had not yet entered my mind. We also did not celebrate birthdays with parties. I honestly do not remember ever having a birthday party.

I was always looking for ways to earn money. I have recollections of mostly handing over to my mother whatever amount of money I made. I have vivid memories of a man who sold and delivered corn tortillas from a wagon that was pulled by a mule. I saw him come in front of our home every day and my mom would always buy a package. They could not have cost more than a quarter, probably a dime. As I watched him one day, the man asked me to go with him on his deliveries so he didn't have to tie down the mule at each stop, and I could simply jump off the wagon and walk up to the door of every home where he delivered tortillas. I remember the names of the streets as if it were ten to twenty years ago. We went west on Buena Vista Street (the street we lived on) and reached Zarzamora Street by dusk. Zarzamora Street was at least fifteen to eighteen blocks west of our home. This is about one and a half miles. We were, after all, being pulled by a mule. I knew it was dusk because already the lights on most homes were on and they were very scattered, as one would see in a sparsely populated part of any town. Today, Zarzamora Street is practically downtown and the city of San Antonio probably extends twenty-five miles farther west. Most of the side streets we went on were not paved. Most were gravel roads. The man probably gave me fifty or sixty cents for my endeavors. This is the year 1938, possibly into 1939. It was in 1939 that I began asking local mom-and-pop stores if I could help with cleaning or other chores in order to earn money.

I want to mention my experiences with both Jovita and Chito driving the one car in our family. I was told a few years later that every time I heard either Chito or Jovita go out the door and walk toward the car, I got in it before they did. I would stand on the back-seat and stretch my arms over the backs of the seats to balance myself. In later years, Chito would smile and remember that I always beat him to the car. I don't ever remember being told to get out of the car.

I rode along. And no, seat belts were not required. In fact, most cars probably did not have seat belts at all.

On one occasion, with Jovita driving, she was involved in an accident. It was more of a fender bender than a serious crash. I have no recollection of how it happened. I do remember Jovita negotiating with the other person about things like who was going to pay for the damages. My sister could stand her ground very well. Not sure if she received any compensation or what the final outcome was. What I do remember is my sister possessing a very serious look on her face and shaking her head in disagreement with the other party.

When I reflect on how tough life was at that time for my family, I base it on the things I have today but didn't have then. I really didn't have any idea that we were poor. When my shoes needed to be replaced, it was only after I had tried different ways to remedy the holes in the souls of my shoes. I was good at cutting out cardboard boxes, cutting them to form-fit the bottoms of my shoes, and I kept my feet dry when I had to walk on wet streets to get to school. Clothes were washed every day, and we had special clothes for Sunday Mass that we only wore on Sundays. My mother did her very best to have us always wear something new for mass on Easter Sunday.

When Lent started every year, we observed all the traditional customs that Catholics of that era maintained. My brothers and sisters always gave up something for Lent as a way of sacrificing pleasures they would otherwise enjoy and attempted to be in a deeper state of grace. I don't think my brothers kept any of their promises, and neither did I. I want to believe my sisters did, but it would only be conjecture on my part.

My mother had many recipes for Lenten food that omitted meat. While my father never participated in this observance, everyone else did. I don't remember my father ever participating with my mother in fasting during Lent. In fact, the only time my father was in church was when we had a wedding or a funeral Mass. I want to say he was an atheist, but I cannot prove he was. He never said a harsh word about the Catholic Church or criticized my mother for being so attentive to her beliefs. He called priests *"El Cura."* A literal translation would be "one who cures," or in more religious terms, "an exorcist."

At this point, and only to make a comment on something that occurred just before the end of the twentieth century, I'm going to jump ahead to the summer of 1998, the year I turned 65. The circumstances in my life at that time, including going through a very costly divorce, forced me to make the decision to retire from the world of work. The issues surrounding this decision will be explained in later chapters. What is significant is that I had been paying into Social Security since 1939, according to the Social Security records, and I had signed my name on the first card as "Bobby Pérez." I retired officially when I was living in the state of Massachusetts and my last position was as principal of Wildwood Elementary School, in Amherst. The Social Security office was in Springfield.

I am sitting in front of the lady who handles the completion of all the paperwork that is necessary to apply for Social Security retirement benefits, and she hands me a copy of my complete record of contributions, from the fifty-nine years of part-time (during my school years) as well as full-time employment. The second I saw "1939," I remembered vividly how, where, and when I applied for my Social Security card, at the age of six. I was born in 1933.

More, on signing up for Social Security at the age of six. Two blocks from our rented house on Buena Vista Street were the first set of railroad tracks that were part of the Missouri Pacific Railroad, where my father worked. The trains that were taken off the main tracks and moved into the Round House used these separate tracks. There is an entirely different dynamic on getting trains off the main tracks and into the "repair shop," for lack of a better term and not to over use the term "round house." Trains go forward and backward. They don't have wheels that a conductor or engineer turns in order to drive them into the shop. If they are taken off the main tracks, there was a change in the tracks they were on. This is usually done by backing them up far enough to change the tracks they are on and now can be moved into the round house.

My father was probably the only one who lived close enough to the round house to be able to go home during his lunch hour. There were small restaurants in the area where others could get a hot lunch. It is difficult for me to call them restaurants because they were more like small cafés. There could be five to six tables and a counter. One such café was named the "Do Drop In." I will remember the day I walked into the café until the day I die. I was all of six years old.

I remember walking up to the counter and having to look almost straight up to talk to the man who was behind the counter and looking down at me. He asked what I wanted. I say this because the man looking down at me was not surprised when I asked if they needed any helpers. I told him I was a hard worker and could be counted on to come in on time every day. It was summer and school was out. Actually, I didn't enter first grade until August of that same summer.

Now, I have to ask the reader to remember this is 1939. People are hustling to make a living. We are still mostly in a state of depression as far as our economy goes. When one looked for a job, it wasn't to make a career out of the job. It was to put food on the table and otherwise be able to survive. Yes, children in this working-class community learned to hustle to make a dollar, or fifty cents, or even a quarter. A quarter would buy you a sandwich, a drink, and probably get a nickel back in change

He tells me that he cannot hire me because I didn't have a Social Security card. He added that he had application forms, and if I could sign my name to the form, he would hire me to wash dishes. I signed a card after he filled it out, got my Social Security number that I used for the next fifty-nine years, and I worked there, as a six-year old dishwasher, for several weeks, until I was "run over by a car" on my way home one evening. Before I explain how I was run over and my first year of school, I have to say one more thing about my Social Security card. I continued using the name "Bobby Pérez" through all my elementary school years as I always managed to find a job during most summers. It wasn't until I was in junior high school that my teachers started calling me "Roberto." I also began noticing all my school records showing Roberto as my first name and having to respond accordingly whenever I was called. While I was never asked to declare a name change by the Social Security administration, all my work experiences were recorded under the same Social Security number. Evidently, the person(s) who first started receiving my contributions to Roberto Pérez and not Bobby Pérez saw no difference in the two first names and saw them as the same name. Thank goodness for that. My records have been straight since day one.

I remember many things about my first year of school. Henry, Elida, and I walked about twelve city blocks to get to San Fernando Catholic School. I entered first grade in September of 1939. Elida was in second grade (but in the same classroom as I was), Henry in fifth, and Jimmy attended a public junior high school far from our school. We wore khaki-colored pants and shirts as our uniforms to attend this school. All our teachers were nuns. I was always well-behaved and the nuns treated me with respect and dignity. I do remember that the kids who misbehaved were spanked. While I was never present in my brother Henry's classroom when he caused disruptions, I also remember hearing the conversations at home between Henry and my father and mother. The nuns would have Henry hold his arms out in front of him with his palms up. His teacher would slam a ruler on his hands. I don't remember how he said this to my parents, but I remember understanding exactly what the nuns did to him. He very obviously did not like getting hit. He played hooky from school a lot. The only problem with this was that Elida and I had to play hooky, too. We never left each other's side.

Remember, again, that this is school year 1939–1940. There was little emphasis on students getting an education and even less on truancy. There were two movie houses in town that opened their doors to show movies as early as 9:00 a.m. Their names were the Joy Theatre and El Obrero, which we fondly called "The O'Brian." Both places were only a few blocks from our school. We played hooky for several days until Elida informed my parents and that was the end of watching all those movies over and over again.

Before school started for the 1940–41 academic year, we moved to a bigger house on the town-side of the railroad station where my father worked. Again, it was two blocks from his job, and he could come home for lunch every day. Elida stayed at San Fernando (from where she eventually graduated because it was a first through twelfth grade school). I went to a public school to enter the second grade. Henry was eleven years old and dropped out of school. He worked at a variety of places where the businesses, evidently, didn't care how old he was. Besides, World War II is looming in the horizon and men age eighteen and older are either being drafted or are volunteering for the armed services. Laborers were in need in all industries. While my parents wanted us to make something of ourselves, getting an education was not something they pushed on their sons. My father would have preferred that all his sons follow in his footsteps and become boilermakers. What he didn't realize was that all of us saw how he looked when he came home from work every day, and to put it mildly, he was not a pretty sight. His coveralls were always black with soot.

I found schooling to be extremely easy. I was a straight A student. I remember the year I entered second grade and the teacher I had. Her name was Ms. Andrews, and I can almost see her in my mind's eye as I reflect on that experience today, some seventy-six years later. I remember when I was taken to her classroom, and she told the adult from the office who walked me to her classroom. "I saw his test results and his IQ is very high." Again, I need to add that this is 1940 and schools are not crowded. Pre-assessments of students' abilities could almost be done wholesale.

I honestly do not recall ever pondering Ms. Andrews's remark, even though I have thought about this fact from time to time as I have progressed through all my schooling years, eventually earning my PhD from the University of Texas at Austin in 1978, when I was forty-five years old. Still, like most of many friends from school, I, too, quit school as I waited to turn eighteen so I could leave home to volunteer for the armed forces during the Korean War. The armed forces would accept seventeen-year-olds if their parents signed a permission form. I do remember rationalizing it this way: I was hoping to learn a skill in the air force that would help me with employment after I left the service.

I need to go back in time now to explain how I was run over by a car. It was during the summer of 1939. We were still living west of the railroad (not the downtown side). I worked the evening shift as the dishwasher at the Do Drop In and was on my way home. Even though it was late in the evening, it was light enough for me to read a magazine as I walked on the sidewalk toward my home. I say "read a magazine," but I was probably just looking at the pictures on it. The café where I worked was only two blocks from my house. There was only one street that I had to cross before getting home. I remember starting to walk across that street and then the next thing I know my oldest brother Chito is dragging me out from under this car that I was under. I had bruises on my arms and upper body. My face was all cut up. I do not remember being hit by the car, the pain, crying, or anything else. I remember waking up the next day being all bandaged up and not being allowed to go out of the house. I remember very distinctly that Chito pulled me out from under that car with some anger, as if having to tend to me was keeping him from going somewhere. Chito was twenty-four years old at the time. I do not remember being hit and the car stopping after running over me, with me still underneath. In retrospect, I was lucky the tires didn't run over me.

Before going forward, a few things need to be said about what it was like in America in the mid to late 1930s. These were the Depression years and unemployment in our country was high. Children who came from middle-class families, or above, probably only had school to worry about. I always had school to worry about, but also how I was going to earn enough money to help my parents supplement what money my father earned, so I could buy shoes and clothes for school. School was never a problem because I learned to read before I entered first grade and found school to be relatively easy.

By 1938, with the birth of my youngest brother Pepe in March of 1936, our family now numbered fourteen. However, Jovita, Carolina, and Chacha were working and living in Monterrey, as was Ramiro, who attended high school in Mexico. They occupied my father's house. Chacha was fresh out of high school. My three sisters were high school graduates and were 26, 24, and 17 years old, respectively. That meant there were ten of us living in one home in San Antonio. My mother and father, two sisters, Graciela and Elida, ages

19 and 7, respectively; five brothers, Felipe Jr., Armando, Jimmy, Henry, Pepe, and me. My brothers, at this time, were 22, 20, 11, 9, and 2, respectively.

There is one particular Christmas that I remember very well. It was 1939. I was six years old. Times were really difficult because I remember that there were no gifts under the tree as late as Christmas Eve. Christmas trees were very inexpensive and everyone could afford one. We could, too. That evening, after it had gotten dark and my parents managed to put together a few dollars, Graciela ("Nena") was told to take Elida and me to a few of the closest stores where they sold toys. They wanted "something" to be under the tree the following morning.

The walk was about seven blocks. We first had to walk past the railroad station and the round house where my father worked, along with about twelve to fifteen pairs of train tracks. There were no homes. It was all stores, and most were closed. It was, after all, Christmas Eve. The one store that was still open was "Touduze and Company." They sold practically everything, from furniture to hardware, clothing, and also a few toys. How many toys would three or four dollars buy? Well, one could go to a movie theatre and buy a ticket for a dime then. So toys like a toy gun or airplane, or doll probably sold for no more than a dollar. I'm not sure if Nena got anything for herself. She had turned 20 two months before this Christmas. Nena was also in charge of maintaining the house and helping my mother with all the chores.

I remember we came home with a single toy for each of the three youngest in the family. That would be Pepe, now 3 and soon to be 4; Elida, 8 years old; and me, age 6.

We were very accustomed to not having very much. Yet our home was always clean, orderly, and chores were distributed evenly among all of us. Nena was an exceptional cook, and she learned to cook by watching my mother. Nena and Jovita (before she left to join Carolina and Chacha in Monterrey) assisted my mother in maintaining a very orderly home environment. Still, Jovita had a job and eventually earned enough money to be the first person in our family to buy a car. She was 27 years old. Felipe Jr. ("Chito") was 23 and

Armando was 21. Chito also worked as a helper in the same round house as my father. I remember Armando mostly partying and getting in trouble with my father. It is also possible that Chito and Jovita pooled their resources to buy that car because I remember both of them driving it at different times. It is now 1940 and big changes are coming not only for our family but for every American family. We are about to enter World War II.

We suffered our first loss in our family in 1943, and it was not a brother killed in action while fighting in WWII. It was my sister Carolina. She had contracted tuberculosis and, unfortunately, had Mexican doctors who made the decision to operate and remove that part of her lung that was spotted with the disease. The operation was not successful, and she died in surgery in October of 1943 at the age of 29. She was supposed to get married the following year. I had spent many days during the summers I spent in Monterrey with her fiancé and her because, like Chacha, Carolina took me on weekend excursions with them. Her fiancé's name was Reynaldo. I was close to them, even though I was only 10 years old when she died. Reynaldo treated me like his little brother, and I became close enough to him to eventually name my second son after him.

Jimmy, born in 1927 in Mexico, turned 18 in 1945 and couldn't wait to register for the draft. Ramiro had turned 18 in 1941 and returned to America to register for the draft. He was drafted and served in the Army Air Corps. Chito and Armando were drafted before Ramiro was and were immediately sent overseas and into combat. Chito was with a Ranger Unit from Texas that joined General George Patton's Third Army in the invasion of Europe in July of 1944. Actually, the first wave of American troops to land in Normandy was on June 6, 1944. I was still only 10 years old at the time but remember vividly the three stars that my parents hung on the front door to our house to show that this family had three sons serving in the war. While Chito marched all the way into Germany after the landing on Normandy Beach in 1944, Armando was seeing action in the Pacific. I remember, too, my mother telling us of the letters of commendation she received from the department of the army for the heroics of Armando in combat. I have no idea what

40

medals he earned because neither he nor Chito ever talked to anyone about what they went through in the war. I do know that the news was not always good about Armando because as many times as the army praised him, there were also notices of Armando being AWOL from duty. No, he never deserted or anything that serious, Armando simply loved to party, no matter where he was. Until his death in the 1970s at age 58, Armando never stopped partying.

By the time Jimmy turned 18 (July of 1945) he had three brothers in uniform and many neighborhood friends were also serving in the armed forces. I remember Jimmy anxiously waiting to take his physical. He was thin, like most of the men in our family were, and he was afraid he wouldn't pass the physical for being underweight. He would eat bananas day and night and drink a quart of milk in one sit-down. The day finally came for his physical. When I got home from school on that day he was spread out on the living room couch and did not respond to my question of how the physical examination turned out. I immediately got the message that the news was not good. He didn't say a word, and my mother told me to leave him alone. He did not pass his physical because his feet were several degrees too flat to be accepted. Everything else was good, but this was enough to be labeled 4-F.

It wasn't until several years later when I turned 18 myself and volunteered for the armed forces that I began to understand what Jimmy was going through. He had to face his friends, most of whom passed their own physicals and either volunteered, as Jimmy was doing, or were drafted. To be labeled 4-F was to be a failure as a man. Jimmy remained lying down on that couch seemingly for days. He eventually got over it. I will always wonder how much of his self-esteem was damaged by this occurrence. Jimmy and Henry were the only two men in our family to not serve in the armed forces of our country. Both would have loved to have served. To have done so would have been a partial fulfillment of being a man. Well, at least in the culture of many Mexican American families at this time in our development. I don't think this is the case today in 2017. I have to also admit that serving in uniform in the armed forces of our country did not mean we were so patriotic that we were willing to put our lives on the line for America. We wanted to be patriotic all right, but we also wanted to join our brothers and friends who were off fighting a war that all Americans were asked to be a part of. Besides, both Germany and Japan at that time were seen as evil empires that had to be stopped.

In 1945, Henry turned 16 on April 5, and he, too, couldn't wait to volunteer for the armed services. However, like Armando, Henry entered the adolescent stage with a passion for getting in trouble through bouts of juvenile delinquency. With his older brothers away, except for Jimmy, who was only twenty-one months older and could never advise or counsel Henry, there was no one at home to keep Henry out of trouble. He began by joining the wrong crowd of young people. It was not long before Henry and his friends were caught stealing and he was sent to a youth correctional facility in Central Texas.

It wasn't enough for my mother to have spent most of the war years praying her rosary every single night while my three older brothers were away at war. Now it was Henry who was making her worry. Having a member of the family get sent away to what was, for all intent and purposes, a prison, was not something my family wanted to share with all our other relatives and friends. Unlike my older brothers who fought in the war, Henry was a bit of an embarrassment. He served a full year at a facility in Central Texas. I remember accompanying my mother on those two-to-three-hour bus rides to get there and to see him. I was 12 years old in 1945 and, because my mother spoke little English, had to do all the interpreting for her. Eventually, Henry served his time and came home to get a job delivering food and supplies for a food company in San Antonio. Did Henry learn his lesson with that stint in that correctional facility? We thought he had, after all, he got a job right away and even bought a car. He also turned 18 in 1947 and was much older than his chronological age.

It was about this time that a milestone event happened in his life that should have been the best thing that ever happened to him. He saw a girl who lived one block away that he simply had to meet. One would think that he would find opportunities to be in places where she visited and then find a way to introduce himself and possibly start a friendship that may lead to starting a closer relationship. They did live only a block away from each other and this could possibly be a start for a friendship that may lead to other things. Unfortunately, Henry thinks of other extreme ways to impress Cruz Rodriguez, a girl he would eventually marry and with whom he would have three wonderful children. How did he impress Cruz?

My brother Ramiro was stationed for a short while at Brooks Air Force Base, a unit only a few miles south of the city of San Antonio. Ramiro kept some of his dress uniforms at home. With thinking that is definitely outside the box, Henry decides to put on Ramiro's army air corps dress uniform (while Ramiro is not home, of course), and go visit Cruz to tell her he's in the service, as a way to impress her. This worked. Henry must have looked like quite the hero, with Ramiro's medals on his chest.

Cruz never told me she believed him. However, they did become a couple, married, and had three children: Henry Jr., Roland, and Elizabeth. Henry Jr., like his uncles, also joined the armed forces during the conflict with Vietnam. Henry Jr. joined the marines and was a machine gunner. More on both Henry's and Henry Junior's lives in later chapters.

There is one incident in third grade that I remember like it happened just a few years back. It's been seventy-one years ago. It was a geography test that I found it hard to believe a test could have been easier than this one was. It was a matching test. One had to identify the product that each country was known to export to the rest of the world. Panama, bananas; Hawaii, pineapples; China, tea; Syria, oil; and so on. Well, I mixed them all up intentionally. Mrs. Martin, my teacher, looked at my paper as soon as I turned it in and gave me that "Bobby? Really?" look.

I remember the years 1941 through 1945, when I was between 8 and 12 years old. I loved baseball. I had my own glove that I took to bed with me every night. I remember using shoe polish so I could keep it shiny and looking like new. We had a team in the neighborhood and played every day, all summer, and after school when school started. I almost always played second base. I seldom struck out when I batted, but I was not a good hitter. I never mastered my swing even though I knew to keep my right forearm parallel with the ground. By the time I swung, I had dropped my arm and almost always got under the pitched ball. I seldom hit line drives. Yeah, I was at best a mediocre player.

Because my older brothers were all Yankee fans, I became a Yankee fan, too. I remember, too, that many major league players left their teams and joined a branch of service to fight in the war. Yankee players like Joe DiMaggio and Gerry Coleman, Red Sox player Ted Williams, and many others, left baseball to voluntarily join a branch of service.

I couldn't hear any Yankee games on the radio, but I could hear Harry Karay and his St. Louis Cardinal broadcasts. So I listened to Cardinal games on my portable transistor radio, although I never became a fan because they were in the National League and I was an American League fan.

I did follow the local double A team, the San Antonio Missions, a farm team of the St. Louis Browns. I remember the 1945 team because there were several very colorful players on the team that I followed. One was a Mexican American outfielder named Ruben Naranjo. He was at best a .240 hitter who would hit a homerun every twenty to thirty at bats. Mission fans loved him. The other two were pitchers. One was a wily veteran who had been in the majors but had been sent down. His name was Sid Jackuki. The other was a young pitcher with a lot of promise. His name was Ned Garver. Garver eventually was called up by the Browns and won well over a hundred games, with a fairly low earned average of just over 3 runs per game, in his career with St. Louis and Kansas City, where the St. Louis franchise eventually ended up as the town could not support two major league teams. While I could never afford a ticket to any games. I still traveled to the park on South St. Mary's Street as often as I could muster up a couple of dimes for the bus fare. I was always able to ask for a transfer to the second bus. I would arrive at the park, and I knew where all the fence knot holes were behind the outfield. There were a few choice holes that I needed to arrive early because other ten-to-twelve-year-old kids knew about them, too.

Since I also had a paper route, I always kept a copy of the San Antonio morning paper so I could read the sports page first thing in the morning. I had the paper route until my bike was stolen. I remember finding other ways to make a buck, like asking at several stores near our home if I could help after school. I almost always found a part-time job. On Saturdays I would go to the golf course at Brackenridge Park and ask golfers if they needed a caddie. I almost always found a golfer willing to pay me a few dollars to carry his bag for eighteen holes. Once, a golfer asked me to be there at the same time on the next day, a Sunday. I went to an early Mass and then took the two buses to get to the park. I knew I was late and was running like crazy after getting off the bus. To my surprise, the golfer held up his group for the few minutes I was late. I could not tell you what the guy looked like other than he was a white guy.

There was a time between 1945 and 1950 that I could name every player, on every team, in both major leagues. I remember a Red Sox team that had six or seven .300 hitters in the lineup. Let's see, Ted Williams, Dom DiMaggio, Al Zarilla, Johnny Pesky, Bobby Doer, and Birdie Tebbets (and I did not look these names up). Check it out.

The month I turned 12, I entered seventh grade and left elementary school, where I was always at the top of the class in all subjects. We had two sections for each grade level in elementary school and our teachers loved to have us compete against each other in language and mathematics. I remember my fourth, fifth, and sixth grade teachers always asking the class who they wanted to compete against the other class' best student. I can still hear my classmates say out loud, in unison, "Bobby." I remember having an ability to remember facts, math strategies, geography, and specific historical data about our state. I found school to be so easy that I would intentionally mix my answers so I wouldn't get a paper always marked "100%." There were boys in my class who resented anyone who did better than they did. No one ever tried to beat me up, but I felt their resentment nonetheless.

I wanted so badly to learn to play a musical instrument when I got to junior high school. I remember lining up before the music teacher as he had each student come up to him and attempt to give low, medium, and high notes to their voices, in front of everyone, of course. I already felt threatened being in junior high school with so many strange students after six years of being with the same group, that I was nervous. When it was my turn I couldn't get anything to come out of my mouth other than what must have sounded like a sick frog. The music teacher shoved me forward and hollered, "Next." I didn't say anything but my mind was yelling inside me "Wait. Wait. Wait. I can do it much better." But the next student was already bellowing out his notes, and I was rushed out of the auditorium, where all the other frog-sounding students were sent. I was not allowed to have *seconds,* that is, any other attempts at qualifying to play an instrument.

I had a reason for wanting to learn to play an instrument. In addition to always playing baseball as a youth between 7 and 15, I also played "guess this tune" with Roger Prado, my closest friend for some eight years. We would whistle tunes to each other and one had to name the tune. Songs like "Night and Day," "Laura," "Begin the Beguine," "Canadian Sunset," "Sentimental Reasons," "Paper Doll" were popular and among the tunes heard on radio. No, there was no television at this time. TV came into our lives, the lives of working-class people like we represented, some seven or eight years later.

In 1947, I turned 14 and entered ninth grade and my last year in junior high school. World War II had just ended less than two years earlier. Husbands, brothers, fathers, and uncles were coming home. I felt a lot of pride in my three brothers. All three came home. I knew Chito had marched into Germany as part of the Third Army with General George Patton in the summer of 1944. Chito went all the way into Germany before he had to be sent to a hospital in England. He wasn't wounded by German fire. He was suffering with frostbite after marching into Germany in the winter of 1944–45. Armando came home unscratched. Like Chito, Armando never shared what he went through. Neither did Ramiro, although he did not have to leave the continental United States during the war.

I was already driving when I turned 15. In 1948, one could get his driver's license at age 15. There was no such thing as a beginner's license. When one passed both written and driving tests, one was issued a driver's license. I memorized every rule in the driver's handbook and received an excellent score on the written driver's test. Now it was time for my driving test. My experience with a police officer was a very unpleasant one, even though I passed the test with flying colors. I arrived with my brother Ramiro, who drove the car to a designated place in front of the building. He then stepped aside and I waited outside the car for the police officer to arrive and give me instructions to start as he would get in the car on the passenger side. We (Ramiro) drove the car to the exact place we were told. It was my first encounter with a mean, ugly adult. I have never forgotten it.

The police officer looked like Ernest Borgnine in his role in the movie *From Here to Eternity*, with a full 250 to 300 pounds of fat on him. He had this really ugly look on his face as he bellowed, "WHO THE HELL TOLD YOU TO PARK THE CAR THERE? I WANT IT OVER HERE." Now mind you, I'm standing several feet from him, and he yells like I was a block away. "Over here" was ten to fifteen steps farther away. There are a dozen people standing around, waiting their turn. I don't remember being scared or feeling threatened. I was, however, left with a lasting impression.

I drove flawlessly. I have always operated very well when I'm challenged. This police officer (at this point I want the reader to know that I wanted to use some very unflattering descriptive words to describe him, and the words are not "Ernie Borgnine").

Between the summer of 1947 and December of 1951, I worked practically every single day in my father's service station. This included holidays and weekends. I was 14 years old and could do anything my brothers could do, including driving a car, which I had to because I had to drive my father home every day after we closed the service station. I don't remember many nights when Jimmy was still around at 10:00 p.m., our usual closing hour. Pepe was 11 years old and wasn't much help. In fact, he was not good with our customers. One negative incident occurred when a customer asked him to check his oil and water levels. Pepe looked at the driver and told him, "For a dollar's worth of gas, you can do it yourself."

This necessitates some explanation. A dollar's worth of gas in 1947 was fully five gallons of gasoline. The price of regular gas was nineteen cents a gallon. You don't believe me, huh? Look it up. I remember this well because I was usually the one who paid the bills when the Gulf Oil Company delivered our gasoline supply. Our cost per gallon? When we started in 1947 it was fourteen cents a gallon. Before I left in 1951 the cost per gallon, as a wholesale price, had risen all the way into the twenties (cents) per gallon.

Jimmy and I were the ones who ran and operated my father's service station. In 1947, Jimmy turned 20; Henry, 18. Henry had a job (and worked elsewhere), a car, was courting Cruz, and needed more money than my father could pay him. Jimmy started seeing Marina but was not anywhere near proposing to her, yet. And he didn't until he found another means for employment. He went to work for the very large department store, Joske's, selling furniture. Nena also had a job there before she met and married Diego Campos. My oldest brother Chito was back working at the Missouri Pacific Railroad Roundhouse and also got married in 1947. He married Esther Cuellar. Armando had his own business. He owned and ran one of the busiest Mexican restaurants in downtown San Antonio, "El Nopal." Chacha married Jesus Vasquez, a skilled Mexican crafts-man, and the two lived in Monterrey, Mexico. Carolina had died three years previously. With both Carolina and Chacha gone from our Monterrey home, Jovita set up her own business of being a women's hairdresser, in San Antonio. She also took it upon herself to become a type of matron-in-charge of family affairs. This was in keeping with her thoughts that my mother had remained very heart broken with Carolina's death. My father put our Monterrey house up for rent.

Ramiro remained in the Army Air Corps. He was a crew chief on small propeller-driven single-pilot fighter aircraft. He was sta-tioned at Brooks Air Force Base in San Antonio for a while. Ramiro asked me to go with him on one Saturday morning to watch him prepare the plane for a flight that afternoon. He could start the plane and drive it out of the hangar and work on it on the tarmac. This included washing the plane and hand-drying it, which he showed me how to do. I still remember his "be sure to circle your motions as you dry the surface" instructions. Ramiro would soon become a brother I would try to emulate in many ways, even though I remained very close to Henry, who was the closest to my age.

Before Jimmy and Henry got married, I remember their Friday and Saturday night partying. They seldom failed to go to this one dance hall called "El Patio Andalúz." I still remember the day after he met Marina because several friends came by to congratulate him on such a great "catch." It would only be a matter of time before he also got married.

As an aside to the story of "when Jimmy met and married Marina," I remember the conversations Cane ("Kahn-eh"), Jimmy, and other friends of theirs had when they conversed at home and I was allowed to listen in on their conversations. During one such occasion, Jimmy had not yet joined the group because he was probably working at the service station, but I was there. Cane contributed this (am paraphrasing now, but remember the distinct essence of how the conversation went) to their dialogue: "Boy! Jimmy sure got lucky when he met Marina. She is really a knockout." Jimmy would have been 90 this past July.

The year was 1948. The color of your skin meant everything in America. The tragic part of this statement is that discrimination of people of color was somewhat improved over what it was like prior to the war. America found out Mexican Americans knew how to fight. I wish I had kept copies of the editorials and letters to the editor that people submitted when the topic came up about sending all these "Wetbacks" back to Mexico. It's funny that the context of this argument was present sixty years ago when there was no drug war, loss of jobs, or concerns with Mexicans coming to America to have babies so they can go on welfare. It was plain and deliberate prejudice against people who looked different than white Americans. No matter how well they defended America against the Germans and the Japanese. Still, there were many letters condemning these racist viewpoints, and most reminded white Americans of the published casualty lists of World War II. Not only that, there were several Mexican Americans who won the Medal of Honor for their heroics during these wars, along with hundreds of other medals.

How far have we come anyway? Well, let's jump ahead sixty-five years. If the All Star Baseball Game of 2013 is any indication, the answer is "not very far." Mark Anthony, a well-known singer and an American of Puerto Rican descent who was born in New York City, sang the national anthem during this game and the hundreds of tweets, perhaps thousands, that followed were an embarrassment to the nation. A typical tweet said something like this one. "WTF! Whoever thought of having a fucking Mexican sing our national anthem?"

At this point in my story I want to inject the experiences I remember between 1941 and 1947 that involve my sister Graciela, or as everyone knew her, "Nena." As I reflect on my relationship with Nena, I remember her during these six years, when she was between 22 and 28 years old, as being a complete 180 degrees from the person she was in her last forty-nine years. Nena was vivacious, full of charm, and wit. She was a fancy dresser and this, in turn, attracted more second looks from young men wanting to get to know her. She was the tallest of my five sisters and as attractive as any of the others.

It was around 1941, when I was about to turn 8 years old, that I remember Nena and I living in Monterrey for the summer. She was 22. In Mexico, there is this custom of people walking around an open park in the evening and greeting people as everyone engages in these walks. When Nena went on these walks, I made it a point to always go with her. I was a little possessive of her, and I also knew that her charm and wit, and capturing smile, would attract young Mexican males. There was one occasion when Nena agreed to walk alongside a couple of guys that I made sure I was between Nena and them. They suggested a walk to a more secluded part of the park to which I answered for Nena and immediately said, in Spanish, "Huh, I don't think so."

Nena enjoyed a good beginning to her marriage to Diego Campos. They had three sons and one daughter—Richard, Ernest, Susan, and Eddie. Still, her marriage failed. Nena became the opposite of the person she had been. In fact, with Carolina and Chacha dying before Nena reached the age of 40, to go along with a failed marriage, my sister became bitter and was in constant verbal fights with Jovita. They sparred with each other constantly. I'm trying desperately to remember a time when they smiled at each other and cannot form a single scene in my mind when this happened. Diego, like Chito and Armando, was a veteran of the war. He and his brothers owned and operated a huge grocery store that employed all of them and was among the largest in the area at that time. With the advent of large chain stores like Handy Andy and H.E.B., the store slowly lost its clientele and had to close. The loss of their livelihood probably contributed to Diego's relationship with Nena and their marriage eventually failed.

Both Nena and Diego were excellent cooks. Nena tried her hand at new dishes, and she had the ability to improvise along the way and improve on the specialty she was making. Nena always prepared all the special meals for our family, even when my mother and father were still alive. One trait of the Perez women was to never let their mother labor in the kitchen as long as they were there.

Now, back to the war years. There were some signs that Chito had gone through some very heavy fighting. In early 1947, an army friend of his who was also a native of San Antonio came by several times to visit with Chito. They had served in the same outfit that marched into Germany. I remember marveling at his new Chevrolet car. You see, this army friend of my brother's had his legs shot off and his car was driven, completely, with the use of his hands. No, he didn't have artificial legs. He had no legs. My brother invited him to come into the house. Took several minutes before he could manage to get his wheelchair next to the driver's door to sit on it. Then it was another hassle to get back in the car when he was ready to leave. He got out of his car only once when he visited.

The first thing we want to think of when we see someone make such an extreme sacrifice for his country is that, certainly, our great country will take care of him for the rest of his life with some monetary compensation after suffering such a debilitating injury. I have no idea what the US Army, through our government, committed to paying him for the rest of his life. However, I do remember Chito, during one moment when he had had a few beers and he wanted to advise me after I volunteered for the Air Force in 1951 at the age of 18. He said to not take any risks, to play it safe at all times. He added that he had been getting a monthly check for suffering frost-bitten legs, something that continued to bother him during cold spells. He was getting a monthly $15 check. In retrospect I wonder what his friend was getting. The following picture was taken shortly after my oldest brother ("Chito") returned after serving in Normandy and Germany in 1945:

World War II occurred near the mid-point of the twentieth century and we are now fully seventeen years into the twenty first, yet I sense a very different attitude toward military service on the part of young Mexican American males today (2018). America did have conscription then, and we do not today. Conscription is defined as a mandatory enrollment for the possibility of being drafted into the armed forces of our country. Also, there were exceptions for those between 18 and 35, while not during World War II but certainly during the Vietnam era. Being enrolled in institutions of higher learning could exempt young American males. At one time, there were very few young Mexican American males enrolled in colleges and universities. So while joining a branch of service may have been inevitable for Mexican Americans, it was also a way of progressing into manhood and, as was the case with me, learning a skill that could possibly result in subsequent employment, a career, and a way to make a living. The GI Bill and college student loans changed the way all Americans, and not just Mexican Americans, now viewed serving in uniform. Like all American adolescents, Mexican Americans now consider going to college much more often than they do serving in the military.

Having stated the aforementioned, perhaps I should add some *qualifiers* as well. It is my humble opinion that the more *working class* a young Mexican American male is, the more likely the option of joining a branch of military service may be chosen. The more middle class a young Mexican American is, the less likely military service is even considered.

It is appropriate at this point to mention that white American adolescents will feel much more patriotic than their Mexican American counterparts to join a branch of service, today. Here again, discrimination and prejudices, both institutional and by groups and individuals across all of America against people of color, make life in uniform unappealing. Still, it has been the military that has led the way to introduce many different forms of inclusion since World War II.

A little more about Roger Prado, my closest childhood friend. We all called him "Kelo." He was the youngest of three boys in his family. The oldest was Raul. The middle one was Joaquin, known as "Cane," pronounced /Khan/ eh/. Kelo was two years older than me. He, too, was an excellent student in school. As soon as he turned 18, with the Korean War just starting, he volunteered for the air force. He became a jet engine mechanic. He ended up in Korea right away. After the war ended, he and I were reminiscing about our experiences during the Korean War. He was there when the action was hot and heavy. I arrived long after it was over. He remembered an incident with a navy jet coming in for a crash landing. He wasn't sure if the problem was mechanical or it had been hit by enemy fire. The emergency vehicles were all in place and Kelo, since he worked on the flight line, was also near the crash scene. He remembers the plane crashing on the runway but the pilot still being able to walk away from the plane. He looked very familiar when he took off his helmet. He was about 6' 6" tall. It was Ted Williams.

Kelo and I went our different ways in our lives. Still, I would always run into someone who had seen him or who knew what he was doing. He left the air force after four years and used his acquired skills as a jet engine mechanic to find employment at Kelly Air Force Base. He eventually retired after working at Kelly some thirty-five to forty years. Kelo's family doctor was another friend of ours with whom we grew up. He was the only person in the entire community whose family hailed from the Middle East. His name is Joe Haney, and he probably still practices medicine there in the west side of San Antonio. There is a tragic end to this story. Kelo went to see Joe Haney about his prostate. He had developed prostate cancer. I was told by a close acquaintance of ours that Joe told Kelo that he came to see him too late to do anything about his cancer. Kelo died of prostate cancer soon after we entered this century. He was probably not yet 70 years old.

Let's go back to 1945 for a bit of news about the Boy Scouts and me. I turned 12 in August of 1945. The elementary schools at that time had grades one to six while grades seven to nine were in what were then called junior high schools. My friends at that time were also my school friends as all students attended schools in their communities. While most of us were dirt poor, we all came from families who were hard working and lived their lives with integrity and respect for all others. The talk among my friends was to join a Boy Scout Troop and learn all the neat skills taught to them. Four or five of us did just that. Our troop met at the same Catholic High School my sister Elida attended and our scoutmaster was a young aspiring lawyer-to-be named Henry B. Gonzalez, who would go on to serve seven terms as a United States Congressman representing San Antonio and ending in 1986. I still remember the very first meeting I attended. Somehow I had managed to save enough money to buy "most" of the uniform items needed and started what became my trademark behavior for the rest of my life. We were asked to be able to recite the "Tenderfoot Pledge" at our first meeting from memory.

It was only 200 to 250 words long. Preparation for such meetings and events became my modus operandi for life. At that first meeting, Mr. Gonzalez asked who was ready to recite the pledge. There were probably fifteen to sixteen of us present. No hands went up. That is, until mine went up. I recited it perfectly. Mr. Gonzales gave me the Boy Scout salute. I liked the feedback. I would spend my academic life, after reaching adulthood, with this same approach. I can do whatever I set my mind to do.

The Period from 1950 to 1955

The most significant thing that happened in America during this period occurred on June 25, 1950, when we entered into the Korean War. As of last July 27, 2017, we remember that it was exactly sixty four years ago on that day the war in Korea ended. The war lasted thirty-seven months and one week. Its occurrence changed the lives of millions of Americans. It changed forever for the 1.8 million American soldiers, airmen, marines, and navy personnel who fought there and for the 36, 574 who died fighting there. In August of 1950, I would have entered the eleventh grade of high school. Many of my friends from junior high school and for my first year at Tech High School were leaving school and volunteering for the marines or the army. Some were 18 and did not need parental approval. For those still 17 (like me), no branch of service would accept them unless a waiver was signed by their parents.

While I had not thought of the military as a source for learning a skill or a trade that would allow me to earn a living, I very quickly had this as a goal for the immediate future. However, there was no way my mother would allow it. World War II had only ended five years previously, and she had very long memories of my three older brothers being in it. In my inquiries with recruiters, I learned that the only thing I would receive training in with the army or marines was how to shoot a rifle, live in the trenches, and hope to come home alive. I very quickly eliminated these two branches of service from my aspirations. I went to see an air force recruiter and quickly learned that this was where I wanted to go. Still, I had to wait until I turned 18 so I could leave without parental approval. Less than four months after turning 18 I was advised by the air force to report to the recruiting office in downtown San Antonio. I went through basic training and in mid-February of 1952 found myself on an air force plane headed for Cheyenne, Wyoming, and logistics school.

I had actually qualified to be a control tower operator based on my aptitude tests that the air force administers to all recruits. I fully expected to be sent to this school and saw myself as acquiring a skill that would help me tremendously after my stint in the air force. The air force doesn't have a way of explaining why things don't happen as they say they will. They don't have to. When one is in uniform, one belongs to that branch of service and one is liable to end up wherever that branch of service wants to send you. At one time during my enlistment there was some commotion about wives being able to reside with their in-the-service husbands and many could not for one reason or the other. While I was not married at the time, I do remember some of the excuses the air force gave for not allowing wives to travel and live with their husbands. One that was popular, and probably also stated sarcastically, was that "if the air force wanted you to have a wife with you when sent on an assignment, they would have issued you one." It was probably stated in keeping with the age-old axiom, GI, or "Government Issue."

The Korean War was raging in the Far East. The year is 1952 and the war is far from over. There are over one million men in the air force at this time and probably as many in the army. The combined manpower in the navy and marines approached this figure as well. Having said this, one should know that the air force had bases all over Europe, Asia, North Africa, Central America, and in many of the Pacific Islands, including Hawaii. It was no surprise that the technical school for training as a logistician was for six hours per day, six days a week, and for twelve weeks. More than that, there were three daily sections of training: 6:00 a.m. to noon, noon to 6:00 p.m., and 6:00 p.m. to midnight. Each section had between 180 and 200 men in training. I was in the noon to 6:00 p.m. section.

We marched to and from the schools every day. The school was in Cheyenne, Wyoming.

Logistics covers the acquisition, storage, maintenance, records keeping, inspection, receipt, and shipment of every piece of equipment and corresponding supplies to maintain an air force base somewhere in the world. The base has to function independently. There are no grocery stores, maintenance shops, restaurants, hardware stores, post offices, airlines, Greyhound stations, bus service, civil engineers to pave roads, plumbers to fix plumbing, hospitals, doctors, dentists, or parishes. All of these are part and parcel to what an air force base has to have in order to maintain its existence. And every base has all of these essential aspects at every installation, anywhere in the world. Realizing this serves to understand what the cost is to maintain one base alone.

Logisticians have the responsibility of maintaining adequate supply levels of all parts and equipment to maintain mission aircraft in the air and ground vehicles in a serviceable condition at all times. One doesn't realize while attending school of the pressure there is to maintain aircraft in the air at all times. If an aircraft mechanic requests any part required to keep the aircraft from being grounded, it is the logistician's job to have it available and very quickly in the hands of the mechanic.

I was very attentive in class and seemed to internalize everything without having to take notes or attempt to regurgitate any of the information. It was somewhat technical, but the procedures and the process were completely understandable from start to finish. I spent evenings and Sundays in the gym and never studied. I knew there was some summary examination at the end, but I had not yet learned to worry about tests.

It was probably during the second week of February of 1952 that I arrived at Francis E. Warren Air Force Base in Wyoming to attend logistician technical school. My flight from Kelly Air Force Base did not leave until midafternoon. The plane landed at night in the middle of a snowstorm. Well, it was a storm for me. I had hardly seen snow in my lifetime and the snow kept falling. It was also unbearably cold. I was put on a military bus and eventually dropped off on the second floor of a two-story barracks. There were some thirty double bunks on each floor. The first floor was full, and I was one of the first to occupy the second floor. The sergeant in charge of the traveling detail instructed me to change into my fatigues and report immediately to the dining hall next door for duty. I never unpacked or made my bed. I took my fatigues out of the duffel bag, changed into them, and reported for duty.

Ever hear of KP duty? KP stands for "Kitchen Police." Well, not fully an hour after arriving in Wyoming, I was on KP duty. I had an unbelievable task in front of me. When I walked into the kitchen of this big dining hall, the very first thing I saw was this huge pile of pots and pans stacked six to seven feet high against a wall right next to four very large sinks. There was a window about six feet wide and six feet in height next to the sinks. The "cook" didn't have to say a word to me. He just pointed at them and said they had to be done by breakfast, which started at 4:00 a.m. for the 6:00 a.m. sections. I quickly found the brushes, identified the hot water faucets, and developed a plan in my mind to get the job done. It was going to take minimally five to six hours. The grease on the pots and pans had grown cold, sticky, and thick. There were no gloves, either.

As I scrubbed them, I remember looking out the window and seeing the snow continuing to fall. I remember vividly thinking "What the hell am I doing here in Wyoming? How did I get into this mess? I want to go home." I don't remember shedding any tears, but I was one sad dude, for sure.

I finished the job before the deadline. I don't remember anyone thanking me because no one was there but me. The morning cooks must have come shortly after I left to go "home." Over the years, I have learned to call anywhere where I laid my bag down and had a bed to sleep in as "home."

In those five to six hours that I spent on KP, more airmen had arrived and were assigned to the second floor where I was. I remember entering the open bay where all the double bunks were and seeing one white airman sitting on his bed with a box of stationary on his lap, and he appeared to be writing a letter.

I was dead tired, but I caught him looking up at me so I said "Hi. My name is Roberto, and I just got off KP." He said his name was Willard Franklin Burns and added, "Please call me Frank." I thought, "Thank goodness." I can remember Frank, but I could hardly tell what his full name was because Frank had that wonderful West Virginia drawl to his pronunciation of English. It took me a while to understand every word out of his mouth. However, Frank was to stay in my life for the next twenty-plus years, and I can honestly say today that his English was close to being perfect. Well, to me, anyway.

Frank and I were in the same class. However, we had different likes and dislikes. He smoked. I didn't. I went to the gym every day and on weekends. He didn't. We both drank beer, so we'd go over to the Airmen's Club for a couple of 3.2 beers on a Saturday night during the eight weeks we were there. The two of us made friends with this huge German kid from Kansas by the name of James Danenhauer. James had a brother who a few years later would graduate from Kansas State University and be drafted by the Kansas City Chiefs of the American Football League. He was an offensive lineman. James didn't smoke or drink when he met us. Frank gave him one habit. I gave him another. He, too, would remain in my life for a few years.

While school was rather uneventful, I do remember learning a lesson about gambling that has lasted me a lifetime. I may buy a lottery ticket once every year or two, but that is the extent of my gambling since then. I learned my lesson about gambling on the very first pay day while in Wyoming. We were not paid by check. It was always in cash. I was a private first class. I had earned one stripe. It came after I completed basic training at Lackland Air Force Base in Texas. The scene on pay day became a routine that I would follow for years: Line up alphabetically for something. On this day, it was to receive my monthly pay of $75.

Everyone was instructed to report outside on the grounds and to line up again by barracks number, at an "at ease" standing formation. As soon as everyone received their pay and formed their individual formations, the first sergeant stood up in the middle of the grounds to speak. I remember this part of his short speech like it just occurred last year: "…if you're smart, you'll use chips…" He added that gambling amongst the troops was not allowed and "you don't want to get caught with money visible at your table." In essence, gambling was expected to occur—and I mean *all* types of gambling, from poker to blackjack to shooting dice. As I walked around the grounds of my squadron, I saw all three types going on everywhere, for most of the day.

As a preface to my story about a lesson learned, I should also say that $75 in my pocket (three twenties, one ten, and one five) was the most money I had ever had in my pockets to call my own. Sure, I used to close the small service station business every night that my father owned while I was in high school. But my father was right there with me to have me hand over the day's receipts every night.

I remember telling myself to not even think about gambling. I would only watch. I did a lot of watching. I slowly began to think that I, too, could win some money as more than a few seemed to be doing. One could walk away with several hundred dollars, if not thousands. I saw the first sergeant himself involved at a poker table in one of the barracks. I finally bought some chips and joined the Blackjack table. It seemed the one that didn't require a lot of skill, only luck.

Well, the one word short answers to what happened are these two: No and yes. No, I didn't win. And yes, I lost every one of my seventy-five dollars. It's a good thing I had a bed to sleep in and free meals. I did without any money for a month. I have not gambled since.

We graduated from our tech school in mid-May of 1952. The top five final test scores received an automatic promotion to corporal. I didn't even know this until I was asked to report to the orderly room soon after our classes ended to be advised that I had earned the top score among all the students. The highest possible score was a 5.0. Mine was a lowly 4.2, but still the highest. Four were tied for second at 4.1, including Frank Burns. I very proudly took all my shirts to a tailor to have my stripes sown on.

My reporting date at Camp Kilmer, New Jersey, was not until June 25, so I had some three weeks to spend at home before departing for New Jersey. I took a Greyhound bus to get home to San Antonio from Cheyenne. I remember that we had a short layover in Denver, as well as the incident I am about to describe. I will remember it as long as I live. It was late May or early June of 1952, exactly sixty-three years ago. I would not be 19 years of age for another three months. I remember traveling with my air force uniform on. I wore my dress blues. I was proud to wear the uniform. Besides, there was a war going on, and I wanted people to know I was doing my part in the war effort. Also, with two stripes on my uniform, I was officially a *corporal*. The "airmen" ranks would not come into play for another six or seven years.

The incident? I still had not started to smoke cigarettes, but I got off the bus just the same so I could stretch my legs and walk a few steps after the long ride from Cheyenne. There were many buses in what seemed like six or seven bus lanes next to the terminal. There were people on every bus. Buses were not all air conditioned in the early 1950s, so most windows were down. This was an unfortunate fact for me. I suddenly felt a semi-peeled banana strike my uniform at chest level and fall on the cement in front of me. I saw no one with their heads or arms out any bus window, but I heard several teenage voices laugh loud on the bus nearest me. I looked long and hard toward that portion of the bus, but no one looked back at me. It was a most cowardly thing to do. I was in uniform. The kids were all obviously white.

The incident bothered me for just a short while. I mentioned I would soon be 19 years of age. Nineteen years is a long time to walk around with one's eyes open and taking in all the abuses that people of color put up with in America. Still, I was too aware of the consequences of being involved in a confrontation while in uniform and what a bad example that would be. Nonetheless, when I looked in the mirror, I still thought I should have boarded that bus and asked who threw the banana at me. I didn't. Perhaps I was the coward.

Frank, James, and I all got the same assignment: Occupied Germany. I was anticipating an assignment in Korea. Still, this is

1952 and Germany was still the same Germany it was six years earlier, in 1946, a year after the war ended. It was occupied by the armed forces of the four major countries that defeated it. The country was divided into quadrants: The U.S., British, French, and Russian. The three of us were assigned to Fuerstenfeldbruck, near Munich, or as the Germans knew it, Munchen. Because the assignment was for three years, we were given three weeks of leave before reporting to Camp Kilmer in New Jersey and then to board a troop carrier ship for the ten-day trip over the Atlantic Ocean to get to Germany. I remember very little about what I did at home for those three weeks. I visited with friends, spent time with my parents at home, and just waited for my day to come so I could leave. I remember riding the train from San Antonio to New York City and then a bus to Camp Kilmer. I was still able to ride free on the train because I was just 18 years old and still eligible for the free pass I could get because my father worked for the railroad. Only my mother was home when Ramiro drove me to the railroad station. Everyone else was at work, in school, or living elsewhere because most of my brothers and sisters were now married. Only Elida, Pepe, and I were left at home. Elida had already decided she would be a nun and was in seminary school at Our Lady of the Lake College there in San Antonio.

This is a good moment to mention we were not a touchy-feely kind of family. I didn't get a hug from anyone, either the day before I left when most saw me for the last time, or from my mother because she was the only one at home on the day I left. When I joined the air force on December 15, just six months earlier, no one even batted an eyelash or think anything of it. We were a family that coped with whatever life brought. The only experience I had with a member of the family breaking down and crying her heart out was when my parents came home from Monterrey, Mexico, after burying my sister, Carolina, there in 1943, and Nena completely losing it. She had been holding everything in for days as she had to stay in San Antonio with Jimmy, Henry, Elida, Pepe, and me when Carolina died because we were all in school and the expense of traveling in Mexico was something my parents could not afford for all of us. My three oldest brothers were not yet home from the war. Only my parents, Jovita and Chacha, were in Mexico for the funeral.

I do remember before getting in the car that I looked back toward the front door of the house and saw my mother standing there. She had the saddest look I had ever seen on her face in the eighteen years of life I had lived. I waved goodbye and got in the car. Ramiro walked onto the train with me and it just so happens the conductor walked by us as he made his rounds to every train car. Ramiro got his attention and told him to look after me. It was twenty-nine-year-old big brother showing some concern for his "little eighteen-year-old brother."

My reporting date to Camp Kilmer was on June 19. Two days later, along with some 2,500 other American troops from all the branches of service, we boarded the USS *Horace Greeley*. One may wonder how that many troops can board one ship in only a few hours and the ship can set sail across the ocean on the same day. Well, American armed services have been doing this for a number of years and the transition from land to ship was quick and orderly. One could carry nothing but one's duffel bag to get on board. All 2,500 of us were prepared and were on board quickly.

It is very difficult to describe what a troop carrier ship looks like on the inside. The living area for that many people is large. Beds are stacked three high and the bed frames are made of steel and sturdy enough to withstand a 250-pound person. I remember having the top bunk. One does not unpack his duffel bag, but one does pull out a cloth laundry bag to tie down at the foot of one's bed where the clothes one takes off daily before showering are placed. We wore our fatigues for three to four days. We were issued three sets.

A few hours after boarding the ship, we reported to the dining area where hundreds of men are fed at one time. There were four to five shifts in three to four different dining areas that could accommodate these many people. There were no seats, chairs, or anything that one could sit on. We all ate standing up. Picture dining tables that are chest high and made of hard smooth-surfaced aluminum. One walked through a serving line where one not only got his tray of food, but utensils, salt, pepper, and whatever else that particular meal called for us to have. When we left our table at the end of a meal, everything was returned, and your area was left clean and spotless.

Soon after having our dinner, a duty sergeant came by to ask those whose rank was corporal or above if they wanted to supervise soldiers on work details or would they rather just be assigned whatever work detail came along. Neither Frank nor James were around when they asked for volunteers. I quickly assumed that both James and Frank would want to volunteer to supervise instead of doing the work, so I volunteered the three of us, without the two of them knowing I was doing this. As luck would have it, Frank and James went on top on the deck watching the sea at night and didn't get back to their beds until I had fallen asleep.

The three of us were picked to supervise army privates on KP. Breakfast was served starting at 6:00 a.m., so someone came by to wake us up and report for duty at 5:00 a.m. When they woke up, James and Frank they both said they had not volunteered, that there must be some mistake. Of course, I had to quickly own up to what I had done, but that I also had no intentions of having them be surprised at five o'clock in the morning on our first morning out to sea. Both took it well and were not angry at me after I told them the rationale I used to justify my actions. Frank and James were two of the most even-tempered people I have ever known.

I was on duty as a "KP Pusher" the entire ten days at sea. My job was deep in the galley of the ship, the lowest part of the ship. It was an extension of the kitchen and where I had some fourteen army troops from Hawaii working under me to "wash all the pots and pans that were used to feed the 2,500 troops on board this hip." I still remember arriving on the scene at 5:00 a.m. on June 21, 1952, and meeting all fourteen of them. I had to quickly set up shifts so that we could have someone always on duty and the majority during peak usage of pots and pans. They were one of the hardest working groups of men I've had the pleasure of supervising. I was asked almost immediately by one them if I was also from Hawaii.

From time to time, when I could leave them alone and be somewhere else on the ship, I would walk up to the top deck and look out to sea. At time of our existence on this planet, that is, the middle of the twentieth century, it didn't occur to me that I was watching a scene that would soon disappear from view and never be seen again. The reader can probably guess what I am referring to, particularly if the history of our oceans over the last fifty to seventy-five years is known.

As far as my eyes could see, I saw thousands of porpoises sailing up and down from the ocean. The movement of our ship could not have had anything to do with this spectacular scene. The fish were jumping in and out of the water hundreds, if not thousands of yards to our left, right, rear, and ahead of the ship. The ocean was just full of fish. I have read in the literature that, because of worldwide fishing of the oceans, we will deplete the oceans of any fish life before too long. I read also that there is some effort to preserve fish life in the oceans, but the effort is not having much success.

I didn't see much of Frank or James during these ten days because, as they would kid me often, I "fixed them up" with jobs to do for the entire trip. The truth was that almost everyone had assigned tasks to perform. There were many jobs that simply entailed scrubbing the decks super clean every day. I have memories of eating our three meals before the troops came because we were on duty while they ate. So there were only a handful of us who would eat in the dining areas before the hundreds came together. I remember the empty space between people eating standing up and our food trays moving twelve to twenty-four inches away and toward us as the ship rocked back and forth. I remember not reaching out to pull my tray back because it would come back to me on its own as the rocking of the ship shifted back and forth. With all this rocking back and forth, I did not get seasick a single time. There was one time when I felt I needed some fresh air, and I did walk up to the deck for a while. But this happened just once.

On the morning of our tenth day at sea, we saw land ahead of us. There were cliffs, as if on the side of a mountain. They were white. Someone said "Those are the White Cliffs of Dover." We obviously had entered the North Sea and headed northeast between all visible land until we saw the White Cliffs of Dover, which are quite a ways northeast via the North Sea after leaving the Atlantic Ocean behind us. We continued going northeast until we landed at the German port city of Bremerhaven. Bremerhaven is the landing site for all troop-carrying ships from America during this time of peace. We stayed in Bremerhaven for only one day as trains were already arranged for our continuing trip to Munich. Furstenfeldbruck is a very short distance from Munich and this last leg of our almost two weeks of travel is finally coming to an end. Frank, James, and I were assigned to the Thirty-Sixth Fighter Bomber Wing of the Twelfth Air Force. My assignment was with the property accounting branch of the supply squadron. James joined the inspection section and Frank the warehousing unit. We lived in the same quarters for our entire three-year tour in Germany.

Our stay in Furstenfeldbruck was short. The entire wing moved to a new base that was finally completed and ready to be occupied within six months of my arrival in Germany. The new base was in the western part of Germany, near the border to France and Luxembourg. It was in Bitburg, near the larger city of Trier. When we moved to Bitburg, a day-long ride by train, the entire wing moved with each airman carrying an M1 rifle and everyone in fatigue uniform.

I was less than two months shy of my nineteenth birthday when I arrived in Germany in 1952. In June of 1955, when I finally boarded a Pan Am flight back to America, I was two months shy of my twenty-second birthday. In today's world, in the twenty-first century, a person between his or her nineteenth and twenty-second birthdays is probably in college or performing an apprenticeship toward a skill from which to make a living. I was doing neither in the middle of the twentieth century. I was part of an occupied force maintaining a peace in a part of the world that now engaged in a different type of war. It was called the "Cold War."

However, my three years in Germany, but more correctly, in ten European countries because I managed to also visit Denmark, Italy, Switzerland, England, Luxembourg, Belgium, Spain, France, and Austria, provided me with life experiences that a similar time period spent in an American college classroom would not have given me. I was exposed to foreign languages, food, music, values, mores, and perspectives from that horrible war that had ended no more than seven years previously that left me with a lifelong lasting impression that to this day defines who I have become as a person.

I also grew as a logistician with tremendous responsibilities in supervising personnel and evaluating individual performances. I may have had only a partial high school education, but I was very proficient in the areas for which the air force held me accountable. I learned to communicate effectively orally and in writing. Because I held responsible positions in property accounting, I had both air force personnel and German civil servants working under my supervision. There were some fifty people working out of my office, equally divided between military personnel and German civilians. The Germans all spoke proficient English. There were only three men among the twenty-five Germans. There were two Jews, one male and one female. The female worked under the one Jewish male. His name was "Herr Bucher," and he was in charge of the local purchases we made of supplies and equipment from the German economic market. Herr Bucher and I worked very closely together. He was the only one whose performance was evaluated by an American civil servant, a "Mr. Hamilton." Herr Bucher and Mr. Hamilton were always at odds, and I became Herr Bucher's confidant for getting things off his chest about our jobs. Not surprisingly, his association with the other Germans in our office was minimal.

I had a warm and cordial relationship with all the Germans in our office. One was a young German lady, "Liesel," whose husband, "Hans," worked at a different American office on the base. The two lived in a very small village near Bitburg, with only a handful of farms around their very simple three-room house just off the main road. They wanted me to visit with them minimally two weekends a month. I consented on a few occasions. Hans drove a small Volkswagen and the three of us would tour the area that they wanted to show me. Several other Germans of their age who also worked on the base would also ask us to visit and Hans would drive us to their homes. I learned to love their German cuisine, their fine beer, and their always courteous manner.

During my three years in Germany, I took short vacations to Copenhagen, Denmark (Kobenhavn to the Danish people); Rome,

Italy; London, England; Barcelona, Spain; Luxembourg City; Brussels, Belgium; and many different cities in Germany. I also took part in a seven-week operation, sometimes called "maneuvers" in military jargon, in Marseilles, France, near the Sea of Biscay. Once a month or so Frank, James, and I would travel to Cologne ("Koln" to Germans), Germany, in the British Zone where we had met some English armed forces people and a few Germans our age who were also friends, to have a few drinks and just hang out.

I do want to single out a few of my experiences in Europe that I still think about today. My first trip outside of Germany was in the fall of 1952 to Rome, Italy. Because air force pilots have to get their flight hours in monthly, there are many scheduled flights to many different parts of Europe by Air Force personnel. I managed to get in on several during my three years in Germany. The flight to Rome was a Friday to Sunday trip on one weekend. I was so excited about visiting all the places that heretofore had only read about, including the Coliseum, the Catacombs, St. Peter's Church, The Vatican, and of course, having some real Italian meals. I remember getting a hotel room, showering, getting dressed, and deciding to lay down for a while before going out because I felt tired. I fell sound asleep and didn't wake up until the next morning. I had blown an entire evening, and I only had two to spend in Rome. I made up for lost time by spending the entire Saturday going to all the places I mentioned above.

The second trip was to Copenhagen, Denmark. I took a seven-day leave to go here and traveled by train. The same train I was on traveling through Germany was placed on a ferry, and I did not have to get off as the ferry carried us on the southwestern most part of the Baltic Sea and up to the port that is Copenhagen. One could see part of Sweden as we landed. I mostly toured the city, met a few Danish people and enjoyed some fine cuisine, as I did in each country I visited.

The most harrowing experience I had while in Europe was during the seven-week maneuvers we had in Marseilles, France. The maneuvers were titled "Operation Vapor Trail," and we conducted it in late summer of 1954. The hypothetical situation was that we had been attacked by the Russians and we had to abandon the base in Bitburg and retreat to a makeshift air base in France. We had to travel by long caravans of trucks. We did not have enough American drivers, so we had to also bring the German civilians who worked on the base as drivers in the transportation unit. As we drove into Marseilles, many French people started coming out of their homes and started yelling at the German drivers. They were not dressed in uniforms but the Frenchmen recognized them immediately and were furious. Fortunately, the yelling and their clenched fists were all that we experienced. The trucks dropped us off at this field unit we called Merrinac Air Base, a very temporary arrangement in the field where we had to live in tents. The maneuvers lasted for seven weeks. Our fighter jets flew missions day and night.

At the end of the sixth week of this exercise, we were given the entire weekend off. It was the first two days in over a month that we didn't have to get up and report for duty. We loaded a few flatbed trucks with beer and headed for the beach. I was never a serious beer drinker. I only sipped on a beer or two and three beers is probably the most I have ever consumed in one day. I never really liked the beer taste or the breath I would eventually get after drinking a few of them. Having said this, this fact probably saved my life. The beach was located on the southwest coast of France. It is known by the French as *le Bassin d'Arcashon*.

Arcachon Bay is a bay of the Atlantic Ocean on the southwest coast of France, situated between the Côte d'Argent and the Côte des Landes, in the region of Aquitaine. The bay covers an area of 150 km² at high tide and 40 km² at low tide.

After having a couple of beers, several friends of mine and I decided to get in the water and do as everyone else was doing, swim out away from the beach for thirty to forty yards and swim back. There were a lot people on the beach as it was in the middle of a resort area. There were a lot of vacationing families with children and rowboats could be rented. I remember the incident that almost cost me my life like it happened ten to twelve years ago. This happened when I was not yet 21, some sixty-three years ago.

I saw what I mistakenly thought was a permanent, round post buried in the sand, near the beach. It appeared to be some seventy-five to eighty yards away. I took the risk of swimming toward it, thinking that as soon as I reached it, I would hold on to it, rest my arms, and then swim back to the beach. I knew how to swim. I was young and strong. I may get a little tired, but I wouldn't try to swim back until I had time to rest my arms a little.

I had trouble reaching it. I didn't seem able to cut my distance to it. I sped up a bit and finally reached it. The minute I placed my right hand on top of this post, it sank. It was just a bobbing round piece of hollow wood that was floating out to sea. I panicked! I looked around me for the first time and suddenly I could make out the lettering on the big ships that were near land. I was out several hundred yards.

Almost immediately, I started swimming back to the beach, an obvious error now that I reflect on my actions. I should have calmly threaded water and used easy breathing and possibly floating on my back to remain afloat. No, I panicked and tried forcing my arms to swim back to the beach. I remember sinking. I remember opening my eyes under water and seeing daylight above the water that was above me. I remember needing to breathe and to cough up the water I had gotten into my mouth. I was very scared.

Somehow, I floated up to the top and rose my head above the ocean water. There was a small rowboat almost on top of me. A small girl, probably no older than ten to twelve, was alone in the boat. I remember being able to get these words out of my mouth, in English (I'm in France), "Could you row me back to the beach?" Her response was one English word. No, it wasn't "Yes" or even "Okay." It was "Surely."

I am not making this up. I remember hanging on to the rear of the boat as she rowed. As soon as I could feel the pebbles of the beach under my feet, I let go. I do not remember saying another word to the little girl, and she continued rowing away from me. I walked (worked) my way to a spot on the beach where I could sit down and reflect. All I could I think of was "What did I just experience? Am I alive? I have to talk to someone and check to see if they hear me. I did. The person heard me and responded.

I do not remember anything else from my seven-week tour of the Arcachon Bay. I do remember being gone from my property accounting office for seven weeks and, upon my return, the entire working staff being ecstatic to have me back. I have been in Germany now two full years, and this is my adopted home and these people with whom I work are the closest people I have in my life. There were four to five German girls my age or a little older who worked here and with whom I socialized. Most were older than me but treated me with respect and dignity. They would often ask about my own family back in Texas and showed an interest in me as a person and as their supervisor. I grew professionally, socially, and also learned about acceptance of one another no matter how differently we look. Emotionally, I was very glad I still had another year left of my tour in Germany. I had adapted to this lifestyle and felt completely at home.

Frank, James, and I worked in different divisions of the logistics operation at our base. The three of us had progressed into being leaders of our respected divisions. I was in charge of the property accounting division. James headed the inspection of all property and supplies received from depots around the world. All shipments went through his division before being issued to users and consumers or before being stored as stock that became ready to be drawn when needed. Frank was in charge of all the storage and had numerous warehouses under his control. The three of us lived in the same dormitory and would often continue our coordination of all three divisions in our dormitories.

We also socialized together. I had mentioned previously that a favorite German location where we visited on weekends was in the British Zone of occupied Germany. The city was Koln, or "Cologne" as everyone but the Germans called. We stayed in military quarters that the British and French troops sponsored and we paid only for our meals. The rooms were free of charge to all allies of the British. We made many friends, British and German, and we met socially at our favorite dance halls and everyone called each other by our first names. Even after leaving Germany in the summer of 1955, I sent cards to a few of them from my home in San Antonio. They were just friendly greetings to people who had become our friends.

Occasionally, the friendly talks would take a serious turn and every now and then some strong feelings would surface. On one occasion, and I'm not sure why we had this subject on the table, the discussion turned to several serious relationships between some German girls and several airmen from our group. Frank and I didn't have such serious relationships going with any girls from Koln. However, this didn't stop one of the girls from telling me that I should consider marrying a German girl and taking her to Texas with me. I remember the incident well because the girl hardly knew me, and she and I didn't have any kind of personal attachment, other than knowing each other through mutual friends. My feelings were hurt a bit when she said something that sounded like this statement: "I have read that Mexican women have a tendency to get fat." I am paraphrasing here but not with the use of the word *fat*. I immediately countered with "This is not true. I never met any fat Mexican women." Now I'm carrying her exaggeration to an opposite extreme. We changed the subject. But later on, and for several years after this happened, I would relive this moment of my experiences in Germany with some of the German people. I introduced this topic as one that caused *some strong feelings*. In retrospect, my feelings passed almost immediately, and we returned to just having fun and drinking that good German beer.

I visited Spain and England in my last twelve months. The trip to England was a two-day weekend visit to London. I spent every waking moment touring Buckingham Palace, the Changing of the Guard, and traveling back and forth using their marvelous subway system. I met a young English woman who showed me around and was almost like a tour guide to me. She wanted me to leave England with a solid impression of her country.

There were many other things about London in the mid-fifties that did concern me. After being in Germany for two years and enjoying exquisite cuisine and a push toward modernity, I saw a London that lacked refrigeration and a people who seemed unhappy, perhaps even bitter. I sensed that the British were already seeing a

Germany that was quickly rebounding from defeat and learning to stand up with some pride in their new found progress in the world.

I traveled by train to Barcelona, Spain. A major reason for going was to be the best man at a wedding of a friend who was also stationed at the same base I was, stay a few days, and then see Madrid and possibly other parts of Spain. Being best man was something I had consented to do for this slightly older sergeant who had been living in Europe for a number of years, had traveled to Barcelona, met a young woman with whom he had gotten engaged, and wanted me to travel there and participate as his best man. I really didn't know him that well. We lived in adjacent dormitories. He knew I spoke Spanish and he would often engage with me in Spanish because he needed to practice it more. He had courted this girl from Barcelona for several years by visiting Barcelona and meeting her family. They had known each other through work experiences. Both appeared to be in their thirties. I had just turned 21.

I met several families who participated in the wedding and was invited to several post-wedding affairs. I ended up staying in Barcelona for the entire two weeks I had planned to be in Spain. There was just so much to see and do, and I had made friends with several members of the bride's family.

All in all, I had a life in Germany, and when my enlistment was about to expire, I was not too excited about returning to America. Yes, I wanted to come home to see my parents, brothers, and sisters, but I had also acquired another life that was very different from the one I lived in America as a person of color who was generally viewed as *suspect*. In Europe, I was everyone's equal. Not only that, I had a position of authority and was treated respectfully. I returned these same compliments to everyone. My life of equity and equality that I had in Europe would be missing in my life as an American. I felt it in the air the moment I landed in New York City in June of 1955.

Having said this, I feel a need to quickly jump ahead to an evening in Maryland and fifty-five years into the future. I am approaching my eightieth birthday. On the evening of July 31, a Wednesday, I perform my (now) monthly ritual of taking my oldest daughter out for our monthly dinner together. My wife, Carol, accompanies us about half the time. My daughter, Maria, is my oldest child. I say "child," but would be 59 in December of 2017. Maria and I are always frank, honest, and no subject escapes us. Maria has been married and divorced and is once again married. Her two marriages have not been "pieces of cake." The subject of our discussion is "Americans who are viewed as suspect," and which I identified fifty-five years ago as a feeling I quickly felt upon my arrival back in America.

Maria quickly made me aware of an incident involving one of the building services workers, who happens to be African American, at the school where she currently works. Maria is the executive secretary to the school principal. She has been at this school now for several years and knows every person who is on the staff. This one worker mentioned loading a 36" HD TV in his car to take and to give to his girlfriend. He had the TV in his car as he drove here in Maryland. A police officer pulled him over for no reason other than "suspecting" the TV had been stolen. The verbal interaction was not pleasant as the police officer quickly "questioned" why he had such an expensive item in his car. The building services worker was "ordered" to get out of his car and to "lie face down on the ground." The worker would not do it. It just so happens the stop was made across the street from where the worker's brother lives and his brother came out to see what was going on. The worker's brother, using non-verbal body language, urged his brother to "do it." The police officer has a gun in his holster, after all. The worker told the officer he would sit down on the curb but would not lie facedown.

The encounter ended when the brother identified the worker as his brother and the police officer ended the confrontation.

I have to wonder, how many times a day incidents such as this happen across America. On this day in 1955, it didn't "happen," I only "felt it."

Welcome home, Roberto.

The Period 1955-1956

I n 1954, one year prior to departing Germany and coming home to end my four-year enlistment (in December of 1955), I received a letter from my mother informing me that my sister Elida had left the convent and was no longer seeking to become a nun. I was not entirely surprised by my sister's decision since I knew Elida always felt my mother's wishes were that she do something different with her life. It is not something that I fully understood about my mother since she was so religious and a very strong Catholic. I would have thought she would be very happy to have someone in the family follow her zeal for Catholicism. Elida was a very private person, and I doubt she shared her views on this decision with anyone.

My mother had another reason to write to me about my sister's decision. She was coming home now. She was also 22 years old and looking for a job with no plans to even go to a community college. She had no transportation to get around. Mom knew I had been saving money during all my time in the air force. In fact, I had close to two thousand dollars in my savings account. I had designated my mother as a co-owner of my account. I instructed her to take one thousand dollars out of my account and give to Elida to get herself a nice, used car to get around and look for a job. Now, remember, this is early in the 1950s. One could buy a new car for under $2,000. This amount would buy her a good used car. Elida did get a very nice used car. She did get a job. For me, having one thousand dollars saved in the bank felt no different than having two thousand dollars saved. I never gave it a second thought. This was a family matter, and I was happy to contribute.

My three-year tour of duty in Germany was coming to an end. I received my assignment to Randolph Air Force Base, only a few miles north of San Antonio. I felt like I was going home for good even though I still had until December of that year before my four-year enlistment would be up. Frank and Jim also go their assignments. I cannot remember where Jim was sent, but Frank was assigned to a base in San Antonio as well. He and I would see each other again. Neither one of us suspected that Frank would enter my life on a more permanent basis once we got to America. As for Jim, I listed him as a reference, as I did Frank, when I applied for a top secret security clearance with the air force because of a job I was pursuing. More on this particular topic in the next chapter.

I could live at home and report for work every day. I could treat my last six months as no more than a job. I received my "separation" on December 15, 1955. All service members during the Korean War had a further commitment, after separating from active duty, to continue as "reservist" for an additional four years. At the end of these second four years, I would get my "discharge." I would turn 22 in August of this year, but I was also quite naive and immature in my thinking.

Naive and immature? Yes, I made one very bad decision not more than two weeks after arriving in San Antonio in the summer of 1955. I, too, needed a hundred dollars to give down on a used car so I could travel to and from Randolph AFB. Then, when I left the service and found a job, I could probably afford the monthly payments and live at home until I could afford to move out on my own. This would have been a workable, sensible plan. However, it was not what I did.

I had this mistaken fear that I could not find a used car that was serviceable and that I could drive safely to and from Randolph. I made the foolish mistake of buying a new car. This was summer of 1955. A Mercury Cougar, with all the extras, cost me just under $3,000 total. I also figured, erroneously, that if I gave $1,000 down on it, the balance of payments would be something I could handle with almost any job I could find after leaving the air force. I remember signing the deal with the Mercury salesman and going to the bank to draw out the one thousand dollars. I still remember the bank clerk saying, "Sir, if you'll wait until Monday, when we will be in July, you'll receive the interest of 6% of your balance added to your account, and that would be $60. This is on a Friday. I could have called the salesman and said, "I'll come close the deal on Monday." Did I do the sensible thing? No, I wanted to drive that new car off the lot and have it for the weekend. How immature and naive can a person be? Stupid is a better description. I would soon regret all these dumb decisions.

Before the month of July (1955) was half over, Frank arrived in San Antonio and reported for duty at Lackland Air Force Base. I picked him up at the railroad station and brought him home to spend the weekend and later would drive him to Lackland. At the time, my mother and father, Jovita, Elida, Junior (Chacha's four-year-old-son—more on where Chacha is residing follows) and I were living at home. We had three bedrooms, so Frank and I shared a room for the weekend.

Tuberculosis Strikes Again

Chacha, married to a Mexican National*, and living in Monterrey with her husband, "Jesus Vasquez" and son Jesus Gerardo ("Junior"), all of 4 years old, was diagnosed to have tuberculosis. The year is 1954 and, other than removing the infected parts of a person's lungs, like one would treat lung cancer, the medical community had found no cure. After leaving her husband in Mexico and returning to San Antonio to be taken care of at home, Chacha had to enter a tuberculosis hospital as a resident because she became contagious. Junior was now being raised by my mother and my sister Jovita.

Frank reported for duty and spent four months at Lackland before he left the air force and went home to West Virginia. While he was stationed here in San Antonio, I took him to Monterrey, Mexico, so he could get a feel for what the interior of my parents' home country was like. What one sees at the border towns is nothing like what one sees in the interior. I suppose border towns have the influence of a "partying America" and the towns are filled with stores that cater to the American dollar. What I didn't realize was that drinking water in Mexico usually affects American stomachs much like taking a laxative would. I was stopping my car almost every thirty minutes on our way back to Texas so Frank could use a bathroom.

Something else happened to Frank while he was here, and it was something I had not noticed. He and my sister Elida started seeing each other and started to go "steady." Before I knew it, *steady* progressed to their commitment to get married. More on Frank and Elida later on in this chapter.

I spent the entire fall of 1955 and into January of 1956 applying for positions, apprenticeships, anything short of going to college and starting to earn a degree. In fact, I couldn't take advantage of the GI Bill and having part of my tuition paid by the government because I had not earned a high school diploma and could not get into a college. I also lacked having a high school equivalency. I will resume this part of my story (Winter of 1955–56) after first retrieving back a few months to June of that same year (when I arrived from my three years in Germany).

*Have to add this remark about Jesus Vasquez: Chacha was the epitome of a mature Catholic woman in her mid to late twenties when she met "Chuy." She attended Mass regularly and it is during a Mass that they met. Chuy was an educated and skilled craftsman earning good money and never entertained the thought of immigrating to America.

It concerns my sister Chacha, her health, and having to be confined to a very restricted environment that was, in essence, very much like a prison as she was unable to have her four-year old son brought for visits because she was considered to be highly contagious with tuberculosis. As I reflect now of this moment in time, I can see why I may have been influenced to buy that new car. You see, Jovita and I took turns driving my mom and dad to this hospital where Chacha was confined. It was minimally a forty-five-minute drive each way. While the visiting hours for family were practically all day long and into the evening, both Jovita and I had jobs and neither one of us arrived at home before six o'clock. My "job" was at Randolph Air

Force Base where I would be until separating from the air force six months later. There was never a single day that either she or I did not drive to this hospital. Jovita had been driving our parents to the hospital every day for several months until I arrived on the scene in late June of 1955. Chacha never left this hospital until that fateful day in November of 1956 when she died while still confined there.

Both my mom and dad were home all day, since my dad had retired, so Junior was supervised and cared for. He could entertain himself and was very much like his mother, calm, courteous, and very well behaved. I could tell Chacha had taught him well. I frequently heard him say "Sí Abuelita," or "No, Abuelito." Also, "Dígame, Tío," and "Mande usted." These are the same courtesies I grew up with through all my developing years. My mother also corrected my Spanish. No, she didn't teach me Spanish. She only spoke Spanish to all of us. We were immersed in this beautiful language.

Disaster Strikes the Family…Again

You know now that Junior's mother, my sister Chacha, died in November of the following year. Junior preceded her in death by a few months. Here is his tragic story:

During late summer of 1955, Junior became ill with what one would assume is a bad cold. He didn't have a runny nose or cough. He did have a high temperature. Since my mother raised twelve children, treating a four-year-old with a temperature was nothing she hadn't seen before. Still my mother didn't think she should make a doctor's appointment just yet. She tried mostly across-the-counter medicine and other well-known family and cultural approaches to handle childhood illnesses such as Junior was experiencing. Nothing worked. The high temperature (102 –104) continued.

It was just a matter of time before she tried a "Curandera." In the Mexican culture, there are many who believe that certain people in our culture have mastered the power to use a type of witchcraft to cure people who otherwise cannot be helped with traditional approaches from doctors and medicine prescribed by these doctors. I assisted her in looking for one. Of course, we inquired of our neighborhood friends and others who might know of a Curandero or Curandera.

But even before approaching one, my mother tried various things she knew of and that had been taught to her by her mother and other family members of her mother's. These included prayers mixed with such unexplainable things as cracking a fresh egg on a hot cement sidewalk, rubbing certain vegetables on Junior's forehead, and other things she tried before I arrived home from Randolph every day. Nothing worked.

We took Junior to the family doctor, a Dr. Urrutia. As fate would have it, Dr. Urrutia was unavailable, and we ended up seeing an associate of his, a Dr. Holly. This unfortunate circumstance cost Junior his life, and it is my humble opinion that this also killed his mother who lost her will to live knowing that her son was dead.

Here is the rest of the story. Dr. Holly diagnosed the problem as appendicitis. He said he needed to operate as soon as possible. We assumed this meant Dr. Holly would, of course, not operate until he brought Junior's temperature down. As all of us lay people do, we trust our doctors to know what they are doing. We assumed the hospital staff found a way to bring his temperature down before the operation was performed. The operation was performed. We found out later that Junior's appendix was very normal. His condition after the surgery was not. Junior entered into a coma from which he never recovered.

He was in the recovery room for a week before Dr. Holly and the hospital staff told us we should take him home to perhaps recover at home, that there was nothing else they could do. My mother, father, Jovita, and I were devastated with what was happening right before our very eyes. And just what is one supposed to do when facing such a tragic dilemma?

Well, we are Christians, right? God is mighty and can perform miracles if we pray hard enough, long enough, make promises of sacrifice, and more. No, our prayers were not answered. We went back to the Curandera. She tried a number of things. Of course, witchcraft is BS and the only thing that matters to these people are the fees we promised to give them.

Before leaving the hospital and Junior's room, I searched for and found the one doctor in SA who was the most experienced with people in comas and unable to recover from them. Luckily, I reached him by phone, explained Junior's situation and what happened to him with the surgery (obviously, a *huge* botched-up surgery that never should have happened). He said he would come by Junior's hospital room, examine him, and then advice the family what to do. He added that his fee would be $25 in cash, payable before he left. The year is 1955. Twenty-five dollars then was probably worth what $200–$250 is today.

I will remember him, his visit to Junior's hospital "door," his name, and what transpired until the day I die. It is also the reason why I am my number one advocate when it comes to my own health. I trust no one. I trust me, and only me.

Dr. William S. Baxter came to the hospital as he said he would. He *stopped* at the door and did not take one more step into Junior's room. He essentially told me, "Yes, your nephew is in a coma. I have heard that some people do come out of these. Well, I have to go now. I'll take the $25, please." Shocked at his actions, or lack of action, I was still composed enough to pull my wallet out, take a twenty and a five out of it, and place both bills in his hand. Life in America and what the almighty dollar does to people are lessons we probably all experience. My lessons learned with this so-called doctor were that sons of bitches come in all colors and professions.

My mother and Jovita cared for Junior, in the coma he was in, for close to a year. They changed his diaper (yes, we had to put diapers on him). The only positive thing that I remember happening in that one year was the day I came home from work and my mother said to me, "Oh Roberto (she and my dad were the only ones to not call me Bobby), his stool today was the same as when he was well and playing around the house. It was smelly and resembled a child's stool who is healthy." You see, my mother never stopped praying and hoping for that miracle that only God could cause. She believed in her God.

Junior developed a bad case of diarrhea. We tried everything to stop it. It would eventually cause his death. It is ironic that this was the cause of his death. It was diarrhea that killed him, after a botched up surgery that never should have happened. A lawsuit? It is not what this family does, or at least, did *then*. I remember Jovita telling me that when she inquired at the lab at the hospital about Junior's appendix, she was told it was a perfectly normal one. Yeah, we could have sued. We suffered two deaths in the family, and we really didn't want any reminders of such a tragic time in our lives

Yes, we told Chacha everything. I was in her room with Jovita and we told her in as loving and gentle a way as we could. I told Chacha I saw Junior take his last breath. It was like a huge sigh. Junior never opened his eyes while in the coma, and he didn't when he took his last breath. Chacha was Chacha. Stoic. Not a tear one, at least not in front of us and while we were there. It was summer of 1956.

Chacha continued losing her health. Perhaps a bit more rapidly now that she had lost her will to live. When that fateful day came, I happened to be the only one visiting her on that day. I called Jovita to come quickly with mom and dad, but she didn't get there in time to see Chacha still alive.

Chacha and I talked very coherently before she succumbed to her death. Her mind was very clear, and she said things to me that I could not possibly include in this book. I am not sure I can ever repeat them to anyone. A few of her comments were about me. Chacha and I had a very unique relationship for a sister and younger brother. She knew I was well read and had no trouble talking to me as if I were only a year or two younger than her, and not the twelve years that I actually was. During those summer months in Monterrey, from 1939, when I was 6 years old, to 1952, when I left to join the military, she was closer to me than even my mother. I remember the look on her face those last few moments. She appeared to not be in pain nor sad that the end was imminent. It was the same peacefulness I always enjoyed being with her. When she closed her eyes and was gone, I felt extremely sad, but still, I felt she knew where she was going. Perhaps, where her son was. There was also the unexplainable feeling of being thankful she is no longer sad and suffering that loneliness that was with her all this time. The date was November 17, 1956.

Now, back to summer and fall of 1955. Know, too, that the afore-mentioned information about Chacha and her son Junior occurred during this same period. I will try to only mention these occurrences where I have to in order to make sense of the information.

My thinking continued in an immature way. I continued trying to find employment and dismissed any thoughts about getting an education. I felt unqualified to pursue an education. In the mean-time, my savings and whatever money I received upon separation were quickly diminishing. I had to do something. I had never asked my father for money, ever, and it was bad enough that I was living under their roof without having to ask for anything else. Also, I had always taken care of myself without asking anyone in my family for any help, and that included my father. I never gave this a second thought.

All my brothers except for Pepe were now married and gone from home. Pepe would be the next to get married, but he was living in Houston. I had not kept in touch with any of them during my four years away from home and only felt close to Henry, who was just four years older than me. Soon after arriving home in the summer of 1955, I met him at a local bar for a drink and quickly realized that my brother Henry was not going to be able to counsel me about getting a job or even suggest ways that I could make a living. Here is what happened.

We met at a bar in the deep west side of San Antonio. It was his suggestion. The bar was a place where Henry and his friends met, probably every day, to drink. These places served only beer. I don't think there was a bar in San Antonio, other than downtown where professionals would meet for happy hour after work, where there was anything else but beer served. If Henry drank hard liquor, it was at his home because the beer "joints" he frequented didn't have the licenses required to serve mixed drinks.

Henry was accustomed to drinking at the bar. We stood at the bar to drink a beer and talk. He didn't ask me anything about my life in the air force or what I intended to do with my life. We

were constantly interrupted by his friends who were curious about
who I was. I was not dressed like they were. My hair was short, my
clothes were cleaned and pressed, my shoes were shined, and I wore
"dress" clothes, that is, dry cleaned trousers and a dress shirt but no
tie. I was definitely "out of place." Once, when Henry went to the
restroom, one of his friends, not much older than me, maybe in his
early thirties, said to me in a low tone of voice, "Man, you're not
Henry's brother. Who are you?" I felt like hitting him in the face with
a clenched fist. Henry came back and I said, "Let's go somewhere
else." I just wanted to get away from his (sorry about this label, but I
was pissed as hell) low-class, trashy friend. Henry wanted to stay, as
if he didn't know of any other place. I told him I was going to leave
and perhaps we could talk some other time, perhaps when he came
home to see our mom and dad. When I came out the door to find
my car, I felt like brushing my clothes off any smell that may have
penetrated into the fabric. It was mostly a marijuana smell amidst all
the smoke in that place.

I started remembering my brother when he was in his teens and
I was between 12 and 14. I remembered taking my mother to visit
him when he was in Gatesville, a prison for youths and very young
adults. I felt a cold sweat on my forehead and thought immediately
that my brother was again hanging out with the wrong crowd, as he
was ten years earlier in our lives. I thought about the bar I had just
left and the people in it, and I wanted to yell back at Henry to get
the hell out of there. Of course, I didn't. Henry was four years older
than me, and I didn't remember anyone ever telling him something
that he listened to.

I didn't see much of Henry in the next few months or years.
This is 1955. Little did I know at this time that his life would end
violently in a very similar environment some twenty-one years later.

Mom and Dad were still alive in 1955. We were by and large a
working-class family with the men earning a living in manual labor
jobs and the women being courted by men from similar backgrounds.
Elida had found someone very different in Frank Burns. Jovita had
chosen to remain single and look after our mom and dad. Nena met
Diego Campos and lived her life as a stay-at-home wife and mother

with three sons and one daughter. Chacha met a skilled craftsman from Monterrey, got married, and had one son.

The oldest, Chito, met and married Esther Cuellar, and together had two sons and one daughter. Armando, second oldest of my brothers, married a girl from a nice family from Monterrey, Mexico, and had one daughter. They would eventually divorce and their daughter died at a very early age from pneumonia. Armando never married again but did live with a number of women in both San Antonio and Houston. One of the women he lived with gave birth to a daughter, Mary Jane, after she and Armando were no longer living together. Mary Jane remains in our lives today. There is more on Mary Jane later on in this chapter.

Ramiro, third oldest brother of mine, only married once, but he had three different families. The first family was with an Italian American girl from New York City, where he was stationed for several years, and with whom he did not get married. He was in New York City long enough to have three children with her. The oldest, Robert, was born in 1945. Ramiro did something that is not easy to write about. He abandoned his New York City family and returned to Texas. That I know of, he never intended to return nor to parent his three children. I will return to complete his story in other parts of this book.

Jovita, who had her own hair dressing business in Monterrey before leaving Mexico for good after our sister Carolina died, worked as a hairdresser at a private salon. She had bought a home and was looking after my mother and father. She had her own car and things were somewhat stable at home. Almost everybody else was gone from home, married, or otherwise making a living for themselves. Elida and I would be the last two remaining at home.

December came and I left the air force without any celebrations, partying, or anyone in our family even noticing. For some reason my family seldom celebrated significant milestones in our lives and they sort of "came and then were gone" while life continued as a routine way of existing. There was one very significant event that happened on December 26 of that year (1955), and this event was my kid brother Pepe's wedding. He married Violeta Rodriguez, and while I do not remember any details about his courtship of Violeta, I do remember that she and her family were also from Monterrey, and I remember that they had an aunt and uncle whose family lived next door to us. It is significant to add that Pepe was born in 1936, so he is all of 19 years old. I will guess that Violeta was probably not yet 19. Their first child was born on the same date in 1956, so a shotgun wedding this was not.

Armando, my second oldest brother, and Pepe were the two family members who were self-employed for the majority of their adult lives. Armando was already the owner of several Mexican-food restaurants in San Antonio. Each had a booming business and my brother should have had a very successful career in this business. He ran an efficient, clean restaurant with good food and employed very good workers. He had successful restaurants in downtown San Antonio as well as in one western suburb. His downfall was that he never overcame his penchant for partying. As I remember, he would get lost for weeks. There is no telling where he went, with whom, nor how much money he "blew away." What the records show is that he lost every restaurant he owned because he abandoned each one. Unfortunately, my father bailed him out of several dilemmas only to keep him out of jail.

He moved to Houston and, although I want to say he was successful in a new work environment (selling fruits and vegetables door-to-door in Houston's middle-class neighborhoods), I remember being asked by him once for five hundred dollars in late 1975. I sent him the money. I did not expect to get it back, even though I already had a family with four children, all under the age of 17. He was my brother. For some crazy reason, I never thought I would not send him the money. I knew he could not go to anyone else. Both my mom and dad were now gone, and he had a knack for not getting along with any of my sisters and other brothers. I felt somewhat obligated. Armando was fifteen years older than me, and even though I knew about his poor decision-making in his personal life, I felt a little pride in being asked.

Pepe and Violeta also moved to Houston. Pepe called Houston home and the city is where he raised his five daughters: Maricela,

Cece, Amalia, Jo Ann, and "Lulu." Pepe and Violeta eventually divorced and he remarried. His second wife's first name was Guadalupe. When Pepe died in 2016, he was all of 80 years old and estranged from his second wife as well. Pepe and Guadalupe had a son, Joe Junior, and he and I have learned to communicate with each other. More on Pepe when I reach this century. I am currently still in the 1950s.

Enter 1956. I am now starting to think seriously about my situation and began changing my outlook on life and what I want to do with it. With so many military bases in the area, one possible avenue was to seek employment as a civil-service logistician at one of these bases. In listing my priorities, this was way down on my list as a choice. I am still only 22 years old. I am also unemployed, living in my parents' home (Jovita's, actually). The best thing I could do while living here is to contribute the best way I could. Monetarily, I could not at the present time, so it was essential that I find a job.

There were none I would accept. Not that I felt I was above being a laborer. It was that the pay was less than minimum wage. I had only enough money to make about three more car payments. That new car purchase was looming in my head as one huge error. Losing the car and the payments I had made so far was not something I was willing to do.

In the meantime, while being concerned with my own personal problems, my family was having it worse. These were the months when Chacha's condition had worsened with each passing week. Not seeing her four-year-old son was bad enough. Her husband Jesus ("Chuy") decided to stay in Monterrey in the job he had for so many years and also attempt to communicate the best he could with my sister and with his son. Still, I managed to find time to still attend a few social functions where I met and made friends. I even started seeing a girl on more than one occasion because we had some things in common.

When it appeared we were getting a bit too serious, we both decided neither one of us was where we wanted to be. We remained friends but decided against seeing each other anymore. Not sure what ever happened to her. I knew one thing. I was getting more and more concerned with my own future and not having direction. These thoughts kept me up at night. That is, until I made some hard decisions for my life.

I never shared my thoughts with anyone, not that I even tried. I suppose I could be called a loner, a person who always looked out for himself. There were no precedents in my life up to this point that triggered this solitary approach to life. I just had this penchant to act on my own, look out for my own health and make serious decisions about what to do with my life. I realized I was at a very uncomfortable place in my life. Twenty-two years old, not really skilled at any one thing that would guarantee a decent wage and the possibility of raising a family.

I knew that I was skilled as a logistician. However, the skills I had as a logistician and the skill level I had acquired after almost four years of experience were at the supervisory level and were not transferable to a civilian job. The starting point at a similar job in a civilian world were at the helper or apprentice level. This would prevent me from going out on my own and meeting all my expenses. This included the car I bought in one very big mistake that kept me up nights on end.

I knew if I were still in the military I could attend college on a part-time basis and pay only 25% of my tuition. This thought lingered on my mind for days. There were, however, some necessary things that had to be completed first before I could even think of taking advantage of college while in the military.

I was informed by an air force recruiter that I could retain my rank as a staff sergeant, my specialty code (as a logistician), and even be assigned again to Randolph Air Force Base. I was also told that a minimum requirement to be able to attend college at the expense of the air force would be to have either graduated from high school or have the equivalency a high diploma. I quickly applied to take the high school equivalency tests. The results came quickly, and I received high marks on all the different batteries of the test. I passed everything.

I immediately reenlisted in the air force.

Reenlisting in the Air Force

The decision to reenlist entered my thoughts by late January of 1956. I was still looking for a job that offered some training and perhaps one that also allowed me to acquire a professional, or at minimum a semi-professional, job that permitted me to be able to live on my own, save money, and feel like I was preparing for the future. Acquiring a high school equivalency did absolutely nothing for me insofar as acquiring a job. This is about the time in my life when I started thinking about long-range goals. Until I reached that final goal, there would be dozens of intermediate goals to attain first. Fortunately, my thinking was mature enough not to feel threatened by my very low starting point. Hey, I just managed to get a high school equivalency, at the age of 22. Yeah, my scores on all the batteries were very high, and I was proud of this fact. It did serve to give me the confidence to always think I could do it and I would eventually reach my long-range goal. No, I never imagined a doctorate. I did imagine a college degree though.

This is also the time in our lives when Jovita and I are spending our evenings driving our mom to see Chacha in that infirmary known as a "state hospital" for the sick who are contagious with certain diseases. I drove four to five days of the week because there were many days when either Jovita or my mom had to stay to look after Junior, still in a coma and needing care on a 24/7 basis.

The decision to reenlist was also greatly facilitated by being assured by the air force recruiter that I would be assigned again to

Randolph Air Force Base. My rank would be restored as a staff sergeant, meaning I did not have to live in the barracks with other airmen but could live "off the economy." This privilege was SOP (standard operating procedure) in all the branches of service. It was part of the military truisms. It came under the banner "Rank has its privileges." I could resume assisting my parents and Jovita with all the driving back and forth to see Chacha. Then, too, because I had not been out of uniform for more than ninety days, the air force would give me a monetary bonus to reenlist. The amount, as I remember, was in the "neighborhood" of $1,500. This helped with the quickly accumulating household expenses.

One would think that with so many members in this family that others would also take their turn in driving daily to see Chacha. Felipe Jr. was raising a family and had two children under the age of five. A third would soon be born. Armando, Henry, and Pepe lived in Houston. Elida's job did not give her freedom in the evenings to participate with us. Ramiro was still in the army and stationed elsewhere. Jimmy did not own a car that was dependable for the long daily runs through the entire city of San Antonio. Nena's family, although they lived next door, had only one car and she had not yet learned to drive, even if she was thirty-six years old. Besides, neither Jovita nor I ever asked any other members of our family for any assistance. It simply is not something either one of us ever did.

What my family and I went through for the period June of 1955, when I arrived back in America after three years in Europe, to Chacha's death in November of 1956 has already been described. I will pick it up from this point forward. First, I do have to mention that I met Grace Campos and fell madly in love with her. It was summer of 1956. I don't know when I found the time to see her, given what Jovita and I were going through with our daily excursions to the state hospital.

Here is how we met. Grace and her family lived on the same block as my lifetime friend since childhood, Roger Prado. He and I would occasionally find time to hang out. On one of my visits to his home, Grace came to the apartment next to Roger's and his family.

She was there to visit her aunt and uncle. I cannot remember her aunt's name. I do remember her uncle's. It was Gerónimo Pérez.

It is worth mentioning here that a third very close friend who "hung out" with Roger and me was a first generation Syrian named Joe Haney. He lived with his widowed mother and an older brother. Their home was somewhat dilapidated like all the other homes in our community. It was my guess then, and now, that the Haney family rented their home like the rest of us did. No one had a front yard that was more than ten feet from the sidewalk to the front steps of our homes. Joe's older brother was a mailman. These are the fifties. Our community is a working-class neighborhood with hardly anyone growing gardens or mowing the grass. It is roughly one mile from downtown San Antonio. Remember, too, that we lived no more than two blocks from the Missouri Pacific Railroad station.

Joe Haney was something of a pariah amongst us. There were seven to eight other boys with whom we grew up. Most of us were from the working class of America. No, I would not classify us as being even close to a middle-class label. Most of us rode city buses to go to school, to go to work, and if not, we walked. Joe Haney did, too. Yet, all of us could tell he was meant for bigger and better things, perhaps because he dressed and talked differently and attended the one major Catholic High School in San Antonio, "Central." He had no accent in his speech. The rest of us did. All of us spoke Spanish first. Joe spoke three languages: English, Spanish, and the native language of his parents. The only other local boy who attended Central, a Mexican American youth, went to college and eventually earned a commission in the army and attained the rank of colonel. He was also a decorated Vietnam veteran. His last name was Martinez. His family owned the one major grocery store in the neighborhood. In the years ahead, I would also learn that this Martinez youth was also a cousin of my brother Jimmy's wife, Marina.

Joe Haney would not only earn his college degree, he would go on to become a doctor. Why did I describe Joe as a pariah? After completing his internship and residency, Joe set up his practice in one of the neediest and poorest communities in the west side of San Antonio. Here we're talking of 100% working-class Mexican

American families. As I reflect today, Joe's stock has gone up even higher. He applied his skills as a doctor where he was needed the most, and not where he could make the most money.

It is important that I not leave this brief respite of related news about my family without jumping ahead to the beginning of this century. Joe and Roger continued crossing paths throughout the fifty or so years that transpired between Joe becoming a doctor and Roger remaining in San Antonio as a jet engine mechanic working at Kelly Air Force Base. Joe's specialty was as a pediatric and adult urologist. Around the turn of the century, Roger made an appointment to see him on a consultation regarding Roger's development of prostate cancer. According to friends of ours who knew both Joe and Roger, Joe's statement to Roger after examining him went something like this: "You should have come to see me long before now. Your cancer has metastasized and has spread to various parts of your body." My childhood friend Roger Prado died before reaching his seventieth birthday.

Grace came from a family of fourteen, just like mine. She had four older brothers: Mario, Rene, Florentino ("Chuy"), and Rudy. All four served in the army during WWII. She also had seven sisters, four older than her and three younger. From oldest to youngest, their names were Alice, Oralia, Olga and Yolanda (who were twins), Grace, Irma, Josefina, and Zulema. Grace was born in January of 1935, so she was some eighteen months younger than me. Although we grew up in the same community and only four blocks apart, I had never seen her before. All four brothers returned from the war and were soon married. Within five to eight years after returning home, all four had left home and were on their own. Grace's father, José Campos, worked in a factory in downtown San Antonio. He was the sole breadwinner for the remaining girls, with the exception of the four oldest, who also married and left home. Now it was just Grace's father, mother ("Cresencia Campos"), Grace (the oldest still living at home), and the three sisters younger than Grace.

In 1952, when Grace was seventeen years old and still in high school, her father was in a work-related accident and his injuries resulted in his death. José Campos, before emigrating from Mexico with his family, was employed as a bookkeeper. Here, in America, the only employment he could find was in low-paying factory jobs that paid only slightly higher than minimum wage.

With her dad gone, and because he was the sole breadwinner in her family, Grace and Irma both left high school after obtaining jobs as waitresses at two different restaurants in downtown San Antonio. Wages and tips all went to their mother to pay the cost of utilities and to put food on the table. Times were so desperate for Grace and her family that they could not even afford a washing machine. The family obtained a multigallon large metal tub that they would use to wash their clothes over a fire in their backyard. They used a broom stick to stir the clothes. They used a second large pail to rinse the clothes in, and of course, they had clotheslines in the backyard on which to hang their clothes.

Unlike most of the families living in this community, the Campos family had bought their home and owned it. No doubt the four older brothers contributed greatly to have their father purchase the home and quickly pay the balance off so their home was theirs and theirs alone.

Still, their lifestyle definitely revealed a family that was among the poorest of the poor in America. Grace's two oldest brothers were skilled craftsmen who worked for decent wages. Mario was an auto mechanic who was now working as an automobile parts specialist. Rudy was also semi-skilled in the mechanic field and earned enough that his wife, Estella, could stay home and not have to also contribute. Rene and Chuy worked at hard labor jobs but earned decent wages. Their wives, too, remained at home.

It is important to note here that this is the middle of the twentieth century. Wives did not go to work to assist in paying bills or to make a living. The American culture, then, was very different from today's. Families could make a decent living with only the male partner serving as the lone breadwinner in the family. My belief is that it was a combination of wages not keeping up with the cost of living and women in America beginning to "flex their gender muscles" and showing us that the title of the song "Anything you can do I can do better" applied to other things as well, that caused this change in our

American culture. Women went to work and the "day care" industry was soon born.

There were other reasons for women joining the workforce. Women who had acquired an education and a skilled profession did not have to get married in order to make a living. Making a life for themselves gave them the freedom to make their own decisions. This is a very different America, and the change began to occur shortly before our involvement in Vietnam.

Grace and I began seeing each other more and more. Her attraction to me grew by leaps and bounds. She felt the same about me. Soon, I was introduced to every member of her family, and she to my family as well. I have mentioned before that the mid twentieth century in America was nothing like it is today. Young men and women did not "agree to live together" without being married. I never thought I had the right, nor could I muster up the courage, to ask Grace to spend the night with me. My thoughts were that if I said anything to suggest this, it would be the end of our relationship. Yes. We are talking of a very different American culture. As a first generation American, I was also very much under the Mexican culture. And when it came to pre-marital sex, this was not condoned in either culture.

The influence of the American culture was already taking its toll on all of us who tried to honor what we could of Mexican mores, customs, and values. One that could have affected Grace and me was to wait at least one year after the death of my sister Chacha. Neither her mother nor mine found it necessary that we should wait a year. We wanted to marry on Grace's twenty-second birthday, January 27, 1957. This was only a little over two months since Chacha's death. There were no objections from any other family members. We had a Catholic wedding in a small Italian church, St. Francis di Paola, only blocks from Grace's home. It was the church the family attended. The majority of parishioners were Italian Americans who also lived near the church and those who started moving to the north side of San Antonio, as most white families had already started to do. Most Italian Americans had moved out of the community by the late 1960s.

Grace and I went to Monterrey, Mexico, on our honeymoon. We no longer had my father's home there as my parents sold it soon after Carolina died some fifteen years prior to this date. What we did have in Monterrey were dozens of family friends, and we visited several. We also visited my sister Carolina's grave, where my parents had laid an attractive tombstone and had hired someone to also maintain the grounds around Carolina's grave.

It is now 2017 and difficult to believe that my sister, with whom I used to "get away" on weekends with her fiancé and her, has been gone for almost seventy-four years…a lifetime!

Grace stopped working. The amount of money she was making was simply not worth the trouble of continuing to be gone for the hours required. She was working at a department store, H. L. Greene, where they also served food. She was the morning waitress and, in fact, opened the store every morning before any departments were open for business. There were dozens of people who arrived early to have breakfast. She developed a clientele who knew her and she knew them. At that time, 1955–57, my Comadre Cruz worked in the downtown area as well. She knew Grace. Grace and I, when we went out or were in the downtown area, would run into several of them. They really missed her and shared with me how amiable and friendly she was and it simply was not that way anymore at H. L. Greene

With both Chacha and Junior gone, my mother and father, Jovita, and Elida lived quietly at Jovita's Elmendorf Street home. Grace and I visited a couple of times a week, as we did with her mother as well. In retrospect, while we managed to save money because we wanted to buy a home and stop paying rent, we probably could have done this sooner if I would have allowed Grace to continue working. While Grace did not mention continuing to work to help us "get ahead," I probably would not have been too keen on the idea. There was something that Latino men do when they marry. It is a silly "machismo" that convinces us (men) that "we can provide" all the money required to make a living.

I am ashamed to continue on this topic because, as I reflect on the way we were, I cannot believe we were so closed-minded. We were. The year is still 1957. I am still in the air force working as a logistician at Randolph Air Force Base. Frank Burns was back and I found out that he and Elida had been planning to get married, and he was going to settle in San Antonio. They did. He found employment right away at Lackland Air Force Base in civil service at a very good pay grade. He essentially was hired at a supervisory level and continued there for almost twenty years. As the foto below shows, Frank Burns was to become a very involved member of the Perez family. Here Frank is shown with (L - R) first son Felipe Perez Jr., sixth (and eleventh child) Roberto, Frank, and Ramiro, third son (and sixth child). All four of us were not only brothers, we were also veterans of the armed forces of our country during times of conflict around the world during the twentieth century.

In the meantime, and still in the year 1957, I inherited additional duties in logistics that I very quickly learned to hate. Here is the story of how I changed my career field as a logistician and was retrained into a different field. It all came about because I was given additional duties handling a classified logistics account. Hardly anyone in our squadron knew anything about this account other than "*one*" person who handled it all, and he was housed in a separate location. It concerned "special weapons." Yes, we also stored nuclear materials. The requisitioning of these materials, the receipt of them, the special shipping of these materials out to other bases or to depots for repair or replacement, everything was handled by one person. The position was so classified that only this person and the commander of the squadron knew about it. Well, this person, also an airman like me, was leaving the air force and the commander had to find a replacement right away. He chose me.

Before I could assume these additional duties, I had to obtain a top secret security clearance. The needed paperwork, the agencies that I had to apply to, and the historical information about who I was, was mind-blowing. I also had to provide the names of a minimum of five people who knew me well enough to be contacted (in person) by members of a top security agency of our government, and answer a lot of questions.

Of course, I listed only people with whom I worked and those who I thought would speak well of me. Frank Burns and Jim Danenhauer were among them. This is the only time I heard from Jim after the three of us had left Germany more than two years previously. He wrote me a note that included this sentence, "I think you will get the security clearance you are seeking." I did. I was cleared to handle top secret materials that were a part of my job.

As I reflect on the above statement (receiving a top secret clearance), it appears like *heck, anyone can get one, all they need is to have four or five people say they are honest, dependable people.* Well, no, not quite. I also listed previous United States Air Force supervisors I had, squadron commanders, and my five-year record in the air force. I listed my technical school record, where I finished first among over five hundred students. I listed my current supervisors and my current squadron commander. The entire process took several months to complete. My understanding was that each interview was conducted face-to-face. At least half of the persons I listed as references lived away from San Antonio. I did not feel particularly privileged. Mostly I felt a bit of pressure to have to be perfect as I performed my duties. Absolutely no one, not even my wife, should know of the material and equipment I handled there at Randolph Air Force Base.

Well, no more than six months had elapsed since I had been given this additional duty when I caused a security violation. When I was informed by my squadron commander of having caused this violation, I could not believe it since I was being so careful. Here's the story:

As a logistician, I supported the military members who were responsible for the maintenance and use of these special weapons. I ordered materials for them and also returned to the appropriate air force depots those pieces of equipment that had to be returned for repair or were otherwise considered obsolete and had to be replaced. The labeling of these materials or pieces of equipment had to be in containers that allowed them to be handled as normal packaging and therefore handled routinely by U.S. mail. The materials were not harmful nor contaminated. They were pieces of equipment and were only lethal when specialists made them so.

There was one occasion when I shipped one piece of equipment back to an air force depot that had, as part of the "To" and "From" address label, a series of eight to nine digits containing letters and numbers that, to me, were necessary for the recipient to know what was in the box. They could not be interpreted as a telephone number, a code that invited perusal, or anything that could possibly make sense to anyone. Yet, in my "decision-making" mind, a way to facilitate for the recipient what it was that was in the box. The receiving depot, or the individual to whom the package was delivered, called the inclusion of these eight to nine digits as part of the shipping label a *security violation*. A special report was made to my commander, who was now obligated to take appropriate *disciplinary action*. Against me.

It is only appropriate that we pause here to consider that we are talking about a branch of service of the most powerful military force ever assembled, anywhere. We didn't become advanced and modern by being mediocre in how we handled all phases of our particular branch of service. Perfection is required in everything we do. I understood that from day one. I did not question the infraction that was called nor the required action that my squadron commander was required to take. This was one of the difficult aspects I had to consider when I made the decision to reenlist. A career in the military means being dependent upon maintaining a spotless record of performance so that a person can expect to be seriously considered for promotion. Promotions are everything insofar as increasing one's wages and extending one's privileges while in uniform.

My squadron commander chose the least, or lowest, disciplinary action to take. He informed me I would receive an Article 15. It is recorded in my personal file as an infraction in the performance of my duties as a logistician. It would remain as part of my personal file for five years. I could just forget about any promotion for this length of time. While I was, of course, very disappointed at getting this "black mark" and it looming *big* in my records, I was somewhat thankful the punishment was not worse than an Article 15.

Being the person I am, I started investigating on the best way to get out from under this five-year lull in my career. There was one way. I could find another career field that I qualified for and submit documentation to retrain into that career field. The new career field had to be one that needed new members because they were critically in short supply and the air force needed them desperately. I found one. There were few applicants and the air force did all it could to attract new applicants. The career field was as military training instructors. Not an easy one to get into, nor easy to complete. The career field called for academic, tactical, use of weapons, survival, and physical conditioning instruction. The failure rate for training applicants was as high as in any other career field. There were other attractive aspects of getting into this career field. There was only one air force base where this training was conducted. It was Lackland Air Force Base, also in the San Antonio, Texas, area.

My application was accepted, and I started this school for instructors in the summer of 1957. There were approximately sixty trainees in my class. The course was two months long, and we attended classes for eight hours a day. The classes were conducted at Lackland. While I was never shy speaking in front of an audience, I also never had to teach an audience to learn from my speaking to them. Basic training is nothing like academic instruction in a school where the learners do not have to apply their learning until months and even years from the time a teacher teaches them the concept. What is learned in basic training has to be evidenced right away. The best example is learning to separate piece by piece, put back together, and then fire an M1 carbine at a firing range and qualify minimally as a marksman. There can be no failures. In many cases, failure to absorb the necessary training can even be fatal. While trainees into the air force are generally between the ages of 18 and 22, many fail the training because they are not physically able to accomplish all the basic training objectives. One is running a ten-minute mile.

I graduated late that summer and was transferred to Lackland. Not only did I leave Randolph, I also left *at Randolph* the Article 15 that I was assessed earlier that same year. Article 15s do not accompany the recipient when he or she transfers out of that squadron. This new career was to eventually be my guide in my future working career and allow me to excel in what has truly become my calling.

The Period 1957-1963

What was life like in America during this period? "Ike" was POTUS. Richard Nixon, a Republican from California, was his VP. They won elections in both 1952 and 1956. Globally, or internationally, we were engaged in a "Cold War." The Soviet Union, a communist territorial giant in Asia that had consumed most of the Northern Asian countries and called them part of their union, showed signs of expanding their influence around the world by forcing other countries to also become a part of their empire. Not only were they attempting to extend into other Asian countries, the Soviet Union would also try to become a part of the Western hemisphere. In due time, the Soviet Union would attempt to make Cuba, only a few hundred miles from our southernmost state, Florida, become a communist state. More on Cuba later in this book. What about life in the American military forces? What role does the air force have? What would be my role as a military training instructor? Did I know what I had gotten myself into?

It is summer of 1957. It would be August before I reached my twenty-fourth birthday. One of the reasons I would later advance, in both promotions while in uniform and in having success in my academic endeavors was because I read newspapers and news magazines like *Time*, *Newsweek*, and *The News* and *World Report*. I always saw myself as being informed and knowledgeable about the issues. My years as a newspaper delivery boy had instilled in me the curiosity to "want to know" about things going on in the world. I watched the news, and it was almost always CBS. If Dan Rather was reporting on some aspect of the news, I would drop everything to watch his report. I even picked up on his colloquialisms. Is it any wonder I have been a life-long Democrat? I did not know it at the time, but I was being influenced to "join" (or go "along" with) the majority culture in America. In retrospect, it was all I knew. My parent's Mexican culture was not only distant and dormant, but it felt like all other "worldly" cultures, *inferior* to the American culture. I subconsciously bought into the American culture, "hook, line, and sinker." This perspective I had unintentionally acquired would also change with time and from living with the abuse people of color, like me, experience in America.

An important point to make here is my selection of this movement *toward the dominant culture.* This was to be distinguished from two other sociological beliefs among Latinos like me and also African Americans. One was *being against* the American culture. The other was *moving, with action, against* the American culture. There is a difference. *Being against the dominant American culture* is tantamount to tolerating the discrimination and prejudice, while at the same time not liking it one bit, like most minority groups in America experience. It is also not taking any action to correct these abuses and intolerances. It's being in the middle of the two extremes. The minority culture that not only tolerates the discrimination and prejudice but also lives within it and just assumes that "this is the way it is going to be." The other extreme, moving against the dominant culture but with action, was to attempt to correct the prejudice and discrimination by "doing something about it." This approach could be peaceful, as in Martin Luther King's approach of nonviolent protests, evidenced in demonstrations and peaceful marches.

Unfortunately, I was in that first group, the one that did nothing about it and just assumed that's the way it is here in America. I wanted degrees, licenses, jobs, and a bigger salary. Yeah, I had trouble looking in the mirror. That was the bad news. The good news was that there were certain movements across America during this period that made me open my eyes and forced me to take stock. I did not like what I saw. I will return to this topic. For now, I will pick up where I left off after graduating as a military training instructor.

Before continuing to elaborate on my life (now) as a military training instructor for the air force, let's look at what was going on in America and the rest of the world in 1957. We were deep into a "cold war" with the Soviet Union. There were hot spots all over the world where there was an expanding influence of the communist countries (the Soviet Union and China, mostly). One in which we were not involved was Indo-China, aka Vietnam. The French had claimed it as a possession and were fighting a war against forces from North Vietnam and were suffering great losses. It is mentioned here only briefly to inform the reader that these conflicts around the world would eventually involve America because we did not want communism to grow more than it had already. It was this fear of an expanding communist threat that would eventually increase our country's defense budget and would prompt our current president to say, before leaving office three years later, that America needs to be aware of an equally expanding military industrial complex. This should be interpreted as Eisenhower's concern for America using enormous amounts of funds to build a defense department instead of using these funds for increasing the quality of life for all Americans. My belief is that we are still doing this now more than halfway into the latter half of the second decade of the twenty-first century.

My new career field was all about preparing young men to put on the American uniform and defend this country. If necessary, with one's life. It was basic training. They arrived daily by the hundreds. They came with only the clothes they were wearing and nothing else. This was standard operating procedure across the country by all air force recruiters. They all came to Lackland Air Force Base in San Antonio, Texas. As instructors, we picked them up at a central location on the base in groups of sixty-five men at a time. Most had been growing long hair, but they also all knew that one of the very first things we did after having them form a group with four columns (we called the groups "flights") was to take the flight to a base barbershop, have each one sit in a barber's chair, and have the barber cut off every bit of hair they had. It is a significant part of their submission to the vigorous training they were about to go through. Once they are completely "hairless," the submission to a voice of authority comes easily. As an instructor, if I said "jump," they would jump. If I said "squat," they would squat.

Before going any further, the reader should be aware that we were trained instructors with only the best of intentions. The intentions are that we respect them as men, as individuals, and treat them with dignity and respect. In my eight years as an air force instructor, I never forgot this aspect of my responsibilities. No, I never said "Please," or use less than an authoritative voice. I commanded the flight to do things with a very high level of confidence that communicated to the men in my flights that I had only their welfare in mind and that I wanted them to learn in such a way that they mastered every training objective the air force had for every new recruit.

After their haircuts, we proceeded to the largest clothing store one could imagine. By the time my sixty-five men came out at the other end, they would have acquired two dress uniforms, including three blue poplin dress shirts, one pair of dress shoes, one dress tie, three work fatigues, including trousers and long sleeve work shirts, one pair of brogans, five sets of underwear, socks, handkerchiefs, a dress cap, a fatigue cap, a raincoat, and an overcoat. Everything would fit into one duffel bag. They would carry the duffel bag into our barracks, a two-story structure with long bays where the sixty-five men would find their "bunks" in their assigned bay. They would have a footlocker assigned for the smaller items they were issued and an open closet against the wall immediately behind their bunks to hang their clothes. All beds were "double bunks" except for one. The one would be for the airman selected as "barracks chief." Each had a shelf upon which to place their dress cap. Everything had to be buttoned and in a specified sequence. The same applied to the contents of their footlocker, which contained toilet articles and their properly rolled underwear. Everything was subject to inspection on a moment's notice.

Starting with the very next day and for the following eight weeks, I would stand at the head of each bay at 5:00 a.m. and holler, "REVEILLE." *Reveille* is defined as a bugle call to summon the troops in the morning in a fort or garrison. I substituted my loud voice in lieu of a bugle call, as did all instructors at Lackland.

Flights were usually assigned in groups of three to four per squadron. We were easily getting four hundred to five hundred recruits per day, so there were enough new troops arriving daily to satisfy one squadron and often two. For eight weeks, the three to four flights in each squadron would compete against each other in all aspects of basic training. I had no idea what real competitiveness was until I became an air force basic training instructor. My flights worked long and hard to be the best at everything, from marching as a single unit with no one ever out of step and a smooth, strong pounding of the asphalt or cement by the flight. Everything was done in unison, including arm swing and eyes focused on the man's neck in front of each man.

In addition to marching and working as a unit, my flights were also taught the customs and courtesies of the armed forces, and in particular those of the United States Air Force. We had PE instructors who taught a daily one-hour class on physical conditioning with a mandatory one-mile run under ten minutes. No one could graduate from basic training unless they accomplished this ten-minute mile. They learned the entire history of Americans in uniform. They learned about the air force in world affairs. They were taught about the chain of command and that their commander-in-chief was always the president of the United States. They learned how to survive a chemical attack and how to live under dire circumstance. I taught them how to fire an M1 rifle, first by breaking the rifle down to several pieces, putting the rifle back together, spending a long day of "dry-fire," where they only simulate firing the M1, as each weapon has no bullets. The very next day, under very strict supervision with several instructors working with a very small group of men, they underwent "wet-fire." Each man had to qualify with at least a "marksman" rating or not be able to graduate from basic training.

During my two tours of duty as a military training instructor, 1957–1961 and 1964–1968, I must have arranged for discharge from the air force at least a dozen men who failed to progress satisfactorily through the eight weeks of training. The reasons ranged from not being physically fit to not accepting the voices of authority that everyone, no matter the branch of service, has to abide by. A few were discipline problems who would not only not accept higher voices of authority, but would even rebel against.

What I did not know about me was how much I always wanted to win, or to be in first place. There were daily inspections of every dormitory (barracks) by squadron supervisors (of training). There were three other flights that started training at the same time mine did. The supervisors would inspect daily, and absolutely everything, from the outside grounds around each barracks, to the cleanliness of the two "latrines," or bathrooms, each also housed six urinals, six commodes, a shower portion of the latrine for six people, and six sinks, three on each side of one of the rooms in the latrine. There was one latrine for each floor. They would then inspect alignment of beds, footlockers, clothes hanging on each airman's wall rack, including equal distance between all coat hangers. Beds would be checked to ensure tight fitting of sheets and blankets, including all corners showing perfect "hospital corners." I usually had three to four days between flights, which meant I trained five flights each of the years I served as an instructor.

It should be noted that I acquired a certain proficiency as a drill instructor that I was elevated to the position of drill and ceremonies instructor for the entire squadron after my second year. I was then responsible for training all the sister flights of the entire squadron for participation in two weekly "parades" that were conducted system wide for all training squadrons. Lackland had fifteen to sixteen training squadrons. Each squadron had twenty barracks, which meant twenty flights could be "housed" at any one time in each squadron. Once I became the D&C instructor, I had a schedule to train, for participation in a system-wide parade, all the "sister flights" at the same time. Each squadron on the base had only one D&C instructor. It was definitely a prestigious position to hold. Squadrons also competed against each other during parades and the one with the fewest demerits, as judged by different supervisors, would be announced. It was really the D&C ceremonies instructor who received the accolades.

These were the years America was building our armed forces to not only be better prepared than ever before, we were building our military to be the best in the world, period. Along with all the other military training instructors, I was "gung ho" and, like all Americans in the armed forces, really proud to say I was an American. I did not think of myself as many Americans think of me, a Mexican American, a Hispanic, a Latino, and to many in the radical right, even *suspect* as an American. In spite of this, my movement toward the dominant culture became more acute.

María Elena was our first child. She was born on December 18, 1958. Grace allowed me to name her, although she agreed the name was beautiful, and she agreed with the way I selected the name. The two of us were watching the *Garry Moore Show* on TV one evening and a woman from a Central American country appeared as a guest. Her name was María Elena. We both heard the name as we watched the TV screen and both of us agreed the name was beautiful. At that time, parents of the unborn waited until mothers gave birth before finding out the gender of their child. I told Grace that if it's a girl, this is the name I would select. Grace agreed.

I had turned 25 the previous August. I have now been functioning as a military training instructor for the greatest air force in the world. What is more, I was also the D&C instructor for a squadron that could train at any one given time as many as 1,300 recruits who had voluntarily enlisted in the air force. Before leaving basic training after eight weeks, each would be trained by me to engage as part of a full military parade with as many as 15,000 other enlistees. Exactly twenty-one months after María was born, Roberto Junior was born. The date was September 29, 1960. I turned 27 the previous month.

The normal tour of duty at a stateside base is four years before one has to anticipate a move. My move was imminent. I continued as a military training instructor until the fall of 1961. María would turn 3 and Roberto Junior 1 when I received my orders to return to my previous air force specialty as a logistician, and I was subsequently assigned to Amarillo Air Force Base in the panhandle of the state of Texas. I would only be there for two years before I would be sent to an overseas installation. Several things would happen in my family that drastically changed things in my life.

It was the summer of 1961, June to be more specific, before I would make the move to Amarillo AFB, that I received an emergency phone call while on duty at Lackland. It was from Grace. She had gotten a phone call from Jovita, to advise me that my father had died on his way to Palestine, Texas, where he had an appointment to see a heart specialist.

Don Felipe Pérez: Born in Piedras Negras, México, seventy-eight years earlier, and called "Don Felipe" because he commanded respect as a professional boilermaker, a land owner, a parent, and because Pancho Villa made him a captain in his army. While he didn't take very good care of his body (he loved to eat), he did live to be 78 years of age. I attribute that fact to how hard he worked most of his life. Although not a Christian, I know he rested his body in a mostly horizontal state on Sundays as he devoured the biggest selling Spanish language newspaper in America, *La Prensa*. He read every page and article, front to back.

Now he was gone. The third of the fourteen members of this family to die. His daughters Carolina and Chacha preceded him in death.

The *head* of the family had been Jovita for some time now. My father was *all there* all the time, still commanding the respect as titular head of the family, but decisions regarding money, taxes, purchases, and more always had to be approved by Jovita. My father was beginning to be *hard of hearing* and, thus, most family members communicated with either my mother or with Jovita, while always remaining very respectful to my father.

Jovita arranged to buy a burial plot for four bodies, my father's, my mother's, hers (Jovita), and a vacancy for probably Armando, who seemed to be unable to find a mate with whom he could share his life. This will not happen as Armando did eventually find a woman who loved him, and although separated at the time of his death, I persuaded the family to abide by her wishes regarding Armando's death. More on Armando in later chapters of this book.

The Move to the Panhandle of Texas

I had traveled to Amarillo to find a home to rent before I would bring up Grace, Maria, and Robert. Both Maria and Robert were not yet of school age. Maria was 3 and Robert had just had his one-year old birthday in September. Grace was some three to four months pregnant with Patty, who would be born the following June (1962) there in Amarillo. A lot happened before June would come.

I had started to again become comfortable with my skills as a logistician. In fact, I benefitted from my years as the noncommissioned officer-in-charge of the property accounting unit while stationed in Germany. In this role, I experienced almost all the roles different workers performed in this major unit because I was responsible for their accuracy in performing their duties. I had no trouble picking up where I left off in 1957.

There were other occurrences in my life that almost immediately impacted us. I received an emergency phone call from home one evening. My mother had died in her sleep, while taking an afternoon nap. It is February 1962. My father had only been gone seven months. Now my mother was gone as well. She was the fourth member of the fourteen to die.

We mourned her death much more than we did my father's. It is just a simple fact of life. Sons and daughters always worship the ground their mothers walk on. Still, life goes on.

My family and I returned to Amarillo. June 1, 1962, came. Patricia Ann was born. Her birth at a small hospital on Amarillo Air Force Base in Texas was uneventful but for the fact that her air force doctor was so short in stature that he need a bench to stand on the facilitate the birth.

On the other hand, living in Amarillo was somewhat eventful. The Panhandle of Texas was known to resemble much of the state of Oklahoma and other mid-Western states in the number of tornadoes that strike this part of America every year. My family and I survived one particular tornado that struck Amarillo in the late spring months of 1962. The four of us (Patty had not been born yet) huddled in the bathroom, which was in the middle of our rented house. The tornado did not strike the ground near us, but we heard it as it roared a few hundred feet above our home. I can never forget the sound it made. It was as if a train, with a very large engine, was going over our heads.

Before spring was over, five of us logisticians working in Amarillo were sent on temporary duty to Big Spring, Texas, to "bail out" an air force account that was in trouble with their records keeping and needed help as soon as possible. The five of us were experienced in this type of work, and we were confident we could assist in solving their problems. What we did not know was how bad off the account was and how long it would take us to straighten things out. The temporary duty lasted five months.

It just so happens that Big Spring, Texas, is located about 150 miles closer to San Antonio than it was to Amarillo. The five of us were all married with families, and we came home for the first weekend (to Amarillo). It did not take me long to figure out that I could spend more time with my family if they lived, also temporarily, in San Antonio rather than Amarillo. For the remaining weeks of the five months, we did just that. I moved Grace, Maria, Robert, *and* Patty to San Antonio. I arrived home for weekends with them some three hours sooner than I would have if they were still in Amarillo. We also made a deal with the managers of the Big Spring account to allow us to start our week at noon on Mondays so we could have three week nights with our families at home. Our work days never ended after eight hours. We worked at least nine to ten hours daily. This continued until I received orders to go to Korea for a thirteen-month tour of duty. I was to report to San Francisco to catch a flight to Tokyo and then to Seoul in January of 1963.

The Period 1963-1964

Before going any further, I must explain what an unaccompanied tour is for a military member who receives orders to serve our country in a foreign nation. "Unaccompanied" means that the tour of duty does not allow for dependent family members to live with the service member in this particular country. Thus, the term to use is *unaccompanied*. All members of the American armed forces are knowledgeable enough about the branch of service they are in to know exactly what is expected of them when military orders are given. Squadron commanders and first sergeants conduct timely briefings monthly, and sometimes weekly, to keep members abreast of all changes. American educators have their in-service and faculty meetings. Military members have the same meetings. They are called "mandatory meetings." Miss one and the circumstances can be devastating, not to mention a call for disciplinary action as well.

Having written the above, I must add that a military member who fails to keep up and to stay informed is usually the person who does not receive promotions and who more than likely will have a short stay in the military. The military expects perfection. Anything less could mean failure. Failure can mean failure of attaining the mission. Fail to attain mission expectations and we then do not deserve to called *the greatest military force ever assembled by man.*

I was not this "gung ho" during my first enlistment, during the years 1951 to 1955, when I was 18 to 22. The Article 15 I received for a security violation and my tour as a military training instructor literally "lit a fire" under me. I adopted a *perfectionist* approach to almost everything I did. I began double-checking myself so much that I must have raised my blood pressure because I worried about every little thing I did or for which I was responsible. Fortunately, this same perfectionist attitude taught me to *problem solve*, so I looked for ways to accomplish things without having to worry about them. That is *without having to worry about them* too much. My personal analysis of my situation is that my perfectionist attitude has allowed me to have huge successes (a 3.5 average for my undergraduate courses, a master's degree from the University of Texas at Austin, and then defeating the ABD syndrome by attaining a doctorate at this same very prestigious university). When I took the competency exam for the E-8 and E-9 ranks, a 150 multiple choice exam that took three to four hours to complete, I was so confident of my score that I thought I must not have missed any problems because I prepared so much for this exam that I honestly didn't think I missed any single item. Evidently I did. My score was not perfect. But it was a 99 percentile rating, meaning that, worldwide in a branch of service that at that time consisted of over one million members, my score was greater than 99% of those taking the exam. There is more on attaining my doctorate further along in this book. Easily, that accomplishment is something I will remember as one that changed me forever.

It was February of 1963 when I reported to Travis Air Force Base for a subsequent flight to Seoul, Korea. Before doing so, my family needed my attention because I was about to leave them for more than a year's time. Grace and I had bought a modest home in San Antonio that we *rented out* when I was assigned to Amarillo Air Force Base in the fall of 1961. The people who rented our home took fairly good care of it. Grace, now twenty-seven years old but only one month from her twenty-eighth—Maria, now 4; Robert, age 2; and Patty, age 6 months. I was not too worried about them because Grace had a fairly large support system with her mother, brothers, and sisters all living in San Antonio. I was ready for a new adventure in a completely different part of the world. I had already spent three years in Germany, with excursions into Austria, France, Switzerland, Italy, Belgium, Holland, Denmark, and England. I had also spent almost a month vacationing in Spain. My three years in Germany were with an occupation force, only seven years removed from WWII. The war with North Korea had not been won but did end in 1953 with a truce that to this day continues to be shaky.

I did not have to unpack my duffel bag at Travis Air Force Base as I was almost immediately put on a *Flying Tigers Airline* plane to Tokyo where I would spend a couple of days before boarding an air force C-47 to Osan Air Force Base in Korea. Most military members, of all branches of service, call Osan by this letter and number designation, *K-55*. Japan, other than the people looking very differently than Americans, was tantamount to being home in America. It was clean, orderly, and while most people also dressed differently, I felt safe and secure as an American. I was able to visit a few restaurants and converse with a person or two. No, I could not speak a word of Japanese. The Japanese were able to accommodate me with their own knowledge of the English language.

Perhaps one of the most interesting sights I have ever seen occurred on my *somewhat slow* flight to Korea from Japan. We were flying a C-47, twin engine propeller-driven workhorse airplane of the air force with top speed at 250 miles per hour. There were no more than twelve passengers. All of us were air force and reporting for duty in Korea for the next thirteen months. There were C-47 airplanes at every air force base all over the world. It was used to transport passengers and also cargo. As soon as we were airborne, the sight of Mount Fuji loomed big and somewhat threatening. It is a volcanic mountain with a height of 12, 389 feet. We must have flown for at least two hours toward Korea, and we could still see the highest peaks of Mount Fuji.

It is the month of February. Snow and extremely cold temperatures are the order of the day, and especially during the months of January and February. When we arrived at K-55, I was assigned to a one-story building with two open bays at each end. Each bay had sufficient room for twelve to thirteen people using single iron-and-spring beds, an accompanying footlocker to place in front of each bed, and open wall racks to hang our clothes. It was very reminiscent of the barracks where my air force enlistees were housed during their basic training. I did not bring any civilian clothes as my assignment briefing informed me that none were allowed. My particular bay was with other noncommissioned officers of similar rank. While I only had twelve years of service, my rank was that of technical sergeant, a rank normally acquired after minimally fifteen years of service. I had progressed with relative speed with promotions because I had an outstanding record in all my assignments.

In the thirteen months I would be here, I would find that South Korea is both the coldest place I have ever lived in, as well as the hottest. Still, my job as a logistician would require me to only work indoors. I was immediately placed in charge of the property accounting branch of the local account. I had some twenty Korean nationals working for me and about an equal number of American air force types who were working their way up the ladder in this logistics field.

In South Korea, there are air force units at some eight different locations scattered throughout the country. All their equipment, supplies, replacements, ordering, turning in, and satisfaction of needs has to go through this account that I have been given the responsibility of managing. There were two commissioned officers above me who were there also unaccompanied and were supposed to be my superiors, or to put it more bluntly, the people I would answer to if there were any discrepancies in the operation of this account. I remember them as "Major Smith" and "Major Jones." These two officers would be charged with the tremendous responsibility of converting this equipment and supplies account from a manual pencil and paper accounting system to a punch card approach where everything would be done electronically with punch cards that would be collected at the end of the day and run through a PCAM (punch card accounting method) for recording and, supposedly, improving on the quality of service all the different air force units functioning all over Korea would receive. The task was to train not only our local staff, both American and Korean, but also call in all our clients from the field, wherever they are located in Korea, and also instruct them on how to change the procedures now in use.

A bit of FYI on what a *pencil and paper accounting system* in logistics in the United States Air Force was like. U.S. Air Force bases function like a town or city does. Every conceivable item of need is available to all people residing there. Fuel (for both airplanes, trucks, and other motorized equipment, food, heating, roads to travel on, technicians to take care of all maintenance, cooks for the dining hall, doctors and nurses to take care of the sick, priests, ministers, rabbi's, and many, many more technicians and experts in their fields to take care of all needs. In general, every function available in a city or town is also available at every American air force base anywhere in the world.

All equipment and supplies are managed by logisticians, including having the most essential of these always available. Think *airplane parts to always have airplanes ready to fly, fuel, combat equipment in the event of an unexpected conflict with a foreign nation* (after all, we are but a few miles from North Korea), *and every item of need to facilitate everyone carrying out their part of the mission.*

Having said the above, the role played by logisticians becomes ever so important. We managed the local account with a series of accounting cards identified by a letter and number. The F1 card was the *nomenclature card.* This card contained the complete item description of the item. The card was approximately three by five inches. The F2 card was the card where all transactions were recorded. This included receipts (credits), issues (debits), and amount on hand. The third card was the F4, the "due-in" and "due out" card. The three cards would be maintained in one pocket of a tray with thirty to forty cards in the tray. The F1 and F4 cards would be maintained side by side as both cards measured three by five inches and fit perfectly. The F2, with recordings that could conceivably have entries made on it several times a day, was ten inches wide and five inches in height. The three were in the same pocket.

The reader should know that most air force logistics offices carry between forty and fifty thousand items that are managed by logisticians. It is one of the most important and, essential, functions of any air force base anywhere in the world.

The order for the change in accounting comes down from Fifth Air Force Headquarters in Hawaii. The justification for this major change is that the account must be made more efficient by converting the accounting methods to a PCAM system. The order comes to K-55 as just that, *an order to do it*. I would say that Majors Smith and Jones began feeling the pressure of having to know and understand the new accounting procedures and to also train the local staff and all clients.

Ever hear of *passing the buck*? In my twenty years in the air force, it is one of the most constant actions taken by people with authority. The entire structure of rank, rank having its privileges, and "figureheads" who have experts doing the work runs rampant in the air force. Well, it did, once upon a time. The two majors had private offices and an NCO (noncommissioned officer) who handled all their mail, prioritized it, did their clerical work, and to (again) put it bluntly, *pass the buck* of their work to those of us who knew how to do it. We'll call this NCO "Sergeant Ryan."

A few days after receiving the order form Hawaii, Sergeant Ryan approached me (but on the QT...brief for *on the quiet*) or put another way, not to be told to anyone because the two majors are going to schedule a conference with me and *they* will tell me it is going to be my job to do. After all, I am really the person in charge of the property accounting office, its efficiency, and supervising all military and civilian employees. Of course, the two majors would ask to conference with me to tell me it is *my job to do*. The year is 1963. I have been in this man's air force for over ten years. I have spent these ten years with my eyes wide open and have internalized everything going on very well. Nearly all problems dealing with anything in the military are planned and problem-solved by the enlisted personnel. Basically, there are four levels of job proficiency in the air force. When one comes out of tech school, we are awarded a "three-level" specialty code. It is the *worker* job proficiency level. After three to five years of experience, and with a displayed job proficiency and the ability to explain one's job from start to finish, such that this person can work independently to do the job, as well as take and pass a five-level skill test, this person can then be elevated to the five-level specialty code. The next level of job proficiency (seven) is only assigned to supervisory personnel. Job proficiency must be in evidence and the commensurate rank, technical sergeant or master sergeant, must also be earned. I arrived in Korea with the seven-level specialty code and the rank of technical sergeant.

The nine-level of job proficiency is assigned only at the "superintendency" level and comes with the "super sergeants' rank of E-8 or E-9." I will show later on in this book my attainment of this E-8 level but declining it so I could retire and join the civilian workforce in 1971.

Majors Smith and Jones were extremely fortunate to have a person like me filling the position that not only had the responsibility to do the job, but who was better prepared to do the job than anyone else. First of all, for most of my military experience, I always welcomed challenges. Secondly, I had filled the position of military training instructor for more than four of the previous six years. I taught some forty to fifty different subjects to U.S. Air Force recruits. Before teaching these subjects, I had to have written a lesson plan and had the plan approved before I could stand in front of a group. Thirdly, of my three years in Germany, I spent the last one and a half years filling the same position, noncommissioned officer-in-charge of the property accounting branch, a supervisory position even though I was only at the staff sergeant rank level. But these were my first four years in the air force and normally a person doesn't attain the rank of staff sergeant until years later. When I left Lackland, in the fall of 1961, I worked at various positions within the Property Accounting Branch at Amarillo Air Force Base. I knew firsthand almost every role that every worker played who functioned in this office. The task, for the two majors, was probably seen as the hardest task they ever had to accomplish. For me, it was a chance to prove how good I was in this role and also fulfill my desire to do an outstanding job. More than anything, I was excited at being given the opportunity to show what I could do. Confident? Forgive me, no. But I was cocky.

I listened to both majors describe the order from Fifth Air Force Headquarters. The order also mentioned a citation of funds that would be provided in the event trainers had to be trained and equipment and supplies needed to be purchased. The complete punch card machines would arrive and be assembled by civilian contractors from the continental United States. After they thought they had told me everything they knew (to tell me), they paused, looked at me, and probably wondered why I had not stopped them to ask questions. In fact, they did ask if I had any questions. While I did not have any questions for them, I did tell them how they could be useful to me in getting this job done.

I told them that I had already checked with other U.S. Air Force bases in Japan and Okinawa to find the one property accounting system that would match ours at K-55. I told them I found one very similar, at Naha Air Force Base in Okinawa. I told them I had already arranged with their local property accounting office to allow me to spend a week (five working days), observing their operation and being allowed to ask questions of every person in charge of every unit. Also told them I wanted to be able to leave with copies of whatever forms they used to do their jobs and to be allowed to contact them by telephone after I left in the event I still had questions about their operation.

Personnel officers during the 1960s filled a similar role as present-day human resources personnel do in most businesses and school systems. While one of the two majors had that role, it was Sergeant Ryan who "took care of business" and get that particular job done in our organization. I told the two majors to tell Sergeant Ryan to make all the arrangements for me to fly there and back. Told them what dates I wanted to use and to get me on flights through Itazuke, Japan, where I had heard had the most flights going to both Naha and Kadena Air Force Bases in Okinawa. In essence, the job of these two majors was done. Their job was to pass the buck to me, and I would handle the rest, with a little help from Sergeant Ryan, a person I considered very adept and knowledgeable about his job. He knew nothing about logistics, but he knew where the buck started and where it stopped. He also knew me and knew this job would be done professionally.

Was it something I would lose sleep over? Not at all, I was excited about the opportunity to do a job I knew I would do well. I didn't think about this at the time (at least I don't think I did), in retrospect, perhaps subconsciously, I knew enlisted personnel are not the ones held responsible when programs fail. Headquarters goes to the top of the chain of command and someone pays for *jobs not well done*. Majors Smith and Jones knew who I was. They placed their trust in me. For that I should be thankful.

I wasted no time. I delegated many of my daily job responsibilities to two or three subordinates to do and most of the supervision of the Korean civilians working in our logistics office I delegated to Mr. Kahn, who already was the supervisor who did all of the interpreting of my instructions to the Korean personnel working in our office and those out in the different satellite units scattered throughout South Korea.

A bit of clarification is in order. Sergeant Ryan didn't call up different airlines to get me to Okinawa. There were no commercial airlines to call. He checked frequently with base operations to inquire of military flights going to Itazuke, Japan. He would then check with Itazuke to check on their flights to Okinawa. It didn't matter if the flight was to Naha or Kadena. I could land on either installation and get ground transportation to get me to the logistics squadron at Naha where I would spend my time.

Sergeant Ryan was very efficient. He got me on a C-54 (four-engine and faster than a C-47) to fly to Itazuke. I would only spend one day there before another C-54 was scheduled to fly to Okinawa. Since I coordinated with all appropriate military personnel at Naha before departing for their base, they were expecting me and facilitated my walk-throughs of every unit I visited. A most pleasant surprise was my discovery that everything I knew about how logistics works in the military was being employed here in Okinawa. While I did not learn anything new, I had this very pleasant feeling that I knew what every unit did to get the right equipment and supplies in the hands of mechanics and other specialists to get the job done and to get all flying aircraft in the air on a moment's notice.

A quick lesson on how logistics worked then (Wow. Fifty-three years ago!). Let's imagine an aircraft engine is being *overhauled*, as they all are on a very timely basis. If not an engine being overhauled, then it could be a case of any of hundreds of different aspects of an airplane being inspected daily and before every *takeoff*. Different specialists who care for the airplane may discover a need to replace *some* part on *some* major assembly, like the hydraulic system, the landing gear, the instrument panel, tires, propellers (if appropriate). This is, after all, 1963. The specialists read their *tech order* (for instructions, part numbers, etc.). Then, is the part available in his tool kit? If not, does *his* logistician have the part in his *service stock?* If not, this where the base-wide logistician comes into play. If it's an emergency because the plane is scheduled to fly within twenty-four hours, the telephone call is made to the *AOCP Unit* (Aircraft Out of Commission for Parts) of the Base Logistics Office. If the item is available in stock, problem solved immediately.

If the plane is not scheduled to fly soon, the request is handled routinely (with paperwork), but still processed quickly, usually on the same day. The delivery of the part may not be until the next day. Now, this is an example of an airplane part. This routine is followed for everything needed on an air force base anywhere in the world. As stated previously, imagine a city or town functioning with thousands of people and what it takes to function daily. As stated previously, the number of items for which the Logistics Office keeps records of is in the tens of thousands.

A record is kept of every transaction. The logistician is the record keeper and the one responsible to ascertain that all needed items to have this city or town function efficiently, and usually combat-ready, are available. Safe stock levels must always be kept in stock and available. The logistician has a formula for maintaining stock at certain levels and to always have replacement items on order.

I followed the routines of stock ordering, issuing the item(s) when available, ordering them when not available, all the record-keeping, job responsibilities, and lots and lots more. It was the same routines I remember from my three years in Germany, my two years at Randolph Air Force Base, my two years at Amarillo Air Force Base, and my short time solving the problems of the air force base in Big Spring, Texas, before coming to Korea. I remember transitioning from manual accounting to punch card machines. Everything fell into place perfectly.

While I spent ten-hour days monitoring and shadowing all the workers involved in logistics at both Naha and Kadena Air Force

Bases, I started writing my lesson plans for the classes I would hold when I returned to South Korea. I contacted Sergeant Ryan to begin scheduling classes on an everyday basis, immediately after work and to also make arrangements to hold Saturday classes for those air force personnel not at K-55 but at remote sites who also depended on us for logistical support.

There is an important point to make here. All of us were on a "remote assignment." That is, none of us went home after a long day to a home, wife, and kids. We went home to a barracks full of other military personnel, most of whom were longing for their tour to end so they could return to their families and homes back in the continental United States. That certainly was the case for me. I welcomed ten to twelve hour days.

I completed my week in Okinawa and headed back to South Korea following the same routines that got me to Okinawa in the first place. Two *airplane hops*, first to Itazuke, Japan, then to South Korea. Both on C-54s. I was excited about getting in front of groups to teach them *how to do things*. In the years to come, some ten years ahead and farther, I would remember having these *captive* audiences and how they leaned forward to hear every word I said about new procedures and how to do things. *That* would not be the case when I got in front of high school students, or even my sixth graders, a grade level I taught for more years than I want to remember. As a matter of fact, my kindergarteners *never leaned* forward to hear me either.

I returned to K-55 in South Korea and honestly do not remember my two majors even calling me in to ask *how it went*. Sergeant Ryan made conversation as a way of inquiring if I had everything ready for my classes since he had set them up. I told him there was one additional chore I had for him. I wanted Mr. Kahn to be paid overtime because I also wanted him every day to sit in on my classes and then meet with all the South Koreans working with us so they understood the new procedures. I also wanted him to attend my Saturday classes with the satellite personnel who would attend those classes.

Mr. Kahn, next to me, was the most essential part of this whole endeavor. I told him he had to write lesson plans, just like I did. I could not risk losing him for some serious illness or unanticipated death and not have someone else pick up the mantle and run with it. Besides, next to me, he was easily the best logistician the United States Air Force had in South Korea.

I told him so.

Everything went as *smooth as silk*. I want to say that attendance was excellent, and no one missed a single class, not during the week nor on Saturdays. But then, there was nowhere else to go, not home or having to run errands for their wives or families. We were all ten thousand miles away from home and halfway around the globe. I learned to pause my instruction when one of the Korean nationals had a question and had to have Mr. Kahn interpret his question to me and to the rest of those in attendance. About half of the Korean nationals had enough command of the English language to have their comments and questions understood by everyone. Mr. Kahn was invaluable.

We conducted classes right through the holidays of the winter that was 1963–64. Remember, this is an isolated tour of duty and *home* was the barracks with other men who, like me, were thousands of miles away from their home and their family. Working, whether it was attending classes or actually reporting for work, was in many instances therapeutic.

The two majors probably stepped into our classes once or twice. They were not logisticians who knew the minute details of property accounting, requisitioning, maintaining stock levels, and records keeping. I checked for understanding quite frequently after short segments of my instruction because all new procedures had to be learned sequentially. I could not have been more pleased.

Time went by quickly, as it usually does when one is busy. I would soon be packing my bags and going home. Several very unique things occurred before my departure. I worked until just before the day I was supposed to leave to finally go home to the states. On my last day in the office, I left the door to my office open and worked quietly on some last-minute instructions for my staff. I incidentally heard Major Jones come into Sergeant Ryan's office and tell him. "Check Sergeant Perez' records. If he hasn't received the

Commendation Medal before, let's start the paperwork to get him the medal."

I wasn't expecting this. First of all, these two majors and I never conversed. They were for all intent and purposes mute. They knew I was the expert here at K-55, and I never considered them support-ive, engaged, or that they even "gave a shit" about our mission there in Korea. What I *did* hear was "*if.*" In other words, there is power in numbers. Two is better than one. Either I earned the medal or I didn't. I wanted to barge in and tell him to stick that medal up his ass. Hey! I was going home. That's all that mattered.

Sergeant Ryan soon walked into my office, which was right next to his. He had a very solemn look on his face. He tells me (asks, really), "You heard everything?" I said yes. I was through packing my stuff. I reached out with my hand to shake his and said goodbye to him. Told him I appreciated all the help he gave me. He thanked me and said, "I'm sorry, Sergeant Perez."

The citation came a few months later, and I will describe the parade at Lackland when I was presented this medal. It is another memorable occasion.

One concern I had during those last couple of weeks was my attendance at Mass every morning at 6:00 a.m. Our chaplain was a Catholic Priest from Ohio, a Father Moese (pronounced /mace/), I became his *acolytus*, or in English, his acolyte (altar boy), saying all the responses in Latin as the world-wide Catholic Church had not converted to the language of the country yet. I thought he was truly a "holy man" because I had never heard him say an unkind word, was soft-spoken, and appeared to be in his sixties.

That is, until I did. We were having a catechism class one eve-ning. There were probably seven to eight of us in a small conference room. Father Moese was retelling some actual story about his priestly duties back in Ohio (Cincinnati I think it was) when he said the "N word" to describe an individual in his flashback story. We were all stunned. There were no African Americans in the group. Still, I was really shocked to hear him refer to someone with such a nasty word as that. My views on Father Moese changed rapidly.

Another concern were the eight to nine other noncommissioned officers whom I lived with.** They drank every night and practically lived in the small village nearest our base. Most of them were "shacking up." All were married and their wives were all back in the USA. We never got along very well because I never joined them nor drank with them. I had my own friends, none of whom lived in my dormitory. The morning I left to catch a plane on the flight line (for Japan and *home*), I took my time packing. Almost all were in the bay (for some reason). Not a word was said. Not goodbye, so long, have a nice flight, *nothing*. We simply did not get along. I picked up my duffel bag, went to the double doors to leave as I carried my duffel bag over my shoulder, and looked back at them one last time. They were all looking at me without saying a word. I paused a few seconds as I made sure they knew I was also looking at them. Still, not one word was said. I wasn't thinking of one particular word, but I was thinking of one particular sentence and hoped they could all read my mind. It was "I hope I *never* run into any of you motherfuckers *ever* in my career in the air force."

** "The eight to nine other noncommissioned officers" does no justice in describing them or the relationship I had with these men over the course of thirteen months of living with them. They were all career military people. They were all white. They all drank to the point of intoxication every day. *But* (and a big but), they left me alone. No, they didn't talk to me more than an occasional "excuse me" to get by. But deep down I knew that *they* knew who I was. They knew the job I was doing in South Korea. When they gazed at me, I always walked a little taller, my shoes shined more than theirs, my area was always cleaner than theirs. In essence, I made sure *they* knew, or at least thought, I *was* better than any of them. There was one southern gentleman in the group. On November 22, 1963, in the middle of the night, like two or three in the morning, this gentleman wakes me up with "Wake up! Wake up! They shot and killed your boy. Kennedy is dead. He is dead." I was, of course, completely stunned and speechless. Just as quickly, this *gentleman* hunched over and started crying profusely, as he left my area. I turned my transistor radio on to hear the news. He was right. Our president was murdered in Dallas, Texas, that day.

Note: I had not thought about this until today as I try to complete this book. I often worry that I *toot my horn* a bit too much. I worry that people may see me as a narcissist who thinks he is perfect. Well, narcissism may exist, to some degree, in all of us. It is possible I may have a bit more than most people. An example of this is my behavior in taking on challenges. I live with a few *credos*. Some are the following: "*Where there is a will, there is a way*" and "*God helps those who help themselves.*" Also, "*If I make my mind up that I can do it, I can do it.*" Finally, I get a big kick out of taking on challenges. I get a bigger kick out of meeting that challenge and overcoming it. And then, I love to reflect and feel good about it. This may all be completely *human* and a part of what makes us unique animals. It was Abraham Maslow, in 1954, who came up with man's basic human needs. After the first three physiological needs are met, *esteem* comes into play. In essence, I'm just a normal human being. Whew!

Finally, make no mistake about this fact. This is only 1963 (exactly fifty-four years ago today). Think back these fifty-plus years and the role South Korea has played in the world. Our country has been modernizing its armed forces every few years to remain the greatest military force in the world, and especially in this part of the world with the threat that North Korea poses. As you read this chapter of my book on an American family of this century, reflect on this Mexican American playing a part in this endeavor. Society, and possibly you as well, can call me by any hyphenated name you want. Still, my thoughts are that I, through my family's actions, have made a considerable contribution to make our air force the best in the world, and certainly in the twentieth century.

Perhaps I was a little harsh in showing a negative attitude toward these two majors. The "if" premise to my having earned the Commendation Medal, after all the work I did on a 24/7 basis, generated these bad thoughts. I am still a little miffed about it all. Nonetheless, here is what I would eventually receive during a military parade ceremony at Lackland Air Force Base, Texas, in 1964.

DEPARTMENT OF THE AIR FORCE

THIS IS TO CERTIFY THAT

THE AIR FORCE COMMENDATION MEDAL

HAS BEEN AWARDED TO

TECHNICAL SERGEANT ROBERTO PEREZ, AF18413909

FOR

MERITORIOUS SERVICE
FIFTH AIR FORCE
15 MARCH 1963 TO 16 FEBRUARY 1964

GIVEN UNDER MY HAND IN THE CITY OF WASHINGTON
THIS   21ST   DAY OF   SEPTEMBER   1964

M. A. PRESTON
Lieutenant General, USAF
Commander, Fifth Air Force

SECRETARY OF THE AIR FORCE

CITATION TO ACCOMPANY THE AWARD OF

THE AIR FORCE COMMENDATION MEDAL

TO

ROBERTO PEREZ

Technical Sergeant Roberto Perez distinguished himself by meritorious service as Training NCO, 6314th Supply Squadron, Osan Air Base, Korea, from 15 March 1963 to 16 February 1964. During this period, the exemplary ability, diligence, and devotion to duty of Sergeant Perez were instrumental factors in the orderly and exacting conversion of the Base Supply Account from a manual accounting system to the PACAF Punch Card Accounting System. The supervision, initiative, outstanding leadership, and personal endeavor displayed by Sergeant Perez reflect credit upon himself and the United States Air Force.

The Period 1964-1968

My tour of duty in Korea ended thirteen months after arriving there in February of 1963. It is now March of 1964. It is actually Thursday, March 26 of 1964. It is a most significant day. I was flown to Tokyo, Japan, on an Air Force C-54 where I then boarded a commercial airline to San Francisco via Anchorage, Alaska. We landed in Anchorage for only a very short stay. It was a refueling stop. No one boarded our plane, and no one departed from it.

Significant day? Getting ahead of myself for just twenty-four hours so I can describe what happened in Anchorage, Alaska, at 5:39 p.m. on Good Friday, March 27, 1964. Here is why this date is significant. This is the exact time the most powerful earthquake to ever hit North America struck in Anchorage. The earthquake measured 9.2 on the Richter Scale. These are the results of this earthquake: 139 people died as a result. Only *fifteen* were as a direct result of the earthquake. One hundred six were killed by the resulting tsunami that struck Alaska. Tsunamis struck as far away as Japan, New Zealand, Peru, and Antarctica. Waves from the tsunami were measured at 220 feet, or 67 meters, in Shoup, Alaska. Five were killed as a result of the tsunami in Oregon and an additional thirteen in California.

For the record, the most powerful earthquake measured 9.5 on the Richter Scale and it occurred in Valdivia, Chile, on May 22, 1960. The third most powerful earthquake happened in Sumatra, Indonesia, and measured 9.1–9.3 on the Richter Scale. This latter one caused deaths in the hundreds of thousands and again, mostly because of the tsunamis it caused to happen.

I had been home now since late Thursday. On my second morning (Saturday, March 28) I woke up to hear the news about the earthquake. I was there in Anchorage less than twenty-four hours before the earthquake struck Alaska. How fortunate indeed.

I am now thirty years old. I have a family with three children, the youngest, Patricia Ann, not yet two years old (but about to be in approximately two months). When I left for Korea, "Patty" was not yet eight months old. For the first few days after my arrival at home, Patty would not get close to me. She would only look at me, probably wondering who I was. However, Patty soon warmed up to me, and we became as close to each other as I was to Maria and Robert.

I want to now go back in time some seven years. Grace and I married in January of 1957. I had turned 23 years of age the previous August. It was the same year I added a new career field to my air force jobs. I spent most of this year and the next two learning how to be the best military training instructor I could be. The old *perfectionist* approach struck again. I learned to be the best I could be *24/7*. And soon, in a squadron of fifty military instructors, all of them non-commissioned officers, along with the squadron commander, ranked me as not only among the best of instructors, but proficient enough to be given the position of "drill and ceremonies instructor." I was elevated to this position in the summer of 1959, when the current D&CI was selected for an overseas assignment. His name was Ralph Hendrickson, and it was his recommendation for his replacement that carried the most weight.

One of the duties of the D&CI was to train every flight to march in parades and in *Retreat* ceremonies. Marching in parades required putting several flights of airmen together in a *mass formation*, usually 12 × 12, or 144 airmen in one formation. The commands given by the *mass formation* instructor were preceded with the preparatory command "Squadron" instead of "Flight." All flights had to participate in at least one parade during their basic training. Several marched in two parades because parades were held on Tuesdays and Fridays of every week they were in training. The Tuesday parade was in fatigue uniform. Friday's parades were always in the Class A uniform, blues in winter, khakis in spring and summer.

Participation in Retreat formations was approximately two times a month. Retreat signals the end of the working day. The *Base American Flag* is lowered in a formal ceremony every week day, unless the weather prevents the ceremony from taking place. All Lackland training squadrons take their turn to participate in the ceremony. There were minimally fifteen training squadrons at Lackland at any one time.

Both parade and retreat ceremonies required instruction by the D&CI. Flight military training instructors would bring their flights to me for this special instruction starting in the first day of their third week of training. We scheduled only two flights at a time. Still, the number of airmen participating was minimally 120. Usually I would find a shaded area where they could sit on the grass while I instructed them on the complete ceremony, be it a parade or a retreat. Retreat instruction only occurred when our squadron was scheduled to participate officially. Participation in parades was mandatory for all air force trainees.

As with everything in the military, competition was always the order of the day. Parades were graded. Every movement made by each squadron was evaluated, from standing in formation throughout the ceremony to marching in front of the reviewing stand. Demerits were given for inappropriate turns by the formation, not taking the required number of steps between pivots by each column of each formation. The commands given by the instructor as they marched in front of the reviewing stand were also evaluated, as were everyone's head needing to be turned forty-five degrees to the right (with the exception of the column of men on the far right of each formation) as the squadrons marched by and the command "Eyes, Right," was given. The results were immediately called in to every squadron and each squadron is told where they placed among the fifteen or so squadrons who participated in the parade.

My formations were always in the top three, and usually *number one*. I wouldn't have it any other way. If I came in less than first place, I would study where our demerits were given and begin strategizing how not to have it happen again. It usually didn't, at least not often. I soon gained a reputation among all instructors at Lackland as someone who not only knew what he was doing, but would not tolerate second place under any circumstances. I was the 3711th Training Squadron's D&CI for two years, until I left for Amarillo Air Force Base in the fall of 1961.

From the fall of 1961 to March of 1964 I functioned as a logistician in Amarillo and Big Spring, Texas, and finally in South Korea. While I could have remained in logistics and risked being assigned anywhere in the continental United States, I asked to return to the military training instructor career field so I could return home to San Antonio. The assignment was granted. Lackland Air Force Base in San Antonio evidently wanted me as much as I wanted to go there.

My tour of duty in South Korea was not only memorable because of my success in converting the logistical accounting of the entire United States Air Force in all of South Korea, from a manual paper and pencil approach to a punch card mechanical methodology, the experience also affected me in ways that proved to be beneficial to my future. I grew tremendously in having the confidence that, if I put my mind to a task that was possible to do, by golly I could do it. I didn't think about this at first. I did, however, alter my thinking about what my future may be like because of this change in attitude, but mostly in having the confidence to do more than I ever thought I could do.

When I reported for duty at Lackland in May of 1964, I was assigned to my old unit, the 3711th Training Squadron. It was a completely different training environment than the one I had left three years earlier. The noncommissioned officers who were now the supervisors of all training had an eight to five approach to everything that occurred. Gone was the competitive spirit that motivated instructors to try harder to not only have the best trained trainees on the base, but to accomplish this feat with consistency. I was again assigned as the D&CI because they remembered what I had accomplished here in my first assignment at Lackland. I began by requiring instructors to stay a little later and to bring their flights to me for additional practice for participation in base-wide parades.

A Master Sergeant Campbell was the noncommissioned officer in charge of both the academic classroom instruction (the unit from which he came from another training squadron there at Lackland) as well as the training of all flights to participate in parades and retreats. Sergeant Campbell was an academic instructor and knew little of the tactical, weapons, marching in formation, and gas chamber training. He had military training instructors under him who took care of this instruction. Of the fifty to sixty MTIs assigned, a handful were here when I was last assigned to this squadron back in 1961. I am sure they informed Sergeant Campbell of who I was and my *notoriety* as one of the best parade and retreat instructors at Lackland. Again, I will toot my horn because I can, and it may be at the bottom of why I had to do what I did below. I was known by many of the seven hundred to eight hundred military training instructors assigned to Lackland Air Force Base. I know because many greeted me by my name when I didn't even know who they were. We were in a competitive field where coming in first was *everything*.

My relationship with Sergeant Campbell got off to a very bad start. He was cold to me and referred to me by my rank and last name. Sergeant Campbell had one more stripe than I did. He never looked at me when he spoke to me. He tried his very best to contradict me at every opportunity. Well, the job of training all flights to participate in parades and retreats was mine. I was the expert. Instructors brought their flights to me, and I trained them. When I stayed past five o'clock to train our flights for upcoming parades, my intent was always to make them the very best among the fifteen or so squadrons who participated.

On one occasion, there were some twelve to fifteen instructors in the lounge getting coffee or some other drink. I was there for a break as well. One of the MTIs, one whose flight was coming to me after the work day ended for additional training, came up to me and said in conversational tone of voice: "Oh, Sergeant Perez, where would you like me to bring my flight this evening?" Evidently, this request, to me and not to Sergeant Campbell, who knew nothing about drill and ceremonies, was more than Sergeant Campbell could handle. In a raised voice, he answered this request directed at me with "There won't be any training required from yours or other flights. They have a schedule during the day when all training is done."

Anger is not descriptive enough to tell how this intrusion on a request made to me made me feel. My immediate thoughts were to say, "Who the fuck said you could answer for me?" I knew if I opened my mouth my words were going to get me in trouble. Insubordination can mean reduction in rank and certainly loss of income.

Before telling the reader what I did, you should know who Sergeant Campbell was and what he looked like. He looked like a white pear. The only thing in his appearance that had shape was his Adam's apple. He easily weighed between 250 and 275 pounds and was just under six feet tall. He spoke with authority all the time. I already knew who he was before arriving here for the second time. He was really a loud mouth know-it-all. Like me, he obtained his college degree by going after work for several years. He knew we all knew that because he told us he did. Having a college degree as an enlisted person is not common among the near one million air force members (at that time, when Vietnam is raging in the far east). He was also a Texan.

Less than two seconds had gone by after Sergeant Campbell's' rude response when I stood straight up from my chair and rushed out of the lounge. I went straight to my car and drove off. I didn't have any training to do for several hours. What to do? What to do? I am in the United States Air Force and putting up with BS from idiots like Sergeant Campbell can be fairly common.

I remembered Master Sergeant Hallet Peace. Hal Peace was also about 6'8" tall and would turn red if he was out in the sun for a long time. He was from Oklahoma. As I remember, Hal Peace and his wife only had daughters. Also as I remember, none were yet in secondary schools. He was big and had a *command voice* like no one had ever heard. He was also the most experienced military training instructor at Lackland. Hal Peace was also my immediate supervisor when I first became a D&CI back in 1959. Hal Peace was now the non-commissioned officer in charge of the 3724th Training Squadron. This squadron only trained National Guardsmen and Reservists. It was the most prestigious training squadron because, across America, all young men of draft age would rather serve in one of these two branches of service because more than likely they would not be activated for duty in Vietnam. Still, the National Guard had quotas and not everyone could get into one of these branches of service. It is also possible that a lot of the men who managed to get into the National Guard *pulled strings* to get in. I drove over to his squadron and hoped he was there.

He was there. I had not yet gone by to see him in the few days I had already been at Lackland. He didn't get up from behind his desk. He asked me to pull up a chair and tell him how it is going back in the old squadron.

I told him everything exactly as it happened. He listened attentively. He asked if I had anything else to say about what happened. I said, "Hal, I've told you everything." He picked up the telephone. No, he didn't call his squadron commander. He called the Base Personnel Services office. He talked to another noncommissioned officer and told him, "I want Technical Sergeant Roberto Perez assigned to this squadron immediately…today." I heard this as I sat there and couldn't believe Hal Peace had that kind of power in what is the only training air force base America has. He put the phone down after completing the call and looked at me. "You're not going back. Is there anything over there that you have to retrieve?" I answered: "Nothing I cannot do without. No, I have nothing over there I wish to retrieve." I did not go back. The 3711th Training Squadron was immediately informed to have someone else assume whatever duties I had because "Sergeant Perez is not returning to your outfit."

Hal Peace is an enlisted person. He is not the squadron commander. However, as I said about my experiences in South Korea, the nitty-gritty things are caused to happen by the enlisted personnel of probably every branch of service.

I wish I could have seen Sergeant Campbell's face when he was informed. He may have had more authority than I had, and he may have outranked me as well. I meant him no harm, and I certainly did not cherish whatever embarrassment he went through and how he justified talking about it when asked by other squadron instructors where I was. I have no idea what he said to them. Still, there was one additional incident at Lackland that affected Sgt. Campbell's squadron (*my old outfit*) and the fact that I left them abruptly. The incident had to do with my performance in South Korea during the 1963–64 period that I was there.

Remember that Major Jones instructed Sergeant Ryan to put me in for the Air Force Commendation Medal "if I had not yet been awarded one during my career." Well, the medal and all the accompanying justification for the award arrived at Lackland and now had to be presented to me during an official ceremony. Official ceremonies were seemingly the order of the day on this air force base. It just so happens that the 3711th Training Squadron was the squadron responsible for the next parade and their commander would have to read the citation at the parade before thousands of troops and then pin the medal on my chest. I would stand on the reviewing stand with the commander of the 3711th and have all the formations salute him *and me* as they marched by. When the parade was over, and before we were dismissed, the commander of the 3711th shook my hand again and added that he was really sorry I had left his organization. I thanked him for his kind words and said nothing else. Sergeant Campbell was in the formation of his squadron as they marched by the reviewing stand.

How fitting, at least for me. I didn't gloat about it. I probably didn't even tell my family about it. There was just a very good feeling inside of me that things happened this way

I did run into Sergeant Campbell again. It happened several years later. The incident had occurred during the summer of 1964. Sergeant Campbell left Lackland on an overseas assignment later on that same year. He returned in 1967. As luck would have it for him, bad luck that is, he was assigned to the 3724th Training Squadron, my squadron, where I was still assigned as the D&CI. I had maintained my reputation as being an excellent instructor and had the respect of all military personnel assigned to this squadron.

Sergeant Campbell knew I was there. I was later informed by one of my trusted sources within the squadron that he told a group, in the lounge again, that he and I were assigned once upon a time to the 3711th Squadron and that he was my supervisor. He added that I just happen to have higher standards than he had, and I had gone to *greener pastures*. Now, this may have taken a bit of added honesty on his part that I never suspected he had. We didn't work together any more even though he was back at his old job as the head of academic instruction. My job now had been changed to be directly under the noncommissioned officer in charge of all training. We only nodded greetings when we ran into each other. He didn't like me. Squadron personnel respected me a lot more than they did him. This must have rubbed him the wrong way. I certainly didn't like him either.

In the meantime, I continued with my duties as the D&CI. We were the only squadron at Lackland who trained the Air Force National Guard. The education level of these trainees was very high. College graduates and graduate school students were more the order of the day than not. Most of the trainees were twenty-five years old and older.

There was one incident I had with one of these trainees that gave me a lot of food for thought as to what to do with my life after leaving the service at the age of 38. This trainee approached me after the day's training was over and asked if he could have a conference with me. This trainee had his own flight military training instructor he could have gone to for a conference. He chose to ask me, and as he said later on, thought I seemed more mature and probably could advise him better than his own flight instructor, who was a few years younger than me.

The trainee was in his midthirties, a graduate school student, and he was facing having to make decisions rather quickly after getting back to resume his *day job* of being a civilian and only having monthly meetings as a national guardsman. He wanted advice on a few things, like his career, his girl that he wanted to marry, and having to spend most of his savings. He was afraid of making the wrong decision.

I really do not remember what I advised him to do. I do remember that we conferred for almost an hour, and I did a lot of listening. I kept asking him questions and also how he felt after responding to my questions. He seemed completely satisfied with his sharing of his so-called concerns and that I treated him with dignity and respect. More importantly, I felt *a real high* myself. Also, I felt his satisfaction with our conference, based on his body language, the look on his face, and seemingly a lot more relaxed than when our conference started.

The food for thought? I saw in me a strength in dealing with people. I should consider a career field where I can advise, counsel, or otherwise *be there* for people in need. But more than deciding on a career, this unique experience made me aware that I needed credentials to make this happen. I needed to obtain a college degree and then pursue a graduate degree that may allow me to also obtain a license to be able to advise or counsel people. I have to start going to college to do this. Not only that. I have to continue my career for the sake of my family and the security of medical insurance *and* also to get a college degree. I had long-range goals now. I also felt a determination to pursue and attain these goals.

On August 17, 1964, I turned 31. I was in my thirteenth year in the air force. I had no intentions of staying in longer than twenty years. I knew, too, that so far I had been so busy trying to make ends meet with part time jobs that I had not given any thought to preparing to go into another field or a different type of work after my twenty years in the service. These were now my thoughts every time I reflected on where I was going with my life. Grace's work experiences were in the service area, either selling in a department store or working in restaurants. Her earnings would not be complementary to mine after allowing for child care. Maria was 5, Robert would be 4 in September, and Patty was just 2 years old. Our plans were that Grace would remain at home until the three were out of elementary school. Still, I had to prepare myself to do something else with my life after my twenty years in the service and continue being the main wage earner in the family. It was an easy conclusion. I had obtained a high school equivalency with high marks and anticipated I would have no trouble getting started in a junior college before transferring my credits to a four-year institution. Grace and I had a plan. It was long term, for sure. This was always our modus operandi. Have long-term goals and never lose sight of them. Also, develop shorter objectives for immediate success that would make the long-term goal possible to attain. I registered for two classes at the San Antonio College on South Main Avenue starting in the fall semester of 1964. I was 31 and for the first time in my life would become a part-time college student. I was still in the air force.

My first two courses were American History I and English I. The English course was British Literature. The history course was America Before the Civil War. I received a C for the History Course, a B for English. My history professor told me that I knew everything I needed to know and my military customs of being precise and brief hurt all my narrative responses on exams. It was a tough lesson to learn and also the next-to-last C I would ever get again in all my college work. My college work over the next fourteen years, acquiring well over two hundred semester hours and three degrees, would only yield one more C. That course was Psychology I and also there at SAC. It was a lecture course of 3-hours-per-session with little discussion. One had to take lots and lots of notes because the final was a 150 multiple choice question exam. It was a high C, but nonetheless, like the history course of the fall of 1964, I could not transfer it. However, I did complete twenty courses while there at SAC and I was able to transfer eighteen of them when I enrolled at Florida State University in 1968. More on that later on in this chapter.

I was only attending classes after work and on Saturdays when a class was scheduled that I needed. I was paying 25 percent of the tuition and the air force paid the remainder. I always looked for used textbooks to buy instead of new ones. Once the class was over, I would resell the book to the bookstore. Money was scarce for us. On average, I completed six courses each calendar year. I always took two in the summer, as I did for the fall and spring semesters.

Grace and I were still very much involved with the Catholic Church. We were both brought up as Catholics. We did not use contraceptives as a way of exercising birth control. Instead, we used the rhythm method. It had already failed us for both Robert and Patty. We continued *trying* to make it work in 1964 and 1965. Well, it failed us again as Grace got pregnant again in February of 1965 and Rey was born on October 7 of that year. Maria had started kindergarten in the fall of 1964. She was in first grade the year Rey was born. I was able to get Robert enrolled in kindergarten in 1965 even though he did not turn 5 until September of that year. Both were enrolled at St. John Berchmans Elementary School.

Having now mentioned the Catholic school where our kids attended, I must now add a few details about how this school managed to get built in the first place. Of course, it is a private school. The public school system located here in this area, the Edgewood Public Schools, did not fund any part of the school. While the Catholic Archdiocese of San Antonio played a big part in funding the construction of this school, a large part of the cost of the school was also borne by the members of the community who pledged a certain amount to contribute to the school being built. This is where my brother-in-law, Frank Burns, and I enter the picture.

We both pledged a certain amount to contribute monthly. What we also did was to volunteer to go door to door to all the parishioners who lived nearby to get them to volunteer to also contribute monthly. My recollection of what Frank and I experienced is that I was astonished at the number of positive responses we got from these parishioners when we knocked on their doors. By the way, Frank and I did all of this canvassing of the community in the years 1960 and 1961. The school was built and opened for students before I returned from South Korea. Maria and Robert attended St. John Berchmans for three and two years, respectively, and Patty for one, her kindergarten year, before all three, and Rey, at age 2, all joined me in Panama in 1968. More on Panama in the next chapter.

Let me take you back to the summer of 1964 when my previous training supervisor (years 1959–1961), Hal Peace, arranged for me to join him in the 3724th Training Squadron. Remember, he said, "You are not going back to that squadron." (I may be paraphrasing here, but that is essentially what I heard him say.)

Starting with that summer of 1964, I functioned as the D&CI with that National Guard Training Squadron for the next four years. It was quite the experience. The war with Vietnam continued, and while I was assured of staying on stateside duty for at least three years, I knew that I would have to go overseas to another assignment somewhere in the world before completing my twenty years. The assignment could easily be in Vietnam. But come February of 1972, I would have twenty years of active duty under my plate. Then, I would retire for sure. This was always part of Grace's and my plan. The one sure thing both of us knew I would keep for the rest of our lives was the free medical coverage because I would be a twenty-year veteran of the American armed forces. It would come to be known as TriCare-For-Life. More on this benefit in later chapters.

So, why was being assigned to this particular squadron make it *quite the experience?* It was because a very high percentage of those able to enter the Air Force National Guard did it because they *knew someone* in government who could facilitate this for them. It was usually someone who knew a senator or member of congress who could pull the strings necessary to make it happen. Among the semi-famous people who arrived at Lackland as members of the National Guard were Alan Ladd's son, who later married a girl named Cheryl, who later starred in the film industry as Cheryl Ladd. There was Jerry Mathers, better known as Beaver Cleaver, of *Leave It to Beaver* TV fame (1957–1963). I had both of them for mass formation drill and for participation in parades. As I remember, Mathers was a very regular young man who did everything he was told to do and had a spotless record in basic training. Earlier, Mathers had tried to join the Marines and actually passed his physical but was denied entrance in to the marines because a prominent NFL player had just been killed in Vietnam and the marines were being criticized for sending that player into combat. They denied Mathers, and he settled for the Air Force National Guard.

A more famous Air Force National Guardsman was Ralph Neely, a two-time All-American football player at Oklahoma University. Ralph was born in Little Rock, Arkansas in 1943 but played his high school football in Farmington, New Mexico. He stood 6'6" and weighed 265 pounds. In 1965, he was a giant of a man and a fine football player who played on both sides of the line of scrimmage. He was selected for numerous awards while at Oklahoma and was drafted very high in the 1965 football draft by both the Houston Oilers of the AFL and the Baltimore Colts of the NFL. He signed first with Houston but then learned that the Colts had traded him to the Dallas Cowboys. He sent the unspent signing bonus back to Houston and then signed with the Cowboys. This signing conflict ended up in the courts and was not resolved for several years. The Cowboys eventually ended up giving several very high draft choices in the mid to upper 1960s.

A towering figure in basic training at Lackland, Neely was immediately made a barracks chief while undergoing training and was also a member of several of my mass formation flights who participated in more than one base parade. His military training instructor was a very close friend of mine, James Claxton, a staff sergeant. Neely eventually left Lackland, returned to playing football, and would only be in uniform in the air force once a month for training meetings and during the summer for two-weeks of active duty. The active duty was conducted inside the continental limits of our country. This was the advantage of being in the Air Force National Guard. In order to be called to active duty, the circumstances in Vietnam needed to turn really desperate. While they were never good, they were never bad enough for either National Guardsmen or Reservists needing to be called for active duty.

Neely would send Sgt. Claxton tickets to Cowboy home games. Sergeant Claxton always included me in the foursome who traveled to Dallas for several games during the 1966 NFL season. We went to several games during the 1966 season. We didn't just attend the games and had excellent seats in the Cotton Bowl (Jerry Jones, Texas Stadium, etc., were a couple of decades away still), Neely had us go to the locker room after the games to join him there. We were in the same locker room where many radio and TV interviews were being conducted. We saw Don Meredith and many other Dallas Cowboys being interviewed right next to us. We would then drive to Neely's house to have a few beers before driving back to San Antonio. I still remember one particular game against the L.A. Rams when Neely got pushed back repeatedly by the Ram lineman Deacon Jones. Jones had Neely on his back a lot during the game. When we arrived in the locker room to join Neely, I remember saying to him, "Tough game, Ralph," and Neely answering me, "You can say that again, Sergeant

Perez." We usually didn't get home until four or five in the morning. None of us had the day off, so we would go straight to work at Lackland after these trips to Dallas.

I continued piling up credits at San Antonio College. It was a very slow process of accumulating college credits, but I never lost sight of the fact that I had until 1972 to complete all requirements for a college degree. As we entered into the year 1967, I began thinking that I would have to go overseas again and that would set me back insofar as attending college on a part-time basis. Another assignment to an unaccompanied location would also mean I would not be able to take any college courses. We were not into computers and online courses yet, even though there were some universities that did allow students to take courses by using the U.S. mail system. Rather than considering this approach in the event I went to another isolated assignment, I decided to apply for an assignment where I could take my family and hopefully also be able to take college courses at the same time.

I was proficient in two languages, being able to read, write, and speak proficiently in both English and Spanish. I only had a couple of courses in Spanish under my belt, but I had remained proficient in the language because of the insistence of my mother and being corrected at home all the time. I inquired into assignments in one of the Spanish-speaking countries in Central and South America. There would be an opening in Guatemala in the summer of 1968 as the Spanish interpreter for the president of Guatemala to all correspondence coming from the U.S. Government. At the time, because of presidents Kennedy and Johnson in the 1960s, America had many programs of military training and assistance with several countries in the Americas. I submitted all the necessary paperwork and a résumé that further elaborated on my skills with the Spanish language. The recipient of my application was an office in the Pentagon that dealt specifically with the Latin American countries. I sent the paperwork on its way and then almost forgot about it because it was a very long shot.

Two months had gone by when I receive a phone call, from the Pentagon. In essence, the caller tells me on the phone that I have made the final list of those who will be called to the Pentagon for an interview for the position in Guatemala. I was given an appointment to come to Washington, DC.

The interview was conducted in the hallway outside one particular office. There was an arrangement of a desk and chairs and there was plenty of space for the interviewer and the interviewee. But I could tell this was a temporary "office," and as soon as the interviews were completed, all the furniture would disappear. Such are the things that happen in the Pentagon. The interviewer was a "Colonel Gomez." The interview was conducted in both English and Spanish. I was relaxed during the interview and found no reason to be nervous about the interview. When the interview was over, I left and flew back to San Antonio to wait for the results. Well, I flew back to get back to work. I wasn't *waiting* for the results. These milestones in our lives come when *they come*.

It is now fall of 1967. A call comes from the Pentagon. "Congratulations! You have been selected to replace the current Spanish interpreter to the president of Guatemala. We are sending you literature to help you prepare for your assignment to Guatemala and also how to handle your family's trip there as well. Your family will be able to travel with you on your flight to Guatemala. As of now, your schedule departure for Guatemala is in June of 1968.

I was excited, of course. Grace was, too. Maria is not quite 9 years old yet, but she understood the gist of everything happening around her. Robert just turned 7 in September. The only other place he knew of besides San Antonio was Amarillo, and even then he was just 1 and ½ years old. He didn't remember anything about Amarillo. I doubt if Maria could recall even where we lived while I was stationed there.

Weeks passed and we began planning our departure. There were things to sell or give away. There was the house. We decided quickly to not sell it but instead rent it out. We had wonderful neighbors just two doors down who said they would look after the house for us until we returned. That we were going to Guatemala became a foregone conclusion. That is, until it wasn't.

143

Shortly after January 1 of 1968, I get another call, but not from the Pentagon this time. It's from the world-wide assignments office, also here in Washington. The essence of the call went something like this (am paraphrasing, but very accurately): "Uh, Sergeant Perez? Uh, hmm, well…your assignment to Guatemala has been canceled. We regret having to give you such bad news because we know your family and you have been planning for weeks, if not months. It was the president of Guatemala's call. He talked to President Johnson and persuaded him to make an exception of extending the current interpreter for another year. The Guatemalan president had gotten so comfortable with him that he didn't want to lose him for the balance of his tenure as president. President Johnson said he would do so."

Of course, I am speechless on the other end of the telephone call. I didn't really feel that disappointed but did feel that an awful long time has gone by believing that I was going to Guatemala with my family. Nonetheless, I am still unable to say anything more than "It's okay. My family and I can handle this." Just as suddenly, my thoughts turned to "Well, then, where am I going if not to Guatemala?"

The voice at the other end of the line then says something I had a hard time believing I heard the voice say to me. The voice utters, "Where would you like to go?" Uh, excuse me. Say that again. We are talking about the United States Air Force. There are currently over one million members of this force. All assignments are controlled by a central office and assignments are made worldwide in a very concentrated effort to replace all personnel in a timely manner. We don't have the world's best air force by asking people where they want to go.

The voice continues, "Before making this disappointing call to you, I have been authorized to ask you to choose from several places around the world where we have vacancies coming up this coming summer. There is a vacancy in Germany. There is also a vacancy in Panama. It will be your choice." I asked to be given time to ponder the request. I did want to share with Grace and also tell her I had already served in Germany, and we would have the opportunity to see a lot of Europe if we took vacations while we are assigned there. She and I talked that evening. Grace said she would leave it up to me.

I was the one who would have the job to do. The last time I worked as a logistician was in South Korea and that was an experience of a lifetime. I knew it would be nothing like that. We concluded that I should tell Air Force Headquarters to send me to Panama.

The very next day, and at the exact time as planned, *the voice* came on the telephone, I told him of my choice. The voice added, "You will not be able to travel concurrently because of a *wait time* for housing in the Canal Zone where you will live." Another item to discuss with Grace. She would have to fly without me to Charlotte and then to Panama City on another flight, and with four children. Maria was not yet 10 (would be in December). Robert would turn 8 in September. Patty would be 6 already and probably the one to "hang on too." Rey was only 2 and ½. Grace said she could handle it. Grace and I knew that Maria was as good as having a young adult or able teenager to assist her. Robert always behaved and followed instructions. She'd have to carry Rey and hold on to Patty. She could handle that.

There were other things that had to be done. I could have my car shipped overseas and drive it while on this assignment. I would have to drive it to New Orleans and deliver it to a ship (on the bay) that would carry it to Panama. I did. I took a few days off from work at Lackland and also planned to spend a day or so with my brothers Armando and Henry in Houston. I drove a 1961 Ford Fairlane four-door in excellent shape. It was as clean as a whistle. The trip to Houston and also spending one-night with my two brothers is an experience I will not soon forget.

About my brothers Armando and Henry: They were very different from my other brothers and me. Armando was a risk taker and an entrepreneur. I honestly do not remember that he ever worked for anyone but himself. This is 1968. He is 50 years old and has always been self-employed. That is, except for his three years in the army during WWII. Henry worked for Armando and was eleven years younger. Unfortunately, Henry had a history of getting into trouble with the friends he kept. This began occurring since he was in his teens. Armando did a good job employing him and keeping him out of trouble. Still, Henry kept his friends, so getting into trouble was always a constant with Henry.

I arrived in Houston and went straight to their three-story house near the downtown area. Why a three-story house? Armando employed twelve to thirteen undocumented workers who sold fruits and vegetables door-to-door in the middle class areas of the city of Houston. He was their caretaker. They all lived in this house. There were at least three bedrooms on each floor. Armando and Henry slept on the third floor. The first thing I noticed about their house was that it was very clean and all the beds were made in every bedroom. While I only saw the top floor bathroom, and it was very clean, I have to believe the other two, one on each floor, were similarly clean. Armando paid their salaries for the work they did. He had two produce trucks. He drove one, Henry the other. Daily, all would rise around 4:00 a.m. and drive some thirty miles to a nearby fruit and vegetable market where Armando would negotiate with farmers and buy their products. They would load both trucks with fruits and vegetables and, using smaller containers in which to sell these products door-to-door, were on the Houston residential areas fairly early selling their products. They had been doing this several years and had many regular customers.

All the workers hit the streets and all knew their routes fairly well. They kept 25% of every sale and Armando got 75%. Seems rather one-sided until one remembers that Armando pays the farmers cash for their products and then has the maintenance upkeep of both trucks as well as the fuel expenses. I have to believe he also charged them to live in that big house. I didn't see any unhappy workers the day and night I spent with them. I slept on the top floor, and Armando had a single bed for me.

Henry knew I was into major league sports and particularly baseball. The Astros were still in the future and the Astrodome had not yet been built. The Houston team was the Colt 45s, and they played in Colt 45 Stadium. Henry treated me to a game, and he bought box seats between home plate and first base. *Choice seats* to say the least. It's been a long time since this happened, but I remember who they were playing. It was the St. Louis Cardinals and their pitcher that night was Bob Gibson. This was a big treat for me. After the game, Henry took me to a steak house for a steak dinner. He was very much a meat-and-potatoes kind of guy. We got to their house around midnight, and when I woke up to leave for New Orleans at five o'clock, they were all gone and the house was empty. And clean.

I delivered my car to the pier address I was given and soon was on my way to downtown New Orleans to get on a Greyhound Bus and get back to San Antonio. I had just a couple of days before I would fly alone to Panama and start a new life in Central America. Grace and our kids would follow as soon as I could find a place to live in the city of Panama. I was on a waiting list for housing in the Canal Zone and the wait would take fully one year.

Living in the Canal Zone (1968-1971)

I left for Panama in June of 1968. I was only three years and seven months from my anticipated retirement from the air force. My plans for "what to do with the rest of my life" were still in limbo. While I am a very serious worrier, for some reason I felt secure that I had enough time to still prepare to do something with my life at the end of twenty years in the armed forces. This particular concern was just simply not on my mind at this time in my life. Getting to Panama, finding a home in the city of Panama for my family and me while I waited for *on base housing* in the Canal Zone, was the only thing I worried about. My full concentration was on this detail.

I arrived in Panama in late June of 1968. I was stationed at Howard Air Force Base. There were two air force bases in Panama. The other one was Albrook Air Force Base. Howard was where the flight line was located and had several squadrons with aircraft that carried out missions in Central America and in a few countries in South America. One squadron had fighter aircraft. I believe they were F-80s. Another squadron had C-47s and C-54s that carried material and training equipment to both Central and South American countries. There was one weekly run by a four-engine C-54 that left Howard Air Force Base and went to every South American country which had a role to play in our mission in this part of the world. The weekly flight was called the *Andes Run*. The C-47s made shorter runs to countries located in Central America. The countries were Honduras, Nicaragua and Guatemala.

Albrook was the home for the Air Force Inter-American Language School. There must have been eight to ten Central and South American countries who sent military personnel from their countries for training at Albrook. They were taught in their native language. All of them were Spanish-speaking countries.

I immediately found that there was a two-year college that offered associate degrees. It was called the Canal Zone College. I took several courses with this college until I discovered that there was also a branch of Florida State University located in the Canal Zone as well. FSU offered courses in a variety of programs. The university was located at Albrook Air Force Base. FSU offered programs of studies that could terminate in bachelor of arts or bachelor of science degrees. I wasted no time in pursuing one program of studies that terminated with a four-year degree in Social Science. Also, most of the courses I completed at San Antonio College were transferable since my grades in all these courses were B or higher. The few courses I completed at the Canal Zone College were all transferable as well.

FSU did not have *semesters* per se. Their programs of studies were all on a *quarter-hour* basis. Instead of having two semesters for a calendar year, as well as a summer program, FSU offered four quarters per year in which students could sign up for university level courses. Instead of going thirteen to fifteen weeks per semester, as is done at universities with semester-hour programs, FSU had courses for a shorter duration and awarded quarter hours. Instead of requiring 120–130 semester hours to qualify for a university degree, the requirement was for completing 180 quarter hours of college courses. Each completed course earned the student four quarter hours.

While I found time to spend with our four children (Maria, Robert, Patty, and Rey), I also never let even one quarter-hour period go by without taking two or more courses at FSU. As I did when I was in San Antonio and taking college courses, I paid 25% of the tuition, plus the cost of textbooks, while the air force paid 75% of the tuition. Grace and I had no other expenses. There were no electrical, water, telephone, rent, or other utility household expenses. Only the food on our table cost us. We were in Panama courtesy of Uncle Sam. We intended to make the most of it.

From fall of 1968 to spring of 1971, I continued taking courses every quarter. I followed the requirement for a four-year degree and did not waste a single course as all were applicable to my program of studies. I do have to *fess up* and admit that I failed one course. It was *Logarithms of Math*. I was hanging in there until the very end, but just barely getting by. However, I did not practice enough homework nor did I have other students with whom to form a support group. I failed it by the *skin of of my teeth*. I immediately signed up to take the class over again. I signed up with others who also failed it and hired a tutor. I passed it with a B the second time. I believe the sum total of quarter hours I earned by the end of the second quarter of the 1971 winter-spring period was 182 hours. I was awarded a four-year degree by Florida State University, Canal Zone Branch. I had met one of my long-range goals that would help my transition to civilian life after twenty years in the military. I felt I would be more marketable with a college degree in my pocket.

I will return to mentioning my involvement with our children after I explain where we lived in Panama City and about Grace arriving with our four children, ages 9, 7, 6, and 2, while also on crutches after suffering a broken ankle in San Antonio before departing for Panama.

First, living in Panama City.

There was no way that I was going to allow Grace to remain in San Antonio alone to care for our four children. I was determined to find a home in the city of Panama while having to wait a year for *on-base housing* in the Canal Zone. Remember that I had my car shipped to Panama, so I had transportation to go into the city to look at houses I could rent, off the Panamanian economy. What I found instead of a house was the availability of apartments that were spacious and that had parking garages attached to the buildings. Also, they were all located in the upper-middle class sections of the city. It was where all the Panamanian professionals lived. The area was clean and very accessible by car from the Canal Zone or Howard Air Force Base, where I was stationed and where I would probably be assigned a home or apartment when one became available.

The apartment I found was on Via Argentina and most of the occupants of these apartments were other American service families waiting for on-base housing themselves. We lived there for a year and made a lot friends. We made friends with one Panamanian family who also lived in this apartment building, the *Quintero's*. Mr. Quintero was a lawyer and his wife was a stay-at-home mother with two very young children. Although a professional herself, she was planning on staying home until their children entered elementary school. Grace and I continued seeing them even after we moved to Howard Air Force Base to live and socialized with them until we left for America in December of 1971.

Now, a few things about my family's arrival in Panama. Grace's arrival at Tocumen Airport (the only airport in Panama City) was memorable, to say the least. She was traveling without me for the first time. She would have to carry Rey in her arms because he was only 2 ½ years old and could not walk down the stair plank from the aircraft. We did not have the gates that we are so accustomed to now for several decades. This is 1968, fifty years ago. It was memorable because Grace and the kids were the last ones off the airplane. Grace did not have Rey in her arms. She had *crutches* under her arms because she had broken her left ankle at home when her brother-in-law dropped an iron bed frame on her foot. Maria, Robert, and Patty walked down the plank okay. One of the two (male) pilots walked down the plank of steps with Rey in his arms until I relieved him of Rey inside the terminal.

I had the apartment ready. It was furnished, and I had filled the refrigerator and pantry with food items. Grace was happy she didn't have to worry about shopping for food for a few days. I had a couple of days off to help my family get situated, so that helped a lot. My drive from the city to Howard AFB was about forty minutes long and the drive had me travel over the long and very high bridge over the Panama Canal. Two incidents occurred on top of this bridge that I will mention farther along in this chapter.

It is now fall of 1968. Maria is 9 years old and in the fourth grade. Robert turns 8 years old in September of 1968 and is in third grade. Patty is 6 and in first grade. Rey stays home with his mother.

I enrolled all three in Canal Zone schools. On military installations all over the world where parents and children accompany the service member, children are never driven to their schools by parents. They get there by riding a school bus. The trouble was that all three had to ride two buses to get to their schools. They boarded the first bus in the city of Panama, and it took them into the Canal Zone, but not to their schools. For their second bus, all three rode different buses. To say that Grace and I worried about this is to put it very mildly. All three made it though. I have to believe these experiences are ones they will never forget.

There was one memorable occasion in October of 1968, while we were still living in Panama City. Panama held elections that fall and one Dr. Arnulfo Arias Madrid won the election. Unfortunately, the people of Panama so distrusted the election results that a coup d' etat by their guardia nacionál (the Panamanian National Guard) ousted Dr. Arias Madrid and one Lt. Col. Omar Torrijos rose to take command and their national guard ruled for several years. During the purge, Panamanian national guardsmen patrolled the Panama City streets with rifles at the ready and there were a few skirmishes with citizens who did not like that their democratic elections were abolished with the coup.

Unfortunately, there were hundreds of Americans living in the city of Panama who were subjected to life in a city being patrolled at every corner by rifle-toting guardsmen. I had Canal Zone plates on my car, and I felt safe because we were not involved at all and the guardsmen left us alone and would simply just wave us forward at every intersection of the city. Inconvenient? You bet. It was also a little scary for our children to be in the car with armed soldiers at every intersection of the city. The day of the coup was especially scary because the order went out to all people that they could not travel the streets of the city, on foot or by car. We were unable to leave for work for some three days. However, our commanders knew of the situation, and it was announced on Armed Forces Radio to just stay put and to comply with the wishes of the Panama National Guard. We did not let our children go to school during this period.

About the two incidents on top of that very famous bridge: One was a tragedy that killed over sixty Panamanian citizens. The other concerned me. First, the tragedy: Panamanian drivers seemed to always be in a hurry. A lot of people in this country cannot afford cars and travel mostly by bus. Buses are everywhere. I have to believe that most people travel to their place of employment via bus transportation. Like most heavily-traveled bridges where there is a lot of traffic, there are minimally three lanes going each way. Some portions on this bridge had four lanes going each way. Most of the drivers who drove on this bridge were Panamanians.

On one particular occasion, two bus drivers were racing each other to see who would get to the portion of the bridge where the number of lanes is reduced to three, from the four lanes each way that they were on. There is a slight curve to the left as they reach this point on the bridge. The bus driver who got to the curve first could not make the turn to his left and maintain all wheels on the asphalt. The bus tilted on its right side and went over the bridge, first on its right side and then with its wheels facing skyward. The bus landed on its roof. The height was probably three to four hundred feet. All were killed.

I have mentioned before that my 1961 Ford Fairlane was in excellent shape. It was. However, while driving in the city, when we were still living in the city, I ran over something that my tires hurled against my fuel tank, and while it didn't damage the tank nor did I lose any fuel, it did disengage the portion of the fuel tank that measures how much fuel I have in the car, and it shows up on my dash board. I lost the ability to tell how much fuel I had in the car. Well, as luck would have it, during days when I was very busy and not paying attention to what my fuel level was, I ran out of gas, on the uppermost portion of the bridge. Fortunately, I suspected this was the problem so I pulled over to the curb on the highest portion of the bridge and raised my hood so a Canal Zone policeman would pull over to assist me. It was a safe lane meant just for this purpose. It was okay to park and leave my car here while a police officer, and I would drive to a service station to get fuel.

Canal Zone police always travel as duos in one car. While one officer and I went after fuel in the policemen's car, the other police officer stayed behind to ensure that people see that the car is temporarily out of commission. The remaining police officer evidently got bored waiting, so he goes up to the bridge railing to look down at passing ships that are either going from or to the Canal Zone locks. The police officer was bending down and looking straight down to the water. Several people who knew me drove by on their way to work, saw my car, and also saw the police officer looking straight down at the water below. One of them told me in the office later that day that he was sure I had (had) enough of Panama and decided to jump off the bridge. It became the joke of the day in my office.

My family and I spent three and a half years living in Panama. For all intent and purposes, *it is* Panama, but we really lived in the Canal Zone. What was it like living in a central American country but essentially still in America? I say *still in America* because the Canal Zone looked like any middle class American community located anywhere in the United States. Yet, one could drive past the perimeter that were the Canal Zone borders, and one could tell immediately that one is in what is essentially a third-world country. Labor for all kinds of menial jobs was available. Americans living here took advantage of this availability.

A bit more about the Canal Zone: It became the Canal Zone in a signed treaty with Panama in 1903. It was known as an *Unincorporated Territory.*

It remained an unincorporated territory until President Jimmy Carter abolished it with the Torrijos and Carter Treaties of 1977. The Canal Zone consisted of 553 square miles through the heart of the country of Panama. It facilitated the construction of the Panama Canal. More on its construction follows.

As the name suggests, a forty-eight-mile man-made waterway (essentially, a *canal*) was built across the isthmus of Panama. France was the first country to attempt to build the canal in 1881. Ships attempting to reach the west coast of the United States had to travel twelve thousand miles to the southernmost point of South America (Cape Horn), which took sixty-seven days to accomplish.

Initially Colombia controlled the construction of the canal. France then assumed the responsibility. But soon the French gave up on its construction because of the high mortality rate among its workers. Twenty-five thousand workers moved one million cubic yards of earth to construct the canal. The United States took over the construction in 1904 after forming a treaty with Panama in 1903. The canal opened for vessels in 1914. Locks were constructed at each end of the canal to lift ships to *Gatún Lake*, an artificial lake created to reduce the amount of excavation required for vessels to cross. The original locks were 33.5 meters in depth. The requirement for most vessels was twenty-six meters. A third and wider lane was constructed between September of 2007 and May of 2016.

In 1914, one thousand vessels used the canal to go from one ocean to the other. In 2008, 14,702 vessels made the crossing. Between 1914 and 2012, more than 815, 000 vessels had made the crossing. As the American Society of Civil Engineers called the canal, it was truly the seventh wonder of the world.

The canal has become a geologist's dream for the study of the earth's crust. In fact, the U.S. Government employed teams of geologists to continue monitoring the endurance and longevity of the canal. Several geologists taught courses on geology for Florida State University there in the Canal Zone. I was fortunate enough to be able to take several of these courses and apply them to fulfill the science requirement for my baccalaureate degree.

In addition to the two air force bases, Panama had a large marine and naval presence. Marines and sailors were stationed at a camp known as Rodman Naval Base. The army was present as well. Most were stationed at a camp known as Fort Clayton. The army, navy, and marines arrived in Panama long before the air force did. When the U.S. government decided to build schools for military dependents, they were built on the army and naval bases. Thousands of Americans worked for the Panama Canal, an American enterprise. These employees, with their families also living in Panama, had their own schools, an elementary, a junior high, and a high school. There was also a very large, and very well known, hospital that was exclusively for Americans, including armed forces personnel. It was known as Gorgas Hospital.

Our daughter Patty spent a few days in Gorgas Hospital in 1969. She was only seven years old at the time and had developed a urinary tract infection that would not heal. Our pediatrician decided the best remedy for this infection was close monitoring in the hospital. Patty spent four to five days there and, even though we were in a foreign country, did not seem to mind at all. In fact, we visited her every day and *every day* had to roam the halls of the hospital to find her because she was out visiting other wards and patients. My sister Jovita visited us during this time and thought her little seven-year old niece must be scared to death being in a hospital in a foreign country. Hah! She didn't know Patty! Getting a little farther ahead in both Jovita's and Patty's lives, many years later the two of them would get to travel in Mexico during one of Jovita's many trips to her country of origin. This time she invited Patty. Patty told me all about it and I hope I can remember to include this adventure that Patty endured. They visited many places and Patty probably has many pictures. Still, one of her recollections of her trip (Patty's) was that Jovita farted a lot during the night. Of course, she added a few other things to make this remembrance a bit more thrilling. It only served to put a smile on my face and howl with laughter.

On another occasion, I was visiting the hospital for another reason that I cannot recall. The hospital was huge and had every specialist one can think of, and it was also an American hospital that took care of all patients, civilian and military. On one visit of mine, I sat waiting to be seen and sat next to a middle-aged American civilian who was also waiting. I introduced myself and he did, too. He was a retired military person who now lived in Ecuador, and not very far from the coastline that is the Pacific Ocean. He owned a large fishing boat and made his living fishing for shrimp. I honestly do not remember the exact city or village where he lived. It was probably Guayaquíl, a coastal city that today has over two million inhabitants.

Before continuing with this gentleman's story, a few things about this part of the world. There is a very heavy undercurrent of Pacific Ocean water that strikes the continental coast of South

America at this point. The effect of this heavy rush of ocean water against the surface of the uppermost northwestern shelf results in the release of earth minerals, iron, magnesium, and other earth products that are essential for the growth of all kinds of fish, shell, and most others. There is probably no better place to fish for shrimp than off the coast of Ecuador.

Back to our conversation: The gentleman told me he came to Gorgas Hospital annually for his physicals. He added that he was staying at a military barracks at Fort Clayton but that his physicals usually took a couple of days to complete and he had trouble getting to Gorgas Hospital because there was no regular bus service to and from Fort Clayton.

I thought I should find a way to help him. Howard Air Force Base, where I lived, was in the opposite direction and probably equal distance from Gorgas Hospital as was Fort Clayton. He told me he still had several additional days to wait before he could return to his home because he also had to wait on the next Andes Run. I told him, *"Why don't you use my car?"*

His first reaction, based on the look on his face, was to show an expression of disbelief. I added "Hey! We are in this place together, to help each other out. I feel I can trust you. You certainly are not going to steal my car. What would you do with it? I'll wait for you to finish your visit before returning my car. I seldom drive it anywhere because I walk to work. You can drive me home to Howard, take my car, and use it until you finish everything. Then, call me to say you are returning my car, and I'll drive you back to Fort Clayton." I added that, "We walk everywhere we go."

Sure enough, three days later, he calls me to say he is finished and is returning my car. I told him where I worked and that I'd be waiting for him. I didn't have very far to take him because he had caught a hop (a "seat") on that day's *Andes Run*, and he would be dropped off on that flight's stop in Quito, Ecuador. As retired military members, we can ride for free on all military flights if there is room. There are never any questions asked. One simply has to have a military identification card. It is the most powerful ID card in the world. Mine has not been out of my wallet in sixty-five years. When

I was stationed in Germany in the early 1950s, my ID card was all I ever needed to cross any border in any country.

Time marches on. I did not hear from him until I am called on the phone one day while at work. It is the operations officer at Howard. It seems a package has arrived on the latest Andes Run from Ecuador and is addressed to me. It is a fairly large box that weighs about twenty pounds. I go by to pick it up. It is a box of frozen giant shrimp, properly packaged so it stays frozen for dozens of hours. A very sincere *thank you card* is also attached. It was from my retired civilian friend in Ecuador.

A very close military friend of mine managed the only military dining hall at Howard, and he kept the shrimp in one of his giant freezers for me. I shared many pounds of the frozen giant shrimp with him and his family.

Our family and I continued with our stay in Panama and living a somewhat routine life. We did take advantage of being in a beautiful country with a wonderful weather. Even though we were relatively close to the equator, I have lived in hotter climates. Texas, Mexico, and even South Korea come to mind. Maria completed the fourth, fifth, and sixth grades while we were in Panama. She was in the seventh grade when we returned to America in December of 1971. Robert completed the third, fourth, and fifth grades and was in the sixth grade when we returned. Patty completed first, second, and third and was in the fourth grade when we came back to Texas. Rey had just started kindergarten when we returned.

All four children were very active in sports. They had many friends in school. All were dependent children of military personnel who, like me, were stationed at Howard Air Force Base. Grace, too, had many friends, who were all wives of military personnel. The only one who was not was Mrs. Quintero, wife of the Panamanian lawyer. The Quinteros loved to visit us at the base, usually on weekends.

Spider monkeys seemed to be in abundance in Panama. Almost all were very friendly and made good, and safe, pets. Still, they had to be kept in cages as they could not be house-trained. Our pet monkey was Maria's to maintain and keep clean. She would have him on a leash and most of the kids had fun playing with him. Maria named him "Bucky," of course.

There was one incident with Bucky that cost me a couple of dollars. Arriving home from my day at the office one day, Maria wants to bet me $2 that she can make Bucky dive into a large pail of soapy water by simply saying, "Bucky, jump in." I said right away, "Daughter, I hate to take your money, but the bet is on." So she takes Bucky out of his cage, while still on his leash. She walks him up to the bucket of warm, soapy water, and says softly, "Okay, Bucky, jump in." That "turkey monkey" did just that: He jumped head first into the bucket of soapy water. There went my two bucks.

The kids played soccer a lot. Soccer was the sport that most kids in Panama played. The sport doesn't require bats, gloves, or bases, like baseball. Football requires a lengthy field to be able to play the sport. Soccer only needs a net and a soccer ball and players to form two sides or teams. Maria was very active during this period of time. Well one day I came home from work to find out she had fallen and broken a wrist. Chalk up a broken wrist for Maria during our Panama excursion.

I mentioned "home from my day at the office" a couple of paragraphs above. But I haven't mentioned what my job at this office was. I am back to being a logistician. However, I have been assigned to a staff position with the director of Materiel Office. The director is a Colonel Welch. Colonel Welch, at the time, was a veteran of over twenty-five years in the army and air force. He was a pilot and was particularly familiar with aircraft maintenance and the logistical support required to keep all aircraft always ready to fly. This last point, *always ready to fly,* cannot be overemphasized in importance. The world's best air force has to always be ready to fly all its aircraft. There can be no inability to fly because of either maintenance needs or the lack of certain parts or assemblies. Colonel Welch was responsible to the base commander to ensure that all aircraft were always ready to fly. His immediate staff of experts, including me, were responsible to Colonel Welch that this was always the case. In my three and a half years there in this position, we never experienced a crisis in any of these areas. Maintenance and logistics were not the only two areas for which we were responsible. Fuel and munitions were the other two areas we overlooked to ensure that we were always prepared.

Howard Air Force Base had several full colonels assigned, along with Colonel Welch. Since Panama was the home of the United States Southern Command that oversaw the activities of all branches of service in Central and South America, including those of the navy, marines, army, and air force, there were also several generals assigned. The highest-ranking general was a two-star general. There were minimally four brigadier generals (one star) assigned to Panama. In all branches of service, anywhere in the world where we are located, generals have an airplane assigned to them at the local air force base to transport them to an emergency meeting called for anywhere in the world. They do not depend on commercial travel.

Since I was a staff person at a high level on the base, I always received private information whenever an aircraft of ours was scheduled to fly to the continental United States and the reason for the flight. During the fall of 1970, I found out that a C-54 was flying to Kelly Air Force Base on a Friday and returning on Sunday, just two days later. Kelly Air Force Base is located in southwest San Antonio, Texas, my hometown. I also found out there were no passengers besides the one-star general who was being flown to Texas. I assumed the general had an important meeting in Texas and was being flown there.

I inquired from the base operations officer on the possibility of getting listed on the manifest. I informed the BOO that my only purpose was to visit my parents whom I had not seen in over two years. I was approved to travel with the general on his plane by the BOO and he put my name on the manifest.

The general, his *aide-de-camp* (a military officer acting as secretary and confidential assistant to a superior officer of general or flag rank) and I were the only ones on this C-54. It was about a six-hour flight. During the entire flight, this lieutenant, probably a graduate of one of the military academies of our country, no small accomplishment, by the way, sat near the general's covered area on the plane, waiting for the general to call on him. By covered area I refer to a small area in the fuselage of the plane that was curtained off from the rest of the plane. The general kept the curtain drawn during the entire trip. He did call on his aide to get him a drink or a snack. This happened several times and the aide jumped nervously each time.

I watched. Mostly I was shaking my head in disbelief. Here was a commissioned officer acting as a "go-fer" for a one-star general. When we landed, a member of the crew (by the way, a five-member crew, at that. The pilot, co-pilot, navigator, and two crew members to handle checking the plane to ensure it was ready to fly) came back to where I was seated to tell me to stay in my seat until the general left the airplane. I was seated next to a window and could see the runway outside as we pulled up to a stop. We were nowhere near the terminal. We were out some three to five hundred yards. I saw a blue staff car pull up near the airplane. When the general stepped down the walk plank, the plank was no more than ten to twelve steps from the staff car. The driver, also in uniform, stepped out to open the back door of the car so the general could step in and sit *himself.*

I was now allowed to step off the airplane. This was as far as the plane was going to go. A crew member told me they were leaving for Panama early on Sunday morning, to be ready to board by 8:00 a.m. I left. Before leaving, I wanted to ask where the general's aide was, but didn't. I was afraid to find out in the fear I would not like the answer. I chose to think he took a badly-needed break himself.

I called my brother-in-law Frank Burns, who came by to pick me up and take me to my sister Jovita's house, where she, my mom, and my dad lived. I spent the weekend, some twenty-six hours, mostly talking with Jovita, my mom and my dad, and enjoying my mom's cooking. I did buy some food products that Grace had asked me to look for and bring back with me.

I was back bright and early on Sunday to fly back to Panama in an *empty airplane.* I wanted to be a smart-ass and ask one crew member if we were forgetting someone (the general). What I asked was "Where's the general?" This crew member told me something he probably should not have. He said they brought this one-star general to his Texas home on a two-week vacation. They would fly back to *pick him up* in two weeks. I said, "Oh." I wanted to say many more things but didn't dare, so allow me to think aloud.

The worst welfare recipients in America are not poor whites, African Americans, and Latinos. I have a feeling Americans are completely uninformed about what goes on in this democratic society of ours. The defense department may outpace *everyone* in getting handouts from the American taxpayer.

One final occurrence that happened to my family is worth mentioning here. I mentioned previously that our children were all engaged in sports. Robert was the especially gifted athletic member of this family. I entered him in a *multisporting event* weekend competition involving ten different athletic events for all ten-year old boys in the entire Canal Zone. There must have been twenty-five boys entered in the event.

Before going further with this information, I should tell you that Robert was throwing baseballs with both arms at an early age. He could kick the ball with either leg, and he was an excellent baseball pitcher who could pitch the baseball into a twelve inch by twelve inch area from the pitcher's mound consistently. More than that, he was an excellent basketball player. Let's face it. Robert played some sport all the time. He even got a trophy in bowling for having the best series for all bowlers over the length of the bowling season.

As the events continued this one Saturday held in the Canal Zone and not on any of the military bases or camps. (This was a Canal Zone-wide event) I kept score for each and every event. By *score* I mean where the athletes placed, like first, second, third, and so on. By the end of the eighth event, I was sure Robert could not be beaten. He "won" the ninth and next to last event. I knew my son had won it all. The crowd gathered for the announcements. Robert had no idea where he stood as far as the standings were concerned. I say this today, forty-seven years later, but upon reflection, I only hope this was the case. Robert turned 57 on September 27, 2017.

The chief judge announced a *different winner*, placing Robert second. I wanted to holler out, "HEY! WAIT A MINUTE." But I only thought this. I didn't say anything because the announced winner was already enjoying his day as the winner, although I knew differently. Later I *knew* others beside me knew who the winner was. I checked my figures. Robert won *going away*. I waited for the right moment, one that would not hurt the announced winner. I looked over at Robert and could tell that first, second, or even third meant diddly squat to him. He was already playing with his friends.

I said (above) that *I* knew *others beside me knew who the winner was*. At the right moment, being as calm as I could be, I went up and asked to speak to the judges. I identified myself as Robert's dad. I showed them my score cards and asked that they re-tally the results. They did. To my surprise, few were surprised that Robert won and did not contest my own score. I added that I would tell my son the final results and that if the judges, Robert, and I were the only ones to know the real score, I was satisfied. They all thanked me and I left. I wanted to say a lot of other things, but as I had already done for more years than I want to remember, I let the white man get away, again, with some serious racist decisions. Robert was the only athlete of color among all the participants. He never thought this, but I did. My son Robert kicked a lot of asses this day. Some day, over a stiff martini, I would like to justify to my son, Robert, the action I actually took that day of athletic competition (in the Canal Zone in the 1960's) in which he was involved.

In the three and a half years we spent in the Canal Zone, we enjoyed going on several excursions in and around Panama. We loved the music of the country. It has become what we now call *salsa music* and with several of our military friends, we would usually spend at least one Saturday evening each month at one of the Panama City night clubs, almost all located very near the ocean where the atmosphere was always festive, the music great, the white rum martinis excellent, and the food equally wonderful.

Grace and I took our kids to a seaside home some twenty kilometers from the city to spend a weekend. It was only several hundred yards from a small fishing village. The house was no more than fifty to sixty yards from the ocean, but the distance was safe. I remember getting up at dawn on Saturday morning when I heard the fishermen talking nearby. I went out to see them as they formed long lines of fifteen to eighteen men with fishing nets that were probably seventy-five to a hundred yards long. They held the nets over their heads and above the ocean water as they waded out into the ocean a good distance, probably until they could just barely touch land. They would then dip the nets down into the ocean water and begin the trek back to the shore. I cannot say that the nets were full of fish, but there was plenty of fish in those nets.

The fishermen were very friendly. I went out closer to where they were and started a conversation with them. I found them to be polite and inquisitive about who we were, where we were from, and how long we were staying. They offered us some fish, but I declined and told them it was their catch, and we would not feel right taking any fish from them. They understood and did not mind our refusal.

As a family, we enjoyed our three-day stay. Being next to the Pacific Ocean with ocean waters that were relatively calm and enjoying unimaginable sunrises *and* sunsets is something that one can only see in a part of the world where both oceans are visible. I'm talking about "both oceans are visible" by simply turning around and looking 180 degrees from the first look.

We had other adventures in Panama and in the Atlantic Ocean that could have been disastrous, but fortunately were not. There is a small island, *Taboga*, located about a thirty-minute *small boat ride* from the harbor of Panama City. Many tourists know about Taboga and boats for the island left every hour on the hour from the mainland. Again, as a family, we toured the island because we heard so many positive things about it. It was close by. It was small, give or take a few hundred square yards, probably no bigger than three square miles. There were no roads on it, so there were never any vehicles on the island. A few people had homes on the island. They traveled on the same boat we did and, when the boat docked on the island, would walk to their homes. There was a small hotel on it, for those wanting to spend the night. We didn't. We walked the island and were ready to return after a couple of hours.

Now that I live in Maryland, I am reminded of Fort McHenry when I reflect on having been to Taboga. A small island, yes, but would you believe there was a small U.S. Navy unit of some three to four sailors who manned an alert radar unit that probably scanned the skies for any possible UFOs (not talking about from outer space here), but as a part of our early warning system for missiles being shot at our country or continent. I saw them from a small distance. They were right next to the ocean in units that were only yards from the ocean waters. I doubt if they used the same boat people used to get there and back from their unit in Panama, probably at Rodman Naval Base.

When Jovita visited us in 1969, we took her to the island. I remember how fascinated she was with a couple of fishermen who we saw catch a couple of lobsters and bring them onto the land. They sat on the island sand near us (we were seated outside a small shop having a glass of wine) and began to cut it up, live and uncooked, and began eating it. They looked up at us and asked if we wanted to taste the lobster meat. To my surprise, Jovita immediately said, "YES." Well, "Sí, por favor." One of the fishermen cut a piece off the lobster and brought it up to Jovita. She took a bite. Looked at me, and said, "Que delicioso."

On the way back to the mainland, we had an adventure I will never forget. Some of the largest ships in the world cross across the Panama Canal from one ocean to the other. The boat we were on was large enough to carry some thirty people on it. That's exactly how many were on the boat—thirty people. The size of the boat was no bigger than the largest school bus made, but as wide as they are long. Next to one of these huge ships, we were on a teeny weeny boat. About five minutes out and headed toward the mainland, a heavy and thick mist engulfed our small boat. I noticed it right away because I remember thinking, "What if the mist stays this thick and we are unable to steer this little boat away from a large ship?" Not a pleasant thought, to say the least. We stayed in the "thick of things" for an additional five minutes or so before the mist rose above us, and we could see where we were going. We were safe.

It is now summer of 1971. Promotions for the two super sergeant ranks of senior master sergeant and chief master sergeant are announced during the early days of June. Both ranks require the earned Air Force Specialty Code of *superintendency*. I had earned that proficiency and was awarded a new AFSC. When promotions were about to be announced, Colonel Welch called me into his office to announce that he had been called by the Southern Command Commanding General to inform him that I had been promoted to the rank of senior master sergeant. Comparing this rank with a civilian position in the business world, it would be equal to a person having the responsibilities of a superintendent. With quarters allowances, number of dependents, and some monetary allowances for other expenditures that one must incur, such as travel costs and cost of living unique to certain areas, my total pay was probably the equivalent of a person earning approximately $50,000 per year, gross. Remember, this is 1971. This amount of money today would be worth three times as much.

This was a true *feather in my cap*. Less than one percent of enlisted personnel attain this rank. Those who do earn the rank and title usually have been in the armed forces for well over twenty years, often more than twenty-five. I still have not been in the armed forces for twenty years. I am already aware that if I accept the rank and title, I must make a commitment to serve an additional four years in the air force. I thanked Colonel Welch for the information, and instead of feeling really proud of this achievement, I started feeling some pressure of having to make a decision about whether or not to accept the promotion. It is not mandatory that I accept the promotion. I added, "Sir, I am going to talk this over with my wife and will make a decision and advise you first thing tomorrow morning.

Before going home from work that day, I inquired into how much more money I would be getting paid, what other privileges I would be entitled to (as an example, for future assignments outside the continental limits of the United States I would be able to travel concurrently with my wife and my dependent children). There were a few other perks. One important one was that when the day came for me to retire, my retired pay for the rest of my life would be considerably more than if I did not accept the promotion. I shared all these things with Grace. She could tell that neither the money or the added perks excited me. She asked me, no, she told me, "You have already made your mind up, haven't you?" I said I cared what she thought. She added that I should do what I want to do. "It is your life."

My thoughts were that I had spent the previous seven years going to colleges and universities after work and on Saturdays so I could have a different life than the one I mostly tolerated as a career service person. Practically, no one I knew had ever heard of anyone turning down a promotion like this. It's more money, more privileges, more prestige, more retired pay (for life), and as a matter-of-fact, I had never heard of anyone turning down such a promotion. My brother-in-law, Charlie Villarreal, also a career serviceman and married to Grace's younger sister Zulema, thought I was a fool for turning it down. He told me so himself.

My mind was made up. Grace, the kids, and I came home to San Antonio and Lackland Air Force Base to process for my retirement. I left the air force before Christmas of 1971 although my official retirement date was not until February 2, of 1972. I was able to use the sixty days I had acquired and saved as vacation days and "sold" them back to the air force so I could leave the armed forces before the end of 1971. I did. I also came home with a bachelor of arts degree from Florida State University.

The Period 1972-1974

It is now December 1971. I am 38 years old and, after twenty years of service in the armed forces, am retiring and about to start receiving $499 per month for life. I gave the air force twenty years of my life, including service in Germany, France, Korea, Okinawa, and Panama. Of the twenty years, 40 percent of that time was spent serving in these countries. Officially it was seven years and seven months.

Being able to retire and receive medical coverage for life at such an early age may have been *the* reason for continuing as a professional airman. Along the way, I also had completed high school, which I had not because I dropped out. But more than that, I attended college on a part-time basis from the fall of 1964 until May of 1971 to complete my bachelor of arts degree from Florida State University. I felt I had gotten ready for this moment, and I wasn't going to have all this hard work go to waste. On my last day in uniform, when I signed out at Lackland Air Force Base in San Antonio, Texas, I went home, changed out of my uniform for the last time *(I thought),* and by afternoon I was waiting in line to talk to an employment counselor at the Texas Employment Commission, wearing white shirt and tie. I wanted to know what my chances were of getting a job right away with my credentials. I got a few leads. I followed up with letters of inquiry and with job applications.

I was working full time within one week, but not in the kind of job I was expecting to acquire. Holy Cross High School, a Catholic private school for-boys-only in San Antonio, was desperately seeking an Air Force ROTC (Reserve Officers Training Corps) instructor right away. The person serving in that capacity developed a serious ailment and was forced to leave the position. I will return to what my duties were at this high school after I mention a few hurdles I still had to complete before I left the air force.

There is a standard process the armed services utilize for all retirees. One must have a physical examination before leaving the armed forces. I was in good health, and I passed my exam easily, as I expected to. I was then scheduled for a conference with certain governmental officials who, evidently, had a copy of my records in front of them and the purpose of this conference was to ask me if I was going to declare some kind of disability due to my experiences while in uniform. These officials would consider the disability and would make the decision as to whether or not I qualified to have a certain percentage of my total retired pay declared as non-taxable income for the rest of my life.

I did not know about this phase of what one goes through upon retirement from the armed services of our country. Declaring a disability due to my time in uniform never entered my mind. Sure, I developed an esophageal hernia that required thoracic surgery and ten days in the hospital during the pressure years of training air national guardsmen during the Vietnam conflict. This happened in 1965. But debilitating me for life? I don't think so. I also saw an increase in my high blood pressure and to this day still take medication for this condition. Debilitating? My high blood pressure is very controlled with medication, as well as by meditating regularly. Debilitating? Again, I don't think so. It also explained why several people who were also retiring and had appointments right before and right after mine came in with lawyers. These retirees were going to declare they developed some type of physical or mental disability and were prepared to have their lawyer support their statement and request. I have no idea how successful these retiring officers were. Officers? Yes, there were no enlisted men who arrived with lawyers.

These were my thoughts: Seeing all this occurring around me forced me to think about it. I quickly concluded, being the good

Catholic I thought I was, then, that to tell such a terrible lie that I considered myself to have a disability due to some injury or condition while I was in uniform to be such a terrible sin that God would certainly strike me with a more severe disability, just for lying. When I was asked if I was declaring a disability and if so, who is your lawyer. I said, "No, and no one."

Stop to think about this scenario, please. Since retiring over forty years ago, I have reflected on this experience and have concluded that Americans would rather eat insects than pay taxes. Think of the hundreds of thousands of army, air force, navy, and marine officers who have arrived at this stage of their military careers and won themselves such a tax break. I know this: Not lying and always saying everything truthfully allows me to sleep better and to look myself in the mirror and be satisfied with the person I've developed into. Sure, I've told many little white lies and many exaggerations. None were about serious things. Most of my lies were in an effort to make myself "look good" to friends and family.

The American Armed Forces have a way of thanking their military members with recognition for their service. Certificates of appreciation, medals, and citations sometimes are overdone. I accepted them with pride for a job done well, even if I never shared these plaudits with anyone in my family. I always thought my three oldest brothers who fought in WWII, my nephew Henry who was a marine machine gunner in the jungles of Vietnam, and my nephew Richard, who was also in Vietnam as a member of the army were the real heroes in my family. Nonetheless, here is the recognition I received in 1971:

THE UNITED STATES OF AMERICA

TO ALL WHO SHALL SEE THESE PRESENTS, GREETING:
THIS IS TO CERTIFY THAT
THE PRESIDENT OF THE UNITED STATES OF AMERICA
AUTHORIZED BY EXECUTIVE ORDER, 16 JANUARY 1969
HAS AWARDED

THE MERITORIOUS SERVICE MEDAL

TO

MASTER SERGEANT ROBERTO PEREZ

FOR

OUTSTANDING SERVICE
3 JUNE 1968 - 21 DECEMBER 1971

GIVEN UNDER MY HAND IN THE CITY OF WASHINGTON
THIS   18TH   DAY OF JANUARY   1972

KENNETH O. SANBORN, Major General, USAF
Commander, U. S. Air Forces Southern Command

SECRETARY OF THE AIR FORCE

AF FORM 2205, JUL 70

CITATION TO ACCOMPANY THE AWARD OF

THE MERITORIOUS SERVICE MEDAL

TO

ROBERTO PEREZ

Master Sergeant Roberto Perez distinguished himself in the performance of outstanding service to the United States while assigned to the staff of the Deputy Commander
for Materiel, 24th Special Operations Wing, Howard Air Force Base, Canal Zone, from
3 June 1968 to 21 December 1971. During this period Sergeant Perez's outstanding
knowledge, devotion to duty, and personal leadership were paramount in the successful
operation and support of the United States Air Force mission in the Canal Zone and
throughout Central and South America. The singularly distinctive accomplishments
of Sergeant Perez culminate a distinguished career in the service of his country,
and reflect great credit upon himself and the United States Air Force.

CERTIFICATE OF APPRECIATION

FOR SERVICE IN THE ARMED FORCES OF THE UNITED STATES

MASTER SERGEANT ROBERTO PEREZ, UNITED STATES AIR FORCE, 3 FEBRUARY 1968 TO 29 FEBRUARY 1972

I extend to you my personal thanks and the sincere appreciation of a grateful nation for your contribution of honorable service to our country. You have helped maintain the security of the nation during a critical time in its history with a devotion to duty and a spirit of sacrifice in keeping with the proud tradition of the military service.

I trust that in the coming years you will maintain an active interest in the Armed Forces and the purpose for which you served.

My best wishes to you for happiness and success in the future.

Richard Nixon

COMMANDER IN CHIEF

DD FORM 1725

CERTIFICATE OF RETIREMENT
FROM THE ARMED FORCES OF THE UNITED STATES OF AMERICA

TO ALL WHO SHALL SEE THESE PRESENTS, GREETING

THIS IS TO CERTIFY THAT

Master Sergeant Roberto Perez 467-40-0597

HAVING SERVED FAITHFULLY AND HONORABLY

WAS RETIRED FROM THE

UNITED STATES AIR FORCE

ON THE *First* DAY OF *March*

ONE THOUSAND NINE HUNDRED AND *Seventy-two*

CHARLES W. CARSON, JR.
Major General, USAF

John D. Ryan
CHIEF OF STAFF

172

Today, should you walk into my tiny office in my home in Maryland, you will see these medals that I earned not in this large form, but as ribbons that I wore proudly whenever I put on the Class A Uniform of the United States Air Force. I also earned the "expert" medal for my marksmanship with the M1 rifle, which I once taught recruits to completely disassemble and put together again.

The medals, in clockwise order, are these: At twelve o'clock, Military Merit; at two o'clock, Meritorious Service; at four o'clock National Defense; at eight o'clock, Good Conduct; at ten o'clock, Defense of the U.N. Charter for service in Korea.

Back to being hired as an Air Force ROTC instructor at Holy Cross High School. I did not pursue the position, as I was not looking for this kind of job. The job requirements were to be able to teach the customs and courtesies of the United States Air Force, as well as the formal drill and ceremonies to a very large group of male high school students. It is the month of January (1972) and part of the end-of-year festivities in May of each school year is a military parade that the students who are members of the ROTC conduct. Before my arrival, the ROTC cadets at this school knew nothing about drill and ceremonies.

It was a case of the high school, as well as me, getting a break with my availability since I had just retired from the armed forces. The school principal must have had a direct line to the Air Force Headquarters in Washington to ask for help. The position I would fill was only for air force retirees with the background and experience in customs and courtesies of the air force, as well as in drill and ceremonies. The air force looked at recent retirees who may fill the bill. Voila! There I was. The air force called me and asked if I was interested. I was jobless, and looking at, generally speaking, everything and anything possible. I asked if I had to make a multiyear commitment because being an ROTC instructor was not in my career goals. I told the air force I would get the job done and may want to leave at the end of the year. Both the air force and the principal said that was okay. They were in a jam and needed a solution now. I accepted the position.

My compensation would be the same as a beginning teacher. This is 1972, forty-five years ago. Fourteen thousand dollars was the going rate for Catholic schools, probably about 80 percent of what public schools paid their beginning teachers. It was only going to be for six months. Besides, I would start getting my retirement pay right away, and that was an additional six thousand dollars a year. My family and I could make it okay. The amount I was receiving as net pay was probably equivalent to four times that amount in today's wages.

Not every student had to commit to being in the ROTC. However, those who did not, had to pay tuition to attend Holy Cross High School. This was not an easy requirement to have to satisfy. The great majority of students at Holy Cross were Mexican American students from working-class families. There were other descriptors of these families that made them different from other inner-city working-class families. Parents were involved in school. This was a religious school. This was a Catholic school. While slightly more than half of the faculty consisted of *Brothers* of the Order of the Holy Cross, there were a significant number of teachers, all male, who were not Brothers. As I observed them and interacted with them, I found out that several, while having college degrees, did not possess teaching certificates. I have already mentioned that beginning salaries here were approximately 80 percent of the going rate in public schools, I found out that the same rate continued and even became lower with increasing seniority. In general, teachers here, other than the Brothers, were here because of a commitment to the Catholic High School, or because they could not find employment in a public school. I knew of at least one teacher who confessed this fact to me over a cup of coffee. He was attending university classes that led to certification. He was expecting to move on after this year. At the time, there were minimally thirty-six hours of teacher-preparation classes that had to be completed, including Texas History and Texas Government. In essence, it is an additional year of college.

As an ROTC instructor, I did not face this requirement. I just had to be able to teach them everything about the air force subjects, as well as how to conduct drill and ceremonies so they could conduct a year-ending parade.

On a daily basis, part of their high school schedule was having two classes with me. There were three groups, so I conducted six classes daily. My classes were unique. I say this because most of my classes were performance-based. They had to perform the skills I was teaching them. While I taught them the complete procedures for a military parade, I also taught them how to conduct an-end-of-day retreat. The interest in military procedures was very high. They were not exactly leaning forward in their seats to hear my instructions with high interest, but neither were they bored and uncooperative. They were all motivated to learn as much as they could from me. I was pleased and felt I was doing a good job. The cadets wore their uniforms every day, as I did mine.

The reader should know a few things about the mood of the country during the years the Vietnam War was going on. America was in the middle of a *cold war* with the Soviet Union. The two major ideologies on the planet that emerged after WWII ended were our form of democracy and communism as practiced by the Soviet Union and China, even though there was a difference between the two countries of this latter belief. America spent billions of dollars expanding and modernizing our defense department. Our annual budget for defense rose to near 50 percent of our annual spending until we finally rose above it. This battle between the two major ideologies grew year by year for over forty years, since World War II ended in 1945.

Here are a few facts about our country in world affairs dating back to the third decade of the twentieth century. During the 1930s, and until Hitler and Germany soundly defeated the French in 1940, France had possession of what we now call Vietnam, along with Cambodia and Laos. The area became known as Indo-China. Control of Indo-China fluctuated between the Vichy* government of France, the Japanese, and local groups of Vietnamese, Laotian, and Cambodian groups. During the time the Japanese were in control, President Franklin Delano Roosevelt stopped the shipment of steel and oil to Japan and this action by FDR was one of the principal reasons the Japanese first bombed Pearl Harbor in 1941 and subsequently British-controlled Hong Kong in 1942. When the war ended in 1945, the French regained possession of this area. However, Vietnam separated itself into north and south during the period 1941 to 1945 and fought each other to control all of Vietnam.

After many years of fighting, the French conceded the territory and left in 1954 and the news quickly spread across the world because of the very large area being affected and the fact that China and the Soviet Union would now begin their attempts to occupy and control the area. Vietnam was already divided between north and south, and the two opposed each other ideologically. The French, before their departure, supported the south.

Dwight Eisenhower (IKE) was president during these years and our support of South Vietnam consisted mostly of arms and training. This continued until the mid-1960s, several years after the assassination of John Kennedy. Lyndon Johnson is now well into his second year since assuming the presidency.

President Johnson and Defense Secretary Robert McNamara began an escalation of the war. Americans by the thousands are now being killed in action. The war had become very unpopular, given the number of American soldiers being killed in a war conducted more than ten thousand miles away.

*Vichy was the name of a small city in France. When France fell to the Germans in 1940, the Germans turned the French government over to *Marshal Filipe Pétain*, who named it *État Francais*. Pétain was a French WWI hero. The French played a part in Germany deporting thousands of Jews from France. Thousands more Jews were saved when Denmark intervened by secretly taking them in until they could escape to America and other safe havens.

Just before my brief venture into information on the Vietnam War, I had written that the reader should know about the mood in America about this war. Unpopular is putting it mildly. Young men are being drafted into the armed forces and possible deployment to the war zone. Young American males are looking for deferments to stay out of uniform and out of harm's way. Being in college was considered a deferment. If one was already a graduate, then joining the National Guard or the army reserve was a possible way to stay out of combat.

I have already mentioned that fighting in what was then called Indo-China started in 1955, one year after the French left the area. I reenlisted in the air force in 1956 and began my career as a military training instructor in 1957. When I returned from South Korea in 1964, I trained Air Force National Guardsmen for four years, between 1964 and 1968, before leaving for Panama. The great majority of these guardsmen were college graduates who had received deferments and now were joining a branch of service *that was usually only involved militarily during emergencies within the continental limits of the United States.* This changed in later years as we entered the twenty-first century and got involved in wars in Afghanistan and Iraq and both national guardsmen and reserve personnel were not only among the first sent over to these war zones, but were apt to go there three or four times while serving in these branches of service.

As an ROTC instructor, I went to work in uniform every day. My high school students were all required to wear their uniforms every day. The school, Catholic and run by the Brothers of the Holy Cross, had a very liberal philosophical attitude and I'm sure the classroom discussions in most, if not all, the classrooms was also very *antiwar* and supported America withdrawing from the Far East, much like the French had done in 1954. The problem was, Americans also hated the communist philosophy with as much passion as they hated being involved in another war. I lost count of the number of times my cadets and I heard "GET OUT OF VIETNAM" shouts from inside classrooms as we oftentimes marched by when we practiced our drill and ceremonies activities. These outbursts were not very frequent, but they occurred from time to time. It was representative of the mood of the country as well. I should add at this point in my story that I did not like being yelled derogatory names and labels when I mostly agreed that America was involved in a war halfway across the globe that had little to do with our security.

It is now spring of 1972. The end of the school year is approaching, and there is simply no way I was going to tolerate another year teaching military subjects and drill and ceremonies to cadets in a very liberal high school where the students obviously didn't want us there and the program was there only because it paid the school tuition for students who were willing to join the ROTC. While I understood completely the attitude of the majority of students at this school and, in fact, did not blame them at all for having developed this attitude, I want to *like the environment* in which I work.

As is happening today in America (2017), and mostly because we had two very disliked candidates vying for the presidency of the United States, a similar mood prevailed during the worst years of the Vietnam War. Over fifty-eight thousand American soldiers lost their lives. As is also happening today, much of the information circulating in our country (then) about the war did not always have a solid base of truth. There were myths galore floating around. Here are but a few:

Myth: The average age of Americans killed in Vietnam was 19.

Truth: The average age of Americans killed in Vietnam was 23. Of the total killed, 11,465 were under the age of twenty, or just under 20 percent.

Myth: Americans in uniform hated the war and would do anything short of deserting to get out of going to Vietnam.

Truth: Ninety-one percent of veterans of this war were glad they served. Seventy-four percent would serve again.

Myth: Americans in uniform during this war were heavy into drugs.

Truth: Research tells us that there was no difference in drug usage between Vietnam veterans and nonveterans.

Myth: Vietnam veterans were more likely to land in prison than nonveterans.

Truth: Vietnam veterans were less likely to land in prison. In fact, only half of one percent of Vietnam veterans landed in prison. Ninety-seven percent of returning veterans received honorable discharges.

Myth: Vietnam veterans had serious problems adjusting to civilian life upon returning.

Truth: Eighty-five percent of returning Vietnam veterans made successful transition to civilian life. These veterans exceeded nonveterans in income by 18 percent. These veterans also had lower unemployment rates than nonveterans. Eighty-seven percent of Americans hold Vietnam veterans in high esteem. Two-thirds of men who served were volunteers. For WWII, two-thirds of men who served were drafted.

I began looking into graduate schools. I had already taken the GRE, and my score was high enough to get me into most graduate programs. Besides, I did not have a science/technology/electronics/math background, so I was not trying to get into one of those programs. With a half-year of high school teaching behind me, I began to look into teaching as a career. It is really what I had done for almost half of my twenty years in the air force. Now I had a taste of high school teaching. I can do this and learn to like it.

I looked up programs that were both affordable and that were with graduate schools near my home. I was not trying *to go away to college.* I am 38 years old, and I have four children. I found a two-year program that paid my tuition. The catch was that I also had a two-year internship that included working in an inner-city environment. I could tolerate this since all I have ever known is attending school while living in the inner city. This program was meant for me.

It was called the Teacher Corps. It had been in existence for six years and was in every major city in the country. The concept was originated by two senators, Gaylord Nelson and Edward Kennedy. For this year, its seventh, one of its selected sites was to be with the Edgewood Independent School District in San Antonio, Texas, *where I lived!* The university sponsoring the program was the University of Texas at Austin. Upon satisfactory completion of the program, graduates would earn a master's degree in elementary education with an optional kindergarten certificate if one chooses to take the additional courses this program requires. I applied.

There were hundreds of applicants and only thirty-six positions. I worried that my age, 38, would hinder my chances. When I interviewed, almost all applicants looked to be under thirty years of age. I gave it my best shot. I remember being calm, confident, and committed to being the best teacher I could learn to be in an environment where students had not, typically, been doing well in school. There were some five members on the selection panel, and I made it a point to always look directly at whoever the person was who was asking me each question so that person would know I was responding to him or her. After I began to answer each question, I also made it a point to look at every other member of the panel so they would also think I was talking to them as well.

Evidently it was good enough for me to be selected. In early June of 1972, I traveled to UT–Austin for my first class. When I reported to the Education Building at UT, I got the biggest surprise I had had in recent times.

My nephew David, who is all of sixteen years younger than me, was sitting in the same classroom. My first thought was that perhaps not everyone was a member of the Teacher Corps. After we hugged and talked for a few seconds, I asked him. *Yes!* David was also selected, at the age of 22 and having just graduated from this same campus with his bachelor's degree the previous month. He got his BA degree in exactly four years in what is a relatively tough university to be able to do it all in just four years. David did it.

We were considered to be full-time students. This would benefit me for my GI Bill benefits because, as a full-time college student, I would get full benefits because I also had four school-age children. My financial benefits hovered around $500 dollars a month. It was actually a lifesaver because, as a full-time student, I had no time for a part-time job to make ends meet. With my $500 dollar a month retirement benefit, my family and I had enough money to make ends meet. I was only getting a net total of $1,000 dollars a month, but this is 1972. Today, the equivalent of this much money is probably in the neighborhood of being worth three to four times as much. We would be okay for two years.

Part of our schedule as full-time students was to teach alongside a certified teacher four days out of the week. Mondays were reserved to attend classes at the University of Texas at Austin. We also had classes in the evening two days a week in San Antonio. Thus we accumulated between fifteen and eighteen hours per semester.

The certified teachers we worked with were called *Cooperating Teachers*. The school I was assigned to was Joseph Guerra Elementary School, a small kindergarten through sixth grade school located on the far west side of the school district. There were a total of some three hundred students dispersed into fourteen classrooms, two each for kindergarten and grades first through sixth. The pupil-teacher ratio hovered around twenty-one students per class, a very manageable number of students. My cooperating teacher was an experienced male teacher who had an excellent reputation as a teacher. He taught fourth grade. Students and teachers at Guerra E. S. had only the highest regard for him. I considered myself lucky to get him for my CT. The first day of school for the school year 1972–73 arrived and the morning went without incident. Students spent the first part of the day mostly covering all textbooks with book covers and listening to my cooperating teacher go over classroom rules, work assignments, student expectations, and then individual classroom responsibilities were then assigned. Before we knew it, it was time for lunch. The students lined up by gender, and we escorted the class down the hallway toward the dining room. Once the students got into the serving line, teachers could leave and teacher assistants on duty took over their supervision.

As we walked toward the dining room, in very straight lines and being very quiet, we went by a new teacher's classroom. One could see inside the classroom because the walls of all the classrooms were made of see-through glass. One could walk down the hallway and see exactly what every class is doing during any part of the school day. My thoughts today about this fact are that it was a way for the principal to look into each classroom to ensure teachers were complying with his or her rules.

The new teacher's name is Ms. Galindo, a recent graduate of Texas A&M University. She has a teacher's aide who is presently escorting their students to the dining room. As the last student in Ms. Galindo's classroom left the room, I see Ms. Galindo lower her head on top of her arms on her desk. A few seconds expired and she continued with her head resting on her arms on her desk.

My first thoughts were that she was sick. No one else appears to be noticing her as my class is the only one walking by in the hallway (toward the lunchroom) and waiting in line right in front of her classroom. I quickly concluded that this new teacher became ill and I should walk into her classroom to make sure she was okay. I did. My class was already walking into the lunch room in a very straight line and not needing any supervision. I entered her classroom, and she immediately raised her head and looked up at who had entered her classroom. "Are you okay? Is there anything I can do to help you?" I said this after noticing that she was crying as well. My assumption was that she may be ill and I should take over her class while she went to the nurse's room to have the nurse's aide help her.

"It was horrible! They didn't mind me. I had to repeat my instructions over and over again. They laughed. They talked to each other. They just refused to listen to me. I tried raising my voice. It seemed to make matters worse. I am so disappointed in my performance. I don't know what to do now."

I told her I was with the Teacher Corps and was interning next door to her and that I would tell my cooperating teacher that I felt I should assist her to get her through her first day. I told her he would understand and that I would be able to control her students. Besides, my cooperating teacher was informing his class of his expectations of their behavior, adherence to rules, consequences of not complying and other administrative details that he had already explained to me. He and I both knew that I didn't have to listen to his first day briefing of his students and that this new teacher needed some help. I did not return to my cooperating teacher's classroom on that first day, nor any day for the rest of my first year in the Teacher Corps. Here is what happened.

First, an explanation of lunchroom rules for this school. Classroom teachers do not have to supervise their students while they enter and go through the serving line, nor while they are eating their lunch. There are other school personnel doing this. They are teacher assistants who have this additional duty and who comply with a *duty roster* that is published a week ahead of time. After lunch, and with the weather permitting, these same teacher assistants then take individual classes out of the lunch room after all in that class have finished their lunch and walk them to the playground for a twenty-to-thirty-minute recess period. It is the only recess period all classes have. It is always after lunch. In essence, the lunch period is about an hour long, including lunch in the lunchroom and twenty to thirty minutes for recess. Most teachers utilize this time to complete their preparations for the afternoon, which usually goes on for an additional two and a half to three hours before the school day ends.

When Ms. Galindo's class was returned to her classroom, I made sure I was waiting by the door as they walked in. The class was a combination third and fourth grade class, with an equal number at each grade level and a total class of nineteen students. Notice I wrote *"waiting by the door as they walked in."* I knew these eight- and nine-year-old students would respect a 6'2" man with his arms folded standing by the door and would walk straight to their desks without saying a word. They did exactly that. Ms. Galindo stood in front of her classroom and watched them all come in quietly and walk straight to their chairs behind their desk. I stood next to Ms. Galindo. I still had my arms folded and looked at every student as they continued to be so quiet that one could hear a pin drop, if one was to drop. She introduced me as "Mr. Pérez," her assistant.

Before describing what happened next, allow me to explain what a combination classroom of two separate grade levels is like. It is a classroom teacher's *nightmare assignment.* Obviously, these class-room teachers have to plan to teach two different grade levels. What was worse in Ms. Galindo's situation was the fact that Joseph Guerra Elementary School was a very low-achieving school where most students were functioning below grade level. In fact, probably over half of the students at this school were below grade level. While normally the age of third and fourth grade students is 8 and 9 years old, respectively, Ms. Galindo had minimally four to five students who were already ten years old, and one of them was still in third grade, meaning he had already been retained *more* than once (if he started school at the appropriate age).

While I did not internalize what Mr. Vidrine, the school principal, had done (in this, my first year of teaching in an elementary school with the Edgewood Independent School District), I very soon was to realize that new teachers always get the worse assignments. It is a bit like the very old army rule of *rank having its privileges.* The problem in doing this in a public school, and even in a private school, is that the inexperienced teachers *should never* get the most difficult assignments. With the welfare of all students in mind, the very best teachers should get the most difficult assignments, as teaching a combination of grade levels is as difficult an assignment as there is. In later years, when I was to become a school principal myself, I would never make such a mistake.

In retrospect, and with the knowledge that classroom teachers all over the country are not well-paid, perhaps a stipend or bonus, should be given to those experienced teachers who voluntarily tell principals that they will take the tough assignments with the added feature of being paid a bonus or a stipend for doing so. Because school districts have no way of paying stipends, perhaps school superintendents of school systems with both upper-middle-class communities *and* low-income areas could help in such situations by pairing schools such that for every low-income school community, it would have an upper middle class school as a partner. Parent-Teacher Associations at the *latter schools* would gladly assist the low-income PTAs who are unable to raise money to pay stipends.

Back to Ms. Galindo and her class. I quickly realized that Ms. Galindo never raised her voice above decibels that were only a few notches above a whisper. If there was noise, of any kind, her instructions were just barely audible. With me standing at the head of the classroom, monitoring every student's move without saying one word, Ms. Galindo was enjoying the quietest class in the building. She got everything done she needed to do, and then some. I stayed with her all afternoon.

When the school day ended and the students were sent home, I returned to my cooperating teacher's classroom and had a serious talk with him about my feelings about Ms. Galindo and her combination third/fourth grade class of low-achieving students. I said I would love to learn under him, but in all honesty, I considered myself already an experienced teacher and the thought of he and I teaching together in the same classroom while Ms. Galindo struggled right next door to us just did not seem right to me. He asked if I would rather do my internship with Ms. Galindo, and I did not hesitate to immediately answer affirmatively. It was settled. I saw that Ms. Galindo was still in her classroom planning for the next day, so I entered and told her I would be back to assist her the next day. She smiled and said, "Thank you."

Almost immediately, Ms. Galindo and I formed ability groups within each grade level, even though the students themselves did not know who were the third grade or the fourth grade students. Two of the fourth grade students only had first grade ability and were not able to read yet. We started the year off by ensuring that all mastered third grade skills, with exception of those unable to read. We formed a group with them and worked with them mostly on a one-to-one basis. We conducted all the language arts activities all morning long, by group. This included cursive writing (letter symbols), writing words and subject-predicate sentences, reading, spelling, and reading comprehension.

I soon began to realize a personal strength in Ms. Galindo's teaching approach. Her students soon began to demand that others be quiet when Ms. Galindo spoke, taught lessons, or gave instructions. They wanted to hear her.

This approach brought a type of serenity to the classroom atmosphere, and I could tell right away that Ms. Galindo was not only more relaxed as she taught, she also presented a calm demeanor and gave more attention to all her students. Still, the slow learners needed a lot of attention and progress with them was slow.

Ms. Galindo was afforded the opportunity to also attend graduate classes with me in our program, as the University of Texas, by virtue of sponsoring this program, accepted all cooperating teachers as graduate students and could enroll in our program in pursuit of a graduate degree in elementary education. Ms. Galindo declined. She was, after all, a graduate of Texas A&M University. She was an Aggie, head to toes.

A bit more about this Teacher Corps Project. It was funded nationally as a graduate program in urban areas across the nation. There were some thirty-eight such projects in about twelve different states. I believe Texas had four. In addition to San Antonio, there were Teacher Corps projects in El Paso, Houston, and Ft. Worth. Nationally, the first year of its existence was 1965. They were funded annually. The number of projects across the country grew with each year as all projects were funded for two-year periods. Ours was funded the seventh year of its existence. Two years later, in 1974, an additional San Antonio Teacher Corps Project was funded for two years. Ours ended in May of 1974. As far as I can remember, all thirty-six Teacher Corps interns graduated with their master's degrees. I added a "Kindergarten Endorsement" to my degree because I had the opportunity to add a couple of early childhood courses and also had the opportunity to do an internship for a year in a kindergarten classroom.

Back to 1972 and the end of my first year as a Teacher Corps intern: For all intents and purposes, it was an extremely busy year of attending courses all day on Mondays of every week. We all lived, and taught at different Edgewood schools, Tuesdays through Fridays of every week. On Mondays, we traveled to Austin to attend classes at the University of Texas, Austin campus. We boarded a chartered bus at 6:00 a.m. each Monday for the ninety-minute ride to Austin. We usually had four graduate classes that consumed the entire day. We rode the bus back to S. A. and usually arrived at 6:00 p.m. In addition, UT professors traveled to San Antonio for two additional classes that were taught evenings, after we taught all day at our individual schools. These classes were usually held on Tuesdays and Thursdays. To say that we had a "full plate" to contend with in this program is to put it mildly. We were very busy.

For my second year in the program, I had to leave Guerra Elementary School so I could work with a veteran kindergarten teacher at a different school. Guerra E. S. did not have an experienced teacher who could qualify to be my cooperating teacher. I was subsequently assigned to Edgewood Elementary School, a school less than one mile from my home. The school year was 1973–1974.

Right away, I fell in love working with kindergarteners. All arrived every morning ready to learn. All were excited to be in school. Ms. Allison, the kindergarten teacher, was superb. She came across as warm, courteous, knowledgeable, and every child loved her. She was calm. Her activities were all "hands on" as the children manipulated item after item and were allowed to make mistakes. Ms. Allison and I taught small groups all day long, and we were careful to notice everything they did we could work on having students repeat some activities. We allowed them to talk all day long, provided their voices were soft and didn't bother anyone else who may be working nearby.

Our classroom was also bilingual. We taught Spanish to all our students. Edgewood E. S. is located in the heart of a Mexican American community, so every student at this school was Mexican American. Every student's first language was Spanish. The first objective in an English/Spanish bilingual classroom has always been to teach Language Arts skills in each student's language of understanding so they can master letter pronunciations. In Spanish, every vowel and consonant among the twenty-eight letters of the Spanish alphabet has the same sound. Spanish is the easiest language to learn because it is a phonetic language. There are two more letters in the Spanish language, but each of these twenty-eight letters has the exact same sound every time. In English, there are only twenty-six letters, but forty-four different pronunciations. Thus, mastery of the English language is, at best, hard to learn and, at worse, very difficult to master. Still, a second, and the major objective is to teach Spanish language speakers English.

As an aside, the assignment of a woman unable to speak Spanish as principal at this school is very difficult to understand. No, not because she is not a Latina, but because Mrs. Anderson did not know one word of Spanish and could not communicate with most parents because most parents at this school knew only Spanish. Mrs. Anderson was also very strict and came across as somewhat cold and suspicious of people who did not speak English as their first language. Our school did not have a parking lot for cars, but there was space for cars to park near the one building that constituted the entire school. There was enough space for some fifteen to eighteen cars very near the building. Mrs. Anderson always demanded to have enough space near the building to park her car. The grounds were all gravel and very difficult to post a sign that would have "Reserved for Principal" dug into the ground. So she had a custodian paint a red "P" near the building that was to tell people who drove onto the school grounds that this particular area nearest the building was reserved for her. All of us who taught here knew this and knew better than to take her parking spot.

The first PTA meeting of the year came and there were several dozen parents who attended, "Several dozen" may be an exaggeration. Perhaps fifteen to eighteen parents attended. Mrs. Anderson arrived just as the meeting was to start. Most parents were already seated in the large all-purpose room that could seat 250–275 people. The seats were permanently bolted to the floor. It was more like a theater than anything else. All teachers were required to attend, as were the four to five Teacher Corps interns. We easily outnumbered parents at least two to one.

When Mrs. Anderson entered the theater, she stopped at the door, put her hands on her hips, and bellowed "WHO EVER PARKED THEIR CAR IN MY SLOT NEEDS TO GET UP RIGHT NOW AND MOVE IT." I wanted to bury my head inside my hands. I was embarrassed for these parents. At the same time I wondered why these teachers put up with this behavior. I just sat there and reflected on the learning environment that was present at this school. It was no learning environment at all. What learning occurred here happened because of a few outstanding teachers, like Ms. Allison.

Mrs. Anderson knew I was transferred from Guerra Elementary School to her school to complete my internship. It was because I opted for the kindergarten certificate and would have to do an internship in a kindergarten classroom. There was no kindergarten classroom at Guerra. Edgewood E. S. was the only school with an experienced kindergarten teacher under whom I could have an internship. I must have spent three and half weeks with Ms. Allison and really loved the kindergarten experience. The children were eager to learn and the activities Ms. Allison and I conducted (conceptualized, designed, and planned by Ms. Allison) were very effective in eliciting complete involvement on the part of the children. Ms. Allison treated me as her co-partner and teacher, and I had my own groups of students for whom I was responsible. I thought this assignment was ideal, and I was learning a lot about early childhood education. Alas, as with Joseph Guerra Elementary School, this was a short-lived assignment.

Just before the end of the fourth week, Mrs. Anderson asked to see me in her office at the end of the day. She "pulled no punches," as she led off with the statement, "I need you to complete your internship at this school with one of my sixth grade classrooms. I will continue showing you with Ms. Allison in order for you to satisfactorily complete the internship in kindergarten." She added that the sixth grade teacher who started the year with this sixth grade group resigned from one day to the next, saying she simply could not control such a rowdy group and her students were driving her crazy. What followed after her were a series of teachers Ms. Anderson hired as long-term substitutes who also told her after a day or two, "No thank you."

She finally hired a teacher who had recently graduated with her undergraduate degree and had not yet found a teaching position. I doubt if Mrs. Anderson confided in her what exactly she was getting into. I would soon find that this newest teacher had the right attitude but not the skills to bring about any change in the rowdy group of sixth grade students. Before continuing to describe the efforts of this new, and very young, teacher, let's describe what a typical self-contained classroom in an urban area like San Antonio looks like.

Typically, across the United States, sixth grade students are eleven to twelve years old, having entered first grade at the age of six. This was a very large group of sixth graders, thirty-five to be exact. Of the thirty-five, it is possible that seven to eight were of the proper age, eleven to twelve. The remaining students had been retained in one or more grade levels for either unsatisfactory grades or for having missed too many days of school. By far, the majority of students were thirteen to fourteen years of age. The year is 1973, and the sixth grade was still the final year of elementary school. We had not yet come up with either sixth grade centers or middle schools that contained sixth through eighth grade. I remember interacting with elementary teachers of grades one to five at more than one school who admitted that they were "afraid of sixth grade students."

I did not hesitate to tell Mrs. Anderson that "of course I would join the new teacher and do what I could to straighten this group out." The new teacher's name was Mrs. Elizondo.

As with Ms. Allison, Mrs. Elizondo and I split the teaching responsibilities. However, we also circulated throughout the classroom while the other taught. This was immediately a beginning strategy that I suggested we follow. My areas were mathematics, science, and social studies. All of my subjects were taught in the afternoon. Mrs. Elizondo taught language arts, which included reading, writing, spelling, and penmanship. Yes. We had a daily fifteen-minute penmanship lesson, with the use of an overhead projector where we modeled writing loops, curls, capitalizations, small case, and upper case lettering.

If we began to have much better control with this very mature group of students, it was because we treated them with respect and dignity. Ms. Elizondo was not a hard-nosed teacher, and while she could raise her voice when she had to, she seldom did. She also did not show signs of anger or disappointment in student performance. There was always some aspect of their performance that could be applauded, even if it was only effort. However, wrong answers or unsatisfactory work was always called out and all students were informed when their performance was not acceptable. We always treated our students as we would have liked to be treated.

We had a successful year with this group. They did a complete turnaround and the trouble they had caused earlier never surfaced again. The year ended and I do believe every intern who started the program two years earlier, graduated with their master's in education and a Texas Teaching Certificate. There were thirty-six of us, along with six team leaders who also graduated with master's degrees. I immediately applied for a teaching position as a sixth grade teacher with the San Antonio Independent School District. I was hired immediately. Male elementary school teachers were in demand then, as they still are today. My nephew David, like me, was also hired, but by the Edgewood School District, where he had gone to school for twelve years. As fate would have it, neither one of us ended up taken the positions we were offered. Neither one of us would spend the school year 1974–75 as classroom teachers. Our story follows below. First, a copy of the degree I earned from the University of Texas at Austin.

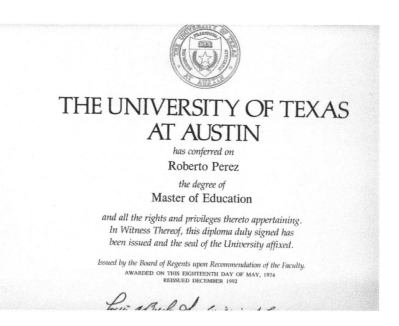

THE UNIVERSITY OF TEXAS AT AUSTIN

has conferred on

Roberto Perez

the degree of

Master of Education

*and all the rights and privileges thereto appertaining.
In Witness Thereof, this diploma duly signed has
been issued and the seal of the University affixed.*

Issued by the Board of Regents upon Recommendation of the Faculty.
AWARDED ON THIS EIGHTEENTH DAY OF MAY, 1974
REISSUED DECEMBER 1992

Pursuing a PhD

T he director of personnel with the San Antonio Independent
School District could not have been more accommodating
to me. By the end of our interview, he told me he was hiring
me. I do not remember saying "I accept" the position. Actually, while
he did hire me, he did not assign me to any particular school. He did,
however, show me where the school may be located. He pulled out
a map of San Antonio and located all the elementary schools on the
map while pointing to my being able to drive to one of the schools
he was considering assigning me to where I would have the sun at my
back as I drove to the school in the morning and also as I drove home
from school in the afternoon or evening.

Let's reflect on the actions of this personnel director. He was
accommodating *me*. A "first-year" teacher would probably find
this very satisfactory and inviting, such that this first-year teacher
would probably want to accept the position without too much
thought. Being, in essence, truly a first-year teacher, even though
I don't remember feeling particularly motivated or impressed with
the actions of this interviewer, I should have found this approach
as teacher-centered and one that would make the interviewee (me)
impressed with a school system that would go to these lengths to
have the new teacher accept the position that certainly is about to be
offered.

I did not accept the position when it was offered. I honestly told
the interviewer that I had applied with several school districts in the

San Antonio area and was going to interview at several others before accepting a position. Job interviews work both ways. The employer wants to make a decision benefiting the company. The job applicant sizes up the interviewer and the apparent professionalism of the company while thinking, "Do I want to work here?" But there was still another reason I hesitated going right into a teaching position right away. The director of this Teacher Corps project from which I had graduated, one Dr. Ernie O'Neill ("Ernie" from this point forward), had already asked me if I would accept a staff position with this same Teacher Corps program because they were submitting a proposal for another two-year project. This time it would not be with the Edgewood Independent School District. The proposal submitted to Washington identified the Austin Independent School District as the school system where the graduate interns would spend their two-year internship and also graduate with a master's in education in 1976, again with the University of Texas at Austin. While Austin is only some seventy-eight miles from San Antonio, the drive to and from Austin, should I decide to continue living in San Antonio, is minimally three hours each day.

Ernie's offer was particularly exciting to me because I would be able to enter a doctoral program and pursue a terminal degree. There are, of course, for most students, questions about being accepted at the University of Texas Graduate School. Not a problem for me! When the Teacher Corps selected me as an intern in a graduate program in pursuit of a master's degree, I was accepted at this same time *as a graduate student* in their graduate school. Besides, pursuing a PhD involves a much tougher task, the submission of a proposal to a committee of five full professors in the UT Graduate School and having *all five* approve of one's proposal to complete a doctoral program.

Is this like pulling teeth? No, it's probably ten times worse. As you will see below, it is bad enough getting *one* professor to approve a doctoral study, in any university, let alone this university, already known to be very tough on doctoral students. More on this aspect of the tremendous tasks that lie ahead for me below.

There was so much more to do before even starting to think about getting into a doctoral program. I was still living in San Antonio. The year was 1974, I was 40 years old. Maria was 16; Robert, 14; Patty, 12; and Rey was only 9 years old. For Maria, I would continue her record of attending a different school every single year between grades one and twelve, a record she would maintain through all of her school years.

There was one other factor influencing my decision to move to Austin. As stated above, the year is 1974. However, we have been back in America only a little over two years. Our four children have been in San Antonio schools only for this length of time. Much has happened with our experiences with the school district to which we belong by virtue of where we live. We live in the Edgewood Independent School District. I enrolled all four of them with the Edgewood public school system, hoping for the best, in January of 1972. None are attending Edgewood schools at this time (1974). Here is why.

Note to the reader: My hope is that this is not too confusing. I am about to move my family to another city, albeit still in Texas, but a major move nonetheless. I want to mention my justification for this move. I am also asking Grace to once again leave her hometown, her mom, and all her siblings. However, it is a part of my story. I have to go back in time again, if only a couple of years.

Immediately upon returning to America in December of 1971, I enrolled Maria, age 13 at this time and in junior high school, with the closest junior high school to our home. Robert was in sixth grade, still in the elementary school, as was Patty, in fourth. Rey was in kindergarten since he had not entered first grade yet. Rey had just turned 6 the previous October, while we were still in Panama. He entered kindergarten in Panama and was still in kindergarten when we arrived in the USA.

The incident I'm about to mention happened at Maria's school, and I almost *blew my top* in anger.

This is school year 1971–72 and in the month of January. I was already working with Holy Cross High School. Grace was a stay-at-home mom who looked after our four children before and after school. She was home when all four came home. On one particular day when all four children had gone to school, Maria felt very ill while at school. She started to run a temperature. The school where Maria attended *decides to send her home by herself,* walking the ten to twelve blocks, in the middle of the day, and already not feeling well. I was not called. Grace was not called. By the grace of God, she managed to make it home safely. However, when I got home and was informed of what happened, I rushed out to my car and drove to the school. To say I was angry would not do justice to how I felt.

I have had one or two occasions in my life when I was so angry about something that happened to me because of someone else's bad judgment that I came very close to doing something physical to the culprit at fault. I have been able to hold myself back and just verbalize my anger. I will resume my visit to my daughter's school after first exemplifying the very first time this happened to me.

It was a day in late November of 1951, in the middle of a regular work week. I had turned 18 on August 17 of that same year. I had received notice by the air force that I should report to their recruiting office in downtown San Antonio on December 15. So I was already counting my remaining days as a civilian. I already owned a car. I was going to just park it in the backyard driveway, raise it up on iron blocks to get the tires off the ground, perhaps even cover it with plastic or a canvas cover, at least until I came back on leave or sold it. My car was a black 1934 Plymouth four-door that was in good shape, and I wanted to keep it. That is, keep it unless someone offered me a good price for it.

My brother Jimmy had relieved me at our dad's service station around 4:00 p.m. and I was driving home. At the time we lived on the 1100 block of Buena Vista Street. By "we" I mean my mom, dad, Jovita, Pepe, and me. Armando was in the car with me as I remember that he wanted to borrow my car that evening. I'm driving south on Zarzamora Street and approaching a traffic light at Zarzamora and Martin Streets. The red light came on, and I stopped as the first car at the light, facing south.

To my left, as the first car facing west at the same light (and on Martin Street), is a car with three drunk men as the only occupants, including the driver. As stated previously, the light turned green for them. The driver was going to turn right and go in the direction from which I was coming (as I sat at the traffic light). The drunken driver *races his engine to burn rubber and make a loud noise.* His car churns vigorously, but he is still able to turn right and then, obviously not in control of his car, slams into my car and me. He had picked up enough speed in those fifteen to thirty yards to really slam hard into my car and cause tremendous damage to both cars. The three men remained in the car. No one got out of their car.

But I got out of my car quickly. I was livid. No, I wasn't hurt, nor was Armando. I hurried up to the driver's side of their car, swung open the driver's door, and I yelled at the drunken driver, "WHAT THE HELL IS WRONG WITH YOU, YOU FOOL?" Now, there were three of them. They were not teenagers. But all three men cowered in fear. I am sure it was not because they thought I was going to hit them, but in fear that the police had already arrived, and they would probably be jailed for public intoxication and the driver charged with driving under the influence. The driver and his two companions knew immediately they were in the wrong. The police officer was there next to me in minutes, and I remember him asking me if I was going to press charges. I remember distinctly answering loudly, "HELL YES!" and the officer asking, "What did you just say?" I lowered the volume of my voice and then said, "Yes, sir."

It is amazing how everything happened so quickly. It didn't occur to me that there were three of them in their car, and they could have come out swinging and perhaps "ganged up" on me when I swung open the driver's door. Or they could have had guns on them. I was just so angry that I lost control of myself for a few minutes. The police officer called for a van and the three men were taken away. They must have really been intoxicated. My car was a total loss. It died a lonely death in a junk yard somewhere in San Antonio. A couple of days later, I reported to the recruiting office and got sworn in to the U.S. Air Force.

It is now twenty years and two months later (January 1972). Let's pick up the story where I left off. It's back to the junior high school Maria attended. There were no school administrators present.

It was after 5:00 p.m. and most of the staff were gone except for the school secretary. I vented my concerns with what had happened to Maria. The woman could only agree with me and say nothing else except to apologize. However, I was angry enough to say that my daughter was not coming back to this very ineffective school, "So please get her school records for me because you won't see her or me again."

The only other school I could send her to would be a Catholic parochial school in South San Antonio, the closest one. It was St. Margaret Mary's Catholic School. The school taught grades kindergarten through ninth grade. I could enroll all four of my children there. I did.

My sister Elida and her husband Frank already had four of their children enrolled there. Michael, as the oldest, was in tenth grade and already attending a different Catholic school, a high school. Gary, Celine, Stephen, and Melissa attended St. Margaret Mary's School. This would make the daily commute easier because the Burns and I could take turns driving all the kids to school. Grace had not yet learned to drive. Frank, Elida, and I simply took turns doing all the driving. The year is 1972 and seat belt laws had not yet been made mandatory.

All the aforementioned occurred during the second half of the 1971–72 school year. I left Holy Cross High School at the end of this school year, as stated previously, and I was accepted as an intern with the Teacher Corps project. Fortunately, I participated in this internship while continuing to live in San Antonio for two more years, until the summer of 1974. By the end of these two years, Maria had now entered the eleventh grade, Robert the ninth, Patty the seventh, and Rey the third.

Back to 1974 and our move to Austin. Grace and I made the decision to make the move. We thought of selling our home since we did not plan on returning to San Antonio, at least not in the immediate future. Still, all of this takes time. We have four children in school. We have to find a place to live. We had to inform ourselves on where the best schools were and where the best, and safest, parts of Austin were so we could try to find a home there. Then too, do we want to rent or buy a home? Grace and I were always savings conscious, so we had enough money saved for a down payment, if we made the decision to buy.

The interview with the San Antonio Independent School District was the only one I actually had, although I had applied with two or three other school systems. I made the decision that if I did not accept Ernie's offer to join his staff and move to Austin, I would accept a position with the SAISD. Grace and I talked at length about the implications of moving again. We had only been back in America just two and a half years, having arrived in San Antonio from Panama in December of 1971.

About making another major move so quickly, I don't know this for sure because Grace did not always express everything she was feeling. My recollections today are that she put all her trust in me and if I thought we, and mostly our children, would be better off in Austin than in San Antonio, then she would be in favor of the move. I called Ernie and accepted his offer. He told me he thought I would accept it because he felt all along that I wanted to enter a doctoral program at UT. He was right. I actually had no idea what I was about to get into.

Before going into detail on our move, a few loose ends need to be tied together about completing my internship, receiving my master's degree, and about my nephew David. David had no intentions of teaching anywhere else but with the school system he had attended all of his life, the Edgewood Public Schools. His father, my brother Felipe Junior, or as we all knew him "Chito," had other things he wanted his son David to consider now that he had acquired a graduate degree from the prestigious University of Texas at Austin. Chito is now only a few weeks from his fifty-eighth birthday. Like our father, Chito had only worked with the Missouri Pacific Railroad. He was a boilermaker assistant, but a "laborer" by any other name. David was his first of two sons. Chito inquired of his supervisors with the railroad if this made his son eligible to train as a railroad engineer with their company now that he has all this education behind him. I don't know any of the details of how David agreed and accepted to do this, or even his willingness to go into a career field so very different from the one he studied for so long and even completed a two-year internship to really be prepared to teach. But *agree, accept, and be willing to do this,* he did.

Fast forward to the year 2018 (today), forty-four years later. David continues as a railroad engineer. He and his wife have visited once with my family and me here in Maryland in the last five or six years. He works (drives trains) out of Laredo, Texas, while living in Houston with his wife. He maintains homes in both cities. David never looked back at a teaching career. My guess is that the pay, even in his first year as an engineer, was at least four times that of a beginning teacher anywhere in America. The money, and satisfying his father's wishes, may have been the reason David left the field of education. His current wife is his second. He had two sons with his first wife. Both sons must be in their thirties today. As I remember, both are professionals as both have college degrees. I believe one has his business in San Antonio, the other in Chicago. I hope to revisit with David and find out how he is doing before I complete this manuscript. He has not answered my phone calls. I intend to keep on trying.

As for the other twenty-four interns who graduated with me, all went into teaching positions all over the country. That I know, David and I are the only ones who did not, at least not right away as is the case with me.

Now, back to the summer of 1974 and our move to Austin. I was asked to report for work with the new Teacher Corps program almost immediately. There were proposals to write and more staff to hire. Ernie wanted me on board right away. I was going to have to commute back and forth between San Antonio and Austin every day. I drove to Austin and returned home to San Antonio every day. I did this with such frequency that it was becoming routine. In fact, while Grace and I did eventually move to Austin, it was not until 1976, a full two years later.

The long drive took its toll, on both me and my car. Add to this the fact that my hours were not exactly 9 to 5 but more like 24/7. We had many evening classes and meetings with the new class of interns and with the professional staff of the Austin Public Schools who comprised the cooperating teachers with whom we worked.

We also enrolled them in the graduate classes and both groups were able to graduate with master's degrees in 1976. Ernie made the decision to step down as the director of the project so that he could fill, instead, the position of program specialist. As program specialist, he would also assume the position of instructor and begin earning "hard money." By *hard money* is meant that his salary would be assumed by the university while the rest of the staff, including the director of the program, would depend on federal funding and the approval of proposals that had to be submitted to Washington every two years. When Ernie stepped down, he also appointed one Ruben Olivarez, heretofore an assistant to the director, as the new director and both of them asked me if I would agree to come on board, not as an assistant but as "associate director" of the program. I agreed. I considered it a *feather in my cap*. Ruben and I, as well as four to five other staff specialists with our program, were all paid with *soft money*. Soft money in this case meant our pay would depend on federal funding of our program

In the meantime, I continued taking graduate classes in pursuit of a doctorate in educational administration. I usually took two classes per semester, including during the summers of 1975, '76, and '77. Ruben allowed me to take one three-hour class during working hours one day per week. The second class I took each semester had to be an evening class. I was quickly accumulating a vast number of semester hours. When the "Research Design" and "Statistics" classes came up, I had to take them as the only classes for that semester because they required a tremendous amount of homework and there would not be time for any other studies.

My duties as the associate director were to complement Ruben and his duties as the director. We planned all activities together and then divided the tasks between us. There were over twenty-five graduate interns in the program, including cooperating teachers already employed with the Austin Public Schools, so we stayed very busy.

I mentioned previously that the drive was taking its toll on me and my car. It was also keeping me away from my family. Maria was now a senior in high school. Robert was in the 9th grade. Patty was completing her final year in elementary school, where Rey was also enrolled. They needed me, and I felt a need to be with them more. We pursued the move in earnest during the summer of 1976. We decided to buy a home in a new area that was going up not more than a couple of miles south of the center of the city. The community was new and all the homes were just being constructed. Total cost of homes in this community averaged around $75,000 with a 2% down payment. A $75,000 home in 1975 is the equivalent of a $200 to $250 thousand dollar home today. We had no trouble with either the down payment or qualifying for the loan from the Federal Housing Administration.

It was a new year of school for all four of our children. Maria and Robert would attend Travis High School some two miles away. Patty was enrolled at Fulmore Junior High School, one of the "feeder schools" for students who attended Travis. Rey entered fourth grade at a school named Pleasant Hills Elementary School, only a mile or so from our home. Things started to settle down for us as a family.

Almost all of the families who were buying homes in this new community had children. They were of all ages. Ours, from oldest to youngest (Maria, Robert, Patty, and Rey), were 17, 15, 13, and 9, respectively. Each had friends of their age. As far as trouble with school requirements, Grace and I have been blessed with very able children who had no trouble, academic-wise, in school. Robert had a tendency to opt for the easiest subjects. The others did very well. Patty complained that students at her junior high school were frequently in trouble because of drugs or other juvenile delinquencies. The year is 1976 and perhaps the beginning of drug use by juveniles and young adolescents in America's schools. One would think it would be present in our high schools, but in our junior high schools? With children between the ages of 13 and 15? Patty verbalized her feelings about all this when she got home every day, and I knew she disapproved of the goings-on at her school. Still, I never once worried that her friends or her were involved in any of this. Patty has her world right-side up all the time.

Also, for the most part, our children have mostly enjoyed good health as well. Maria has had asthma most of her young life and has learned to live with it while always taking the necessary precautions.

As for my graduate studies, I am now in the planning stages to enter the most serious part of my doctoral program. The Research Design class, as well as the Statistics course, were the last academic classes I had to complete as a part of my doctoral program. Now comes my selection of a research "problem" to pursue. Topics ran the gamut from A to Z in all education topics, from kindergarten to high school, and I could even enter research topics in higher education. I wanted my study to be an important one that perhaps, if I did a good enough job, I could publish it as an original work that no one else has done. My problem was that I had no idea what that research topic was going to be.

In the back of my mind, I always thought I could very easily fall into that pitfall of becoming another member of that now burgeoning number of *All But Dissertation* club and never quite get the job done. I began to feel that I needed to make some changes in my daily work routines. If I stayed on with what I was doing, I would certainly become an ABD. I took a bold step. I told Ruben I was resigning without revealing to him of my reasons. I just said I needed to make a change, and this was true. What I didn't realize was that I also hurt his feelings because my reasons for the change only benefitted me. Still, I resigned.

I went home. I told Grace. While Grace never offered me any advice, she always listened to me. Often this was all I needed. However, there was still some pressure I was feeling. We had bills to pay. When I resigned, I immediately stopped earning a pay check. I did a lot of reflecting on what my next step should be. Would I look for another position? I have a teaching certificate. Should I apply with a local school system and finally become a public school teacher? Then again, could Grace and I make it if I did not work for a full year while I finished my dissertation? It is only the first week in June. I would have the summer and two more semesters to complete my dissertation. What about the house payment? Grace is working with the Marriot Hotels as a supervisor and earning fairly good money. It was enough to pay our utility bills, buy food for a family of six, purchase fuel for our car, pay our monthly credit card bills, but not enough to make our monthly house payment. More reflecting on what to do.

In the next few days, Grace and I finally made a decision on what to do. I was about to put a lot of pressure on myself. I would have to get everything done within the next twelve months and then return to a full-time job and continue supporting my family. We were in our second Austin home now. We had sold our first home after living in it for only two years. We bought another new home some twelve to fifteen miles south and west of the city of Austin. It was a bigger home in the small town of Menchaca, Texas. There was an empty lot immediately east of this home that was filled with trees and was also for sale. The house and the lot were the only two on this block. Buying the lot would give us a lot of privacy. There would be no neighbors on either side of our home.

We qualified for and were able to buy both the house and the empty lot. How did we handle making the house payment? I stated (above), "I was about to put a lot of pressure on myself." Well, what I did was submit an application for a $10,000 student loan to my credit union. It was immediately approved since we had an excellent credit rating. For the next twelve months, we cut our spending, took no vacations, did not buy new clothes other than the school clothes our children needed, and we lived a very frugal existence.

Financially, with Grace continuing to work with the Marriot Hotel and she and I watching every purchase we made, we were okay and would eventually make it for the next twelve months through May of 1978.

The completion of my dissertation was another story. Here it is, June of 1977. I have not-quite twelve months to get it all done. I don't have a topic yet. I don't even have a committee of five full professors to approve of my proposal and eventually my completed dissertation. The steps to follow are just now beginning to form on my mind. I expected the task of completing a PhD study at UT Austin to be difficult. However, I had no idea what it would really be like. Consider my pending tasks:

Identifying five supervising graduate school professors who would agree to be my "supervising committee" representing the

University of Texas. I had three full professors in mind, all members of the educational administration department at UT and with whom I took the majority of my graduate classes, and who I thought had given me encouraging feedback when I submitted papers expressing myself as a possible educational administrator. The selection of one of the two other professionals to make up the required number of five members of this committee should represent another related department within the university to make the committee representative of topics upon which I would base my study. I selected a full professor from the Curriculum and Instruction Department.

The fifth member could be from outside the university but needed to be a practicing professional educator who also possessed a PhD. I had already asked a trainer with the Educational Service Center there in Austin who did some training of our Teacher Corps interns on certain topics during the time I was associate director. He gladly confirmed he would do it. It was also a feather in his cap. Being on a doctoral committee could open some doors for him there at UT Austin.

Before formally approaching them, I would need to provide all five members with a proposal for the study. The proposal needed to state, in a clear, concise, and professional manner, the following topics:

1. A statement of the problem to be studied
2. The significance of the problem
3. Definitions and limitations
4. Organization of the study

I had a long-range goal (complete the dissertation by early spring). I now needed a series of short-term goals that would eventually lead to the completion of this long-range goal. It is still early June of 1977. Questions on my mind centered around the four topics above. This would be my first task. Select a problem upon which to focus my study. While selecting the problem, keep in mind its significance to the field of education. The Department of Educational Administration could not have been more cooperative with me as I began my study. The clerical staff knew me because, as the associate director of the Teacher Corps project, my office was on the same floor and we often talked about relevant topics that concerned all aspects of education. There were extra offices on the floor, and I was given one. That meant I didn't have to work on this tremendous task from home. I immediately planned to get up every morning as if I had a job and left early for the university to work on my dissertation. I was given a filing cabinet, desk, and an executive chair. I had the most modern "typewriter." Please remember, the year is 1977. Computers were not yet in full usage in offices, schools, or classrooms. The typewriter remained cold and silent as I had nothing to type. I needed a *problem* for my study. I reflected on this task of mine day and night. I probably lost a lot of sleep over this unmet need.

The thought of ensuring that the problem in education I was looking for should be *real* and not just *made up* in my mind began to enter my thoughts. I now had six years of experience in education. I left the *military training instructor* and *logistician* roles six years ago. So, "Roberto, what problems have you found in education in the six years you have been in this new profession of yours?"

That was it! I have a problem! In the six years I have been in education I have found a management philosophy of *top-down* authority. Every school system has a *central office*, where all the decisions are made and then sent *down* to the schools. Teachers hate this with a passion. Many believe these decisions are ill-founded and will probably be reversed in a year or two if teachers will just be patient and not pay attention to them.

Yes! I have direction. I have topics to look up in the literature to see if anyone has done any studies on the topics of centralization, decentralization, and job satisfaction. Along with looking for previous studies, what does the literature say about these same three topics? If there are studies that have already been done, what are their findings? And if I find studies, what are the conclusions reached?

Obtaining my PhD 1977-78

I had topics upon which to do research in probably the best-equipped university library in the country. Well, perhaps the second best, since everything I read about university libraries gives that particular nod to Harvard University. I spent most of what remained of the summer of 1977 in the Educational Psychology Library of UT. It consisted, at that time, of five floors. I had, generally speaking, three topics on which to base my research. Each one took me in dozens of directions. Centralization was included in government, administration, private companies, and schools at every level. The list was endless. After spending a couple of weeks reading how decisions are made at all of these organizational levels, I started concentrating on organizations that had decentralized their decision making.

Voila! An almost immediate consequence of decentralization of decision making, in almost all of my readings of different organizations, was the concept of *job satisfaction*. I spent a considerable amount of my research time reading about organizations that had benefitted from making this change. The more I read, the more I realized that none were public or private schools. Still, the concept of job satisfaction came up in most of the studies on decentralization of decision making. The more I read about my three research topics, the clearer, in my mind at least, it became that I had three topics to investigate as I worked on my dissertation.

I now had already spent the better part of three months working almost exclusively in the Ed Psych Library. I had fifteen to twenty file folders full of information on my three research topics. I knew I would need to list all the publications I had read if I was to reference them in my narrative. By the time I was to finish this work, I will have referred to well over 150 different authors of applicable professional work on these topics. While citing many of them in my narrative, I felt I should also list those from whom the information I obtained from reading of their expertise allowed me to write with authority and knowledge, even if the narrative did not include references to their particular work.

Now comes the most difficult part of attempting to do a research study that ends with the completion of a dissertation: *Getting the five members of my committee to approve of my work.* The initial approval had to be of my written proposal. Part of the written proposal had to be the completion of, and an elaboration of exactly how I was to accomplish the task, the following items I have already mentioned in the previous chapter:

A statement of the problem to be studied
The significance of the problem
Definitions and limitations
Organization of the study

It took me several weeks to get all five members to approve my proposal. I really have no idea if the university compensates them for their participation as members of doctoral studies. I have to believe they do receive pay for their involvement. The PhD trainer with the Education Service Center, and the fifth member of my committee, did not get compensated. He was doing me the favor of being on my committee and reading the vast amount of documentation I would be submitting to them in the coming months. Of course, he would also be able to list this activity in his curriculum vitae. I got their approval. I was now ready to start on my dissertation.

But first, a few words first about obtaining my committee's approval. While doing this work, eventually completing it (and able to earn the title of Dr. Roberto Pérez), it did not occur to me that these five individuals had to also commit to being a part of this task, albeit doing nothing more than reading every chapter, giving me feedback, and eventually signing their name approving my work. Still, each had to judge whether or not I was up to the task of truly conducting a professional scientific study and proving my hypothesis. There are (by far) many more doctoral students who only get this far and then fail to get all five full professors to approve of their work and earn the title of being a PhD. They end up earning the title of ABD, or "All But Dissertation. My wild guess as to the ratio of ABDs to PhDs is minimally 8 to 1, or worse. I was determined to become a PhD, even though there were many a night that I didn't sleep more than a few minutes worrying about it. These particular nights came after I had submitted each of the seventeen chapters to my committee and then it took weeks to hear from some of them. You should know that I am at heart a fatalist, so I always thought the worst, like, "They don't think my work is good enough!"

How I obtained the statistical data: There are two kinds of studies one makes to complete a dissertation. One is a field study where the candidate conducts the study in person and in the environment where the data is gathered. The other study is done through the completion of a questionnaire that, hopefully, is provided by the respondents who completed it and then returned the instrument. This latter model is the one I used for my dissertation.

Now, the work begins. A dissertation requires the field testing of this data-gathering instrument to prove its all-important validity and reliability. I had taken the two most important courses to prepare me for the statistical requirements of a dissertation. First, the questionnaire my respondents receive and respond to would provide the crux of my statistical data. I spent more than a week, working practically 24/7, on three pages of questions that would provide me with *all* the data needed to prove my hypothesis. It was that "the greater the involvement of teachers in certain areas of in-service education, the greater the job satisfaction." Thus, my dissertation is titled "A Comparison of Centralized and Decentralized In-service Education

Programs: Teacher Involvement, Program Characteristics, and Job Satisfaction."

I had to read the literature to learn about obtaining statistical data that would make *field testing* this instrument (questionnaire) valid and reliable. The first thing I learned was that I would need to select a population of educators that would be representative of the same population to whom I would eventually send this questionnaire. This task consumed three weeks of my time. I am starting to feel some pressure now. Will I ever get down to data collection? How can I if I have to prove so darn many things before I "get to work on the nitty-gritty of this study?"

Next, the selection of respondents (to *just field test* the questionnaire): The actual respondents would be the professional staff at public schools, elementary, middle, and high schools. I needed to select similar personnel for a short test of the instrument to ascertain the data would be similar, and thus reliable and valid. Public schools all over America are strikingly similar. I selected a handful of public schools near Austin. I asked their school principals for permission to approach randomly selected members of their professional staff and received quick approval. When I applied the mathematical formula in order to determine predictability, the percentage was upwards of 80 percent, thus making my questionnaire completely suitable to elicit the data I was hoping to get and also making it reliable.

Yes! Success! I can move forward with my study.

Next was the selection public schools. The state of Texas has one of the largest number of public school districts in the nation. In order to make my study scientific, I would have to conduct a true random sampling of *all* the public schools in the state of Texas. This was my next task. How do I select randomly the correct number of schools in one state to make it a scientific sampling?

I listed all the school districts by number and applied what is called "The Monte Carlo" application of determining a random sampling. One hundred fifty-six school districts were listed as needing to be approached for a true random sampling. Again, identified with a number only and each number identifying a school district by name on my list, I now had the school districts I needed to approach. Some of those identified had several hundred schools, thousands of teachers, and hundreds of thousands of students. What do I do now?

Again, with the Monte Carlo method of statistical application for true samplings, each selected school district was inserted into the mix and the product that was "spat out" of the formula were the names of schools within each of the 156 school districts. This gave me another opening for continuation of my study. I have names of schools within each of 156 school districts. Now, the selection of one school within each school district and, again, applying a mathematical approach so the selection is also scientific.

DONE!

Next is communicating with the individual school principals, identifying myself and the purpose of my request, and asking for permission to send a selected number of professional staff on their faculty the questionnaire for participation in my study. Of course, I am using the University of Texas at Austin stationary and attempting to impress these recipients of my mail as being representative of a truly professional study worth their involvement. I received approval from all the chosen principals.

I then asked each principal to select, randomly and with my instructions for random selection of staff, and provide me with names of teachers and other professional staff members in order for me to send them the questionnaires through the mail. Again, I received the information from all of the schools. Now, I cannot be sure the principals did the selection of faculty members to participate. I want to think they did it personally, but whether or not the principals did the selection or their administration secretary did it does not alter the fact that they were still selected with my instructions for a true random sampling. I am ready for the next step.

There were a total of 1,400 names selected in the 156 schools that I approached. I sent each recipient the three-page questionnaire with an accompanying introductory letter with instructions on how to complete the document. I had to make both my introduction and the instructions very brief for fear they wouldn't read it and just "toss it." Surprise, surprise. My hard work is beginning to pay dividends. *I got an 80 percent return!*

Okay, this is hard to believe, at least in today's world, in 2017, that such a high return could even be dreamed about. Trust me, reader, *I got an 80 percent return*. Now, let me add a few things to how my legal size envelopes looked when I dropped them off at the post office. First, I bought first class stamps that I pasted on each envelope myself. I *never* placed any of my stamps perfectly on the upper right-hand side of each envelope. They were never symmetrically perfect. They were usually slanted and a few I gambled and smudged them a little with a drop or two of a coffee stain. I wanted these professionals to know I was one of them, albeit one going for a doctorate.

I placed an identifying two-digit number on each answer sheet so that I could credit returns and keep an accurate record and be able to cite in my dissertation the validity of my study. I didn't come up with the 80 percent return by guessing. It was perhaps the most accurate statistic of my study. As an aside to all of this, one of the very brief statements I made in my letter to each recipient was the statement that I wanted their very honest evaluation of the extent of their involvement in decision making at their school. I had an idea that some would consider this a risk that perhaps their principal may be apprised of what each faculty member of theirs said about this and perhaps get upset. I asked that they trust me. It was strictly between each individual participant and me, and I was only documenting numbers to determine the extent of their participation.

Well, of the 1,120 returns, *one* person found the two-digit number on her answer sheet and wrote me a note on her answer sheet. I am paraphrasing now since this occurred thirty-nine years ago: "AH HA! You said this was strictly confidential, between you and me. What is this number for?" I took the time to hand scribe her a letter explaining the process I was using. And to please trust me.

By early October (1977), I started my first two chapters. The first was the introduction to my study, which took very little time. The second was a review of the literature. The second chapter took me several weeks to complete. The completed questionnaires were being returned now, and I was busy compiling data. I was surprised by what I was seeing in their answer sheets. I was beginning to worry that the results may make my study invalid. Almost to a school, there was no teacher involvement in decision making, at any of the 156 schools.

I soon began to realize a trend that was developing with the return of the chapters I was submitting. I reviewed the feedback I was getting on my first two chapters (approved by all members of the committee). With the exception of two of the professors (who always questioned several of my findings or recommended more readings for me to do, the others gave me approval with no more than two or three comments, most of which I handled right away and were not burdensome. I reflected on this revelation and decided I was going to take the lead on requiring them to return my work. For the members who were procrastinators, I intended to make it tough on them by *not asking them* to return my chapters, approved or not, by a certain date. *I told them by what day I needed my chapter back because, if not returned, I was going to consider the chapter approved, and I was going to move on to my next chapter.* I have to be honest about how I worded my statement to the committee. Yes, I exaggerated the urgency of my having to move forward with my study because I had resigned my job to get this done. I also mentioned I had gotten a large student loan to get this done. I mentioned having four children still in school and the fact that I only had twelve months to get it all done. While presently I feel I exaggerated a bit, all of this was true. I did worry about it, and it was mostly because this twelve-month period to get this done *was it*. If I didn't finish my approved dissertation, there would be no "tomorrows."

But I am also a person with confidence of what I can do. I did not doubt that my work would be better than satisfactory. During one of those nights I could not sleep for thinking about this, I also decided, "What the hell! I will have given this my best shot. If I didn't get it done, well, I didn't get it done." It will not be the end of the world for me. Having said this, the reader should know that deep inside of me, I knew I would earn my PhD. I knew I would, but I never told anyone of my confidence. I never discussed this with Grace because I would have her at a disadvantage. She would approve of anything I said I would do.

All five complied with my wishes. Getting my committee members to comply with this request was perhaps the single most important milestone in this endeavor of mine. I have no doubt that many doctoral candidates lose their patience with committee members who either neglect their commitment to the candidate or else are just too busy with their own jobs to worry about the task at hand. If they fail to approve of the chapter that the candidate has submitted presently, there is no one to remind them or to get after them for not responding in a timely manner. In retrospect, I felt all five members of my committee knew I was a serious person. I did not refer to them as "Carl," "Ben," Leonard, Tom, or "Hal." I always referred to them as Dr. Ashbaugh, Dr. Harris, Dr. Valverde, Dr. Horn, or Dr. de Shong. When my note to them said, "If not returned, I am going to consider the chapter approved...," I believe all five knew I meant it. The year was 1977. I had already turned forty-four. They were not dealing with a green-horn college student.

Having mentioned the above, and sort of castigating committee members for not responding to the doctoral candidate, the burden really rests with the candidate. If the candidate is attempting to complete his or her dissertation while also holding down a full-time job, this task can be overwhelming. In my case, I was not. I spent my days and nights, 24/7, doing almost nothing but working on my dissertation. To complete each chapter and obtain approval by a committee of five full professors whose job it is to ensure that the narrative provided by the candidate conforms to what was in the proposal, can become more than one can handle. It would be very easy for a candidate to say, "NO! I've done enough. This is impossible to complete. I've gone as far as I can go." I never gave this a second thought. I did give it a lot of *first* thoughts though.

On this last thought, I have only told a few very personal friends of mine, perhaps one or two, that I became a different person when I was finishing my candidacy. The pressure was almost more than I could handle. I planned to complete it. My committee was returning my chapters approved. I started to breathe more easily. I could feel the completion of this immense task. It is now April of 1978. My committee agreed to hear my defense of my work. A conference was set up at the University of Texas, and I was more than well prepared. I knew what was on every page of my 239-page dissertation. I went into the meeting not just prepared. I was confident I would answer every question any one of the five committee members would ask.

The day came. We met for several hours. There was not one question that any one brought up that I was not able to direct them to a certain page for the answer. Each of the five professors left the meeting only after congratulating me for the job I did.

To be perfectly honest, I knew the moment I walked in that I was not going to have a problem. All five were sitting at one table and all faced the podium where I was asked to stand to field their questions. Of the five, only Dr. de Shong was relaxed and sort of sitting back to wait his turn to ask me about my work. Dr. de Shong had read my dissertation and was ready to ask about any concerns he may have. The other four, all full professors, were hurriedly skimming through my document. I surmised that they were looking for items in my report that they were informed about and wanted me to clarify items I may have included in my dissertation. The first five to six questions were about areas in which I had spent a lot of time, like finding similar studies from chapter two, the Review of the Literature. This was an easy question and one which I could elaborate on for a long time. I found none. My study was unique. No one had heretofore published a study that measured job satisfaction in the areas of centralization and decentralization of decision making on the part of classroom teachers as concerned their own in-service education.

I was able to refer them to specific pages in my dissertation where I explained in detail the exact response I was giving them orally as I stood behind the podium. The deeper we got into the defense of my dissertation, the more relaxed I became. The longer we continued in this venue, the more confident I became. Finally, Dr. Valverde, the youngest of the group and also a Mexican American like me, asked me if I had found *any* programs in the 156 school systems that I could classify as having *some* elements of decentralization. I answered, "*None.*"

At this point, I could feel my heart skip a beat. Hmm, does this mean that my research, because I found no programs upon which to prove my hypothesis, is invalid? Dr. Valverde followed up with a positive statement that immediately set me at ease. "Not proving your hypothesis does not make your study invalid," he added. Your study becomes a perceptual study in the minds of the 1,120 respondents who answered your request.

The meeting lasted only a few more minutes. There were only a few kudos expressed for the thorough job I did. Still, the positive remarks, while only a handful, came from each of them, nonetheless.

Evidently, all had done this before. Each came up to sign the first page of my dissertation, shake my hand, give me a smile, and say, "Congratulations, Dr. Pérez." The date is May 19, 1978.

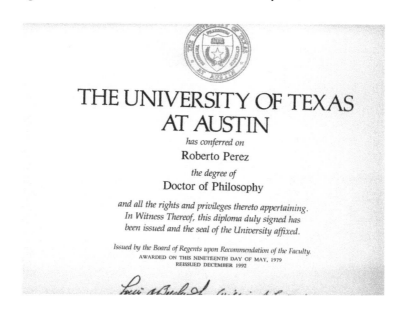

THE UNIVERSITY OF TEXAS
AT AUSTIN

has conferred on

Roberto Perez

the degree of

Doctor of Philosophy

*and all the rights and privileges thereto appertaining.
In Witness Thereof, this diploma duly signed has
been issued and the seal of the University affixed.*

Issued by the Board of Regents upon Recommendation of the Faculty.
AWARDED ON THIS NINETEENTH DAY OF MAY, 1979
REISSUED DECEMBER 1992

St. Edward's University (1979)

I did not feel any different. Yeah, I have earned a title. I could now prepare calling cards "Roberto Pérez, PhD." What I have done is reach a milestone in my life. Still, I have, hopefully, many years ahead of me as a professional educator. The only thought I had after graduation and receiving my doctorate was to apply as a professor at a university. As luck would have it, I did not keep this thought in my mind for very long. I did not submit any applications or ask that my résumé be reviewed for a possible position at any university. Instead, I received a call from the academic dean at St. Edward's University, only a few miles south of the University of Texas, right here in Austin, Texas.

After the usual introductions, this came from the Dean: "We are setting up a Teacher Corps Project in South Texas, and we need a program development specialist. Are you interested in this position?"

Before elaborating to the reader of my response to the dean at St. Edward's, a few words are in order. Oh if only a person could see the future! If this was possible, I would have seen the next two years as among the very worst of my forty-plus years as an educator. With the dean excluded, I went to work in an environment that was not only hostile to me, but also as unprofessional as any I had worked with up to this time (1971–1981). More on this, below.

In most ways except two, the offer by the dean was "just what the doctor ordered," so to speak. The position called for this person to come on board as a member of the St. Edward's University professional faculty and also as "assistant professor" on a *tenured* track. The Teacher Corps projects across the nation, now in their fifteenth year of funding, had recently reduced the number of Teacher Corps Interns for each project to only four. The programs could be at either the graduate or undergraduate levels. This project was at the graduate level. The interns would be placed in a small rural school district in South Texas, only a few miles west of Kingsville. The priority for bringing in hundreds of new teachers into our profession was no longer a priority for Teacher Corps Projects. Emphasis was now on the introduction of new ideas for teaching and learning and experimenting with approaches to impact both areas.

My position as program development specialist would require me to teach all of their graduate courses except those requiring a subject specific instructor. These particular courses could be taken during the summer at midpoint of their internship on campus at St. Edward's. The four interns would live in South Texas near the schools were they would work. As PDS, I would spend one full day on site each week. I would spend a half day observing them in the classroom and also conducting post-observation conferences with each intern. I would also teach two courses during the other half of my day in South Texas.

The *two ways* in which this hire, and my assignment, are not ideal are these:

First, and the reader will find this very hard to believe (and possibly wonder why I even took the job), my annual salary was going to be $19,000 per year. For crying out loud, this is lower than a beginning teacher's salary, and probably in any school district in any of the fifty states. The dean warned me when we talked that private Catholic universities like St. Edward's paid very little and thus usually had great professor turnover. There are other factors concerning high professorial turnover that seem so detrimental to the university's effectiveness, and I hope I can mention them further down in my narrative.

The second detriment in my acceptance of this *professorial* position was that, just like at the University of Texas at Austin, tenure would be based on the federal government continuing to fund this

Teacher Corps project. I had already learned to dislike UT because their commitment to improving teacher training was only based on the university continuing to receive federal dollars. If the *feds* ever stopped funding these projects, a *whole lot of people* would just simply be out of a job, and that would include me.

The one advantage I personally would enjoy was to not have to make a move to another city or state. I could *stay put*. It is summer of 1978. Maria is 20 and attending college. Robert is, too, but about to drop out because he was making good money working part-time, something he always did, even when in high school. Patty was in college at Ohio State on a grant. Rey was just 14 and about to enter high school. Let's face it. My children needed me to be *available* to them.

There was really a third reason, had I known in advance I was going to experience this while at St. Edward's, for me to say to the Dean, "No, thank you." It was the fact that I was coming on board with this new Teacher Corps project as the program development specialist, not as their director. They had already hired a person to be director. In retrospect, I have to wonder how they ever determined to hire this person to be the director. Before elaborating on this person, a few descriptive adjectives are in order about this Teacher Corps project to be conducted in South Texas in a small school system consisting of 98% Mexican American students. The project would be a bilingual *English-Spanish* program with the objective of teaching Spanish to ESL, "English as a second language," students in this school district with the ultimate objective being to *facilitate the learning of English*. I hope I can justify this program description and show why the theory behind this approach is effective.

The four graduate interns are to be of Mexican American descent and fully bilingual, as, of course, I am as well. This is a most definite requirement. We began the selection process for the four interns, and we chose the best four of all the candidates who had made it this far in the selection process.

First, a few words need to be said about learning English as a second language and why we teach Spanish-speaking students in American public schools in Spanish if the objective is to learn English. Here are the facts from the research on this topic. Students who have mastered their first language, if it is Spanish, can more easily learn English because they can transfer the learning of letters and their pronunciation, including consonants and vowels, because Spanish is a phonetic language and among the easiest to learn because of the consistency of this fact. When students have been taught under this theory, the research found that the learning of English occurred more rapidly. Another fact from the research was that, of the twenty-six letters of the English alphabet, these twenty-six letters, in combination with each other, have more than forty-five different pronunciations. There is the *silent* /e/ when used in four-letter words and the letter *e* is the fourth letter while the only other vowel is the second letter and is always pronounced with the *long* sound of the letter, as in /kite/, /rate/, /hate/ etc. There are /ie/ combinations, as well as /ea/, that give us one vowel sound in English. In Spanish, every letter of their alphabet is always sounded in speech. It has been shown to facilitate the learning of English because of its consistency.

Now on to the St. Edward's University Teacher Corps project: Had I known this about the director of this project, as well as what I was getting into, I would have said to the dean, "Thanks, but no thanks." My suspicions today, in reference to the selection of this person, are that he surely must have been the only candidate. The director chosen for this job was an African American gentleman who spoke absolutely no Spanish. When he and the dean interviewed me for the job as PDS, I thought it a little weird that this man was the director, but perhaps he had other skills that made his selection pertinent and the most appropriate of all the candidates. My intentions from the beginning were to be the best PDS I could be and to make this project successful, and if the director was to get all the credit, well, that is as it should be.

I was given an office next to his. We were both in a different building than the one with the clerical staff (two women, both near middle-age) and the dean. The two women had other responsibilities, besides all of the administrative support for the now funded Teacher Corps project. All the mail that came in for the Teacher Corps project, addressed to me or to the director, went to these two women first. One of them, the most senior, made the decision as to whether or not the mail came to us or to the dean, no matter to whom it was addressed. I should have realized from the get-go that this was *no way to run this railroad.* I immediately noticed that business mail addressed to me always arrived at my inbox already opened. Strange, to be sure. At first I began to wonder if this was a Catholic university policy or a way to ensure that everything was *on the up and up.* After all, this is a Catholic university.

This procedure would soon bite me in the ass. But more on the specifics later. Let's get back to the director of the project.

As I did with my study for my dissertation, I always arrive at my office very early in the morning and usually stay late, definitely until after five o'clock. I want no surprises or calls to me or my office after I'm gone. So if I stay late, I usually field those calls and solve them before leaving for home.

The director usually arrived at his office just before noon, and usually just in time for him to go out for lunch. I was never invited to have lunch with him. In fact, we seldom communicated in a personal way. When we did talk, it was always about my schedule for classes or about my supervision of the four interns. In other words, it was always business. We must have worked together in adjacent offices at St. Edward's for a year, from the summer of 1978 to the summer of 1979; and I never found out if he had a family, a wife, girlfriend or anything personal about him. In the beginning, I suspected he had other duties at the university that kept him away from our building until late in the morning. I found out he had no other duties. Being the director of this Teacher Corps project was the only duty he had, and *he did very little of that.* I handled it all. I had many years of experience, planned and taught all the graduate level courses the interns had to take to graduate, made all the onsite visits, met with the superintendent of schools down in the valley, as well as with the school faculties and with the parents of the children where our four interns served. The director did *diddly squat.* And very little of that as well.

I asked to talk to the dean about how lopsided our duties were. He hesitated to agree with me that our director did very little and that he was, for all intents and purposes, worth about as much as *tits were on a bore hog.* I caught on quickly that this dean was not going to come down on this person in any way. I left the dean's office even angrier than I had been before walking into his office.

This is a good time for me to pause and write a few things about my penchant for resolve. I do not work very well in environments that are not functioning at maximum efficiency, and especially if I am being treated with no respect and dignity. I want resolve, and immediately. If I am unable to get resolve and I've tried everything possible to find resolve, I usually do not stick around to be a part of it. I once walked out of being treated as a fool by one air force master sergeant supervisor when I was an instructor at Lackland. I waited for the very next opportunity when the director would be in his office. I knocked and asked "Can we talk?" I closed the door behind me. This man must have felt the vibes and the seriousness of my tone of voice. He was a man in his forties, also a PhD, and in retrospect, I have to believe he didn't perform any differently anywhere else where he worked. We are all creatures of habit.

I went right to the point of how I felt about the way he was fulfilling the role of director. I tried getting him to look into my eyes because I kept looking at his even if he did not look at me directly. I told him I was sure he was earning more money than I was, but I was doing everything. I said, "Jim, you do diddly-squat around here, and I'd like to see some changes."

I was not nervous. I was not afraid of him. I didn't know if he would be so angry he would take a swing at me. And the reason I was not *any* of these things is because I was *right* in voicing my concerns. He was a bigger person, physically, than me. But hey! We are both professional educators and I have a concern that he could at least try to answer and prove me wrong, right?

Wrong! He walked out of the office and left me standing there. He didn't even close the door behind him. He just left. I knew this was the beginning of the end. I walked back to my office and typed my letter of resignation, effective immediately. I walked it up to the dean's office and handed it to him and also told him I would leave things in order before physically leaving the campus. There would be nothing left undone and whatever action needing to be taken care of by me for this project, at this moment, that was my responsibility, it would be accomplished. I was giving up on this tenured track position as an assistant professor at this prestigious university. I had just spent thousands of dollars to acquire my PhD and in less than a few minutes of venting to a person posing as my professional superior, I told him and for all intents and purposes, this university, to kiss my ass.

Grace and I were making ends meet. She was a supervisor with the one Marriott Hotel there in Austin, and I had my air force retired pay. We could make it for a few months even if I stopped getting a check from St. Edwards. But I would have to get a job. I had previously thought, if only in my mind alone, that I would rather pump gas at a service station than work for someone or some agency that treated me with less than dignity and respect. Well, it's time to *pay the man, Shirley*!

I still had some cards up my sleeve that I could call on. There was a doctoral student at UT who went through all the same things I went through to get his PhD. His name is Peder Matthews, from the state of Washington. He had been on a year's leave of absence from the Austin Public Schools and was already back with the Austin schools as a principal of one of the largest elementary schools in the city, if not the state. At the time, sixth grade was still being taught at the elementary level. Peder's school had *six* sections of sixth grade. I knew he was looking for sixth grade teachers.

While at UT, we talked professionally on many occasions. His PhD was in curriculum and instruction and had a Spanish language component to his field study. We shared many things as we both did our doctoral work. I called him. It is summer of 1979. I told him everything. I asked him for a shot at one of his vacancies. I added that he could call the academic dean at St. Edward's University and ask him for my academic references and anything else that Peder may want to know about the job I did while at St. Edward's. I suppose Peder may have wondered if I was crazy or something. I had practically quit my job, leaving the university in a bind, so to speak, and now I'm asking Peder to call the dean to ask about my performance while there. I added this when I talked to Peder about calling the dean. "Peder, all I ask is that you call me after talking to the dean and in your own kind words, tell me what he says to you, about me."

Crazy? No. I know who I am. I am the *perfectionist* people call *crazy*. But when you want something done professionally, all the t's crossed and all the i's dotted, it is people like me you want to do the job. I had confidence the Dean would tell Peder who I was professionally as an educator.

I was still cleaning up my office when Peder called. It wasn't more than thirty minutes after our last conversation. "The dean used the term *prolific*" (In the American Heritage Dictionary, *prolific* means producing abundant works or results) "to tell me who you are and the job you have done there." Then Peder added, "Roberto, you are hired. Get over here so I can introduce you to the other sixth grade teachers and members of our faculty."

Teaching Sixth Grade (1979-1982)

I remained at Williams Elementary School for three years, as a sixth grade teacher with a doctorate in Educational Administration (but also certified as a K – 8 classroom teacher). I would spend all three years teaching under Peder. He left for his home state of Washington after our third year (in 1982). Peder was also a very private person and while we both respected each other as educators, he never shared very much of his personal life with me. In fact, he never stopped by during my planning periods to talk or to share aspects of our school. We did more talking when we were both doctoral candidates at The Univerity of Texas at Austin. Then, too, Peder had close to 2,000 students, ages 5 to 13 or 14, a faculty and staff of close to 150 professionals, and one tremendous responsibility to not only have an effective school where children came to learn, but also a school that guaranteed to all parents that their children were safe.

A school principal is every bit a chief executive officer, a CEO, having to make crucial decisions almost every minute of every day. I started at $36,000 per year as an experienced teacher with an advanced degree. Peder earned no more $25,000 above my salary. All salaries of educational personnel are published in the media because we get paid with tax dollars.

Peder was another perfectionist. I can still remember the first day I was in his office. His desk was clear, with only a notepad, pencil, a *to-do* list, and an inbox on the left front of his desk and an outbox on the right-front. He was so demanding that soon after he left for his home state, several of the really outstanding teachers there at Williams, while always respecting Peder for the *prolific* person he was, still complained that he expected the same from all his teachers and their evaluations usually reflected the fact that most were not the outstanding educators that Peder expected all of them to be. One of them sat with me over a cup of coffee one day and confided in me that she had a lot of respect for Peder, but it would take her a few years to get past the less than "outstanding" teacher evaluation reports Peder wrote on all his teachers. This fact would probably keep her from moving into an assistant principal position she really wanted.

Peder observed me teach. I really came into my own as a teacher during this period. I taught between thirty-three and thirty-six sixth grade students in a self-contained classroom each of my three years at Williams. To say that our school was overcrowded is to minimize the problem. We were severely overcrowded. I pushed my students to read and write so much that at one *back-to-school* night, probably in September of 1979, one of the parents, an Asian-American who was also a science professor at UT, expressed a concern to me, in front of a classroom filled with the parents of my students, that it appeared his daughter was going to spend a very busy year being in my classroom, adding, "Will your students get a chance to play and go outside?" I had just exemplified a typical day in my classroom for my students. This UT professor was a bit out of line with his question. I had just walked-them through a typical day for my students.

I don't remember what my response was to satisfy him. It was probably something like, "We have a thirty-minute recess period immediately after lunch every day. And just prior to their recess, they have thirty minutes for lunch with their friends." I didn't add anything else. But afterwards, I thought of all the things I put my students through every day that I could have said. On the days we have spent an inordinate amount of time doing academic work, and I can spot a face or two showing signs of duress, I would say to the class, "Everyone put your pencils down, leave your notebooks and textbooks open to the page you are working on, and line up at the door. Let's file out and stay in your lines once you are outside."

(Before going further, the reader should know that all of the sixth grade classrooms were in portable buildings. *Stepping outside* is stepping out into an open field. Our portables are fully 150 to 200 yards from the fence that borders the entire school grounds.) My next set of instructions to my class was "Okay, I will race all of you to the fence and back. You cannot run back until you have touched the fence. Last person back has to clean the chalkboards after school." I always made it a point to fall back and be the last person back every time we did this. We would then rest a couple of minutes and enjoy a drink of water before going back into our classroom.

I just had a flashback to one of my outstanding students during that 1982 school year. It was the daughter of that Asian-American professor from UT. Speaking of the word *prolific*, she—I could name her if I wanted to just use a name; truth is, I would be lying. I don't remember her name—was a prolific writer. And the reason I remember this incident is because she and several of my students wrote personal notes to me on their weekly book reports. (Regarding this requirement of mine: Each student was required to read a complete story book, each week. I took them to the library every Monday to ensure they selected one from *that* library. The book report, with complete references to book title, author, and more, was always at the top of their report. A three hundred to five hundred word synopsis had to follow. The report ended with a 150–200 word reaction by the student. It was the only homework they ever had over a weekend. They had homework every day, minimally for forty-five minutes to an hour. All book reports were always due first thing on Monday.

Well, several students would write outside the body of the lined paper, usually from bottom to top, with a personal note or two. This student I am referring to was the first to do it (and she may have told others that she did it and that I responded to her). Her note was "Mr. Pérez, how was your weekend? Our dad took us to the coast, and we had a lot of fun. I hope you had a chance to spend it with your family, too." I am, of course, paraphrasing, but right on target with her note.

(Note: All of my students wrote in very legible cursive writing. For the one or two students who had problems with their cursive writing, I would have them practice over the weekends and hand in their practice papers to me on Monday. Almost all the girls in my class had beautiful penmanship.)

(A few words on calling me "Mr. Pérez." Everyone on the faculty knew Peder and I had PhDs. They started calling me "Dr. Pérez." I immediately told them I was "Roberto." They all knew Peder as... Peder. In the years ahead of this year, and in the fourteen consecutive years I spent as principal in three different states, my professional staff always called me Roberto. From 1999 until I retired from the world of *paid/compensated work* as an adjunct professor at two universities in the DC area in 2015, I had a hard time convincing my graduate students to call me Roberto. I got tired of saying, "I'm one of you.")

The reader has to remember that I took a lot of graduate courses in education. My guess, without having to look at my transcripts, is that I acquired well over sixty semester hours for each of both my masters and PhD. I acquired 184 quarter hours for my undergraduate degree at Florida State. So all this is to say I knew what worked in the classroom that would motivate students and I also knew from my dissertation how to work on job satisfaction. On this latter point, substitute the construct motivation for job satisfaction because I had it down to a science on how to make school interesting for my students. There were few dull moments in my classroom.

The most successful of my instructional strategies was to have my students have a major say in most of the things we did. Of course, I always had veto power. They knew that first hand. I asked them to evaluate everything we did. Most of the time it was a short response survey, and it was always anonymous. Sometimes, on a Friday, usually, I would ask them to individually evaluate my performance. One of my favorite surveys was to have them complete this sentence by filling in the blank lines: "Mr. Pérez reminds me of_____(any animal) because _____." Nine of every ten were mostly complimentary. There was one, one year, that I will take with me until the day I am cremated. "Mr. Pérez reminds me of my cat because he is easy to fool."

Now, I did not feel embarrassed for one minute. I sometimes would act as if I didn't know some things that were going on in the classroom, especially if I could get extended mileage from my *playing dumb*. I remember very well who the student was who wrote this. She was one of my outstanding students (and *not* the Asian American girl I have already referred to). It was a student who felt no one was as good as her. In fact, she may have also walked around our classroom with her nose uplifted a bit. I loved having her in my classroom. She initiated so many discussions on boring topics that, in my mind only, I would think "*Yes*. I just knew *she* would bring this up."

I have already written that our school had close to two thousand students. Yet, every morning, all of us, in classroom formation, would sit on the large gym floor until the beginning of the school day. Then one of the teachers on duty would call the gym to attention, we would all say the Pledge of Allegiance, someone would read announcements, and we would all file out by grade level. (There was a duty roster for professional staff; three of us each school day) to supervise all of them as they sat on a very clean and polished gym floor.)

One morning when we were all waiting for the school bell to ring to start our day, I entered the gym only a few seconds before the bell rang. Everyone was waiting for the bell. The gym, if you can believe this, was in dead silence. I had been absent for six or seven days with a severe case of the flu. When I walked up to stand in front of my class, *all* of my class members stood up (usually no one stands until the leader says, "Please rise.") and started applauding my presence. No one else in the gym had risen, only my class. It took everything I could muster to not start crying. I did feel my eyes moistened a lot.

The other five members of our team were all outstanding and experienced teachers. All knew the sixth grade curriculum from A to Z. We were *self-contained,* so we taught all subjects. We taught pre-algebra. Our science curriculum included a lengthy unit on "Endangered Species" of animals. I tried my very best to not ask too many questions about the essential objectives needing to be mastered by our students. What I did was to observe them a lot. We met every day after our students went home and I was an ardent participant at all our meetings. I listened attentively and picked up a lot of information from them and was able to apply most of it.

Teaching high school Air Force ROTC at Holy Cross High school during the spring of 1972 was a completely different experience. Those students were fully in the adolescent stage. I now have preadolescent students who are still trying to figure out who they are. Here is where our team was truly outstanding. We shared everything about our students. Some came from tough home environments. We talked about how to help them. Our sixth grade student body alone numbered slightly over two hundred students. There were times when our team was still meeting at 6:00 p.m. and even later. School let out at 3:30.

Most sixth grade students are eleven to twelve years old. A couple may have started school late because of their birth month and could even be thirteen. Then there was the occasional fourteen-year-old who may have been retained for one or more grades. Such was the case with Edgar. He was also quite husky, but not fat. He had a specific learning disability, a processing problem when he received information that he could not connect to prior learning. He may have had dyslexia but was never diagnosed as having it. He was very well behaved, a good listener, and had the most positive attitude of any student. Edgar was also our "fixer-upper." He could fix overhead projectors, recorders, practically any of the few technologically advanced instruments we had in any of our classrooms. Nearing the end of the school year, Edgar's last at Williams Elementary School, a member of our team asked, "What is going to become of Edgar? What will he be doing six years from now? Ten years from now? Or even in later years?"

Another member of our team almost immediately answered the question. "What Edgar will be doing is probably supervising half of these students who get As and Bs as most of them will be working for him. I see Edgar as making it big inspite of his learning disability." No one on the team disagreed with this prediction.

During Peder's last year as principal, he was absent for at least eight to ten days during the school year. He wasn't ill or doing other school business. I suspect now that he was interviewing at some schools back in the state of Washington in his efforts to go back to his home state. While our school had an assistant principal, and I always thought she was an outstanding administrator, Peder always asked me to substitute as principal while he was out. The lady who was the assistant principal never complained or seem to mind that Peder preferred I fill in for him while he was out.

I did have one memorable experience as Peder's substitute. I have mentioned how the entire school sat as individual classrooms in our huge gym every morning. We are talking of 1,800 students here. Still, the gym was big enough to fit all of us easily. The sixth grade classes sat right next to the kindergarten classes. This was not by design or for any other reason. On one morning, a five-year-old kindergarten boy had two $20 bills in his tight right hand that his mother sent with instructions to give to his teacher. They were not in an envelope, inside an 8 × 11 ½ sheet of paper, or inside anything else. They were just two $20 bills in his tight right hand. When he got to his classroom, he was minus the two $20 bills. When the teacher asked the boy if he had something his mother had sent to school, the boy said he had some money but he must have dropped them somewhere. The teacher came to the office to inform me that she didn't think the boy dropped the money. She suspected one of the sixth grade students sitting next to her class had taken the money. I took the boy to this sixth grade classroom and asked him to identify the student who had taken his money. The boy could not. He did not remember. Although this was not my sixth grade class, I knew everyone in the class. I picked five students to come to the office to talk to me about what they saw. I talked to them individually. Each denied having anything to do with this theft.

I spent the entire morning talking to them individually. I had been around students of this age long enough to know that one of them had stolen the boy's money. One finally confessed that he had seen Joe H. take the boy's money. I dismissed them all but Joe. Joe denied he was the guilty one. Joe looked at me with the straightest look, not blinking an eyelash even once. He was very convincing. He was not going to admit he had taken the money.

It is now early afternoon, and this is the only task I have been able to work on all day. I finally decided I would call Joe's father and tell him his son was accused, that he was seen taking the money. I knew I risked getting yelled at by a parent for simply taking the word of other students of the same age. What if they had a bone to pick with his son? What if they were covering up for themselves? Joe's father said he would be right over. When Joe's father walked into our office, Joe was sitting in the same office and had no idea his father was coming to see about this accusation. As soon as Joe's father walked in, Joe stood up and yelled, "I did it. I did it. Don't let him hit me. I did it. I did it." Case solved. Thank you, Joe's father.

Joe's father wanted me to give Joe three swats across his buttocks with a paddle. Texas was one of over twenty-five states (at that time, not sure if this is still the case today), as well as the Austin Public Schools, that permitted corporal punishment with parental approval and a professional witness present for the swatting. I told Joe's father that Dr. Matthews did not permit corporal punishment in his school; therefore, I denied his request. I suspended him from school for three days. The parent said something like, "A lot of good that will do. Joe will enjoy not being in school." This remark by Joe's father is one that I would remember when I became a principal.

During these same three years I spent at Williams, I also took four graduate courses at Texas State University in San Marcos. The four courses, along with a completed year-long internship as a school administrator, would allow me to be awarded an administrative certificate to qualify me as a candidate for either an assistant principalship or a full principalship. Peder volunteered to supervise this internship. The internship was meant to last one full year. The required experiences by the intern included everything in which a principal may need to engage. Because I was also teaching sixth grade while doing the internship, I did not feel I had found the time to do everything required of interns. It was all on a trust basis. Peder told me to complete the forms whether or not I had done them. I didn't. I told TSU to give me an incomplete and I would finish the other experiences during the second year. One of the unmet tasks was riding the school bus with students several times, both morning and afternoon. I got both experiences in during my second year.

Before the end of my third year as a sixth grade teacher, I was selected as an assistant principal at Odom Elementary School there in Austin. My one year at Odom would be 1982–83. Odom had a thousand students and grades K through sixth. The principal I would work under would be a very conservative and experienced principal named Carol Moring. Carol was the epitome of a *School Marm*. More than that, Carol was every bit as tall as I was (6' 2"). Almost every teacher had to look up at her when they talked to each other. She was also a lady of "*few words*," telling me once when we conferred about something I was tasked to do that she was much more *economical with her words* than I was with mine.

On another occasion, there was one parent of two children at Odom who was "deathly" afraid to talk to, or with, her. This parent told me once, "I couldn't do what you do when you talk to her. You stand right next to her and converse. I could never do that. I am very afraid of her."

(Note: The years immediately after completing my doctorate were especially hard years for me. That one year spent on my dissertation was a year full of risks. The experience at St. Edwards also had me wondering about my decision making and my penchant for *going out on a limb* only to prove my philosophy and demand that everyone had to treat me with respect and dignity, as I did them. The thought of everyone having *peaks and valleys* in one's life was something that never entered my mind. I wanted everything to always be perfect. If it wasn't, then it was because of me. Resigning from a tenured professorial position, one that probably hundreds of PhDs who were recent graduates would have *killed* to get, was really a huge risk. But not in my mind. I felt relieved of not having to contend with people who only posed as professionals but were really people I had to *carry with me* as I did my job and more than carried my end of the bargain.

As an aside to this last comment about resigning from St. Edward's, I had shared my hiring with my family. All my brothers and sisters were proud of me. Since none had attended college, few of them understood the work it took to complete my dissertation. Carolina and Chacha would have been very proud of me. But they had been gone for so many years, Carolina for thirty-five years, Chacha for twenty-two. But there was Jovita. She had an idea of how much work it took. She had no problem telling her friends, especially her clients where she worked as a hairdresser. I never heard her say anything, of course. I was never there at her shop. By the way, it was called the White House Beauty Salon...because the shop was in a white house. All her customers were also white ladies. She was known as "Jo."

Well, after telling Grace and my four grown children of my actions, it was time to tell Jovita. She was, of course, disappointed. I suppose she would have to tell the truth if one of her customers or the lady who owned the shop were to ask her how her brother was doing, she would have to tell them the truth. My family is that kind of a family. We seldom lie. I do remember her reaction to me when I told her I had quit my job at St. Edward's. "What's the matter, Bobby, couldn't you do the job? Was it too hard for you?"

I didn't tell her the real reason I quit. I just said something like, "Jovita, I doubled my salary by returning to the classroom. Remember, I have a family." And that was exactly what I said to her.

But I started questioning everything I did. Suddenly, after attending college on a part-time basis, after work and on Saturdays, for fifteen years while earning an undergraduate degree from Florida State University with a 3.5 average and two advanced degrees with an even higher grade point average, I was really a very *unhappy camper*, and my mind started thinking in ways I had never thought before. I was now 51 years old. There was a song made famous by Peggy Lee that had lyrics that said something like, "Is that all there is...?" That song would pop up on my mind frequently, day and night. I never suspected I was going through some change of life. But I was. I left Grace, my family, and went out on my own. This was not something I was proud of, or something that I later did not regret.

I would be remiss if I tried fitting all that I went through and the lives I hurt if I just tried fitting this part of my life into the middle of a period when I left the classroom after three years of teaching and entered the administration field called the *principalship*, so I won't. I will dedicate my last chapter to this shameful part of my life and attempt to keep it all in its proper context.

Now, back to Williams Elementary School, Odom Elementary School, the Austin, Texas, Public Schools, and school year 1982–83.

On Being a Principal in Austin, Texas

I have already mentioned that I came into my own while teaching at Williams Elementary School as a sixth grade teacher who taught all subjects. My class membership was never less than thirty students. Williams was a bit more middle class than Odom Elementary School was. Williams also had more white students. The breakdown at Williams was in the vicinity of 70% white, 25% Latino, and 5% African American. Williams was also in one of the newer sub divisions of Austin. There were more new homes here than at Odom. Odom was several miles closer to downtown Austin, so the minority population was a bit higher. The white student population at Odom was more like 55%, Latinos at 30%, and African Americans students at 15%. Both schools were very *middle class* and the number of students who were on free or reduced lunch status at Odom was just under 30%. The free or reduced lunch student population at Williams was under 15%.

Mrs. Moring and I met for an extended meeting once the administrative placements were announced. She knew I had been an associate director for a Teacher Corps project at UT for several years and had supervised internships for dozens of graduate students while there and then again at St. Edward's. I had several years of experience observing teachers teach and also conducting pre and post observation conferences and writing formal evaluations. She told me she wanted me to take charge of that aspect of the supervision of Odom teachers. The professional staff at Odom, with its one thousand students in grades kindergarten through sixth grade, special area teachers, special education teachers, counselors, and other teachers who serviced students with special needs, probably numbered between seventy-five and eighty educators. I would need to formally observe each one twice during the school year. The observation process had several parts to it. The teacher and I had to meet for a pre-observation conference wherein the teacher would identify the lesson, objectives, date, and time. This would not take long. The observation itself was usually forty-five minutes to an hour. The post observation conference, where the teacher would get feedback on whether or not I thought he or she realized her objectives for the lesson, usually took thirty to forty-five minutes.

By the way, the observation of classroom teachers is a course taught in Departments of Education at graduate schools. I had received the same training during the summer of 1974 at State University of New York (SUNY) at Buffalo, New York, for a one-week, eight-hours-per-day activity when I joined the Teacher Corps project at UT, Austin. I will never forget my instructor because of his last name. His full name was Lou Sinatra.

The supervision of classroom teachers involves much more than formally observing them in a teaching sequence. Administrators, as instructional leaders, have the responsibility of also being in all the school's classrooms every day by doing *walk-throughs* to quietly and without interrupting observe teachers teach and, if necessary, and under confidential conditions, provide them with feedback for improvement. My procedure, if the teacher and I met in a personal conference if we needed to, was to always give them kudos for all the good things I saw while in the teacher's classroom. Then, after pausing and ensuring I had my consulting face on, I would ask what he or she thought of certain areas that I thought could have been better (but would never tell the teacher these thoughts of mine). I wish I could say that the teachers always mentioned areas they could have done better. They did not. Some did, but they were not the norm. If it was the latter, then I could expect an improvement because the teacher himself or herself identified the area needing a change, and they would own the change. If it was the former, I often made sure that on my subsequent visits to the teacher's classroom, on walk-throughs, I could observe if the teacher improved. If not, my consulting perspective would take on a more direct approach with me stating what I really thought of something the teacher was doing. Even then, the feedback approach has to be nonthreatening. My aim was to see better services to students (through better teaching), not to punish the teacher. None of us are perfect.

Note: The walk-throughs and formal observations of classroom teachers has been a regular part of teaching and learning in all public school classrooms in our country for several decades, probably dating back to the 1960s. I mention this here to emphasize that teachers have been the most supervised licensed professionals in our country. The improvement of teaching skills has always been a responsibility of administrators and supervisors who function in our public schools and are compensated with tax dollars. While teachers are the primary service providers, the interaction between teacher and student is exactly that, an *interactive process* by two people with equal responsibilities, one with teaching, the other with learning. One is a professional who, for the most part and what I have learned to be the case in every school and state where I have worked as a teacher and administrator, works diligently at a 24/7 pace because they *care*. They spend tens of thousands of dollars to earn their degrees and licenses. Yet, easily, they have the most difficult jobs in America attempting to provide a good education to all students. Their pay is not commensurate with their job responsibilities. Many students, at every school, do not interact with the service provider (aka *teacher*) with the best of learning intentions because they (students) are not ready to learn. Their parents have not prepared them to come to school ready to learn by teaching them manners and being responsible.

Further along in this chapter I will mention how I functioned as an assistant principal at Odom Elementary School. It was my only year as an assistant. Yet, it was probably one of the years I grew the most as an instructional leader because of the many functions I took on. Starting with the following school year, 1983–84, and for thirteen consecutive school years, I would function as the principal at five different schools in three different states. One of the items I always covered with all the parents of all my schools at our very first meeting during each of these thirteen years was the item on *responsibility for learning*. I never had a script or notes to look at with this item. I doubt if I ever displayed vocal pauses or even be at a loss for words. I believed in the school responsibility for teaching and learning. I believed equally that our school was not *solely responsible* for this task. Here is what I would say: "My most recent experience as a classroom teacher was with students eleven to fourteen years of age. They were all sixth grade students. I usually had thirty-three to thirty-six students assigned to my classroom. It was during these three years, working under an outstanding principal, that I learned the art and science of teaching and learning."

As the classroom teacher, at every back-to-school night, when I identified myself to parents as their child's teacher for that year, I informed my students' parents that I would assume full responsibility for *teaching* them all they needed to learn while in my classroom for six hours a day for 180 days of the school year. "The responsibility for the *learning* I would share with *them*. They have a responsibility as well. When you send your son or daughter to my classroom to learn, I want you to prepare them by having them show *good manners and respect* for the space other students need in the classroom and also with an attitude that shows their individual responsibility for learning. I can apply disciplinary procedures when I have to, in order to continue teaching, as I would have many other students that I would also have a responsibility to their parents to teach them to the best of my ability. When I have to stop teaching to ask a child to show good manners or show a responsibility for learning, I am failing every student in my classroom."

At Odom, now functioning as an assistant principal, in addition to taking the responsibility for all teacher observations and formal evaluations, I also served as the Spanish interpreter to assist those parents who needed help understanding their responsibility for their children's learning at our school. For some reason, interpreting for Spanish-speaking parents, although it came up at both special education meetings and at parent-teacher conferences, the number of times I had to be involved in this endeavor was but a fraction of what

I had to do six and eleven years later in Maryland and Massachusetts, respectively, when I served as the school principal in those two states.

The reader should know that, as a self-described perfectionist, I wanted to be in on every aspect of the principalship. An added task I took on by myself was the administration of the annual skill tests. At Odom, we administered the Iowa Test of Basic Skills (the ITBS, as known throughout the country) to all students. The tests were administered over a four-day period, Monday through Thursday, and only in the morning, usually in late April of every school year. As stated earlier, our school had over a thousand students. The number of classrooms, for every grade level, was between four and six different sections. Potentially, these skills tests in reading, mathematics, science, and social studies were administered to students in some thirty-five classrooms. Each of these four days, I had to be in school ready to distribute the hundreds of tests and answer sheets to every classroom teacher and also ensure that at the end of testing, each day, I received every test and answer sheet back. Of course, the test booklets did not have any student's name on it. The answer sheets did. At the end of each day, I had the responsibility to secure everything under *lock and key.* It took several hours of *checking.*

Not sure if I have already mentioned that I was a Boy Scout for four to five years. Well, I learned their motto and perfected it. It is *be prepared.* On the weekend before the testing started (it was spring of 1984), I spent Saturday and Sunday at the school preparing. On Monday, all classroom teachers received instructions first thing in the morning to visit my office and obtain their testing materials. For Monday's testing, I prepared over the previous weekend; for Tuesday's, Wednesday's, and Thursday's, I prepared the night before.

I never asked Carol Moring for any help. She never asked if I needed help. She walked around the school building all day long with her eyes wide open. She knew everything was always *copacetic.* And if I may throw in a special note following this last statement, the reason I was here as her assistant only one year. At the end of this one year, she recommended to the superintendent that I be given my own school.

I did get help from our counselor because she didn't see any students over the four days and had time to give to me. Mrs. Moring didn't tell her to help me nor did I. She was just one of those professionals who knew what the task was like and wanted to give me a hand. I welcomed it because I knew what an outstanding person she was, and I could count on things being done correctly, the only way I would accept her help. Still, I am one of those people who usually does things himself if he wants them done perfectly.

I am remembering my one year at Odom with many fond memories. Some were even humorous. There was the time I was working on some document in my office, probably completing a teacher evaluation form, when out of the corner of my eye I see a very small figure on the sidewalk outside our school building. It is moving slowly from right to left. It was a child, probably no more than 2 to 2 ½ years old. Not a big deal, right? Our school is surrounded by private homes on all sides. But wait. I am expecting a larger silhouette to follow right behind this small figure. Mom! Or even, Dad, right? But no, I wait two to three seconds to see if the parent is going to come running after the child before it attempts to cross the street or even get abducted. I stand up, go to the window, and look both ways. There is no one but this child out there on the sidewalk all by itself.

Remember *be prepared*? I knew I couldn't run out there to secure the child by bringing her/him to the school. The child would probably run away, maybe out into the street, as it would be afraid of a man, a stranger, trying to *save it. I* stormed into the outer office where all the clerks were working and quickly asked one of the female office workers to run out there and talk to the child to ask who she/he is and where her mother is. The lady who went out there talked to the child.

Office lady: "Where's your mother?"

Child:

Office Lady: What is your mother's name?"

Child: "Honey."

The child only had a one-word answer for the second question. The lady from our office stayed with the child to see if an adult would come running after her. Sure enough, a lady did come running after the child. The child, a girl, recognized its mother, ran to her, and allowed her mother to pick her up. The mother looked at our office lady and apologized for being so careless.

Another humorous story that occurred during the year was this one about a male student in first grade. He simply could not stop talking out loud in his classroom. His teacher was at her wit's end. Mrs. Moring and I ended up seeing him almost daily, often just long enough to allow his teacher enough time to teach a lesson. The student was all of 6 years old and to say he was verbose is to put it extremely mildly. As I reflect on counseling this young boy, or even observing Mrs. Moring talk with him, I have this image of the boy talking without ending a subject/predicate sentence and *just running them* all together. I joined Mrs. Moring this one day and simply forbade him to talk while I cautioned him that he had to also practice listening. As soon as I paused, he started up again. This one time we had had him in our office long enough, and I sent him back to his classroom. He had been to the office so many times he had a well-worn path in the hallway to both our office and his classroom. This time, Mrs. Moring and I stood just outside her office door to watch the young boy walk to the outer office door to leave the greater office area. The three or four office ladies who also worked in this greater office area also stopped working long enough to watch the boy walk (gingerly, at that) to open the other door. The boy stopped before opening the door, looked back at both Mrs. Moring and me, as if he knew we were watching him, and said loud enough for all in the office to hear him. "You know, you two are the very best principals I have ever had." He then walked out and went merrily on his way back to his classroom.

For two to three seconds, there was complete silence in the office. All of us were making sure the boy got far enough down the hallway to *not* hear all of us bust out laughing.

There were other humorous events, though, and I will get to one more after explaining that the end of this school year is quickly approaching.

By early May of that same year, 1984, the Austin Public Schools announced their principal and assistant principal appointments beginning that summer. My name was on the list. I was being assigned as the new principal at Bryker Woods Elementary School. The school was only a half mile from the University of Texas at Austin. Like all Austin Public Schools, Bryker Woods served students from two or more communities, as schools were paired in order to achieve a racial balance. Students in grades first to third who lived on the established radius of De Zavala Elementary School in East Austin (where mostly families of color and Austin's poorest families lived) would join students in the same grades at Bryker Woods, and were bused to my school. The fourth, fifth, and sixth grade students from the Bryker Woods community would join De Zavala's students in these same three grades and attend De Zavala. These are the years that public schools took on the tremendous burden of expensive busing of students to comply with the law on heterogeneity of all classrooms in all of the Texas public schools.

However, it is still May of 1984, and the current school year has not ended yet. I am still the assistant principal at Odom Elementary School. The administrator assignments are made public, as they also appear in the Austin newspaper, *The Austin American Statesman*. Very quickly, the Odom staff and faculty, and the residents in the Odom community, begin their plans to bid me farewell. The staff and faculty planned a farewell party in which the highlight would be a film about me in that one year I was there. Because I was in and out of everyone's classroom daily (I really could only visit six to eight classrooms per day because I had other duties, most of which involved the required solutions to disciplinary problems as presented mostly by our fifth and sixth grade students), the film revealed a humorous, *but untrue*, manner in which *all* classroom teachers treated me as I walked into their classrooms for my walk-throughs and formal observations daily. A typical depiction was one of me walking into a teacher's classroom quietly as the teacher is conducting a lesson. As soon as I found a seat in the classroom, opened my clipboard to begin writing my observations, the teacher would say something like this to her students: "Okay, boys and girls, it is time for us to have our morning (or afternoon) recess and go outside on the playground. Please begin lining up as you know how." Of course, I'm sitting there, pencil in hand, with nothing to write about. I would soon be all alone in this teacher's classroom. There were four to five examples of this in the film and when the staff and faculty saw the film they couldn't stop laughing. The media specialist, a really savvy tech person for the times (1984), had gotten videos of me (secretly) to provide teachers with the needed sequences to make the video really funny.

It is now summer of 1984. My first meeting as a new principal is with the director of personnel for the Austin Public Schools, even before I went to Bryker Woods and reported to the director of all the area schools of which my school is one of its members. I have still not seen my school. The DP's name is Perry Jackson, and I would find in the next few years that Mr. Jackson was one of the most dedicated personnel directors I would find in Texas, Maryland, or Massachusetts. More on him as we continue with my experiences as an educator. Why see the DP first? All principals have to staff their schools and be ready for the start of the next school year with every service provider present and ready for the opening of school. I have to work on staffing as the very first and most important aspect of starting a new school year. Perry had already selected ten to twelve teacher applicant files and had also separated them to select those applicants who best fit my student population. He told me this the very first time we met in his office. I immediately formed (*cemented*, really) this bias about America's public schools. I just knew we had the very best schools of any country anywhere. We had professionals with only the very best of intentions. No educator I have ever known has worked for the money they make. It is a pittance.

I'm going to take a brief pause from this sequence to mention why I thought Perry Jackson was one of the most dedicated professionals I had ever met, or ever will. I'm going to move forward one full year. It is now summer of 1985. A few significant changes have occurred with my role as a school principal, but more on this later. First, summer of 1985: I go through the same routines to prepare for my second year as a principal. I visit with Perry and get files on prospective teachers. I pursue them, set up selection committees, interview them, *hire some of them*, and prepare for the first day of school for the year 1985–86. During the week prior to the opening of school, which is on the Tuesday after Labor Day, our staff and faculty prepare every day. There is training of all kinds, new programs to learn, school schedules to memorize, lots and lots of coordination meetings to have our school run like clockwork. I would have it no other way. On Friday morning, I had our last faculty meeting before the first day of school and went over every minute of that first day with the entire staff and faculty. I can still hear one of my third grade teachers say loud enough for all to hear: "It's like being read a story." I had rehearsed my presentation several times during the night to ensure I covered every hour and minute of that first day of school.

It is now 3:00 P.M. on this same Friday before the Tuesday, with most staff and faculty eager to start a three-day weekend, and many teachers are completely ready for the first day of school and are getting ready to go home (I had told them to leave as soon as they could as they have had a tough week). I write this knowing full well that already at least six or seven teachers have already asked me if I would be here on Saturday as they want to come in and put the finishing touches to their preparation. There is a knock on my office door. It was one of my new hires, a lady in her early forties who was late getting started on a career because she stayed home with her young children. She walks in on my cue, "Hi, Mary. Come on in." She closes the door behind her. My first thoughts were that she came in to ask for some help getting ready for the first day of school next Tuesday. I intended to spend Saturday here at school and even Sunday. I anticipated an easy problem to solve for her.

Mary gets emotional and, without raising her voice, states unequivocally, "I CANNOT DO IT! I CANNOT DO IT. I KNOW I CANNOT DO IT. I DO NOT THINK I CAN TEACH THESE FIRST GRADERS. THEY NEED A TEACHER. I AM NOT READY! I CANNOT DO IT."

For those who know me, they know I did not get startled. I did not equate her in emotions. "Mary, sit down. Let's talk. I want to hear everything that is on your mind. I will help you get ready. I'll come in and go over that first day with you tomorrow. If we have to, we can repeat it on Sunday."

This came next. And no, Mary did not sit down. I now sensed that Mary had a plan to quit and absolutely nothing was going to stop her. "NO! NO! I HAVEN'T SLEPT ONE NIGHT THIS WEEK WORRYING ABOUT FAILING. DR. PEREZ, I QUIT! GET SOMEONE ELSE." She then stormed out of the office and within minutes I saw her go out the door with a couple of personal bags and was gone.

Before telling the reader that I solved this problem, there are a few more things the reader should know. Ever hear of *par for the course*? Principals all over our country face similar problems, not just every year, but every month, every week, and several times a day if not every hour. Later on you'll hear of the parent at one of my schools in Massachusetts who was getting out of prison and was going to come after his son, who attended my school, "and no one is going to stop me from taking him." A conference with the child's mother put things in much worse perspective than one of my teachers quitting. But alas! I regress. You'll hear about this second case soon enough. It is several years away.

And no, I did not go after Mary. Ever hear of "There but for the grace of God go I?" Yeah, things could have been worse. This could have happened in the middle of the week in our second or third month of school. I sat back in my chair and reflected. Do I start the year with substitute teachers? No way. Now what. Hmm. It isn't 4:30 yet. My man Perry Jackson must still be in his office. He didn't strike me as the kind of guy who left early for the weekend. Sure enough. I called. He answered. Had probably let all the secretaries go and start the long weekend early. I told him the whole story behind Mary quitting. Told him everything, as well as my reason for calling him. "Perry, I want to see if there are any outstanding teachers left that we didn't hire. And may I come up right now to check folders, take their names and phone numbers, call them, and see if I can interview some of them tomorrow, or even Sunday."

"Come on over. I'll have some coffee ready."

It was between eight and nine o'clock that night before I got through reviewing the *best of the last*. All four of my selections came in for interviews the next day, a Saturday. I had called two of our teachers to ask if they could give up their Saturday morning to assist me with these interviews. They were two teachers who I considered *gung ho* and would do anything for children. Both said the equivalent of "Dr. Perez, what time do you want me to come?" (and the reason teachers are special people in my book). All of you out there attending these book club meetings have them to thank for your ability to participate socially.

My three-person committee selected a person who became a great teacher. I told her I would be in school Sunday and Monday to help her get her classroom ready and also brief her on all the school procedures so she wouldn't miss a beat. My three-day weekend turned out to be three additional long days of work before I started my short week of only four school days that first week of school. Actually, while I have not mentioned this before, there were some renovations made to my school (Bryker Woods) that would not be finished until end of day Sunday, just two days before the start of the school year. When the contractors left on Sunday, my school was "in shambles." Tables, desks, cabinets, *every piece of furniture*, was doubled up (on top of each other) or otherwise just "everywhere. The rooms affected were the dining room, the all-purpose room, and all the hallways. The classrooms were not affected, and all were ready to receive students on Tuesday morning (as far as classrooms being set up). Yeah, my teachers were worried when they left on Friday. But I told them, "Don't worry. We will get the rest of the school ready."

It is important for the reader to know that principals, teachers, all support staff, and custodians are on annual salaries. They (we) do not get paid for overtime. Yet, my two custodians were there early on Monday morning (Labor Day) to assist me in setting up the all the furniture in all the required rooms and hallways. They also swept, mopped, and waxed the floors so that when parents and students walked in on Tuesday morning, they found the school they wanted their children to attend. My staff and I saw to that.

(From a couple of paragraphs back: "A few significant changes have occurred with my role as a school principal, but more on this later...") Well, here is what I meant: At the end of my first year as Principal at Bryker Woods, I am given a second school, Pease Elementary School. Pease is on Twelfth Street, very close to downtown Austin. It has less than two hundred students and only about eight classrooms, grades kindergarten through third grade, just like Bryker Woods. Obviously, with my three hundred students, the total is barely five hundred students, if that many. Surely I could handle it if Pease had an assistant principal who could carry out the duties of a principal, but under my supervision. Pease was not a problem at all. I had an excellent assistant who did an outstanding job. I tried stopping by the school at least once a day, but often could not when there were pressing problems at Bryker Woods. Still, I did not worry about the school because of my assistant.

It was during the second year of my principalship experience that things really changed. A ruling came down from the Fifth Circuit Court of Appeals in New Orleans that eliminated the need for busing in order to have a racial balance in all of Texas' public schools. The new ruling made all schools "unitary." I cannot explain the court's interpretation of how they defined the term. Webster's says it means *having the nature of a unit, a whole.* My interpretation was that all Texas students had to attend their neighborhood schools to make them unitary or "whole."

I was opposed to this action by the courts. My students from De Zavala were all progressing because of the heterogeneity of the composition of students at my school. Of the three hundred students, about half came from De Zavala. The other half were the mostly middle class students from the Bryker Woods community. There was one exception to the attempts to have heterogeneous groups with the busing of students: Kindergarten students *had not* been bused. At all schools in Austin, kindergarten students always went to their home schools. My students who lived in the Bryker Woods community were exemplifying proper language, courtesies, and even offering help to many students from the De Zavala school who struggled with their lessons. I told my supervisor that sending my De Zavala students in grades one, two, and three back to their home schools would only delay their progression. But there was no stopping the new court order. I felt so bad for my De Zavala students that I told the superintendent in a private meeting that he may as well send me to East Austin, too. He didn't hesitate. He did exactly that. Evidently my conference with him was not at his pleasure and, while he didn't oppose my strong request to send me, too, moving me out of Bryker Woods could possibly cause him some problems with the local community. I could tell he was doing something he had not planned to do.

Before revealing my experiences in East Austin for the next three years, a few more details about my second, and last, year at Bryker Woods. The students from De Zavala presented me with most of the classroom disruptions. Of the 150 De Zavala students, only 3 to 4 percent would act up in the classroom and cause teachers to have to stop instruction. They were really not a bad group of students, just very behind in their academic progression. The majority of the disruptive students would act up because they simply had trouble coping with the lessons presented by their teachers and would get frustrated. There were no teacher aides to assist, and I had no assistant principal to assist with attempts to help the classroom teacher. There were no parent volunteers in any of the classrooms who could help struggling students with one-on-one help with difficult lessons.

One of the methods I used to assist teachers was being aware that the majority of the disruptions occurred in the afternoon, after all our classes had been to lunch and also to outside recess. I soon realized that both the lunch period and recess had to be under closer supervision so that there would be no disruptions that would *carry over* to their classrooms when the students returned for their afternoon lessons. Because of this, I supervised the first, second, and third grade students in both the lunchroom and on the playground to ensure proper order, language usage, and to ensure that all students showed respect for the space of other students and it was always maintained. Students knew they had to keep their hands to themselves. Their voices had to be in *conversational* tone. The afternoon lessons were usually science and social studies. Both subjects required intense reading on the part of all students. The De Zavala students were our weakest readers and would often have to receive help. When some did not get help, it was often because they felt embarrassment that they needed help. The acting up would begin.

Before citing one particular incident with a very disruptive student who acted up almost daily, a few words on the concept of *corporal punishment* (CP). These are the mid to late 1980s in America and CP was still allowed in some twenty-one states. As of school year 2011–2012 (the latest data on this subject in the literature), there were still nineteen states that had CP as a deterrent against disruptive behavior in our public schools. My source, Google, adds that as far as private schools are concerned, all but two states in 2011–12 allowed CP in their schools. The list includes all of the southern states plus Arizona, Colorado, Idaho, Indiana, Oklahoma, Missouri, Texas, and Wyoming. The five states with the most paddlings for 2011–12 are (# of paddlings and percentage of students are inside parenthesis) Mississippi (31,236 and 6.3%), Texas (28,369 and 0.6%), Alabama (27,260 and 3.2%), Arkansas (20,033 and 4.2%), and Oklahoma (9,972 and 1.5%).

While the Austin Public Schools allowed CP to occur, with parental approval and administered only by the principal with one professional staff member present as a witness, Peder Matthews (Williams E. S.) did not allow it at his school. Carol Moring at Odom did. I should add that CP was administered only for the most serious of offenses, as in intentionally hurting another student seriously.

Most of my faculty and staff did not approve of paddling students. They knew I respected them and would certainly respect their wishes. But they also knew, after I told them, that there are special cases of student behavior that sometimes reach the last resort. If I chose to paddle a student for a very egregious act, then the staff and faculty knew it must have been just that, *a very egregious act*. Before doing so I would first get the student's parents to approve of my decision. Absent their approval, there would be no paddling. In my two years at Bryker Woods, it had only happened once. This one time, the student's misbehavior was not an egregious act that required a paddling, but the student got a paddling nonetheless. Here is the story.

Arnold, a third grade student bused to our school, was a frequent referral to our office. I went to his classroom to remove him at least two or three times each week. This time it was after his teacher had given him several opportunities to stop his disruptive behavior. This particular offense on his part was particularly ugly because he used profanity and yelled it at his teacher. When I counseled him in my office, he started to do the same with me. There was only one thing left to do: Suspend him from school for the rest of the day.

(Allow me to take a brief respite from this sequence to confess to my readers what my philosophy on suspensions was. I was frequently confronted, by parents, teachers, other educators with "if you remove him from school, the student isn't being taught and is probably happy he is going home." I'll concede that this is what happens, but it doesn't change my mind. I have experienced similar situations in three different states in fourteen years of being a principal. What I would have already done is placed him in *in-school suspension* with academic work to do. This has required another staff or faculty member to supervise him. Another strategy is to keep him in my office with work to do and me sitting behind my desk working on paperwork. This last one is not my MO. I never sit behind my desk while students are in school. I am out in classrooms observing teaching and learning. What I will have done with this *home* suspension is this: I have given a classroom teacher with as many as twenty-five other students the time to teach them and not have to quarrel or otherwise attempt to discipline a disruptive student.) The other students have a right to be taught as well. No, the situation is certainly not good for this one student, and a fact that I always share with this one student's parents.

More. I called Arnold's home to have someone come to school to pick Arnold up. I was going to ask for his mother or father so I could explain all that has happened. The father is home and answers the phone. He is not pleased. "I'll be right over, Dr. Perez," and he hangs up. In less than fifteen minutes, Arnold's father is at school. I've been waiting on him. He is very angry. I ask him into my office and close the door behind me . His voice is now several decibels above conversational tone: "THE REASON ARNOLD MISBEHAVES IS BECAUSE HE DOESN'T RESPECT YOU. HE ISN'T AFRAID OF YOU. HE DOESN'T ACT THIS WAY AT HOME. WHAT HE NEEDS IS A GOOD PADDLING FROM YOU." The father pauses for a second or two.

I tell him, "Do you want me to paddle him?"

The father's answer comes quickly. "YES!"

"How many swats, or licks, would you like me to give him?"

"GIVE HIM THREE GOOD ONES!"

I asked my secretary to come in and be the witness. I kept my paddle hidden in the closet. No one had ever seen it. I called Arnold in. I told him, "Your father has requested I paddle you for continuing to cause disruptions in school. Stand over here. Now reach forward and touch your ankles." (I never let him see the paddle. I held it behind me.) As soon as Arnold bent over to touch his ankles, I gave him three quick hard swats on his buttocks. He straightens up, grimaces, and goes out into the outer office. I look over at his father and what I see causes me to close the door so that only he and I are in my office. My secretary had already left the office.

Arnold's father had already started making the face of a man about to start crying. And crying profusely he did. I told him I could leave him alone in my office if he chose or I could talk to him about my philosophy on spankings. I told him, while I had not spanked anyone at this school before, I had spanked students at another Austin school who had caused severely egregious acts of violence against other students, that warranted paddlings and, had done so only with that student's parent's permission. In all previous cases, the students had violently harmed other students. None of those cases were for misbehavior in the classroom. Those students, however, were between fourteen and fifteen years old.

The year was 1985. It was Austin, Texas. I tried never sharing the things that happened at my school with other administrators, but one. She was the area superintendent, and I always thought I needed to keep her informed so she never got calls about things going on at my school without hearing first from me. In my four years under her supervision, I only got kudos from her. Still, I had many administrator friends from all over Austin. On one or two occasions I heard them talk about corporal punishment. A few believed in CP. Most did not. In retrospect, I wanted to say after my last experience at Bryker Woods that I would find other measures to take before suggesting to a parent that we paddle her or his child. What I wanted was to teach my students to read, write, and compute. I am not a psychologist, psychiatrist, social worker, or miracle worker. I know what I have to do to teach and cause students to learn. Before ending my story, I will mention other confrontations with some really troubled students who didn't get spanked. You may wonder why they didn't. All I can say is every case *has its own merits*. You will soon find out what I mean.

I continued being a principal for almost four more years in Austin, at De Zavala Elementary School. Before the end of school year 1989–90, I was driving a large U-Haul with an attached car carrier pulling my car on my way to Rockville, Maryland. That story comes next. But first a little about my remaining years in East Austin as a school principal.

I was the principal at De Zavala Elementary School for school years 1985–86, 1986–87, 1987–88, 1988–89, and half of 1989–90. I had the good fortune of having a wonderful and talented staff and faculty. Of some four hundred students, only two were white. Latino students probably represented 75–80 percent of all students and African American students the remaining 19 percent. I remember having an outstanding media specialist, called librarian at that time, who was probably the very best with whom I ever had the pleasure of working. Her name was Susan Sanders. She read to every student in the school during their "library period" once a week. She had contests that elicited their involvement in reading endeavors, as well as other student behavioral programs that brought the school huge dividends with student comportment. One of her programs was called (am paraphrasing now) "Caught You Being Good."

More about "Caught You Being Good": The staff and faculty received instructions about our participation in the program. We were all given colorful stickers to always have with us any time we saw a student do something good, we would talk to the student only long enough to tell him or her "Caught you being good (and the reason for the recognition)." We would give the student the sticker. The student would keep the sticker in his or her possession until their class had the once-a-week class in the library with Susan and would at that time, upon being asked, turn in all the stickers they had earned since the last time they had the class in the library. Susan, in turn, pasted the stickers on all four walls of the library. Students could see their stickers on the walls of the library any time they were there. I remember that the walls were almost completely full by year's end.

There was one particular time when we received two visitors to our school who came at the end of the school day. They were two ladies who came to see me, and I honestly cannot remember the reason for their visit. What I do remember is that both of them told me how amazed they were at the courteous and complimentary manner shown by our students as the two of them worked their way from their parked car in front of the school and walking up the sidewalk to the schoolhouse door. Both told me they were greeted by almost every student who was walking toward them and away from the school. The "Good afternoon, ladies," "Hellos," and even "I really like that dress you are wearing" to one or even both ladies came from more than just one or two students. I was very pleased, of course and told them those students had a reason for their compliments. They were expecting a sticker from each of the two ladies. I added that if we had time, I would elaborate further on how our school is reaping dividends from this school program.

While De Zavala will always remain on of my mind as one of the schools I will remember with fond memories, there were other less-than-positive experiences I had while there as their principal. Yeah, I continued growing and learning as a principal. Mostly I learned about caring for every student and not only about their learning at our school, but also their well-being, safety, and treating other students as they would like to be treated.

There were other memorable experiences. Like the Friday, I stayed late after school was over. (I almost always stayed late because my MO was to be in classrooms all day long and only in my office after the students had gone home. I returned every phone call and reach a conclusion on each call no matter how late I had to stay in school.) The time was probably around 6:30 or 7:00 in the evening. There were one or two other teachers who also worked late frequently planning lessons for the next school day. This one time, one of them found two of her tires slashed and completely flat. She and I happened to be leaving at the same time, and I also found two of my tires also slashed flat. The reader should know that our school had no parking lot. Our school took up a whole short block in the city of Austin. Anyone visiting or working at this school had to park on the street on the school side of the block. Our tires slashed were the ones nearest to the curb. I am not sure how soon this teacher (I remember name as *Kathy Ward*) was able to get her husband to change her tires. I had to buy two new tires and wait for a service truck to change mine. It was close to ten before I got home.

Another memorable incident at De Zavala occurred when one of our troubled students physically attacked me as I tried talking to him in my office. He was a year or two older than most of the other fifth grade students in his class. He was a special needs student and one who was frequently in my office. I do not remember saying anything to him to offend him. This was never my MO. Still, he suddenly starts swinging his clenched fists at my chest. I will remember to this day hearing the "thud, thud, thud" pounding on my chest but not really feeling any pain. I quickly restrained him and held his arms behind his body. Not sure how I was able to quickly tell my secretary to call the police. This student was completely out of control.

In retrospect, this was my first major mistake as a principal. A police officer arrived within minutes. The student then attempted to hit the police officer. The police officer not only restrained him but also knocked him down to the floor, headfirst. The student's face was the first to hit the floor. It was a concrete floor and blood came shooting from his nose and mouth. We had a nurse on duty. She came in to assist. The police officer left with the student.

I could not have done a worst job than this in handling a difficult situation. I should have tried to get the school custodian or one of two male teachers in the building to assist me. My first thoughts were that this student was going to hurt someone or himself. I thought the police officer's presence would calm the student down. I was completely mistaken. His aggressive behavior toward the police officer escalated everything to heights I didn't think possible.

The student was held in custody until his legal guardians came for him. I suspended him from school for ten days. After ten days, he was admitted to an educational facility for aggressive students. He had either a teacher or an instructional assistant always with him at his new school. He was never left alone. He never returned to my school.

For weeks on end, I thought about him constantly. I tried to rationalize that I had done the best I could under a very difficult situation. But in the middle of the night and in my gut, I always thought I failed him. Still do, to this day.

One last remark about Susan Sanders. I have mentioned what a student-centered and outstanding librarian/media specialist she was. Well, here is an example of how much she gave to the students at our school. Each of the summers she was assigned to De Zavala, she would come to the school during the months of July and August. She met with as many of our school's students as remembered to be there on the days of the week she had informed everyone she was coming. She would then walk all of them to the city library that was some three to four blocks away where she would read to those who asked her to and also to have them check out books to read on their own.

I have now remarried and have two wonderful children, Josef (born on April 5, 1986) and Sofia (born on February 15, 1989). Josef was not quite 3 when Sofia was born. Their mother developed a condition that required major surgery and also having to be immobile for several weeks. Their mother is a native of New York and her parents were unable to assist us in caring for Josef and Sofia or their daughter. I had no one to turn to but *myself*. The Austin Public Schools would allow me a leave of absence on an emergency basis, with pay, if such a situation came up. I had no choice but to ask for one. It was approved. I stayed home to take care of a baby and a three-year-old for six to eight weeks during the spring of 1989.

While I was able to take care of my family problem, I also was forced to leave my school, my students and their parents, my staff and faculty, and also would require a substitute principal take over my school. While the new principal was the one who was there before me and had retired, my decision to do this did not go over very well with my staff and faculty. I believe most thought I left them to take care of someone who really didn't need being cared for. My relationship with my staff and faculty began to sour and was also irreversible.

While I had experienced, I thought, a strong relationship with the hierarchy of our school district, I soon heard from my area superintendent that the superintendent was concerned about my school's morale and teachers now suddenly being unhappy with the principal they have had for soon-to-be four years. The superintendent asked her to supervise me closely to ensure things got back to normal at my school. When I had a one-to-one conference with my area superintendent, and she informed me of this, I tried my best to re-assure her things would return to normal. I said this, knowing that working toward a reconciliation between the staff and me is not something my school needed. What my school needed was a more effective teaching and learning environment for teachers and students. Any other goal or objective is unwarranted and unnecessary. It was time for me to go somewhere else.

With this experience with my wife's health behind me, I reasoned that my best bet would be to apply to schools in New York, Pennsylvania, and Connecticut. These were all areas that were near my children's mother's home and should I need help from members of her family, this would now be possible.

Before sending my résumé and curriculum vitae to school systems, I first had to apply for certification to both teach and to be an administrator in these states. None had *reciprocity* with the state of Texas when it came to the certification of teachers. In other words, receiving certification in Texas to teach and be a school principal was not recognized in these three states. To my dismay, I found very few states where I applied for positions that recognized certificates from Texas as valid. This took me most of the summer months of 1989 to obtain. Through the submission of letters of recommendation and my college transcripts, I received certification as both a classroom teacher and a school administrator in all of these states. I could now apply to work there.

My son Rey will now play a big part in my ability to travel to all of these states, and to several school systems within these states, to interview for vacancies as an administrator. Rey has now been a flight attendant with USAIR for two years and his mother and father, Grace and me, can fly on a space available basis for free. Rey informed me how to check for availability of seats on different flights that would get me to my destination. I must have taken advantage of this benefit some eight to ten times. I could not have flown anywhere at my expense as I never made more than $40 thousand per year all the years I was a principal. I have remembered to always thank him for giving me this privilege.

I did not apply to the Montgomery County Public Schools (MCPS) in Maryland as a principal. I did apply there as an administrator doing in-service training of teachers. I had five years' experience at the University of Texas at Austin, my two years at St. Edward's, and now seven years as an administrator with the Austin Public Schools. Still, it was MCPS who called me first. I was a little surprised that they called to ask me to come for an interview for an open principal position. I should have realized the circumstances were unique because the call came in October of 1989. Did the principal there die? Perhaps get fired? I would soon find out.

On Being a Principal in Rockville, Maryland

Here are the circumstances behind the call that I got from the director of personnel for the Montgomery County Public Schools (MCPS). The first thing that was strange was that I did not apply to MCPS as a principal. They did not recruit nationally. Their principals were all locally trained and generally moved up after first being an assistant at one or more schools, and this was usually preceded by having been selected as an intern for at least one year at one or more schools. This may not be the case anymore. The year was 1989, twenty-seven years ago. Since then, I am sure the five to six different superintendents MCPS has had may have changed how they select their principals.

I immediately did some research on MCPS and was astonished at the size of the school system. At the time, MCPS had thirty high schools, probably sixty to eighty middle schools, and I was astonished to read that they had more than 120 elementary schools. Further research on MCPS revealed that this school system ranked in the top ten in the country on reading and math scores.

Since MCPS requested that *I come for an interview*, they were paying for my travel. However, travel was all they would pay for. I set myself up on flights that would have me arrive on time for the interview and also catch a late flight to get back to Austin before midnight of the same day. I was absent from work only that one day.

I was surprised at the composition of their interview committee. There were seven members on it. All seven were area superintendents. MCPS was divided into seven areas. Their entire line of questioning centered on my prior experiences as a school principal, my philosophy on teaching and learning, and my ability to lead a large cadre of educators to ensure success for every student. Their questions came rapidly, and there were a few follow-up questions by other members of this committee. The one thing I never got around to asking was how and why they selected me since I was not a candidate for a principalship position with this school system. The committee was also very structured, and when they said the interview was over, it was over. My travel for the interview was a one-day occurrence.

At least a month later, after I had now been to several school systems in these three states to interview for vacancies that were coming up at the end of the current school year, but had not been notified of being selected, MCPS called me again. Would I come up for a second interview? I said I would come. The interview was set up for mid-November of 1989.

A little more background information on this move: My second wife and I had bought a home. It was my third home purchase in Austin, Texas. Knowing that I would surely be offered a job somewhere in one of these three states, I put the house up for sale. I sold it quickly and found a home to rent fairly close to where we had been living. My family and I were ready to make a move if and when the opportunity presented itself. While I continued as principal at De Zavala, the school climate was quite a bit different than my first four years there. I continued giving it my very best shot at being the most effective principal I could be. I did not lower my standards and every student, parent, teacher, and staff member was treated with respect and dignity by me. This has always been my MO. Still, the fact that I was traveling to northeastern states to interview for positions did not go unnoticed. Everyone knew I would leave at the end of the current school year.

I came back to Maryland for the second interview. The interview committee was huge. There were at least eight members of the Twinbrook Elementary School staff and faculty. The area superintendent chaired the interview. A couple of other MCPS elementary school principals were also present. Everyone had at least one question to ask of me. After a few questions about my philosophy on teaching and learning, the entire focus then quickly turned to my doctoral dissertation and what this group called site-based management. I came to realize that they were comparing the pros and cons of centralized versus decentralized management, from my dissertation, to their program on site-based management This group was aware of my doctoral work before I was called to come. My dissertation, I told them, was on a comparison of teacher involvement in numerous areas of decision making at their schools. Regarding my study, and based on the responses to my questionnaire by my respondents, I did not find any schools in the entire state of Texas that exhibited the traits that define teacher involvement such that they had a say in decision making at their schools. Thus, I was unable to prove my hypothesis. Questions about this comparison between centralization and decentralization and site-based management now came at a faster pace. The teacher involvement that I did not find in Texas in my study was the *modus operandi* for the school this group was interviewing me to join as their principal.

The reader should know a bit more about why the questioning by this committee centered on my doctoral work. At the time, some ten MCPS schools were engaged in a special program on site-based management, including the one interested in possibly hiring me as their principal. The essence of this ten-school, site-based management program was that a committee was formed at each of the schools that not only consisted of the principal and assistant principal, but also a representative of each role group that was part of the school and community, including an involved parent with children attending that school. Each member of this *leadership committee* joined other members to arrive at a consensus in making decisions concerning the direction the school would take on all their educational programs. For my second interview, it was this committee that conducted the interview, as led by their area superintendent.

Again, the interview ended. I left and was on an airplane back to Austin before the sun had set. The call came the next day. "Dr. Pérez,

the committee has selected you and want you to be their school principal. How soon can you make this move?" After a few seconds of
complete silence from me, I managed to say, "I thought all along this
job was to start at the end of this school year. I am the principal of a
school now, and I cannot just *up and leave.*"

Now comes a more complete explanation of what has happened
at Twinbrook and why the hiring of a principal for this school is
urgently needed, not just for the school system, but mostly for the
Twinbrook community. The principal who had been there for a
number of years was fired. He was accused of sexual abuse by several
teachers. You would think that a school system with such recognition
as MCPS would certainly have more than one current principal who
would accept the challenge and volunteer to come in as principal at
Twinbrook and help this school and community. I was told later that
none did. MCPS, with all its recognition and notoriety, had no one
on board who would come in and give this school and community
relief for all their concerns.

Here we are again, decision-making time. I did not answer the
question right away about *how soon I could make the move.* Initially,
it was out of the question. I considered it unprofessional to resign
for selfish reasons in the middle of the school year. (This thought,
if only on my mind, became weaker and weaker with each passing
day. I began thinking the staff and faculty at De Zavala were ready
to see me go and to get someone else.) Another thought, and probably only in my mind, an almost two week break in our school year
is coming up for the Christmas holidays. De Zavala has the school's
former principal to call on again should I depart at midyear. Then,
too, there were several hundred more students at Twinbrook (than at
De Zavala), who needed a principal.

As one can tell by the direction this argument is taking (if only
in my mind), I started rationalizing numerous decisions that favored
me. Probably the strongest variable that pushed me to accept the offer
from Maryland was that the Twinbrook School and Community
wanted me. I had been interviewed twice and these people *wanted
me.* This approach, *site-based management,* was indicative of a school
system willing to try innovative programs to improve on the delivery

of services to students. This certainly had me thinking more positively about making this move. Everything in Texas was *top-down insofar as management is concerned*. The more I thought about these facts about MCPS, the more I thought I would be heading into an educational environment that reflected more flexibility and innovations than existed in my home state. What is more are the references to my dissertation, now more than ten years after I completed my statewide study. Yes, I had been recognized for *advancing the literature on in-service education* by the Texas Education Agency in 1984, but now I'm being recognized by a committee of educators and parents from a school system 1,500 miles away. This fact was not lost in my mind.

Before the end of the month (November 1989), I notified the Austin Public Schools that I was resigning my position at midyear. I informed the MCPS DP I would *report for duty* on the first school day after New Year's Day 1990. I continued at De Zavala for some three weeks, until the holiday break started. It is at this point that I can pick up where I stopped when I wrote that I would now be driving a large U-Haul van with an accompanying automobile carrier attached.

Maria and Rey played a part in the completion of my wholesale move to Rockville, Maryland. Maria had recently gone through a divorce and was ready to make a new life in Maryland. She accompanied my family and me in this move. Josef was just three months short of his fourth birthday. Sofia was not quite one-year-old baby. Rey and I coordinated the approximate time of our arrival in Rockville, and he was waiting for us at the home I had arranged to rent. Rey was living in Columbia, Maryland, at the time and continuing to work for USAIR as a flight attendant. One of his roommates came to help as we had a large U-Haul filled with our furniture and all our other belongings.

I was immediately impressed with the professionalism displayed by the Twinbrook teachers. I found a more student-centered school environment than I was accustomed to in my Texas experience. The school started every day with a school-wide television show that not only led the entire student body, staff, and faculty in saying the

Pledge of Allegiance but also in making announcements. On my very first day, I was introduced as the new principal on television. Because the Latino percentage of over six hundred students was at near 30 percent, I made several statements in Spanish after first introducing myself in English and stating how excited I was to be their new principal. Before the end of that first day, I visited every classroom in the school and made a more personal introduction of myself to both teachers and students.

Twinbrook, like all MCPS schools, was a local community school. There was no busing of students other than because of distance and/or because they had to cross very congested streets with heavy traffic. The composition of the Twinbrook community was made up of mostly working-class families. There were probably as many home owners as there were families who paid rent to live here. There were also several multiple-floor-housing development buildings where families receiving assistance lived. The majority of people who lived in these housing development buildings were Latino families. However, as I found out when making home visits, I found a high number of White and African American families also living here.

The student population at Twinbrook was between 650 and 675 students. The classrooms included two pre-kindergarten, and four sections each of the following: kindergarten and first through fifth grades. There was also a self-contained classroom of twelve students who were labeled category 4 special needs students. Category 4 students required the school to offer a self-contained classroom environment where students received all their instruction from a specialist with special education credentials and who was assisted by two instructional assistants. With a growing emphasis on inclusion already getting a lot of attention, self-contained special education classrooms for instruction were already starting to be phased out of existence. The number of credentialed teachers, to include counselors, physical education, music, orchestra, and band teachers, plus speech therapists, physical trainers, and one or two more in specific areas such as reading specialists, the professional staff numbered well over sixty people. I also had an assistant principal, one who had been here at Twinbrook for a several years and who helped me tremendously understand the problem that had occurred with the firing of the man I replaced. He was not considered as a replacement for the principal who was fired. In retrospect, this man came to work every day and was a loyal employee. However, as I reflect again on working with him, there were some signs he resented not being given the opportunity.

I had come to Maryland from a very good school system in Texas. Austin, like the rest of the state, and as I found out in my study, was very centralized when it came to all decision-making regarding educational programs. The fact that I was taking over a school involved in site-based management already made MCPS very different from my experiences in Texas. I was eager to learn how it worked. The School Leadership Committee was not supposed to get involved in personnel issues or student disciplinary problems. They also did not get involved with Building Services, an area reserved for the building services manager and the administrators. It took me a few weeks to get into the habit of running educational concerns through this committee. I was decision maker at all my schools in Texas. It was difficult to get out of this habit. Decision making was done by consensus even though we still voted on important issues. Still, when things go wrong at any school, site-based management or not, it is the principal whose head goes on the chopping block. I knew that much from experience. It was no different here in Maryland.

MCPS also had a strong union participation. Every school had a member each from grade levels kindergarten to third grade and from fourth and fifth grades. There was also one additional slot for a representative from the special area teachers. What I didn't find in my study in the state of Texas was alive and well in these ten MCPS schools who were field testing the concept of site-based management.

The ten schools involved in this program met as a group at least once a month and shared the goings-on at each school as a way of everyone learning from each other how they handled certain problems and also got immediate feedback from the other nine schools. There were two high schools involved in this endeavor, along with two middle schools. The other six were elementary schools, including Twinbrook.

Time marches on. I am now well into my second year at Twinbrook. The Leadership Committee had obviously gained a lot of power, locally, as they met frequently and considered themselves sort of the power brokers of the school. Problems began to arise when issues started surfacing regarding areas that I thought were reserved for my decision making because the issues included either staff or students that I thought should be considered confidential and thus, I was the only one that should be handling the issue. Most members of the committee did not see it this way. I began to sense that the more they were in existence, the more authority they felt they had.

This did not go well with me. If there is one major area that principals in every school in America have as their major job responsibility, it is *decision making*. I continued participating with this Leadership Committee. I had to. I was informed of this program and the school's participation in it when I was hired. I thought frequently that of all the things on our agendas, at every meeting, I had just one vote, like every other member, including the parent, the building services representative, and each teacher. But *none of them are ultimately responsible for bad decisions the committee may mak*e. I am.

I continued attending these meetings but not enjoying them. I had no choice. They were so accustomed to having a substitute principal after theirs was fired, that there were times when I thought I was ignored after I made contributions to our discussions. Well, it was just a matter of time for something to go very wrong. A personnel matter came up. It was tabled for a later day because we lacked a quorum for making decisions. The committee selected a date in the near future to meet again to discuss this issue. I informed them that the date they selected was not a good day as I had other things on my calendar that prevented me from being present. I told them to pick another date. One of the members, one who talked as an expert on all issues very often, said as she looked at me, "It's okay for you to be absent on this day, the assistant principal will be here and he can participate in making this decision" (I am paraphrasing what this person said).

That did it! I am the principal of this school. I am being told by one member of this committee that I can be absent, and *they will make the decision*. I stood up. I had had enough of this so-called *site-based management*! I pushed my chair back. I looked at every member present, and said "I AM NOT RETURNING FOR ANY MORE MEETINGS WITH THIS COMMITTEE. I AM NO LONGER A MEMBER OF THIS COMMITTEE. NO BINDING DECISIONS CAN COME FROM THIS COMMITTEE WITHOUT MY INVOLVEMENT, AND I AM NOT RETURNING FOR ANY MORE MEETINGS."

I stormed out. I went to my car and drove home. I remember telling my wife to recall the time I told her I would rather pump gas at a service station than work anywhere where I am not treated with respect and dignity. Then I said, "That day may be here. I just killed Twinbrook's Site-Based Management Program and this will probably piss off the superintendent, the School Board, and probably my staff and faculty and the entire Twinbrook community so much that they may have to fire another principal from this school."

Before going further, know that the area superintendent who played a part in hiring me was still my immediate supervisor. However, each of the seven areas had roaming supervisors who frequently checked their schools to ensure everything is going well. MCPS is a huge system. There were over 150 thousand students and, at the time, an annual budget of more than $750,000 million dollars. Another item I failed to mention was that my pay as a principal was fully $25 thousand dollars more annually than in Austin. I am sure the annual budget for this school system is way past one billion dollars today.

I was at my school the next day after my exit from the Leadership Committee. The roaming supervisor arrived not much later than I did, and I was always the first person at school. She had already heard from one of the members of the committee and wanted to know what happened. Calmly I told her everything and how it had come to this. Somewhere in my explanation I must have said to this lady, "I am either the principal of this school *or I am not*. Twinbrook Elementary School is no longer a *site-based management school*. They have a principal making the decisions, just the way over two hundred other schools in MCPS do."

The area supervisor stayed at my school the entire day. She was told by the area superintendent to stay there and gauge the atmosphere at the school. Were teachers angry? Were parents lining up at the school house door to complain about me? As for the first question, some may have been. I don't know, to this day. As for the second question, there was one parent who complained. She was a member of the committee. No other parents did. The area supervisor did nothing with this parent's concern.

I carried on with my regular duties, visiting classrooms, conducting meetings previously scheduled with staff and faculty, returning calls to parents, and more. Time waits on no one. Days, weeks, and even months came and left. Neither my area superintendent or the superintendent of schools had called me to report to them or anything. I suppose the essence of what ended transpiring was that I, as the principal at Twinbrook, took my school out of this select group of ten schools, *because I could*. I began feeling like I was truly the principal of this school.

A few thoughts to keep in mind as I continue with this factual story are these: First, my guess is that there are over fifty million public school students across all of America. There must be over two hundred thousand public schools. With only a handful of exceptions, every one of these schools has a principal who is charged with a tremendous responsibility of overseeing schools that are safe and are also centers for learning. And not just to the parents of hundreds of children, but to the students themselves and to the staff and faculty of each school. Secondly, none of the role players under site-based management who had become serious decision makers on behalf of all these students, parents, and staff have been trained to exert such an important responsibility. I have been trained, and I accepted this responsibility, a long, long time ago. I have the scars to prove it.

Finally, upon further reflection and the action taken by all of my supervisors, to include the system superintendent and the School Board, the school and community who hired me, and after I abruptly ended a program that they obviously wanted to succeed as they tried to improve on the educational services to students, I have to believe they trusted me to have done what I thought I should have done. They saw me as the true decision maker. In fact, one other principal went up to me at system-wide administrator's meeting and quietly said that he and several other principals have talked about thanking me for not letting site-based management get out of hand and that they now saw an end to this experiment in MCPS.

The school year continued. Parents, students, and the majority of the staff and faculty appreciated the way I ran the school. There was actually more teacher involvement now than there was while the school was being managed by this committee. I formed many committees and also empowered them to make decisions with me regarding almost every aspect of an elementary school in America. School years three and four came and things kept getting better insofar as the school climate at my school. The school climate went from solemn to the enjoyment of things going well. I began feeling support from all role groups, and I felt secure that I was doing a good job as principal and also felt everyone would go to bat for me if anyone in the school system wanted to remove me as an administrator.

There were many incidents of student misbehavior. I sometimes felt like assigning number cards to students when they were referred to the office for causing disruptions and then calling them in some kind of numeric order. There were that many. I was seeing a behavior I seldom saw in Texas schools. Here are a couple of examples: A very husky fifth grade student, probably some forty to fifty pounds overweight, got into trouble almost daily. The worst thing he did was come up behind another fifth grade student, a girl, and rapidly pull her jeans down below her knees. I suspended him from school for three days.

There was another student who was also frequently in trouble. On this occasion, his classroom teacher buzzes me on the intercom and says in a frightened voice, "Dr. Pérez, you have to come quickly. James is sitting in the middle of the classroom and has thrown almost every desk away from the middle of the classroom and is hollering obscenities at me and at the students. All the students are up against the wall and seem to be very afraid. You have to come now."

I hurried to the classroom and saw him sitting on the floor in the middle if the classroom now throwing pencils and small items at the students. I stopped at the door and said with a stern voice, "James, come with me, NOW!" James (in a louder voice that could be heard down the hall): "FUCK YOU!" I hurried over to where he was sitting, not really knowing what I was going to do, but knew immediately what to do when I get next to him. I turned his body around so that I was behind him. I then leaned forward and brought his arms behind his body, and picked him up. I am now carrying him out of the classroom as he tries to butt me with his head . He did get one slanting blow with his head and hit me just below the mouth. I had a cut lip for a few days.

My secretary, Carol Parker, saw me coming and I quickly said to her, "Go to your car and drive it to the front of the school. James and I will get in the backseat, and I want you to drive us to his home." All this is happening at rapid pace. The three of us were in her car and heading toward James's home in a matter of minutes. James's mother, Marie, was in the front yard of her home when she saw us drive up to her home. James's teacher had already called her to describe what he was doing. I still had James under control as he couldn't do anything but perhaps try kicking me or continuing to try to butt me with his head. I rushed into her yard and up to the front door, which was open and then I also opened a screen door. I released James into his living room.

I had no idea what Marie would do. I had already experienced a similar situation with one white student in Texas who hit a younger girl student with a heavy rock only because the little girl called him by his wrong first name. James and this boy in Texas were definitely two birds of one feather. Marie was known for being in school frequently and for yelling at teachers for attempting to correct her children's behavior. "I'm sorry, Dr. Pérez, I am sorry for James's behavior." I looked at her and said, "Don't bring him to school until I tell you he can come back." Carol and I got back in her car and drove to school.

These words from Marie were not what I expected. I expected a flow of obscenities, as was her custom when she had to respond to teachers at our school when they called her to make her aware of her children's unacceptable behavior at school. Upon further reflection, I can only conclude that this was, for Marie, a sudden realization that her son behaves at school very much the way he behaves at home. She realized, too, that I acted as only a school principal knows how, remove the danger at school that can only hurt other students, if not the misbehaving student himself.

Okay, let's put all of this in its proper context and perspective. By system policy, principals can only suspend students for a maximum of ten days. I suspended James for five days, until the following Monday. I called Marie and told her James could return to school on Monday. I was calm with Marie. I treated her with the utmost dignity and respect. My teachers who had run-ins with the entire family (three children and Marie) always wanted me to *do something*. Most of them, although they were not James's teachers, would have run-ins with him when they were on duty supervising student behavior before school started, during duty as a lunchroom or playground supervisors, or at departure time at the end of the school day. They would almost always march James into my office and quickly tell me what he did wrong (use of profanity, not following a rule or policy, hitting someone), and quickly leave. He was always my problem to solve.

The School Board, as well as the superintendent, do not like to see the suspension of students. A common excuse for not wanting students suspended is *"How can students learn if they are sitting at home and not being taught to read and write and compute?"* My response to this comment is that I, too, agree with the comment. However, I would add that if the student is going to attempt to injure other students and disrupt instruction by yelling obscenities and yelling at his principal at the top of his lungs to fuck himself, neither will he or any other student who are subjected to this unruly behavior, *engage in learning to read, write, and compute at my school.* Often, I thought of what I would say if Marie, or any of the other parents of unruly students, would go before the MCPS School Board to complain about me. I always wanted this to happen. I wanted to elaborate on what my responsibilities were as the school's principal. Yes, it was to ensure to parents that their children would all grow academically, psychologically, emotionally, socially, and show progression each year they are in my school. After pausing for one or two seconds, I would tell them that another responsibility I had that I considered just as important as the above was to ensure to all parents that their children were safe at my school. When I suspend a student, it was to ensure that I take this responsibility seriously, and when I tell our parents that their children attend a safe school, they can believe me.

Then again, I do not mind being questioned. Did I arrive at my decision when I was angry and wanted to just *punish* James? Did I arrive at my decision just to get him out of the way so his teacher, and all the other special area teachers who have to contend with him every day, could teach in peace and quiet? Well, yes and no to the first question, and a qualified yes to the second question. I *was* angry at what happened. I was already taking a risk by putting James in Carol's car and driving him home. Part of a principal's credo is to never *ever* put a student in your car or in any car. I was throwing all caution to the wind because it was James who was acting up, and if I have learned anything in my many years in instructional leadership, one must take risks to get the job done. There was never one year when I did not take risks at least a dozen times, in three different states, so I could get the job done.

Actually, Marie had four children at my school. I had her home phone number memorized (of course). We talked frequently. I made more home visits to her home to talk about her children than any other ninety or a hundred parents combined. While we could have talked on the phone, I felt Marie listened to me, and she started to sense that I went to a lot of trouble to communicate with her. I began to feel that she started to believe that we were all truly on her side and would do whatever it took to get all four of her children to *like* coming to school.

As an aside to all of this, the reader may be wondering about my mention of making home visits as if this was also part of my job description. No, it is not. I would ask the reader to remember I came on board as a teacher in 1974, now twenty years ago, and making home visits has always been a part of my philosophy, first as a teacher, and then again as an administrator. I learned about their effectiveness when I was trained as a Teacher Corps intern on the west side of San Antonio's poorest schools. I saw the difference it made on parental attitude toward their child's teacher. The one constant from all these years of making home visits was that I formed partnerships with these parents. We were in this endeavor *together*.

The one thing that soured and never improved was my relationship with my area superintendent and the superintendent of schools. All of my requests for assistance from MCPS to fund certain programs for my students, teachers, and even the school were never approved. The superintendent treated me very unprofessionally at a meeting attended by at least ten other principals. We were all part of a special consortium of schools and the superintendent was informing us of some changes that were being made. At the appropriate time, when there was a pause, I raised my hand to ask a question. He called on me. I asked the question. It was on how the changes would be funded. After all, my school stopped receiving funding assistance ever since I pulled out of the site-based management program. He *ignored* my question completely and, instead, called on someone else. I was embarrassed more than anything else. No, I wasn't angry. I had been getting the cold shoulder now for many months.

I had one or two extremely weak teachers that I tried working with to improve their performance. One of them transferred to another school to get away from me, the other couldn't go anywhere because no one wanted her. She did not report for work more than once without the benefit of leaving lesson plans for a substitute teacher to take her place. This is one of the biggest no-no's for a classroom teacher. Yet, she did this several times. Well, an opportunity came up that would allow me to possibly get her to transfer to another school.

I am already starting to feel guilt and embarrassment at even suggesting that I would not, instead, just get her fired. The teacher had more than twenty-five years of experience. I did not hire her to teach at our school. She was transferred to my school without my approval. I wrote evaluations on every teacher each year. After her first year with me, she received an evaluation that she earned. In other words, her mediocracy at delivering services was in her evaluation. Still, my evaluation of her effectiveness only caused me to meet with her regularly so she could improve. She did not improve. I needed minimally three years' worth of attempts to get her to improve before I could declare her to be incompetent and to have the school system fire her. MCPS just did not fire teachers because of one bad evaluation.

At the end of school year 1993–94, our student population went down. We would have to lose one classroom teacher. The MCPS policy was that the one with the least seniority would be the first to go. All of our youngest teachers were outstanding. The one having to go would not necessarily lose her job. She would be transferred to another school. I remember lying awake at night thinking of how I was going to *not* designate one of my very best teachers to transfer out but to get my weakest teacher to, instead, volunteer to go. MCPS would approve the transfer if the teacher volunteered.

My weak teacher already had one low evaluation in her records for the previous year. She was about to get another weak evaluation, but it would not be weak enough to have the system take any action. If I took her down several notches lower than I was planning to do, she would be reclassified in grade level and this would affect her pay. The loss was in the neighborhood of between eight to ten thousand dollars for the next year. However, she would continue as one of my classroom teachers with a classroom full of students.

The time came for our end-of-year evaluation conference. I wrote *two* evaluations on her. One was the one I had already prepared. It was showing all her areas needing improvement, and it showed all of her weaknesses. But I would continue attempting to help her improve and she would remain a member of our faculty. I put this evaluation in my desk drawer and did not show it to her.

We had our conference. I showed her the weakest of the two evaluations. In retrospect, the evaluation was not very far off target. It would, however, cause her to be reclassified. She would lose a significant part of her salary. She was, of course, very disappointed. She did not attempt to talk me out of it or try to justify to me that I should make some changes because she deserved better. This teacher knew me, and she knew herself. I reminded her of the many times she put the school and me in trouble with her absences. She remembered how I had to counsel her often.

Both of us said nothing for a few minutes. Deep inside of me I wanted to just say, "Okay, okay, Louise, I'll raise the evaluation just enough to have you continue receiving your normal pay. But you have to promise me you are going to change…" But I didn't. She continued speechless for a few more seconds. I suppose she was waiting for my good side to come out of me. It did.

"Tell you what I will do, Louise. I will change your evaluation enough to have you keep your current pay grade on one condition. I will change it if you volunteer to transfer to another school. As you know, we are losing one teacher allocation because of a declining student membership."

One split second after I finished this last sentence, Louise said, "I'll do it. I hereby volunteer to transfer to another school." I asked my secretary to prepare the paperwork. After Louise left my office, I asked my secretary to come in and close the door. I told her everything I had done. Yeah, I had solved our problem and kept all our young outstanding teachers. I was still going to have to look in the mirror and wonder if I even knew that guy I was facing. To this day, twenty-two years later, and until now, only three people knew what I had done. Louise was not in good health. Perhaps that was the reason she had so many absences.

There were numerous incidents that particular school year (1993–94) where I continued being at odds with my area supervisor. While my relationship with my area *higher-ups* continued to be shaky, my relationship with other divisions within MCPS could not have been better. I have mentioned once before that MCPS trained its own principals before appointing them to principalships. Well, for school years 1990–91, 1991–92, and 1992–93, I had a principal intern assigned to my school for an entire year. All three became principals upon ending their internship under me. All three were females, and all three helped our school as much as our school helped them.

My area superintendent received a promotion within the school system, so our school now had a new person taking over. She reminded me a lot of Carol Moring back in Austin because she was also very much of *old school* vintage. She, too, was tall. She could easily have been a sergeant in the army in another life. Once, in my school to *check things out*, she asked that my Building Services supervisor accompany us on a tour of the school. We looked at every nook and cranny. At one time we were in a girl's restroom when she asked Joe Green, my BSS, why he hadn't replaced a window glass partition that was part of that restroom. Joe answered that he had called it in but was told it wasn't bad enough to be replaced. She then reached over to pick a hard container sitting on the floor and banged it against the partition and broke the glass into dozens of pieces. "Call it in and tell them it's an emergency. They'll replace it now."

This new area superintendent also brought with her to this new position an administrative supervisor who knew Carol Parker through another supervisor for whom Carol worked. At the time, the secretary I had at Twinbrook transferred to another school, and I was recruiting a new secretary from the voluntary transfer list. Like for certificated personnel, those with more years of experience are first in line to be considered by the gaining school. Still, the vacancy is posted nonetheless. It is the law. I had many people wanting to come to my school to be our secretary.

The supervisor of whom I refer was a person named Dr. Neil Shipman. He knew Carol through Dr. Naomi Plumer, Carol's supervisor at one of the central offices within MCPS. Naomi Plumer and Neil Shipman were colleagues with MCPS, and their individual staff members, because they worked closely together, knew each other very well. Neil Shipman also knew I was recruiting for a new administrative secretary and knew Carol was interested in such a position.

Neil called Carol and told her that Dr. Pérez at Twinbrook was looking for a new secretary and that Carol should look into possibly being selected. Neil probably told her my school was a good school, and he would call me to put in a good word for her. Carol did in fact volunteer, and I received her name among the five or six people who also volunteered. Neil did call me to recommend Carol Parker.

Carol was a fairly new employee within the system. She was probably last in line as far as seniority is concerned. Being an administrative secretary is a tremendously important position within a school. Most principals rely heavily on them to maintain financial records, cumulative records on all students, and just be the second most important person in any school building. Administrative secretaries must also maintain confidentiality on all matters regarding students, parents, staff, and faculty.

When Neil called, I did not tell him that there was a *fat chance* that I would be able to select Carol because she was down on the seniority list. But his words on Carol did not fall on deaf ears. Now it was up to me to pull off another miracle. Just *how* is another story. Without ever having seen Carol Parker, I wanted her over all the others because she came with a recommendation from a supervisor of mine.

I came up with a plan, and while I wasn't sure the Personnel Office would approve of it, I fully intended to use my plan and then be as convincing as I could be to get the Personnel Office to approve it. I scheduled interviews with *all* the candidates. Also, I did not have any other staff people join me as members of a selection committee because this would ruin my plan. What if every other member of the selection committee wanted someone else and not Carol? I would not take that chance. I am doing the interviews by myself, and if someone complains, I can say this person is to be in on confidential information about personnel and students, and I want to be the sole judge of who it should be.

I called Rochelle Kraus, the person who handled classified personnel and told her I was selecting Carol Parker, and I wanted her to report ASAP. Ms. Kraus asked about all the others who had more seniority than Ms. Parker. I told her I had interviewed all of them and the only person I thought could do the job here was Carol Parker. Ms. Kraus said okay and she would take care of everything else. Carol Parker became my administrative secretary. Carol and I developed a good working relationship, and because Twinbrook was a tough school, she got involved in more activities that are foreign, to put it mildly, to any type of secretarial work, anywhere. She had to referee serious arguments between staff people. She assisted me with student problems as has already been described in this chapter. There was a time or two when things were not going well in the office with inefficient clerks or in the school in general when the office did not coordinate or communicate well with some teachers or other staff. Once, I sort of took it out on her by raising my voice (in the confines of my office, of course). I found out Carol could also be direct with me. She went on to prove to me that the dozens of personnel problems, as well as the student and parent issues that developed in our school, were always kept in strict confidence. I soon learned to trust her more than I did my assistant principal. We became a team, and I shared more and more things with her.

In the meantime, I was seen by some MCPS administrators as *not being one of them*. This comment requires some clarification. Because most principals are products of this school system, and I was not a product of MCPS. I had not learned to always abide by the orders, or whims, of higher-ups. This trait was very peculiar to MCPS. All policies that come down from the central offices must be mission-oriented to the local school systems and its students. Principals have an obligation to ensure that this is always the case. When it isn't in the best interests of the local community, its parents, and students, then the principal of that school should question the policy when it is not.

During the five years I was at Twinbrook, there were an unusually high number of policies that came down from the central offices that put my school at a disadvantage. I questioned each of them at the time they were sent down. It was not a belligerent decision of mine, and I did not mean to be unprofessional. The associate superintendent for Special Education, who was responsible for one particular policy change sent to my school, told me in person that *I was not one of them*. I would have preferred a discussion and his ear to my explanation as to why my school would have problems with this change. I got neither a discussion or his ear.

School year 1994–95 started and the central office continued ignoring my requests for changes. There was one incident that was, obviously, meant to embarrass both my school and me. I called my immediate supervisor, the assistant superintendent for my area, and when she said there was nothing she could do about it, I said (am paraphrasing but essentially what I said), "Fine! I'll do it alone then."

I felt secure in my school and community. My staff and faculty would never allow either the superintendent or the school board to overstep their authority when it came to either disciplining me or even firing me. It is true that I had a rough start with them when I stopped our participation in site-based management, but I soon won their plaudits for a job done well.

During my tenure at Twinbrook, MCPS was involved in a number of law suits by parents of students who were labeled "*Special Education Students*. In almost all cases, it was because their needs were not being met at their assigned schools and these parents wanted MCPS to fund their attendance at private schools where their needs would, supposedly, be met. In something of a paradox, the superintendent and the School Board left me alone, while also ignoring me and my school's needs. It was time for me to move on.

I started looking at professorial vacancies at four-year colleges nationwide. And I was not going after assistant professor positions. I had just turned seventy a year ago. I went after associate professorships, if any were posted. I was a member of the *Association for Curriculum Development*, and they always listed vacancies from all across the country. I also subscribed to *Education Week*. EW had a special multiple-page section to their weekly newspaper with dozens of vacancies. Because I was still trying to get close to my second wife's home state of New York, I applied to Bridgewater State University, at the time (1994) graduating more teachers at all levels than any other university in the northeastern United States. Bridgewater had multiple programs in Liberal Arts Studies and in all the science areas. It was a prestigious university. The university is located some thirty miles west of Boston, Massachusetts.

I did not restrict myself to only colleges and universities. I also applied to school systems in the states of Pennsylvania, New York, and Massachusetts. I had already received certification as both a teacher and as an administrator in the first two states. When one sends applications on a nationwide level, one has to also attach a curriculum vitae, which is a summary of one's education, professional history, and job qualifications for the potential employer to peruse. My college transcripts, for both undergraduate and graduate programs, over 130 semester hours and over 180 quarter hours at Florida State University, were for the most part *almost exclusively As.* I had university experience at the University of Texas at Austin and St. Edward's University. While I also attached personal letters of recommendation from people who thought highly of my work, I also listed every place where I had worked as a teacher and as a school principal. I have no idea if any of these places where I applied called the Superintendents of MCPS or the Austin Public School System. Likewise, I have no idea what they could have told the people *inquiring about me* from the places where I applied. The people against whom I *ranted* for treating me disrespectfully were not the ones who would receive an inquiry asking *who I was.*

What I do know is that several places contacted me to inform me that my application had been accepted and that I had been placed in the top five of the candidates on this nationwide search. This included Bridgewater State University and Wildwood Elementary School. This latter school was located in Amherst, Massachusetts.

As I waited for something to develop, I continued working very hard to make Twinbrook the best elementary school in what was already an outstanding school system. I developed a strong professional working relationship with all staff and faculty members. I remember each of the three administrative interns who (each) spent a full school year under me giving me very positive feedback about their experience training under me. I was unconsciously developing a learning approach that I would eventually bring to full fruition some fifteen years later when I would become a university adjunct professor at two Maryland universities: American University in Washington, DC, and McDaniel College in Westminster, Maryland.

Both Bridgewater State and Wildwood Elementary School contacted me to come for personal interviews. For the former, I was now in the top three of all the candidates. For the latter, I really do not know if anyone else was asked to come for a personal interview.

I went to Amherst to interview for the principalship first. The group who comprised the audience for the interview was enormous.

It was tantamount to being a staff and faculty meeting, except that there were parents of Wildwood students also in the audience. It was a long interview because there were so many questions. They wanted to know who I was and if I was truly the person they wanted. Their school was preschool through sixth grade and the number of students was well over 650. It was one of four elementary schools that made up this particular school system. All four schools would then feed into a middle school and high school that comprised a separate school system from this one. There was also a fairly large Latino student population. No, it did not compare to Twinbrook's thirty-plus percent, but it was certainly in the middle to upper twenties. As with many of the schools where the interest in me was high, my bilingual ability was always a part of my repertoire that made me a desirable candidate.

After the interview, I could sense that I made a good impression, One or two of the questions that were asked of me bordered on the very personal. One that made me sort of *gulp* (after responding) was one that asked who has been the most important person in my life. I immediately thought of my father and said so almost immediately. I had no idea I would get a little emotional about remembering my father, but I sort of choked up a little, and I could feel my eyes moisten. They certainly remembered my introductory statement when the first question was "Who are you?" When I answered, I also mentioned that my father was fifty when I was born and my mother forty.

It was less than twenty-four hours later, when I was already back in Maryland, that I heard from the superintendent who informed me that he was told by the Wildwood School and Community that they had made up their minds and that they wanted him to call and offer me the position. I told the superintendent I had committed to an interview with Bridgewater State University. That interview was coming up in two days. I would call him after that, one way or the other.

Bridgewater State had four faculty members and the chair of the Search Committee conduct the interview. It was a complete change of pace. It was all about teaching and learning. It was also an area in which I was very interested and was spending more and more time reading about and in which I was doing research. We are talking about two notches above a beginning professor and not having to worry about engaging in necessary publishing to compete for tenure. I would be hired with tenure.

The interview lasted between two and three hours. I was then asked to go to lunch with them and the interview would continue in the afternoon with the University Chancellor. I did not have a return flight until that evening, so I immediately said I would do it with pleasure.

A pause here to review what *chancellor* meant to me: A one-word answer is *nothing*. I was to find out later that the chancellor was the university president. What the Interview Committee did not state (up front, to me) was that they were recommending that the university hire me. Being referred to the chancellor was indicative of their recommendation. True, the committee did not have the authority to hire me. But they were highly recommending me to the chancellor.

The chancellor and I conversed for several hours about teaching and learning and the university's role in preparing teachers to teach. He showed me around the university and even recommended real estate brokers to contact. I left feeling like a *million bucks*.

My second wife was evidently not expecting the news that I was hired by Bridgewater State and that I had accepted the position. She was already planning to go to Amherst and, possibly, had already contacted people there that she may have known previously to say that Wildwood wanted me, and she was certain I would accept the position.

A few words about being offered an associate professorship: It would be the culmination of fourteen years of a part-time college education that eventually led to my earning *the* terminal degree, a doctorate, or as is most commonly known, a PhD. Also, each of my three degrees were earned with part-time attendance. It is true that I earned my masters by going two straight years, but even then I worked as a teacher four days of the week for two years. The undergraduate degree from Florida State University was the culmination of seven years of part-time attendance and, with the exception of two and a half years of part-time attendance at FSU, the other semester hours were earned at community colleges. I paid up front for every college semester hour I earned, utilizing the 75 percent tuition assistance the military offered me. I did, finally, borrow money to stop working and complete my dissertation. None of this was a *piece of cake*. I cannot tell the reader how many sleepless nights I spent just looking at the dark ceiling and asking myself, "Roberto, what the hell are you doing? Do you even know?" Oh, I knew. I would fall asleep dreaming of finishing everything. I never lost the zeal to do it. The zeal never left me.

I told my wife I was hired, and I had accepted the position. Well, I may as well have hit her across the head with a two by four! She almost immediately broke down and started crying. My immediate reaction was that maybe she heard that I did *not* accept the position and she was terrified at my having done that. Seconds later I heard (am paraphrasing here but not by much), "But I wanted to go to Amherst," as she continued crying.

Obviously, I did not end up going to Bridgewater State. And honestly, at that time I did not get upset at her for acting like she obviously had all of her life in her family. This woman was all of thirty-seven years old but acting with a very well learned behavior. I also knew who she was (will come back to this knowledge in a moment). She cried or whimpered for, seemingly, hours! Now, mind you, the breadwinner in this family has reached the pinnacle of his career. In doing so, it is also the end of a hard-fought battle with individual incompetents, school systems, and universities that gave me so much hell that I began to believe that hell *is* right here on earth in the form of constant battles to live up to one's philosophy of life and the purpose of life here on earth.

I said I knew who this woman was. Well, the most precious things in my life at the time were two people, one was named Josef and was all of 9 years old. The other was named Sofía and was 6 years old. I kept imagining she would take off with them and keep me from ever seeing them again. I considered her capable of doing just that. And that was something I was just not going to let happen.

I was awake all night wondering how my good fortunes had turned into a living hell. Bridgewater had a hard time accepting my change of mind. They could not believe it. The chair of the Search Committee called me and asked to talk seriously with me. She said I should tell my wife that we *were* going to Bridgewater and that she soon would accept that fact and be satisfied. She tried her very best to convince me. Then, too, as I listened to her, I knew that she and her committee had gone to great lengths to recruit me. A lot of time and hard work had gone into this endeavor. Still, Josef and Sofia were everything to me.

I would be lying if I said I have stopped thinking about this milestone event in my life. It happened twenty-three years ago. Over the years I remember waking up in the middle of the night after having a really bad nightmare in my sleep. The nightmare? The nightmare on more than one occasion was this same event with Bridgewater State University and my second wife. And yet, today, now 2018, I have come to realize it is who I have been all my life. When I walked away from that air force sergeant in Texas in 1964, he could have had me court-martialed for insubordination. When I told my immediate supervisor at St. Edward's University that I expected him to carry his weight and then I resigned a tenured professorship there, I threw all caution to the wind even then. But I have always put having integrity first. Upon reflection of other times in my professional life, I have been here before. I seem to always act this way. Perhaps my decision to not risk losing my son and daughter is indicative of the person I have been all my life. Besides, it was my decision, not my second wife's.

On Being a Principal in Amherst, Massachusetts

The move to Amherst was not too unlike the move from Austin to Rockville, with the exception that Amherst was less than one-third the distance from Rockville, this time *just* 450 miles. Neither of the gaining school systems, in Maryland and Massachusetts, provided any funds to facilitate the move. I had a house full of furniture and a family to move to a new residence. Again, I rented the largest U-Haul trailer and, again, with an attached automobile carrier. I not only drove on perhaps the busiest highway in this part of our country, Interstate 95, but I also had to go through New York City.

The recommendation to me, upon reaching Amherst, was that perhaps I could rent a trailer for a few weeks while I chose a home to buy. We did. Josef and Sofia were only 9 and 6, respectively, so we did not need much room. Nonetheless, it was quite an experience. Fortunately, we were only in that trailer for less than three months. The trailer park was fairly large and had all the accommodations needed to make living there comfortable. We had placed all our furniture in storage while we waited.

Wildwood Elementary School was quite similar to Twinbrook back in Maryland. As stated previously, Wildwood's grade levels spanned from prekindergarten through sixth grade, while Twinbrook only accommodated up to the fifth grade. Wildwood had several hundred more students than Twinbrook. Test scores at Wildwood were fifteen to twenty points higher for grade levels third through sixth grade. Still, almost all School Board meetings had test scores, or related topics concerning test scores, on their agenda. Our test scores at Twinbrook never got close to the test scores at Wildwood. The difference was that the Wildwood school and community worried more about test scores than they did in Maryland.

Upon reflection on this topic (test scores), I am privy to the consistent, or not, involvement of parents in their children's progress in school. While I would never use the label *helicopter parents* to describe the Amherst community, I have to believe that this same *push* parents applied to their school, they also applied to their children to excel in their studies. I was only on duty a few days when I noticed the difference between Wildwood and Twinbrook parent involvement. I could measure this difference visually by comparing the number of parents attending *Back-to-School Night*, attendance at parent-teacher conferences, and by the number of parents questioning me about the existing educational programs for their children. The Amherst parents were twice as involved as the Rockville parents were. Achievement and progress, generally, proved my point. Again, upon reflection, in the six years I had been in these two states as a school instructional leader, I have grown two to three times as much as I would have in an educational environment, such as the ones in Texas, where decisions affecting students are made on a top-down learning atmosphere. I learned, make that *I grew* as an educational leader, by the ages-old axiom, *experience is the best teacher*. As a principal, I had to make twice the number of decisions in Amherst and Rockville than I did in Austin.

Different schools, in different states, yet the one thing that was a constant in these two states, and in the state of Texas as well, was that all of the students, in all three states, looked very much alike. They were between the ages of five and twelve. They dressed similarly. They all acted their age. I observed intelligent, kind, well-mannered, and caring students. This group usually comprised 80 to 85 percent of the students in all three states. Some 15 percent required extra attention because they lacked the foundation to connect the new learning to prior learning. Our teachers and I had to strategize daily to find ways to meet their needs. About one third of this 15 percent of students also came to school with behavioral and/or emotional problems. It is this group that consumed my time.

A pause here is appropriate. I taught as a sixth grade teacher with thirty-three to thirty-six students in a self-contained classroom environment for several years. I had five to six students who required my individual attention two to three hours a day. These were two to three hours a day that kept me away from the rest of the class on a daily basis. This required very careful planning. The behavioral problems would sometimes conclude with keeping students after school. But this required coordination with the student's parents to ensure he or she would be picked up an hour or two after the end of the regular school day. More loss of *time on task* with my students.

Having said (written) the above, it was at Wildwood that my growth as an instructional leader developed in a more versatile and risk-oriented manner. I employed a strategy that I first used extensively at Twinbrook. This strategy, one that I initially tried to use at De Zavala in Austin, was to try to nip in the bud negative student behavior by supervising them closely in the lunchroom and while on recess immediately after lunch. If I suspected there would be disruptions in some of the intermediate grade-level classrooms (fourth through sixth) that afternoon, I pulled the students before they had a chance to spoil their teacher's afternoon lessons.

Student misbehavior was the same in all three states. It was the same five to six students per classroom who came to school with behavioral or emotional problems in all the schools. There was never a single case where I did not engage the student's parents to form a partnership with me to attempt to change the student's behavior. It would not do the particular situation any good if I corrected the behavior of the student at school if the student went home every day and the only reinforcement the student got at home was negative and he or she arrived at school the next day just as angry and emotional as the day before. I could only help the situation if I made a home visit and convinced the student's parents I was interested in their child having success at school. Sometimes it took me weeks to just get to *first base*, so to speak. That is, getting parents to meet with me may take some time. But as I have said before, *time waits on no one*. The last day of school comes. All the students go home for the summer. The building is emptied. And as I looked in the mirror, I always reflected: *Shoot, Roberto, a miracle worker you are* not.

I have to switch now to my personal life in Amherst because this is the place where my life fell apart. I am including as a last chapter to this offering, of my autobiography, an explanation as to how I came to be thrice married. It will be brief, and I will endeavor to not use accusatory language. Most of the participants who played a part in this very low point in my life are still walking around on this planet. I will attempt to use Jack Webb's famous *"Only the facts, ma'am, nothing but the facts"* approach. I believe I have already mentioned that there have been moments of my life of which I am not proud. And they have to be included here. The last chapter of my memoir will be something of an *epilogue* and will attempt to explain a few personal things. I will probably have to repeat a thing or two from this part of this chapter.

My daughter number one once told me, when the two of us were being honest with each other and spilling our guts out (mostly mine, as she had little to spill), "What goes around comes around." Yes! My second wife found someone in Amherst with whom she supposedly fell deeply in love. She made no bones about it. She didn't exactly tell me this, but I could tell she was walking on cloud nine every time this person was in view. By the way, *this person* just happened to be a teacher at Wildwood and, thus, was a member of my staff.

Still, I was not exactly heartbroken. My thoughts were with Josef and Sofia 100 percent of the time. They became my one major concern. I would tolerate almost anything to not ever let these two gems of mine out of my sight. And I did. The truth was that I had plenty to worry about. I started to feel loss, the loss of Josef and Sofia, two very special people in my life. On top of that, what I didn't know about Massachusetts was that the woman, in almost all divorce cases, usually came out of these things *smelling like a rose*. The men are generally taken to the cleaners. After you read more about my divorce in

Massachusetts, you'll understand why my son-in-law Bob Young said to me, "Roberto, you got fucked in Massachusetts!"

If these goings-on were not so comedic, it would really be worse than tragic. Having my second wife leave me for another person was not really a great loss, yet I lived in fear because of Josef and Sofia. Yeah, I lost a lot of sleep over this. I could not see a life without them. I had already spent many years of just the three of us experiencing going on excursions, both while living in Maryland and the one year in Massachusetts. There were very few Saturdays during the years 1992–94 that the two of us did not head for Washington, DC, to visit as many museums as we could. I would often drive all the way to the mall and try to arrive as early as possible to find all-day parking so we could spend the entire day there. I capitalized on one of the two three-to-four-day breaks that students got during the school year to take off with them to Albuquerque for a short vacation. I will mention some really "comedic" occurrences that happened during another vacation in Texas that involved their mother in my epilogue. Another hilarious story concerning my children's mother's newly found partner involved still another member of my instructional staff. More on this dilly below.

A short reprieve from the flow of this part of the chapter is again in order. My children's mother did not work for a living. She had a degree from the University of Texas at Austin and a Texas Teaching Certificate. She kept trying to prove to me that she was going to make a good living with her art work. From all indications, she was good at her art work. I told her it was okay to not contribute to our living expenses. I told her to work on her art work and get really good at it so she could capitalize on her expertise. My Saturday field trips with Josef and Sofia were, initially, meant to give her a break from having to look after Josef and Sofia and concentrate on her art work. I knew, too, that my children's mother had a difficult time getting along with her parents, especially as concerned financial assistance. Having said this, I already had it in my mind that I was going to file for divorce and seek full custody of Josef and Sofia. My foolish, and now quite obviously, completely uninformed, expectations were thoroughly destroyed when I did get my divorce. The Commonwealth of Massachusetts favors the woman in most divorce cases. I had no chance to get my kids.

This next action by me will be seen as foolish by the reader. In fact, for the many of you who have gotten into an *us vs. them* litigious confrontation, it may even be seen as stupid. However, this action by me should also be seen *as me being me*. I am a fair-minded person. I gave my children's mother a $4,000 check to fight me in court because I was going to file for divorce, and I was going to seek custody of Josef and Sofia. Given her infidelities and actions right in front of me, her children, and the Wildwood school and community, I expected to win. It would be *a piece of cake*. My thoughts were that she would get no financial help from her parents and, thus, would it be fair of me to fight her for custody of my children when she had no money to get her own lawyer to fight her case? No, of course not. I told her to get a lawyer. "Here are four thousand bucks."

In retrospect, and if you have been reading this book attentively, it is *truly* me being me. I am a fair person who marches to his own drumbeat. I have my beliefs, my standards, and I have thrown caution to the wind many times in my lifetime already. The reader may be shaking his or her head and saying, "Man! What a fool!" While I saw myself in the mirror daily and knew who that guy was looking at me, and, too, I slept very well even though I was completely broke and not only did all my savings disappear at the age of 56, I could not pay my monthly obligations. I simply did not have enough funds to make ends meet. Not even close.

As an aside, here I am at 56 years of age, and I have only had a single occasion in my entire life when I accepted a very small loan by a relative of mine. I never received financial assistance from my mother, father, brothers, or sisters. Not even when I went colleges and universities all those years. Let's face it. I come from a working-class family. We lived pay check to pay check. The one occasion? During the time Frank Burns and I were practically inseparable, when we only lived one block apart on Hatton Drive and Darby Boulevard in San Antonio, Frank handed me $300 dollars to get out of one particular debt that was accumulating a high interest rate. This was *vintage Willard Franklin Burns,* born in the hills of West Virginia with a heart as big as an elephant.

Frank also advised me on preparing my annual income tax returns so that I never paid more than what most Americans pay. When Frank decided an expense was deductible from his income, *it was deductible.* He would always tell me that if he got audited and an error was discovered on deductions that should not have been listed as such, he would curl his lower lip and tell the auditor while showing the saddest look on his face, "By golly, sir, I cannot believe this error got by me. Well, it certainly was an error on my part. It won't ever happen again. No, sir. Gosh! I can't believe I made such an error." Frank was never audited. He had another belief that I also adopted. He believed that the only people who are audited are those who make silly errors on their returns. His returns were always perfect, and to the letter. And so were mine. Always.

What I did have going for me in Massachusetts, however, was an outstanding lawyer. He was expensive. But I was still utilizing him to keep my children's mother straight some twelve years after the divorce. More on this in my next chapter when the shit hit the fan once again.

There is still more on my stupid mistakes in this divorce. My children's mother's father got involved in going after me. I had already been convinced by him to buy a $150,000 insurance policy, from him, to protect my family. During the separation and while in the Discovery Phase of the pending divorce, my children's mother's father forged my signature on this insurance policy, probably but I'm not certain if this is the case, to take cash value out. I found out about it as I always check daily all my debits and credits to my accounts. No, I didn't call him on it. I contacted his employer with a long letter. His employer happened to be this same insurance company. They responded with a long letter apologizing to me. I was satisfied with that.

I had also bought a used car from him that I paid for monthly. He told his daughter to ask me what I was going to do about the car I was buying from him. Now, I have forgotten how long I had been giving him, without fail (my MO), a monthly amount to pay for it.

I assumed my children's mother's father knew who I was—a man who lives by his word. After all, we'd been in this family together now thirteen years. I knew who he was. He *knew who I was*. It is this knowledge that prompted me, upon hearing from my children's mother that her father wanted to know what I was going to do about his car (*his* car?), that prompted me to drive *his car* to her drive way with a note that the car keys were in the car. I left no other note.

The worst thing that happens to the male in a divorce in Massachusetts was that I was going to have to leave my children's mother living in the same comfortable lifestyle she had been accustomed to while married to me. It was standard operating procedure for the Commonwealth of Massachusetts. Two married people get divorced but only the man suffers the consequences. During the *discovery phase* of the pending divorce, she would take the children with her, and I would have to give her *one-half of my gross earnings every month*. We are not talking about net earnings here. The only income she would not get was my air force retired pay, and Grace Paul was already getting half of three-fourth of that sum. My children's mother earned no money, so all the bills would continue to be paid by me, as was occurring before the divorce. One of the objectives of the court in Massachusetts was that the divorce should result in the woman resuming the lifestyle she had been living. There is no consideration or favor made for the *breadwinner*. There is simply no miracle that can happen to allow me to resume my previous lifestyle. I was screwed. Royally.

But first, the other comedic occurrence at Wildwood School. There was a third person involved in this mess, also a member of my staff, a woman who hailed from Alaska but who had made the move to Massachusetts to be near the one person who made her heart flutter. Of course, the person who made her heart flutter happened to also be my children's mother's newly found partner. I found out about all this because this third person did not mind telling everyone about her feelings toward the person with whom she was madly in love. She asked to meet with me, in my office, but for a completely different reason.

Here is her story. She makes an appointment to see me. We meet in my office. "Dr. Pérez, I want you to supervise a one year internship for me in educational administration with the University of Massachusetts at Amherst as my principal and my supervisor, starting this fall. Would you approve my request?" She then quickly made me aware of her previous relationship with my wife's partner. If I chose to not supervise her internship, she would understand. She never uttered one accusatory word, only praise and the continuing crush she had for this second person in this triangle. She added that she would take this person back in a minute.

I remember sitting in my office maintaining eye contact with her and even wondering if I should say, "Say what?" I can be the coolest person ever and not be influenced by dramatic turns in a conversation. I quickly came to a decision about what to do. "Of course I will supervise your internship. None of what you told me need go any further than with you and me." And supervise her internship I did.

Back to the divorce. My lawyer's name was Steve Monsein. He was recommended to me by one of my sixth grade teachers, Peter Gervickas, who had gone through a divorce and was represented by Steve as his lawyer. Peter and my assistant principal, Fran Zyperstein, had previously been co-principals at Wildwood until I arrived. Along with Jo Ann Bruhn, probably the very best special needs teacher I had the good fortune to work with, the three of them were my closest allies at Wildwood.

I will now regress (with a couple of short paragraphs) to my last year or two at Twinbrook (because that experience fits perfectly with what I am about to describe) to bring up the fact that I grew very close to the instructional staff there. Their friendship and closeness to me would impact me and what I was going through at Wildwood and in Amherst. Even though I ended Twinbrook's site-based management program, what the staff got instead was much more satisfaction with the way I led the school. I could feel the *camaraderie* between staff and me long before I left. Well, after I arrived at Amherst I started getting phone calls from two or three members of the Twinbrook staff. The calls were friendly. We were always on a first-name basis.

I was always "Roberto" to them, and I called everyone also by their first names. Because teachers did not have telephones in their classrooms and cell phones were not quite "in" yet, I am sure they would come to the office and have Carol Parker call me and then Carol would hand them the telephone. It was almost always, "How are you doing, Roberto?"

While I never shared exactly what I was going through, I also didn't let them know that I wasn't sleeping very well. I was flat broke and, based on Steve's advice, seriously considering filing for bankruptcy. *That* is what worried me. *Me.* Filing for bankruptcy! Man! I had bought and maintained four different new houses in San Antonio and Austin, plus another home in Maryland and still another one in Massachusetts. To say I was miserable is putting it mildly.

I had already gone from 176 pounds down to 160. I must have looked terrible. Maria was sending me packages of "Ensure" to take. About Carol's calls, I am not sure if she could tell I was down. She asked the same question everybody asked, "How are you doing, Roberto?" Carol would always ask about Josef and Sofia, now 10 and 7, respectively, as well. I remember feeling like I didn't have a friend in the world, except for Peter, Fran, and Jo Ann. Carol's voice was friendly and I could visualize her smile, not to mention the sincere reason for calling. The calls from Maryland always came at the end of the working hours for the day. Therapeutic? You bet.

I planned to move out of the house. The house payment was going to continue to be paid by me. Still, I just had to move out. I would move as far from Amherst as I could, fully forty-five minutes away to a little town called Shelbourne Falls. I found a house for rent that practically stood alone on a hill. But I could walk anywhere I needed to go in town. I asked one or two male members of my staff to give me a hand on a Saturday morning for my move. Amazingly, ten to twelve teachers also showed up without my knowledge. The female members of my staff practically set the house up for me.

I had one neighbor. She was a middle-age woman who lived alone. She was friendly. I took only the necessary furniture to outfit two bedrooms and enough pots, pans, and dishes to be able to cook meals for myself and for Josef and Sofia when they were with me twice a month. I took a couch and a dinette table with four chairs. I lived here for some eighteen months, until June 30, 1998, when I retired. I would then turn 65 in forty-eight days. I planned to be as far away from Massachusetts as I could get. Josef and Sofia were already living in Syracuse by then, having moved with their mother and her partner about a year earlier. The word I got from one member of my Wildwood staff was that my children's mother and her partner were not welcome in Amherst any more. I have no idea how this *unwanted attitude* was manifested. I never cared to find out.

At that time in my life, now twenty years ago, I had begun a routine of exercising every morning before going to my school. I'd rise at five and do four to five miles on the treadmill every single day. I was on my second NordicTrac. Brought it with me. I was maintaining my health. Maria and Patty would visit me more than once in this short time I lived alone in Shelbourne Falls. Before Josef and Sofia moved to Syracuse with their mother, they were with me twice a month on weekends for probably close to a year. Even though they had moved to Syracuse, their mother was obligated to meet me halfway every two weeks so they could spend the weekend with me. I usually cooked our meals but made it a point to take them out for at least one meal during each weekend they were with me. Their mother and I met in Albany, New York, every other Friday. I would then drive back to Shelbourne Falls until I returned to Albany that Sunday afternoon to return Josef and Sofia. I would then drive back to Massachusetts.

Back to 1997 and Shelbourne Falls: Josef and Sofia loved my newly rented house. It was sort of off to itself and had plenty of yard and an unfinished wilderness to the north of the house. A very healthy-looking porcupine lived only a few yards from the house in the wilderness. It visited our front yard often. We also had toads, frogs and grass snakes everywhere. Somehow, often, I'd find one of these creatures in Josef's jean pockets when he retired for the evening. I didn't mind the toads or frogs. The snakes were not welcome at all. The house was also full of field mice. After my first night of staying in my new residence, I woke up to find mice inside my shoes, under the bed, and throughout the kitchen. I bought dozens of traps and declared war on them. Eventually, in a matter of several weeks, I got rid of all of them and knew that the house was clean of mice when my traps showed up empty every morning.

As an aside, I shared the nonconfidential goings-on of my life in Shelbourne Falls with my instructional staff at Wildwood. I still remember the seriousness in one of my teacher's voice when she said, "Well, certainly you're trapping them (the mice) and ensuring that you drive them *alive* in your car at least twenty-two miles from your home so they won't find their way back. That's our standard way of ridding our homes of field mice." My response to her: "Why, of course, Alice, that's exactly what I've been doing." Of course, all along I have two fingers of each hand crossed so I can be forgiven for stating such a big lie.

I had an attached garage and would drive my car into the garage every evening when I came home from school. I then walked into my bedroom and then down the stairs to the kitchen, dinette area, and small living room. The front door opened to a small front porch and then a spacious front yard. There was one major problem with this attached garage. It had a ninety-foot concrete driveway that lead UP to the garage door. The concrete driveway started just inside the road that led to my house. Notice the capital letters for the word *up*. Oh it was up all right, at about a forty-five degree angle. No, the car I was driving now had no trouble going up to the garage door, but only as long as there was no ice and snow on the driveway. One Friday evening, when I worked late at school (as I almost always did), I could not get my Nissan Sentra (actually Carol Parker's Nissan—but more on that below) to go up more than a foot or two. I had to abandon the car and try walking up to the garage door to be able to get into my home. I was mostly on my hands and knees as it was snowing, and I could not maintain my balance. I finally made it all the way up to the garage door. I was soaking wet. And yes, I was wearing a suit, white shirt, and tie.

I will now go back some ten paragraphs to that call that Carol Parker made, probably in response to one of my former Twinbrook teachers saying, "Let's check on Roberto." It was probably the worst day ever in my life. Oh, I had my health. I always managed to give my job as principal my full attention and would let nothing else interfere with giving it 100 percent of my time and always concentrating on doing the best job possible for my students, my instructional staff, and the parents of my students. But the days all come to an end. The dust settles. The people all leave. Now, one can hear a pin drop. Now, one is all alone. I pick up the phone. Yes. It's Carol.

"Carol, before you say anything, are you busy this weekend?" Before she can answer, I add, "I wanna come down for a two-day visit. I want to catch a plane this evening and be in Maryland for a couple of days before returning Sunday evening. I can stay with Maria and Bob. However, can I see you over the weekend?"

"Is anyone picking you up at the airport?" comes from Carol. "Well, no. You see I don't know which airport I'm flying in to…yet. I am flying standby with USAIR and there are three possible airports I can fly to. I can call you and let you know before the plane departs. Is that okay?" Carol: "Sure. I can pick you up myself."

We had a plan. Still, there was so much more to do. Call Maria and Bob. Check flights. And oh yes, how do I get to Hartford, Connecticut, to the airport to catch a flight? I had just returned *my children's mother's father's car* that same day.

I had an unbelievable staff and faculty. There was one teacher who, while she never stopped questioning everything I did, she always did it with class, courtesy, and politeness. I would ask her if she would give me a ride to Hartford, Connecticut, and drop me off at the airport. The trip was fully ninety minutes away, so she was looking at three hours beyond her work day before going to her own home. Jo Ann Bruhn did not hesitate. She said, "Yes! I'll take you." A few things about Jo Ann. She was a special needs teacher who was very student-oriented. She lived with a guy named Larry Smith. Both were outstanding friends. The year is 1997. Here we are, the year 2017, and Jo Ann, Larry and I are still the best of friends and we stay in touch.

A little more information on my *flying standby* with USAIR. My son Rey has been working for USAIR (now American Airlines) since the fall of 1989. I have capitalized on his employment with the airline to take advantage of being able to fly *gratis* if there are any empty seats. Over the course of twenty-plus years, until around 2009, I seldom bought a plane ticket whenever I flew alone. Since we have been married, I have tried taking Carol with me a couple of times, and she did not like the suspense of not knowing if there were any empty seats. Most of the job interviews I had in the northeast were facilitated by flying standby and not having to pay for a plane ticket. I can probably count on the fingers of one hand the number of times I failed to get a seat. Still, there were a few, and I had to spend the night at a hotel if it was on my way back.

Right before I received that call from Carol that had me asking her if I could see her that weekend, I had spent several miserable months in a semi state of depression. I was hesitating filing for bankruptcy. Josef's and Sofia's mother was taking more than 60 percent of my net earnings, which was really 50 percent of my gross, and it was according to Massachusetts law. But I had all those deductions to my pay, income tax, both federal and state, social security, medical coverage, and more. My children's mother had none. I remember having an appointment with the clerk in the central office who handled pay and she had asked to see me because she couldn't believe there was not some kind of error in what I was paying in alimony and child support. It was all there in black and white, and on paper. She shook her head and wondered how I could make it at all. I was not making it. Something had to give, and soon.

I had trouble sleeping. My doctor put me on antidepression drugs with the intent to get off of them as soon as possible. I did. My doctor's name was Andrew. I was Roberto to him, and he was Andrew to me. He knew I was drinking two stiff martinis every day and the last time I saw him, sometime in early 1998, he said, "Roberto, you can give up on these meds, as you have, but you must not give up on your martinis. They are doing you a lot of good."

And of course, I believed him and have ever since.

Picking up where I left off: Jo Ann drove me to Hartford. I flew in to DC. Carol picked me up. We went to Maria's and Bob's home first so I could check in with them and thank them for putting me up for a couple of nights. Still, I spent most of the other hours with Carol. I told Carol everything I had gone through. I left nothing out.

I started to find out who Carol was. Before we called it a night, she reached inside her purse, took out her car keys, and said, "I want you to take my car back to Massachusetts."

Just like that. Without hesitation. At the time, Carol's three adolescent children were still living with her, and they had a second car in the family. However, all three were about to go away to college. Randy was going to Harrisburg, Pennsylvania, to attend Messiah. Melanie was going to Frostburg in Western Maryland, and Vicki was about to leave for Arizona State University. Carol's car was a four-door Nissan Sentra in excellent condition. It was their very best car. All three knew who I was because they had come to visit their Mom when she was my administrative secretary at Twinbrook. I'm sure Carol explained the circumstances and all three understood.

I started seeing Carol almost every weekend after that first time. I mostly flew to Maryland on a late Friday night flight and would return on a late Sunday night flight. The drive to Amherst from the airport was about ninety minutes, but I lived in Shelbourne Falls. While Shelbourne Falls was another forty-five minutes from Amherst, I didn't have to drive through Amherst to get home. There was a more direct way, and it saved me about forty-five minutes. We kept this hectic pace for more than a year.

I had gotten my divorce. Josef and Sofia went to their mother. I would see them twice a month, on a Saturday and Sunday each time. The monetary compensation would now be reduced to child support, approximately $934 a month for both children, as well as an additional $200 a week for their mother. Her alimony would continue for 155 weeks. The total alimony amount for the 155 weeks would total $31,000. The child support would continue until each reached the age of 18.

Of course, it is now the Wildwood School and Community that is becoming aware of what my plans must be now. After all, Amherst is a small community. At the time, there must not have been more than 25,000 people living in Amherst. Everyone knew everything. They also knew I left the school every Friday right after the students left so I could drive to Hartford and then *fly home*. Fran, Peter, and Jo Ann knew how much I hated being there in Amherst.

They knew I had gotten from the state of Massachusetts exactly what my son-in-law Bob Young said I got.

As an aside, my children's mother and I started this routine when all of us were living in Amherst. We continued for an additional year when I started living in Shelbourne Falls and they were in Syracuse. We continued the twice-monthly exchanges after I moved permanently to Maryland in June of 1998. We started exchanging the kids in Wilkes Barre, Pennsylvania, from July 1998 until February 2007, when Sofia turned 18. I never missed a single visit. Not a one! Usually, I couldn't wait to see them.

As I reflect on this chapter, I notice that my personal life and the tragedies it brought while I lived up here have consumed almost the entire chapter. The truth is that I do not remember ever enjoying my job as a school administrator more than the three years I spent in Massachusetts. Upon further reflection, I now understand why. I was having success. No, not the success of having a school where everyone was in attendance every day and all Wildwood students were learning to their utmost potential. Not sure such a school exists anywhere.

What *was* happening was that I was having success solving problems. I was meeting the demands, requests really, of the teachers on our faculty. The few heavy discipline problems we had were also being solved. I remember suspending one particular student because other students were not safe being around him. Suspending students from school was a definite no-no. The School Board frowned on this action by school principals. I doubt if any of the other principals had suspended any students for several years. I remember a male school counselor on our staff who was very student-oriented and was a much sought after adult on our staff. He walked into my office one day to thank me. I was a little puzzled at first, until he added, "I know that you know that our school system frowns on any student ever being suspended from school. I also know that this particular student's presence in school put the safety of others in jeopardy. So I do appreciate your going out on a limb over this." Of course, I am paraphrasing what he said, but this is exactly what he meant to say.

Here is the thing about being the school principal. This is the person responsible not only for the teaching and learning at his school, but also for the safety and security of hundreds of children and a somewhat lesser number of staff and faculty members. I never lost sight of this responsibility. I read all the appropriate professional periodicals concerning what was happening at the thousands of schools across the country. I always kept in mind the potential that this same occurrence could take place at my school. I remember reading, not in an educational periodical, but in the newspaper, that a five, six, or seven-year-old student was found walking alone on a sidewalk some two or three blocks from the nearest school and that the child "just simply walked away" from his class at a time when his teacher did not have all of her or his students within view.

How about having to call a parent when, for whatever reason, a teacher walks into my office, scared to death, to inform me that she cannot find Little Joe or Mary or Alice, and a search of the entire school and the accompanying grounds reveals no child anywhere? Being a fatalist at heart, I always imagined the worst of all things and I tried, on a 24/7 basis, to not ever find myself in such a situation.

I never neglected to inform the parents of all my students how seriously I took this position of being principal at the school where their children attended. They knew I had tough standards and would not hesitate to pick up the phone and describe for them exactly what their students were doing in school that was considered inappropriate. There was one parent who became angry about something in school and came to school asking for a conference with me. I was always busy and seldom not involved in something very important concerning a student. We had a large number of students who were identified as having special needs and they seem to occupy most of my time. I could tell this parent was angry, and it would not help matters any if I kept her waiting and denying her attention. I put some things on hold that simply could wait another ten to fifteen minutes while I met with this parent in my office. I always closed the door to my office to facilitate a more honest exchange of concerns. I never sat behind my desk for any conferences—never! I had soft chairs only inches apart and the parent and I usually sat abreast of each other and only inches apart. She and I could look closely into each other's eyes and be frank, bold, and honest.

"How can I help you, Mrs. Smith?" (not her real name). This parent must have had a child in my school who was between 6 and 12 years old. Most of these parents were in their late twenties to late thirties. The moment I finished my introductory remarks, the parent used a series of four-letter words, none were f-words but many words rhyming with *spit* and *dam*, and she used them several times. As soon as she paused (being careful not to interrupt her because I wanted to hear what other choice words she would use to tell me what she thought of the school and me). The pause came. I stood up, looked at her eyes, and said in an increased-decibels voice, "Mrs. Smith, this conference is over. I don't allow the use of this type of language at our school by anyone. I am not going to start allowing it with you." I walked to the door and opened it, while repeating once again, "This conference is over."

Mrs. Smith, obviously embarrassed, and also speechless, walked out and I never saw her again. I began preparing myself to what I was going to say to the School Board when this lady came to them to complain about me. I started to relish the idea that she would go the School Board. I knew I was correct in considering the school environment to be somewhat sacred because of the ages of the children who attended here. However, the lady never did go the School Board, and as far as I can remember, her child kept coming to our school.

I remember driving to my school (I am now driving Carol's car) almost giddy every day because there was never a dull moment at my school. Besides, after the hell I went through to get divorced and now finding myself looking forward every day for the weekend to arrive so I could drive to Hartford to catch a plane to visit in Rockville and to be with Carol Parker. Yes. I almost hummed myself to work every day, right after I used the NordicTrac to push and pull several miles. My mental health was also returning. I may have been almost broke, but I was still enjoying the new life I was living, both here in Massachusetts and on weekends, in Maryland. When I reflected on the fact that I had to file for bankruptcy to get out of paying the huge house payment, I would then get gloomy.

Still, I thoroughly enjoyed all the challenges that being the principal at Wildwood brought to me. There was one particular case where the parent of a second grade student came to see me about a major concern she had for herself and for her second grade daughter. She had divorced her daughter's father because of abuse by him. While not remembering all the other details behind her ex-husband also being sent to prison, he was now getting out of prison and had communicated to her that he was coming "for his daughter to take her with him, and no one is going to stop him from doing this." She made me aware of the harshness by which he had treated her once upon a time and why she left him, taking her daughter with her. She let me know in no uncertain terms that she was scared and did not know what to do. One thing she was not going to do was run away and hide with her daughter. She wanted me to help her cope with this problem.

One of the things that Wildwood had going for the school that was probably unique was that we had many true professional educators, counselors, special needs teachers, therapists, and other special area people. We had a weekly Wednesday meeting, two hours before school started, to discuss issues that the entire team could be made aware of and that they could contribute to solving the problem with their recommendations through their expertise. The team decided we would assist this parent by ensuring that we would provide a "safe haven" for the second grade student by implementing a plan at school that would guarantee her safety.

In implementing this plan, we would need to involve the Amherst Police Department. They would be on call should the student's father make an appearance at school. The second grade classroom the student was in was very close to the front door. Up until this plan was implemented, all school house doors were closed, but not locked. As an aside, this is 1996. America's schools have not yet experienced the locked doors approach to ensuring all students are safe. For Wildwood, all doors are now locked except one door on the east side of the school. This unlocked door was at the opposite end of where the child's classroom was located.

Know, too, that all of this planning is taking time and time is of the essence. A few of us were key personnel in the plan. We had planning meetings at least twice a week, and they always included the chief of police of Amherst. We discussed the plan at our Wednesday morning meetings to update everyone on where things stood as of that moment.

The man never showed up at school. As far as we knew, he never showed up at Amherst. Perhaps it was only a threat to scare the child's mother, who was probably the one that caused him to go to prison.

As I have all my life, I simply stood up and said to myself, "I'll get through it." But first things first. The year 1998 enters my life. And it was a good year. I continued seeing Josef and Sofia twice a month. They were in Syracuse, and I was still in Amherst. So I drove four times a month to Albany, New York, to have an exchange with their mother. It was really two visits a month, but each visit required two trips to Albany. But I would not be in Massachusetts for long. I submitted my letter of resignation to the superintendent of schools and told him I loved my school. I loved the students. I had a wonderful faculty and staff. But I hated living in Massachusetts. It has done me wrong. I could not wait to get the hell out of this state.

Carol asked Randy (my stepson) to come up to Shelbourne Falls and help me load a U-Haul truck as I made the move back to Maryland. I retired for the purpose of starting to draw my Social Security benefits on June 30, 1998. I remember visiting the Social Security office in Springfield, Massachusetts, to begin the process. I also remember the lady who looked me up in her records and would later print my record of contributions. She handed me a copy showing my contributions to Social Security over all the years I worked. The earliest entry dated back to 1939. That's right, 1939. I was only six years old. And I could still see (in my mind's eye) the man behind the counter at the *Do Drop In* in San Antonio, Texas, who filled in the form for me when I asked if they needed a dishwasher and he answered that they did but I would have to also have a Social Security

Number. He told me he would arrange for that and asked me what my name was so he could fill in the form and I could sign it. "Bobby Perez," I told him.

Well, I now had a record of it in my hands.

My Newly Adopted Home State (MD)

I have retired again. Again? Did it in February of 1972 when I retired after twenty years in the US Air Force. Did it again in 1989 when I retired after ten years with the Texas Public Schools (TPS) as both a classroom teacher and as principal. With the TPS, I was able to buy five additional years because of my time in the military during both the Korean and Vietnam conflicts. I retired in 1995 after only five years with the Maryland Public Schools. Since I was sixty-two years of age at the time, I was vested and could draw retired pay for life, although not very much. I would now begin drawing retired pay for forty years of professional work, five of which I paid cash for an additional five years credit for contributions I would have made at the beginning of my tenure with the Texas Public Schools. I would also have my Social Security. It's a matter of being alert, informed, and security conscious, and not to mention your own best advocate.

Upon returning to Maryland around July 1 of 1998, I put all my furniture in storage and moved in with Carol. We would get married on July 31 of that year. She had bought a townhouse in Damascus, Maryland, and we lived there until the summer of 2001. We saved money together so we could cover the down payment on a home we were having built in Mount Airy, just fifteen minutes north of Damascus. You should know that the only reason we were able to get a bank loan for the purchase of this home was because of Carol's good credit.

I knew I had ruined my credit for a minimum of five years. I wouldn't be able to buy anything on time because no business, or bank, would trust me. However, I have patience and know how to save money for months, or even years, in order to buy whatever I needed with cash. It is now twenty years later, and I have not bought anything other than by buying it with the total amount paid for in cash. I also do not ever *not* pay the entire credit card balance when their statement arrives once a month. Here is the bottom line: *I have not paid one dollar in interest in these twenty years.* It is amazing at the savings I have been able to realize because of this fact.

A little justification for not ever charging anything since 1997: After being proud for most of my adult life for having the ability to easily buy things *on time* because of my excellent credit, what I went through in Massachusetts brought me only embarrassment and shame. When I arrived back in Maryland in the summer of 1998, I tried to establish credit early on with Sears and perhaps one other major department store and was denied. It was one of the most embarrassing things ever in my life. Instead of being the sturdy upright guy I have always been, I was now being denied credit. And with Sears, a store I had always done business with. I never again asked anyone, anywhere, to sell me anything on time. Then, too, my marriage to Carol started to turn things around for me, and quickly.

Note: Before I continued with this manuscript today (February 9, 2017), I paused long enough to ask Carol when the last time was that she bought anything on credit. Before going further, Carol and I split all the expenses, on a monthly basis. Carol's answer: "When we got married on July 31, 1998."

Because I continued working after arriving back in Maryland in 1998, and because Carol had already received her bachelor of arts degree in accounting from the University of Maryland and was earning good money, we were both able to not only continue to never carrying balances forward each month, we were both able to save money every month.

Initially, my plans were to start a personal educational consulting business. I had five hundred business cards printed professionally so I could distribute them *far and wide*. I spent the months of

July and August of 1998 trying to distribute my business cards any place I thought would give me some exposure. I never did try to distribute them locally, in Montgomery County, or with local schools. I simply burned too many bridges just before I left here to go to Massachusetts. The superintendent was the same person who was in this same position in 1995, when I had all those confrontations with local administrators. One of them told me to my face he didn't think I *was one of them*. This ended up being a bigger setback than I imagined it would be.

I got many calls to interpret, tutor, and to also teach Spanish at the middle and high school levels as a substitute teacher. The going rate for tutoring was $15 dollars an hour because almost all tutoring requests were made through a tutoring conglomerate who also received a portion of the fee. It was probably a like amount that the tutor received. I did try to establish my own clientele, but it would have taken me at least a few years to earn a reputation as an effective tutor. Tutoring on my own, without joining a tutoring resource, meant having fewer students to tutor. Then, too, I was restricting myself to the few middle and high schools that taught Spanish when I substituted as a teacher. The most I could net, if I worked five days a week, was a gross of $100 a day. I never was asked to teach Spanish more than two to three days per week. So I started substitute teaching at all grade levels, kindergarten through high school. During the years 1998 and 1999, I actually taught at all of these grade levels.

I had to expand the areas in which I was eligible to teach. I applied at American University as an adjunct professor during the summer of 2000, while still doing substitute teaching in all the public schools of the area. Almost all the calls I got to substitute came from Montgomery County schools and, in most cases, from teachers who knew me when I was a principal in the school system. I received requests almost every day. Still, the net pay of $100 a day was demoralizing. I seldom worked less than an eight-hour day, thus I was earning under $13 an hour.

The dean of the Department of Education at American University called to ask if I was interested in an adjunct professor position. The résumé, or curriculum vitae, I had sent them had all the information I had accumulated while at the University of Texas at Austin, my assistant professor position at St. Edward's University, and my selection by Bridgewater State University as an associate professor in 1995. The dean asked if I was interested in teaching a graduate level course in educational psychology. I answered affirmatively. The dean wanted me to teach one three-semester-hour course during the fall of 2000, one evening per week, for fifteen weeks. At AU, I would have the freedom to also choose the textbook my class would use. I just had to advise the university bookstore so they would have the textbooks available at least one week before classes started in the fall. This is academic freedom at its best. I knew I was going to like teaching at the college graduate level. Also, when I interviewed with the dean, she had another professor participate in the interview. Both asked questions that would reveal my love for teaching at the college level and my philosophy about teaching and learning. This second professor on the panel added that he had informed other members of the faculty of my candidacy and how impressed they were with my credentials. He also added that he made copies of my curriculum vitae and had shared them with all members of the department. I felt wanted. I felt good. Finally, something to feel good about.

However, there were some drawbacks in accepting this prestigious position. The key phrase to remember is *adjunct professor*. I had no idea of the difference in pay between a college professor who is in a tenured position at the university level and a professor hired to teach as an adjunct. I was about to find out.

The dean tactfully *eased* into finally telling me. "Roberto, the bad news is that American University can only pay you $2,000 per course." I was being asked to teach one class. The last class for the semester would be taught during the second or third week of December. The first class would be taught during the first or second week of September. I would receive a check in the mail sometime before Christmas, if I were lucky, for a total amount of $2,000. Meeting once a week for fifteen weeks, for three hours, provides a total clock time in classroom hours of forty-five hours. $2,000/45 = $44 an hour. "Not bad," you say? Trouble is it would take me minimally an additional three to five hours per week to plan my lessons.

Let's say it is just three additional hours of planning per week. Now it's twelve hours per week, total, and for fifteen weeks. It is now $15 \times 12 = 180$ hours. It is also $2,000/180 = $11.11 per hour. I hope to elaborate a bit more on this ridiculous situation in my epilogue. Then, too, I lived fifty miles away from the Nebraska street address in Washington, DC, where AU is located. There would be no compensation for mileage. I received no benefits. As an aside, but completely related to the ridiculous situation people who spend a fortune getting advanced degrees and end up accepting positions like I accepted, it is the reason some fifteen years later I participated with other adjuncts in this area in starting a union of adjunct professors who would qualify for food stamps and other assistance in order to make a living.

As long as I was only teaching one class per semester, I spent four to five hours per week preparing. Being the perfectionist I have always been, I had my presentation outline for every weekly class meeting *written in stone* in my brain. I seldom had to look at notes to follow a sequence of instructional items on my agenda. Teachers and college professors who know what they are doing and who elicit feedback from their students, end up being excellent teachers and professors because they seek feedback to make them better teachers. I was in this group. The last thing I wanted was to be seen as a mediocre professor. Unlike other professions, all college professors are required to have their students evaluate the class at the last class meeting and one of the students is tasked to conduct the evaluation, sans the instructor's presence, and then, while ensuring the instructor does not see or read the evaluation results, obtains the instructor's signature that the activity was conducted and then mails in the results to the university office that handles this aspect of teaching at the university level.

Students themselves do the evaluation. Lately, public school teachers are also having their students do likewise. If you can recall my experiences as a sixth grade teacher in Austin, Texas, it was par for the course for my sixth grade classes while at Williams Elementary School back in the early 1980s.

I entered a second year of teaching at AU. I was continuing to teach that one course. Of course, in order to earn a decent living, I had to continue also substitute teaching in the area's public schools. That $2,000 check I received in the mail from AU in December, while seeming to be a good sum of money, but after working for 180 hours, was tantamount to earning a minimum wage.

Fortunately, Carol was now earning very decent wages in her own chosen field, and with my own retired pay, we were able to purchase our home. I had finished paying alimony to my children's mother. We were doing okay financially. It is now the fall semester of 2001. For the current semester, I was teaching Spanish on a long-term basis at Walter Johnson High School in addition to teaching at AU one night per week. I was in the middle of a morning class on September 11 when another teacher from our department who happened to have a planning period interrupted my class to ask me, "Have you seen what's going on?"

I told her I had not, but that my class would soon be ending and I, too, had a planning period and would plant myself in front of a television screen somewhere in the building. I did. It was very hard to believe the things we were all seeing. Amazingly, there was little discussion among faculty members during this day on how we allowed this to happen in America. A better discussion on this tremendous tragedy should be discussed under separate cover.

Changes were being made at American University. The university had taken on the responsibility of providing the graduate level instruction and subsequent teacher certification of a fairly large cadre of graduate students who had been selected by a national program to identify recent graduates who would commit to teaching in inner city public schools for a selected number of years. AU would get involved from the very beginning by joining the DC Public Schools in setting up selection committees to interview candidates and choose between thirty-six and forty graduate students (per year) to begin a two-year program of instruction that would result in a master's degree from AU and certification to teach at either the elementary or secondary levels. I was subsequently selected to participate on one of the selection committees. I was also selected to teach several graduate courses that were a part of the curriculum. Obviously, in order to complete the program within a two-year period, students would have to carry a full load of classes. The university then started condensing the graduate classes into two class meetings per week and requiring a minimum of forty clock hours of instruction per class. If each class meeting was for two and a half hours of instruction, five hours would accumulate per week and each class could be completed in an eight-week period.

With this in mind, classes could now start at varying dates and months of the year. An example would look like this: If each student intern started his/her four classes per week on the Tuesday evening after Labor Day each September, say perhaps on September 5, meaning that eight weeks of instruction would end during the week of October 23–27. A second tier of classes could then begin the following Monday or Tuesday, October 30 or 31, or even one week later. A similar schedule of classes could permeate the other months of the year. The objective would be that all students complete their programs of studies within a two-year period.

Since I had now established myself as an adjunct professor, and I was receiving excellent student evaluations, AU asked me to also teach undergraduate classes. I taught the undergraduate version of educational psychology for two or three semesters. These classes were in addition to teaching in the graduate program.

It is appropriate to look at what a typical school day looked like for these interns involved as graduate students in this program. Each went to class four evenings a week. Classes usually started at 5:30 p.m. to give students sufficient time to get to their class after teaching all day in one of the DC Public Schools. This alone can be a very difficult chore because traffic congestion in this area is among the worst in the country. Classes had to be three hours long in order to satisfy the two and a half hour requirement per class, plus a short break that would split each class in half. If the class did not start until 6:00 p.m. because many students could not arrive on time, then I would have no choice but extend the class until 9:00 p.m. Many evenings I would ask for their approval to skip the break and go for two and a half hours of straight instruction and interaction.

If the reader has been following along this path I have described, then the reader also knows that I am no longer teaching just one class per semester. In fact, perhaps we should not call them *semesters* any longer. I am now averaging four to five classes taught each period that heretofore we were calling semesters. The $2,000 check I was previously getting in late December now comes upon completion of each class and is now multiplied by four or five for each period.

Obviously, I had to stop substitute teaching in the Maryland Public Schools. I was having to go 24/7 each week because of the now extended planning required for *two* classes per week, *and* each one is taught twice per week. I was planning lessons on Saturdays and Sundays. I continued teaching that one undergraduate class during the day at American University. My class started at 8:30 each morning. We met daily for seventy-five minutes. Having seven to eight hours before my evening class started allowed me more time to plan my evening class while at AU. I shared an office with another adjunct professor, and she was rarely there when I was. I usually planned in the library anyway because I had access to as many publications and written resources as I needed.

Again as an aside, my undergraduate seventy-five-minute class each weekday morning started at 8:30. My routine for all my classes has always been to enter my classroom a full thirty minutes before my class starts to ensure all my audio-visual equipment is available and each piece is functioning. I usually use multiple visual aids for every class as well as the overhead projector to walk students through the agenda for that one class. In order to arrive at AU by 8:00 a.m., I have to be walking away from the Metro train to get on my shuttle bus (at the "Tenley Town/AU" stop) no later than 7:45 a.m. Since it's a thirty-minute Metro train ride from the Shady Grove Stop, I have to get on a train that leaves no later than 7:15 a.m. It's a forty-five-minute drive from Mount Airy to the Shady Grove Stop, meaning I have to leave home by 6:30 a.m. This is the reason Carol and I are up between 5:00 and 5:30 each morning.

If my evening class ends at 8:30 p.m., one can do the math to ascertain what time I will get home that evening. I left at 6:30 in the morning and started my class at 8:30. Anyway one looks at this schedule, it's two hours each way. I would be home by 10:30 each of the four evenings I have classes at American University. I never (ever) scheduled a class to teach on a Friday. No, it is not a day of rest. It is a day to start planning for my Monday class.

I started teaching at AU according to this schedule in the fall of 2002. I grew as an instructor. Remember that at the college level all classes end with students evaluating their instructor. I took their feedback seriously. I seldom got a critique saying anything negative about my presentations. What I did notice for every class was their involvement, or interaction, with me as we discussed all important concepts and objectives of each of my classes. The feedback was almost always complimentary and some even signed their names to the evaluation. They didn't have to.

The program continued past 2007, but I finally concluded that I was devoting too much time to get the job done and also to adhere to the schedule. I was working seven days a week, counting the planning time required. My classes did end by mid-December and mid-May every year. But then we had summer classes (had to have them in order to acquire the number of semester hours needed to graduate). I would usually have two to three weeks off before classes started again. By then, Carol and I were doing okay financially. What we did need was to maintain our good health.

I started looking for other colleges and universities in the area who had similar teacher-training programs. I found several. I sent them my résumé and curriculum vitae. McDaniel College, formerly known as Western Maryland University and located in Westminster, Maryland, and only thirty minutes from Mount Airy, asked if I could join them as an adjunct professor. The adjunct compensation was the same as at American University. When I talked to the Dean at AU that I was going to resign my adjunct professorship there and now start teaching at McDaniel College. She convinced me that I didn't have to, that I could teach at as many colleges and universities as I wanted to. For a year or two, until 2009, I did just that. But I never signed up to teach more than one evening class at American University. I finally settled on only teaching at McDaniel College.

What did happen was that I started demanding a better compensation for each class I taught. And I received it, too.

The situation at McDaniel was very similar to the program at AU, with a few differences. McDaniel offered advanced degrees in several areas in education. The university also offered supervised internships. McDaniel quickly noticed my doctorate was in educational administration and asked if I would join the graduate school team of administrators who supervised interns seeking certification in educational administration throughout the state. Between the years 2008 and 2014, I must have supervised as many as twenty-five interns. I did this in addition to teaching two classes. One class was titled *Teaching and Learning* and was a derivative of the old *Ed Psyche* class that was part of my required classes back at UT Austin in 1972–74. This modified version was a class on the cerebral functioning of the brain, at varying stages of development, and how humans learn.

I remember reading in the literature that aerobic training, when done regularly as part of a daily exercise program, actually builds millions of brain cells through the rapid surge of oxygen that is generated while doing these exercises. My students were, of course, all graduate students pursuing an advanced degree and required courses to qualify for a specific certification. They were all practitioners. The tuition at McDaniel was not cheap. Each graduate level class (it is my guess) was in the neighborhood of $1,500 per class. Still, it was lower than at most colleges and universities in the area. McDaniel offered big discounts when a school system, anywhere in the state of Maryland, recruited a cadre of fifteen or more teachers (to sign up for the class) while also offering McDaniel a classroom on one of their campuses where the class could be taught. I traveled to the far corners of the state of Maryland to teach my classes. I was paid 25 cents a mile for my travels.

The second class I taught was only for teachers seeking to be administrators. It was titled "Observation and Supervision of Classroom Teachers." I only taught the class four or five times during the time I was at McDaniel as there were few teachers who wanted to go this route.

In 80 percent of the my classes, I had at least twenty teachers. Yes, they were all teachers who had now been in the classroom for minimally five years and wanted to earn more money by acquiring a master's degree, or additional specific certification in a special area. In my seven to eight years as an adjunct professor, I remember only four or five teachers who had trouble meeting my class objectives for the course. A final grade of B in a graduate class is the lowest grade a professor can give or the class must be taken again.

These teachers were all paying for the class from out-of-pocket-money that they earned from their teacher's salary. They seldom missed a class, and I was always very specific in my requirements (for them) to earn an A+, A, A-, B+, B, or B-. If they earned less than the points required for a B-, they failed the class. I had no failures, only an occasional B-, but plenty of Bs and B+s.

Because all programs required my class as a course in their program of studies, I taught the *Teaching and Learning* class minimally six to seven times each year. I had the syllabus memorized and etched in stone in my brain. But I still read the literature in order to stay current, and I never hesitated to add new twists that I learned. I learned to love the class and always looked forward to teaching it. The university usually asked me how many sections of the course I could handle. I picked no less than three sections to teach per semester.

A few side issues about teaching in a graduate program. I started teaching at this level only because substitute teaching in the public schools did not pay much money, and while I thought I would teach at the undergraduate level, the need was really in graduate programs. I treated this privilege with much respect and always performed as the consummate professional I thought I was. As with all college courses, I was evaluated at the conclusion of each class I taught, and anonymously. The dean of the college would always make it a point to give professors feedback. The feedback I always received was outstanding. I worked at being good. I practiced not using vocal pauses. I was always well-groomed, wore starched shirts with attractive ties, modeled good eye contact, and always involved all my students. As I learned from twenty years in the military, my shoes were always shined. I had a trick map (in my mind, for every class) that allowed me to memorize every student by their first name before the first class ended. Before I left home for all the subsequent classes I had with any one group, part of my preparation was to check my memory to see if I still remembered each person's first name. My students, however, had to cooperate by always sitting in the same seat, for every class.

I joined a professor's union. It was started by a rather young recent PhD graduate who did not get a tenured position upon graduation and had to settle for an adjunct position. He advertised his intentions by posting an item on one of our faculty bulletin boards. Six or seven of us met one evening. The *originator* of this union had some data to share. Colleges and universities were no longer hiring very many professors as tenured members of the faculty. Why should they? Young, bright professors could be coaxed into accepting an adjunct position for 15 to 20 percent of what the college or university would need to pay a professor coming on board in a tenured position. We had several meetings after the first one. We had no one to go to to complain or who would even listen. I stopped going to meetings and considered it a lost cause. Let's face it. America simply does not like unions of any kind. Never mind that they gave us the eight-hour-day, the forty-hour work week, vacations, sick leave, medical coverage, and on and on . In the minds of many un-informed Americans, unions only exist to make sure the youngest and latest addition to the workplace is always the first one to get laid off or fired. The simple minds of many people function exactly like this one mind. I gave up. Who has time for this?

It is now 2014. It's time I really retired. I am now 81, and soon to be 82. Carol would continue working for another year before she, too, would retire. I applied with the Frederick County Public Schools as an interpreter or translator, but only as a volunteer. I did not want to get paid for my services. I found out the greatest need Frederick Schools had was for interpreters and translators. But they are part of the system's annual budget and interpreters and translators are paid an hourly wage. They are used twice a year for perhaps two or three full days during parent/teacher conferences and also for meetings to discuss student progress for those students who have Individualized Education Plans, the famous IEP. They convinced me that they needed me and "Would I please sign up as one?" I did, but on the condition the school system would also allow me to volunteer without pay to help Latino students who were struggling in school.

It was not long before I get a call from the person who manages (schedules?) school volunteers. "Dr. Pérez, we have a twenty-one-year old high school student who has struggled for five years to get her high school diploma. This coming year is her last chance to complete the two courses she needs.

Without really knowing why she had spent five years in high school and still was unable to earn enough credits to graduate, I responded with "Of course I will help her." It is the beginning of the fall semester of 2014. I met the volunteer coordinator (VC), whose office is in the Frederick Middle School. We met at the high school where Maria Lopez is a student. That would be Frederick High School, which is adjacent to the above referenced middle school. Maria also met with us at the same meeting. The VC introduced us to each other and quickly left for another meeting.

I basically interviewed Maria to find out all I could about her and to come up with a schedule for me to help her. After listening to her tell me where she thought she needed help, I would then come up with a schedule to meet with her. First, though, I wanted to know who she was, so I asked her in Spanish because she appeared to speak little English (while at the same time noticing that this girl needed an intense class on learning the English language). Nonetheless, I listened attentively. She told me who she was all right, and it took her about thirty minutes.

She was brought to America by her parents when she was fifteen years old, so she had not been in America very long. The family easily could have declared themselves to be *refugees* as they were fleeing El Salvador where the family was constantly threatened and money taken from them almost daily. Maria, her parents, and a younger sibling, left in the middle of the night and headed north, hoping to reach America. The family crossed into Guatemala on foot and then, also on foot, walked the length of Mexico to reach the American border. They crossed illegally and worked their way to Maryland where her mother had some relatives living. The year was 2010.

With the help of friends and her parents working two jobs each, they were able to rent an apartment and begin making a living. Her parents soon earned enough money to buy a used car and to get around easier. Her parents then took her to school, and it was determined that she should be in high school at that time. She was taught by bilingual teachers who were attempting to transition her into the English language. They had some success, as she was starting to communicate now in both languages. Truth must be told, Maria did not speak either language very well. El Salvador did not care enough about their children to require them to go to school. Many did not, ever. Maria did not say to me that she went to school during her many years of living in El Salvador. What I knew was that she spoke a very poor version of Spanish.

Maria was soon 17, and still struggling in school. Her parents had problems in their marriage and soon divorced. She was already working after school most days of the week to help her mother pay bills. She met another Latino with whom she worked. This Latino boy had already been in America a few years, spoke much better English, managed to graduate from high school, had a job that allowed him to also have a car and pay rent and live alone, in Frederick, Maryland.

They met. Soon, Maria left home and moved in with her boyfriend. He was teaching her to drive when she had an accident. It was a horrific accident. Her boyfriend thought she had learned enough to be allowed to drive on her own, and risk doing so as she did not have a driver's license. She went to a shopping center to buy some groceries and parked the car right in front of a fast-food place as she went to do her shopping. Upon returning, Maria climbed into her boyfriend's car, started the engine, and thinking she was reaching for the brake pedal before backing up, she stepped hard on the accelerator and the car lunged forward, jumped the curb, broke through the very large window glass of the fast food place and she soon found herself, and the car she was driving, well inside the fast food place while the people who were inside had managed to get out of her way and were mostly safe and unhurt. Maria sat in the car, stunned, scared, and of course, speechless.

The police soon arrived and, when she couldn't show any papers, of any kind, much less a driver's license, the police took her to the police station. She was about to be locked up when her boyfriend showed up. Then, her mother also arrived as Maria had texted her on their cell phones. After much negotiating, an overly friendly police officer, as well as an understanding restaurant owner, Maria was not locked up. She did, however, make all the Frederick newspapers and her story was on all the DC and Baltimore TV News Stations. Maria never did explain to me who paid for all the damages she caused.

As we all know, time manages to march on, no matter what our life experiences are. Maria is 20 years old and if she turns 21 and still has not met the requirements to graduate, she will have to leave the high school and perhaps work on obtaining a GED. She had somehow managed to pass most of her other classes, but usually by the *skin of her chinny-chin-chin*. Enter Roberto Pérez, who sat and listened attentively to this fantastic story. It was now going to be up to me to get her to the finish line.

I must give the Frederick High School teachers a lot of credit for working very hard to get Maria to not only speak better English but also get through the basic courses she was taking. She earned only Cs and Ds but these grades are enough to get you credit. She did not do as well with her English, mathematics, government (or civics), and science courses. Still, in the five years Maria had been there now, she continued getting Cs and Ds and getting ever so close to earning enough credits to graduate. However, there were two courses she had failed two times. The courses were tenth grade English and twelfth grade government. These were the courses I would have to help her with.

I told her that probably the best thing for me to do was to take these courses with her and hear what the teacher is requiring her to do as well as because I didn't know if she could tell me what she had to do. Maria didn't think this was a good idea. She had already learned how high school students in America can be sensitive about their peers seeing how inept they are. Let's face it, Maria needed help. I vowed to the VC that I would get her through high school.

Okay then, I would meet with her every week day except Mondays and Fridays for two hours. Her teachers would know who I was and my method of getting Maria through each assignment would be to tutor her through the completion of each assignment for two hours each of three days of the week. Her assignments would all be on her computer, and she and I would do the assignments together. Fortunately, many of the assignments required multiple choice responses. We would have to work a very different approach for those requiring a written narrative. Maria had no idea how to put together a subject/predicate sentence. I knew I had my work cut out for me.

For the multiple choice responses, I would ask that she do them herself while I observed the response she chose. She almost always chose the wrong response. In reality, because I eventually received every paper or assignment she got, it was as if, together, we took the tenth grade English course in the fall of 2014 and the government class in the spring of 2015. Fortunately, English was one of the classes I did very well on when I was in high school, back a few *centuries* ago. Also, fortunately, I had not forgotten anything. I could still diagram sentences, knew all the tenses, idioms, *everything*.

But what about narrative responses? I told myself that the only way Maria will get through this part of the course would be for me to do the complete work for her and then she would simply put her name on the paper. *No way!* Her teacher would know immediately and then I would be the one who failed the course, for doing the work for her. Besides, it seemed very unethical.

There was one way. It was still stretching the truth, but at least not blatantly. Already, for the multiple choice responses, I would not let her turn any tests in until I corrected them, and I had to correct all of them. Also, before correcting her responses, I would also inform her why I did not recommend the other *wrong* responses, as a way of also instructing her while doing the work for her.

Still, I refused to think I was really doing the work, only correcting it. Yeah, I know. It's a bit of rationalizing a white lie. I got her through the class. She earned a B+. Maria was very proud and told all her friends she earned a B+ in tenth grade English.

One down, one to go. We tried using the same approach again, although the twelfth grade government class required more narrative responses than replying to multiple choice tests. I then did this with Maria: Knowing that there was no way she was going to write subject predicate sentences, paragraphs with main ideas and supportive information for those main ideas, and that each narrative had flow and was fluid and made sense. Deep inside of me I knew that Maria would not be able to do this any time soon. So I had another trick up my sleeve. I would write the narrative at home the evening of the day she got the assignment. I would write it in a way that was consistent with the skills Maria was exhibiting with me. (And this was no easy trick. Maria did not have command of the English language.)

However, I would require her to return the paper I wrote back to me and turn in a copy she wrote by copying every word of the paper I wrote, and put her name on the paper. I would then also go over all that I wrote. This happened a few times until there were only a few days toward the end of the semester. Maria then stopped returning my papers and instead, began *turning them in with her name on it*. I had wondered if she was ever going to do something dumb like this but dismissed it when I also thought that her teacher would notice, and since she knew who I was and how I was *carrying her through this course*, she would certainly advise me. She did not.

My first thoughts were that "I cannot allow this to happen." I met with the teacher who supervised her after-school homework time (the two hours I spent with her three days a week). I never quite got to the main reason I had asked him to meet with me. I did not tell him I was disappointed in Maria. This teacher began our meeting by telling me he had such a very high impression of Maria and was aware of her background in El Salvador, the accident, everything. This teacher spoke very highly of her and all that she had been through, not to mention supervising her the five years of struggling to earn her diploma. I *did not* tell him what I thought Maria had done. It just did not seem as the right thing to do.

I saw Maria mostly from a distance after this. I did notice how proud she was to be a high school senior. Still, we never interacted again.

There was one more time when my experiences with Maria would come up, not for a discussion on the experiences of school year 2014–15, but upon being recognized by the volunteer coordinator and other Frederick Public School supervisors at the end of the school year, in the early summer of 2015, when all the interpreters and translators met for an end of school year get-together. Everyone brought a plate of food from their home country, and we shared our year's experiences. The MC at the event asked me to stand and be recognized because of the job I had done with one high school student. She added that I, in fact, had taken two classes with her and got her through high school. I did not contribute anything else about my year with Maria.

So, why did I not feel very proud of this experience? Easy. I'm not sure I taught her anything. She and I both cheated.

Ces't le vie.

It is now summer of 2015. I had stopped teaching at the college and university level. I was waiting for more requests to help struggling students from the Frederick Public Schools (FPS), but the requests would only come after the school year started in the fall. Once school started in both the 2015–16 and 2016–17 school years, I was asked to interpret at many parent/teacher conferences. However, I have not had to volunteer to help struggling students.

This would be a good time to inject some thoughts and reflections on the many parent/teacher conferences I have had to interpret for both parents and teachers. I will guess that I have done this interpreting two full days each semester. I do three to four every hour, so that I must average between sixteen and twenty students each of the two days. Let's round it off at fifteen per day, thirty for the semester. I would interpret on sixty occasions each school year. I have been doing this now for minimally two years, so I have experienced interpreting for well over one hundred students during this length of time. By the way, I cannot do this *gratis*. FPS insists that I get paid for my services.

The only reason I am mentioning these experiences with Latino students here in Frederick, Maryland, is because of this fact of the over one hundred students we have discussed during these conferences, I do not remember a single case wherein the classroom teacher had to inject the thought that the student we were discussing was uncooperative, a discipline problem, bothered other students, or that the teacher was otherwise seeking help from the parents we were conferencing with to help curb such behavior at school. On the contrary, I am having a hard time remembering a single conference where the teacher did not say she or he loved having the child in her or his classroom. There were several conferences where the teacher did identify academic areas where the student needed to improve, but negative attitudes toward learning were never a part of the discussion.

Since I was a principal here in Maryland for five years, and for three more years in Massachusetts, I can echo these same thoughts from my eight years of experience in this part of our country. Another thing I am noticing is how proficient students at all grade levels are getting at learning the English language. Still another fact I am noticing is that those students who excel in their studies and make an extra effort, also manage to speak the English language with a more heavily concentrated desire to speak it perfectly. And we are seeing that more and more often.

It is summer of 2015. I would soon be 82 (and some twenty months ago, as today is now August of 2017). As I complete this chapter of my memoir, I am reflecting on the fact that I seldom have had a day when I did not have four to five objectives to accomplish during that day. It is a habit, but upon reflection, a very healthy habit. Because Carol and I have a little over two acres of land, and we maintain vegetable and flower gardens, both of us stay very busy throughout the calendar year. As a matter of fact, seldom does a day go by that Carol doesn't ask, "What's on your plate for tomorrow, honey?" Carol did retire during the month of her sixty-second birthday. Let's say, "officially retired." She continues working for the Montgomery County Public Schools as an auditor. However, she works when she wants to, and lately she has *wanted to* quite often. Again, habit.

The two of us still live our lives with daily objectives to accomplish and a need to end each day as a productive day. If we work on our vegetable and flower gardens, our fields, rearranging furniture, cleaning the refrigerator (or freezer), vacuuming, cleaning the hard wood floors, and most importantly, ensuring that we also ran five to six miles (Carol), and for me, power walked two to three miles at less than a fifteen-minute-per-mile clip, *each day*, we call it a *good day*. I also add fifteen to twenty minutes of lifting twenty, thirty, and forty-pound weights. One final daily exercise I have been doing now for some fifty-five to sixty years is leg lifts and stretches on my back, as therapy for my diagnosed scoliosis (an abnormal lateral curvature of the spine), first discovered during my first enlistment in the air force in the early 1950s. It is these daily leg lifts that have allowed me to go mostly painless all these years and also maintain an excellent *gait* to my walk. I was taught by an air force physical trainer in the middle of the last century. The following pictures reveal my life today.

Epilogue

This epilogue is being written as an addition to this memoir as a way of giving purpose for having written this document. The epilogue also hopes to answer a few questions that the survivors of the twelve children who were born to Felipe and Amalia Pérez may have after reading about the first generation Americans of their family. By including this narrative separately, the author is able to focus on a few specific questions that readers of this work may have without, hopefully, being influenced by the protagonist who is telling this story.

These are the questions this epilogue will attempt to answer:

1. Why write this experience of one immigrant family as a memoir?
2. Are there any other family experiences that are a part of the narrative that are significant to this story of first generation Americans?
3. How did the author intend to influence the survivors of the twelve children of Felipe and Amalia Pérez?
4. Is the information on first generation Americans of Mexican descent vital to other Americans?
5. The protagonist (author) reveals what he considers racist attitudes on the part of a significant number of Americans. Is it necessary to include this in the narrative of this story?

6. Is it important, or even necessary, to mention the issues on education in America?
7. The author reveals his concerns with beliefs, as in religious beliefs. Is this necessary for a memoir?
8. The concept of unions for American workers is a pet peeve of the author. Is this necessary to mention in this document?
9. Who are the human contributors to this memoir?
10. What comedic occurrence took place when my two children, Josef and Sofia, took a four-day vacation trip with Carol and me to San Antonio, Texas, in 1999?
11. Why did Steve Monsein, my lawyer in Massachusetts, have to intervene again on my behalf some eleven or twelve years after I divorced my children's mother?

Question 1:   The thought of documenting the lives of this family first entered my mind when I began researching my dissertation topic for my terminal degree in 1977. While I knew we were an exceptional American family, I had not thought of putting our story in writing and subsequently publishing it for all Americans to read. My first thoughts were to leave our story for our children and grandchildren to read and to know exactly who they are. However, the deeper I got into who this family is and what they have done as citizens who contribute very positively to this country, the more I felt a responsibility to tell our story. But why as a memoir? It is not easy to toot one's horn. But yes, it is also my story. From high school dropout, to outstanding military record for twenty years, to raising four children and teaching them to be responsible and law-abiding, to then marry a second time and raise two more children in a likewise manner (by the way, this is no easy chore while living in this country), to attaining three college degrees from two prestigious universities, including a doctorate, to then being a school principal in three different states and finishing my professional work with fifteen years as an adjunct professor at two different universities while teaching practitioners. There is a purpose in telling my story.

Question 2:   The very best examples for me to emulate came from my five sisters. The oldest, Jovita, born in Mexico in 1912 and who lived to be only fifteen months shy of 100, taught me about being responsible and putting one's feet flat on the floor each morning, and going to work at whatever one chose to do with one's life. She brings to life that commercial for the armed forces of our country that says *be the best you can be.*

Question 3: The technological advances of the twenty-first century have brought us a type of social media that has allowed my own sons and daughters, grandchildren, nephews, nieces, grand-nephews and grandnieces, and other relatives, a way to *stay in touch* at almost a moment's notice, such as with Facebook. I keep up with almost all of them by being friends with them on Facebook. More importantly, almost all of them communicate with me frequently with their postings.

Questions 4 and 5: The *surprising* election results of 2016 has given Americans much food for thought about our country's immigrant population. As I completed this first sentence of this paragraph, I suddenly felt a strange feeling that this question may be difficult to answer. On the one hand, we are all immigrants. That is, unless one was born from Native American parents and has only lived in a Native American reservation all of one's life without the benefit of having any other type of blood in one's background. If one is "this person," then this person is not an immigrant but a full Native-born American. Otherwise, welcome to our club, you immigrant you.

The winning Trump administration has ridiculed, demeaned, and otherwise accused my ancestral background as a culture that breeds criminality and abhorrence for the rule of law. The problem with the constant publicizing of this canard (unfounded, deliberate, and misleading story that is repeated publicly every day and several times a day) is that Americans tend to be gullible and will believe almost anything. Racism already exists in every corner of our country. No help is needed from Donald Trump. Perhaps the most bizarre justification that the Trump Administration has for allowing foreigners to migrate to America is that *they love us.* What happened to coming to America to make a living for our family and because it is the land of opportunity?

Question 6:   In a word, *yes*! The author (protagonist?) spent most of his working life as an educator. Like with everything else in my life, I put my heart and soul into being the best teacher I could be, the best principal I could be, and the best adjunct professor I could be. That meant doing the appropriate research into areas of *teaching and learning* that work. It meant doing a lot of *leaning back and reflecting* on how best to implement activities that my students could engage in to connect the information I wanted them to absorb. Add to my penchant for perfection the urgent need to make education meaningful for all students, particularly the ones who heretofore had not been successful in their educational pursuits. I was always interested in doing what works. I always attempted to make the interactive process of teaching and learning one that involved the honest interest of teacher and learner.

Question 7:   In those areas where I mentioned my loss of faith, I did it with honesty and sincerity. I also attempted to be nonjudgmental. While I continue to believe in a physical world, I have progressed in my beliefs to the point that I now believe there is a place for some elements of some religions who teach empathy, assistance for the unfortunate, and for people who have special needs. Still, these same elements, of some religions, have to also inform learners that everyone is entitled to their own beliefs and must be respected, whether or not it is a belief. With artificial intelligence coming into play, there is no telling how much this step into our future will affect our religious beliefs. My position at the moment is to appreciate all religions, while at the same time speaking against those religions who think theirs is the only one that is true.

Question 8:   My baptism into the world of workers' unions was positive, and I am sorry to admit that I was already an administrator when I was confronted with concerns by my staff members who were urged by their unions to make demands of me. Just yesterday I was telling my wife and first daughter how I thrived on having problems to solve and always looking forward to arriving at a solution. I cannot remember a single problem that I was made aware of that I didn't feel the solution to the problem would make my job, as well as my faculty's, better and more efficient. It's like having an oil leak from the crankcase of one's car and having to find it. Then when one finds it, one fixes it and the problem is solved. The same goes for a water leak or an air leak out of one's tires. Find it. Fix it. Problem solved.

With unions, I enjoyed reminding our staff of our mission as teachers. Just today, one of the teachers on my faculty at Wildwood Elementary in Amherst, Massachusetts, was reminding me (in an email) of my telling her once (twenty years ago) when she expressed a concern to me and how I reminded her of our mission, *with a question for her*: "Is this the best thing for this student?"

It is only a starting point for a meaningful discussion. I was always patient. I won as many debates with members of my faculty as I lost. I welcomed unions. They are necessary for the benefit of a happy workforce.

Question 9:   The memoir mentions, for the most part, the most immediate members of my family. All have contributed to this work by having been a part of my life. The most unfortunate thing is that all of my siblings have passed away. My mom and dad both passed away before I took my first college course in 1964. Yet they were a big part of my motivation to do something with my life. The possibility looms that I may have to write a second book so I can include all my nephews, nieces, their significant others, as well my great (grand) nephews and nieces and their significant others. I feel I am close to all of them.

My brothers, especially my three oldest, who were drafted into the armed forces of our country at the beginning of WWII, modeled a type of bravery and resolve that also said if I want to live in this country, then *there are dues to pay and fighting for our way of life in which to engage. I would do the same when my turn came.* I followed their lead. I have already mentioned my sisters, who really made me the person I am today.

While I have remained close to all six of my children, my first four have allowed me to grow in very meaningful ways through my mistakes. This has made me a much better parent to my second two, Josef and Sofia (the second picture, below). The first picture shows my first four children, L-R, Patricia Ann, Robert, Maria, and Rey is standing. I also have four grandchildren, Ana Gabrielle, daughter of Patricia Ann (who raised her by herself and is in the third picture). Ana is seen in her graduation from Texas State University recently. Aiden Lovine, son of Josef, is in the fourth picture. Aiden is 11 years old. I also have two granddaughters by my son Robert. They are Jordan and Jade, both in their twenties. I made the decision to not post their pictures without permission.

Question 10:   It is the year 1999. Josef and Sofia, along with their mother and her partner, are now living in Syracuse. I remember promising Josef and Sofia that I would take them on a trip to the South Western United States, to either Texas, New Mexico or Arizona, on a short vacation when they had a break from school. I did. We traveled to San Antonio and Albuquerque. While in Texas, I noticed right away that both Josef and Sofia had small bags around

their necks in which telephone numbers to call their mother or someone in New York were written. Their mother included them in the event I decided to leave the country and take off for Mexico (with them in tow, of course). They had these bags hanging around their necks like one would wear a necklace. If this was not so tragically comedic, I should have gotten angry. But paranoia raises its ugly head in many ways in our family. I just dismissed it and did not give this a second thought. In a day or two, Josef got tired of this "thing" hanging around his neck and dispensed with it. Again, I did not give this any serious thought. We are talking about my son and daughter at ages 13 and 10, respectively. They tried very hard to follow their mother's instructions.

Question 11: It is now the year 2009. Sofia has turned 20. Josef is 23. Josef is no longer in school. As long as Sofia remains in college, she would continue being my dependent for purposes concerning life insurance. Sofia then drops out of college. I ask their mother for a signed form and subsequent release from having to declare her as still being my dependent for purposes of my Texas Teacher Retirement life insurance. She does not answer my request. This declaration prevented me from declaring my wife as the beneficiary in the event of my death. I finally hear from my children's mother as she informs me that she will not release Sofia from being my dependent until she becomes self-sustaining in her life. I go back to Steve Monsein, in Massachusetts. Again, I have to plop down a $1,500 retainer fee to get him to get her to sign the release. It is no easy chore, but Steve Monsein's firm gets it done. And again, it cost me money.

Finally, there is Carol Parker-Pérez, my wife of nineteen years, who puts up with me and my perfectionist behavior. She has modeled being a wonderful and caring wife. She loves and cares for my own six children and my grandchildren. All members of my family feel her love for them. Without her support and encouragement, this work would not have been accomplished.

Roberto Pérez

About the Author

Roberto was born during the Depression of the 1930s in San Antonio, Texas as the eleventh of twelve children of Felipe and Amalia Perez, immigrants from Monterrey, Mexico. In Mexico, Don Felipe was a professional engineer and could drive coal-fed trains. Pancho Villa recruited him and made him a captain in his army. Villa and Don Felipe subsequently lost almost everything they owned when the Revolution ended. Villa was assassinated. Don Felipe survived and kept only his home. Roberto was born six years after his parents arrived in America. Only Mexican Americans lived in Roberto's community and were the only students with whom he went to school until reaching high school. Prejudice and racism against Mexican American children were evident in subtle and institutional ways. While he always recognized that he was an excellent student, problem solver, and very quick to learn new concepts, Roberto was nonetheless unsure of his strengths to learn.

After quitting school at 17 to volunteer for the armed forces as America was engaged in the Korean War, Roberto was sent to Wyoming to attend the Air Force Logisticians School. There were 580 air force enlistees in his class. Roberto was recognized as having the best academic average among the near six hundred men and was awarded an automatic promotion to corporal as his reward. Based on his successes and accomplishments in the air force, Roberto attained his high school equivalency and, at the age of 31, confidently began attending college on a part-time basis. He didn't stop until he earned a BA from Florida State University at age 38, a master's from UT–Austin at age 41, and a doctorate, also from UT–Austin, at age 45.

At age 84, Roberto only recently retired again as an interpreter and translator with the Frederick Public Schools in Maryland.

CPSIA information can be obtained
at www.ICGtesting.com
Printed in the USA
BVHW02s1701200418
513783BV00027B/502/P

9 781633 386259